PRAISE FOR BRENDA S. ANDERSON NOVELS

Pieces of Granite

"*Pieces of Granite* is an emotionally poignant story that flawlessly weaves together sensitive and tender moments, delivering a flawless tale of the depths and power of redemption. Fans of Karen Kingsbury will love th⸱ ⸱hristian women's fiction!"

—KE⸱ ⸱ES GILBERT, Author of the *Texᴀ⸱* ⸱ the *Sun Valley Series*

"One of my ⸱ng in a multilayered look at a far fᵤ ⸱ach character has early issues that cause proᵤ ⸱ life. Real-life kinds of interactions between the paᵤ ⸱ and children with plenty that a reader can learn from and apply in their own lives."

—CHRISTINE DILLON, author of
Grace in Strange Disguise and sequels.

"Brenda Anderson's realistic, flawed characters and messy life situations drag the reader on a rollercoaster ride of emotions in this story of what happens when the strong one everyone leans on begins to spiral. A page turning tale of one woman's journey of relinquishing control and finding her true self."
—Award-winning author, SHANNON TAYLOR VANNATTER

The Coming Home Series

"Anderson does a fine job exploring the nuances of Christian faith with its common companions guilt and grace."
— *Booklife/Publishers Weekly*

"*Hungry for Home* is more than a series finale—it is heartfelt, heart-wrenching fiction at its best, exploring relationships and family, love, faith and forgiveness in fresh, life-changing ways. I see myself in these endearing, enduring characters, their weaknesses and struggles and hard-won triumphs."

— LAURA FRANTZ, author of *A Moonbow Night*

"Anderson thrusts her readers into the gritty underbelly of family life and she doesn't mince words or shy away from the difficulties that complicate relationships. The reoccurring themes of grace and restitution are delivered with heart-wrenching honesty. These compelling stories celebrate the joys and sorrows of ordinary living with an extraordinary God."

— KAV REES, BestReads-kav.blogspot.com

Where the Heart Is Series

"*Risking Love* is a touching story of love and loss - and risking your heart! I can't wait to read the next in the series!"

—REGINA RUDD MERRICK, author of *Carolina Dream*

"*Planting Hope* is a lovely wrap-up to the Where the Heart Is series. The strength, or lack thereof, of a family unit has a profound impact on all of its members. Brenda Anderson expertly illustrates that in this story, and all of her books, as she deals honestly with the idiosyncrasies of families – the good, bad, and ugly. *Planting Hope* is about the hope God plants deep in our hearts, and the lengths we'll go to for those we love."

—Award-winning author, STACY MONSON

BOOKS BY BRENDA S. ANDERSON

THE MOSAIC COLLECTION

Pieces of Granite, Coming Home Series Prequel

A Beautiful Mess

A Beautiful Christ-mess, a short story

Hot Cocoa Summers, a short story

THE POTTER'S HOUSE BOOKS

Hands of Grace

Song of Mercy

Season of Hope, (Coming December 2020)

Long Way Home

Place Called Home

Home Another Way

WHERE THE HEART IS SERIES

Risking Love

Capturing Beauty

Planting Hope

COMING HOME SERIES

Pieces of Granite

Chain of Mercy

Memory Box Secrets

Hungry for Home

Coming Home, a short story

Pieces of
Granite

Coming Home Series Prequel

BRENDA S. ANDERSON

VIVANT PRESS

Minneapolis, Minnesota

VIVANT PRESS

Pieces of Granite
Copyright © 2014
Brenda S. Anderson

All rights reserved. No portion of this book may be reproduced, stored in a retrieval system, or transmitted in any form or by any means—electronic, mechanical, photocopy, recording, scanning, etc.—except for quotations in reviews or articles, without the prior written permission of the publisher.

ISBN-13: 978-1-951664-04-6

Library of Congress Cataloging-in-Publication Data is on file at the Library of Congress, Washington, DC. Library of Congress Control Number: 2014920526

Scriptures taken from the Holy Bible, New International Version®, NIV®. Copyright © 1973, 1978, 1984, 2011 by Biblica, Inc.™ Used by permission of Zondervan. All rights reserved worldwide. www.zondervan.com The "NIV" and "New International Version" are trademarks registered in the United States Patent and Trademark Office by Biblica, Inc.™

This novel is a work of fiction. Names, characters, places, and incidents either are the product of the author's imagination or are used fictitiously. Any resemblance to actual events, locales, organizations, or persons living or dead is entirely coincidental and beyond the intent of either the author or the publisher.

Cover Design by Think-Cap Design Studios

Printed in the United States of America

2 3 4 5 6 7 25 24 23 22 21 20

To Mom and Dad ~

You demonstrated the true meaning of family and faith, and you always encouraged my dreams. I am tremendously blessed!

Miss you, Mom!

Welcome to

THE MOSAIC COLLECTION

We are sisters, a beautiful mosaic united by the love of God through the blood of Christ.

Each month The Mosaic Collection releases one faith-based novel exploring our theme, Family by God's Design. We share stories that feature diverse, God-designed families. Our contemporary stories range from mystery to women's fiction, humorous fiction, and literary fiction. We hope you'll join our Mosaic family as we learn together what truly defines a family.

To keep informed about The Mosaic Collection books, subscribe to Grace & Glory, the official newsletter of The Mosaic Collection. You will receive monthly encouragement from Mosaic authors as well as timely updates about events, new releases, and giveaways.

Subscribe:
www.mosaiccollectionbooks.com/grace-glory/

Learn more about The Mosaic Collection at:
www.mosaiccollectionbooks.com/

Join our Reader Community, too!
www.facebook.com/groups/theMosaiccollection

Books in

THE MOSAIC COLLECTION

Learn more at www.MosaicCollectionBooks.com/Books

See, I lay a stone in Zion, a tested stone,
a precious cornerstone for a sure foundation;
the one who trusts will never be dismayed.
(Isaiah 28:16)

Chapter One

One more slam should drive away her fears. Debbie Verhoeven raised the hammer, her tongue poking from the corner of her mouth, and eyed the nail's head. With Handel's *Water Music* floating through the background, she swung the hammer down, transferred her strength to the nail, and implanted steel into oak. She skimmed her finger over the small metal head now blended smoothly with the wood's surface. Perfect.

Just like this little one. She patted her stomach and imagined the dime-sized heel floating unseen beneath her fingertips, a mere seventeen weeks alive. Absolutely perfect.

She took off her safety goggles, blew a brown strand of hair from her eyes, and removed a lawn chair from the open-stud garage wall. Time to relax. She unfolded the chair and placed it where her Mommy-van usually sat, where antifreeze had dripped Rorschach-like blotches onto the concrete. She collapsed onto the chair and smiled. Driving nails was great therapy.

But then, there was always clean up. A warm breeze blew through the garage's open door and a car puttered down her normally quiet street as she examined the butcher block workbench spanning the back of the garage. Next to her woodworking project, a Minnesota spring bouquet of lilacs and dandelions cuddled together in a Pepsi can, adding a splash of color and refreshing fragrance to the un-Sheetrocked area. The bouquet would stay, but tools needed to be hung on the pegboard and wood scraps awaited recycling. As for the granite stones scattered on the bench, she must have an empty coffee can around somewhere.

It could for tomorrow. Friday morning would be soon enough to clean her bench. She massaged her belly. Baby Verhoeven needed rest.

The door to the house opened, and her husband peeked through the crack. "About done?"

"For the afternoon, anyway." She stood, brushed dusty hands on her jeans, and wiped perspiration from her forehead. Even with the garage door open, the air movement did little to cool her pregnant body. "Kaitlynn still napping?"

"At the moment." A rare smile lit Jerry's face as he stepped into the garage. He wound his way in front of their decade-old Ford Escort wagon, cradling a Hostess cupcake in each hand.

Her stomach growled and she licked her lips. "Snack time already?"

"Maybe an hour or so past."

"No, it's not ... " Her gaze flew to the saw blade clock mounted on the pegboard above her workbench. Five forty-seven. Jerry had been home two hours already? No way. Maybe one. And a half. Maybe. And Kaitlynn never napped this long.

It was far past time for snacks. Supper should have been started over an hour ago.

But if Jerry wasn't complaining, why should she?

He set the cupcakes on her bench and ran his palm across her wood project. "What are you making?"

She grinned and covered his hand. "Something for my garden."

"A secret something?" His other hand blanketed hers.

"Yep."

"I have a secret." He circled his arms around her waist. "I love you," he whispered in his luscious tenor. His subtle Halston cologne drew her nearer until his lips briefly met hers, his goatee-mustache tickling her mouth. He drew back and smiled again, with creases accenting his green eyes. The years-old burn scar mapped over his cheek blushed a brighter shade of pink. Shoot, he was gorgeous, even with the fluorescent light reflected off his smooth head.

"I like your secret." She drew a finger down the front of his polo shirt. "What's the occasion?"

"Two minutes of quiet with my wife now, so you can sleep in tomorrow. Don't worry about getting up with me. Get in a little rest before Kaitlynn wakes up."

Oh, that sounded heavenly. If only it were that simple. "What about Kaitlynn's party? I've got a cake to bake tomorrow. A house to clean—"

He pressed a finger to her lips. "Party's two days away. Take it easy tomorrow. I'll help when I get home. No worries."

Girl, stop arguing. She plopped back down in her chair. "Thanks, hon." No sane pregnant stay-at-home mom would be dumb enough to turn down extra sleep and help.

"You're welcome." He handed her a cupcake.

She nibbled the devilishly good chocolate treat, skirting the crème center. Always save the best part for last.

Jerry downed his in two bites. He didn't need to savor the taste. Calories hated him and never stuck around. Life wasn't fair.

Licking his fingers, he leaned against the bench. Familiar

worry lines wrinkled his forehead. "Any word from Ricky?"

The cake suddenly tasted like sawdust. "He's flying to London tomorrow." And Granite Creek, Minnesota, wasn't exactly in the flight path of New York to London.

"I'm sorry, hon." Jerry opened a folding chair, faced it opposite hers, and took her hands. "You know it kills him not being here, although I'm sure Marcus is quite happy."

Probably. "Those two. I think they're beyond hope." Why her older brothers couldn't get along . . . ? She shook her head. "I keep reminding myself how lucky I am to have two older brothers who love me, who love us, and maybe someday . . . "

"It'll happen. They're good guys; they've just got a little growing up to do." He leaned over, raised her bare feet to his lap, and massaged the ankle that revealed her one foray into rebellion during college. Her poor mother still rolled her eyes whenever she noticed the diminutive lily permanently inked to Debbie's skin. An act Debbie never regretted.

Besides, Jerry loved it. Said it was sexy, and his gentle caress affirmed those words.

With a sly grin, he traced the lily with his thumb. "Where are your shoes?"

"My feet were hot." She pointed beneath the bench where ankle socks lay tucked inside tennis shoes.

"Didn't you teach Kaitlynn to always wear shoes when working in the garage?" His grin expanded.

With a huff, Debbie crossed her arms. "She's napping."

"Rebel."

Hardly. "Yep, that's me." Maybe in an alternate universe.

He chuckled, then concern leveled his lips as he nodded at her stomach. "What do we tell the family this weekend?"

Debbie caressed her baby. This little one would be loved, no matter what the diagnosis. "We'll tell them I'm pregnant, but the rest? I don't think we should, at least until we know for sure."

"And you've heard nothing from the doctor?"

"Not yet. Every time the phone rings . . . " She glanced at the cordless phone lying silent on the workbench. Three weeks had passed since the amniocentesis. It was well past time for the doctor to call with the results. This nervous anticipation was hard on both of them.

Especially Jerry. The corner of his lip quivered. A sure sign he was holding back his fears. "How do I keep myself from worrying?"

"Ah, Jerry."

"Seriously, Debbie. I'm scared to death."

Not a surprise. "I know. I'm scared too." But for different reasons.

"I wish I were strong as you."

Sometimes, I wish I could be weak. "God's not asking us to be strong."

"What if I can't handle it?"

"God doesn't give you more than you can handle."

A sarcastic laugh escaped his throat. "Right. Tell that to my dad. To my ex-wife." He pinched the bridge of his nose and looked down.

Debbie grabbed his hands. "Look at me."

He peered up, his cheeks flexing.

"Whatever happens, we're in this together. Do you understand that?"

He nodded like a guilty child accepting a scolding.

"Good, because I am *not* your dad. Nor am I Francine. You're stuck with me through everything. Got that? You have my word that I will never walk out on you."

His arms wrapped her in a trembling hug, clearly unconvinced.

God, please give him strength.

The phone rang as if in answer to her supplication.

She reached for it, but Jerry grabbed it first.

"Hello." Jerry massaged the left side of his chest. "Yes."

"Doctor Haugman's office?" She mouthed.

His gaze focused on the ground, he did one slow nod.

Please God, for Jerry's sake, and for me and the baby, let the tests be negative.

"Monday." Color leaked from his face.

No. Debbie laid her hand on Jerry's arm.

"I understand. We'll be there."

With a heavy sigh, he lifted his chin, clearly trying to appear brave, but red streaked the whites of his eyes and tension hollowed his cheeks. His lip twitched as he slid his hands between his knees, and cracked his knuckles.

"Dr. Haugman wants to see us Monday." An appointment meant one thing: they had information that couldn't be delivered over the phone.

Chapter Two

$\mathcal{F}$riday's noon bell rang, and Jerry eagerly excused his class for recess. Just in time to preserve everyone's sanity—his and his students'. He turned to the whiteboard and erased the division problems that the kids had struggled with this morning. Fridays and spring were a poor combination for student concentration.

Add to that, it was gorgeous outside. Seventy-four degrees and no mosquitoes. Yet. They would be buzzing and biting soon enough. After the harsh winter, the kids were antsy and needed to run off all their stored-up energy. He needed a break from youthful humanity.

His whiteboard clean and ready for the afternoon discussion of *Holes*, Jerry slumped in his chair, ran his hands over his bald head, and gazed at the flax-colored brick walls adorned with nearly a year's worth of children's artwork. Their dreams brought alive with paper and crayon.

Would his new baby live to share her dreams?

Monday would tell.

He tugged open his screechy-bottom desk drawer and pulled out his lunch. Not many adults carted a Mickey Mouse lunch box. When he first brought it to work, his colleagues had snickered and tossed wisecracks. Frankly, it didn't matter what others thought. He cherished the gift from Kaitlynn.

No surprises hid inside it. Peanut butter with homemade strawberry jelly, a Honeycrisp apple, and two Oreos. He took the sandwich out of the plastic baggie and heard a knock on the door. Harvey Peters stood in the doorway, absent the wheelchair-bound child he normally tended. Even while working with the four other special-needs students assigned to Jerry's classroom, Harvey wore a perpetual smile.

Drove Jerry nuts.

"Need some company?" Harvey leaned against the doorframe.

Rubbing a hand over his goatee, Jerry glanced at his lunch. There must be a diplomatic way to say, "Beat it." One would think his colleagues would get the hint when he didn't show up at the teachers lounge during break this past week.

"Got stuff going on?"

Jerry nodded. "If you don't mind, I'd rather . . . "

"Hey, I hear you." Harvey stood straight, still smiling. "Sometimes you need that quiet time."

Jerry's mouth curled up. "You've got that right."

"Well, I'll leave you be, then." Harvey walked out, and then peeked back in. "By the way, I wanted to pass on that we're all rootin' for you for the principal's position. I can't imagine anyone doing a better job."

"Thanks. I appreciate it." Several other teachers expressed the sentiment during the past month. He prayed the school board would hold an identical opinion. "I'll rejoin the world next week." Until then . . .

The closed-top desk drawer called to him. No. It needed to stay shut. Instead, he picked up the five-by-seven family portrait anchored on the desk's corner. Their church directory photo. Debbie sat holding Kaitlynn on her lap. Jerry stood behind, the photographer's way of adding height to Jerry's five-foot-nine frame. Debbie's height equaled his. At least she had hair. Thick, chestnut hair she complained about, that he loved. Her gray-blue eyes always had a way of seeing into him, the way she seemed to read everyone's heart.

He'd love to see those eyes when her surprise arrived today. His true secret from yesterday. He glanced at the clock above the whiteboard. Maybe the gift was already there. He owed her something good.

And this present would keep her mind off of Monday. He set the portrait back in the corner where he could always see it. With this new baby coming, six years stood between Debbie and returning to her career as a marriage and family therapist. Was he being selfish, keeping Debbie to himself when she had the gift of healing hurting families? Or were they the epitome of a strong, tightly woven family? Lord, let it be so.

He leaned back in his chair, pressed his chin to his chest, and exhaled. His eyes closed for a minute before he shook himself awake. Waiting until Monday for the test results played havoc with his body. He could go home and sleep forever.

So, why couldn't he sleep at night?

He bit into his sandwich, and then threw it down. Tasteless.

His desk drawer summoned him again. This time he answered. He slid the metal drawer open and removed a framed family portrait. His former family. He'd studied this photo a lot this week, while awaiting his new baby's diagnosis. How sad that this picture had been relegated to a closed drawer. This family had worn sincere smiles then. But only weeks following the portrait sitting, the unthinkable had happened. He hadn't believed he'd ever smile again.

Then, it got worse.

God doesn't give someone more than they can handle. Right.

The person who coined that phrase hadn't lived through what he had.

Jerry stared at his sandwich. That first bite sat like a rock in his throat. Even the Oreos didn't appeal. Why couldn't he be strong like Debbie?

He examined the photo again, at the family he'd torn apart. With closed eyes, he lifted a prayer that he'd be stronger this time, that God would guide him through.

Debbie believed.

But life had taught Jerry, sometimes God was absent.

DEBBIE TAPPED THE BOTTOM of the mini-loaf pan, and cake dropped onto a board covered with tinfoil. Another perfect chocolate rectangle. So far, no problems.

She dipped the butter knife into warm water, then into a container of store-bought vanilla frosting, before spreading the frosting over the cake.

"Help now?" Kaitlynn, seated on the top step of a folding step stool adjacent to the table, pleaded for what had to be the hundredth time. Her daughter always wanted to help, and Debbie loved that fact, but if she wanted to complete the cake today, Kaitlynn had to remain a spectator.

"One moment, precious." Debbie placed the cake loaf behind a train of six others and frosted half of another. She centered the half on top of the final piece, stepped back to view her creation, and pumped her fist. *Yes.* That end piece even looked like a caboose. Not noon yet, and she'd baked and frosted a cake without her harvest-gold oven burning the bottom. Maybe sleeping in this morning was exactly the medicine she needed.

"Now, you can help." Debbie tore open a package of M&M's, dumped them on the Formica table in front of Kaitlynn, and pointed at the cakes. "Pick one car."

"Can I put on the candles?"

Debbie laid three twisty candles next to the candy. "When you're done decorating."

"Okay, Mommy." Kaitlynn took one M&M at a time, and assigned each a specific location. The candy pieces would end up lined in near-perfect rows, not scattered and clumped. That inborn precision should occupy her daughter for at least another ten minutes.

Just enough time. Debbie cut a red licorice stick into one-inch lengths and stuck those between the train cars, coupling one piece of cake to another. She took a chocolate bar, broke it into equal pieces, and placed them on the train cab and the caboose for windows. One-half of another chocolate bar angled on the front of the engine depicted the iron pilot, or cowcatcher, as her brothers put it. Circular peppermints—white with red stripes—formed the wheels on both sides.

Debbie tore open other packages of candy and laid the pieces out by the car she wanted them to go on. The task would occupy Kaitlynn even longer.

She walked the short length of her galley kitchen and snagged her toes on an upturned crease in the once-white linoleum. Stupid floor. She flexed her toes. No damage. Well, with another baby coming, she'd have to live with the cracking floor for a long time. No sense complaining about something she couldn't change. She opened the refrigerator door with her usual prayer that it last another five years. No hot dogs in the crisper drawer. Plenty of ketchup, mustard, and relish, though.

"Precious, Mommy's gonna go downstairs for a second, make sure we have enough hot dogs for tomorrow." If not, she would add that to her already budget-busting grocery list. "Can you be careful?"

"I'm careful." Kaitlynn planted a hand on a hip, cocked her

head to the side, and wiped her straight brown hair from her face.

Love the attitude, my dear child. "Of course, you are. I'll be right back."

Leaving the basement door open, she hurried down the wooden steps, past spider-webbed walls, and across the dusty concrete floor, to the chest freezer. She raised the lid and a faint knock sounded on a door upstairs. Great timing. Well, they would have to wait two seconds. She counted out the packages of hot dogs, and heavy footsteps pounded above her.

Who in the world? Had to be her brother Marcus, or maybe her mom or dad. She slammed the freezer shut and hurried to the stairs. Well, whoever it was, she sure didn't appreciate—

Kaitlynn screamed.

Chapter Three

*G*od, please no. Debbie's heart galloped as she leaped up the steps, two at a time. She should know better than to leave her doors unlocked. Even in a small town, things happened. She opened her mouth, but "Kaitlynn" came out in a rasp. Her foot missed a step, and she banged a knee on the wood. Wincing, she pushed herself up and limped up the remaining steps.

Please, God, please.

Never had the thirteen steps seemed so long. She'd been gone one minute at the most. One lousy minute. What kind of maniac breaks into a house and hurts a toddler? Panting, Debbie limped through the door.

Her tear-filled gaze flew to Kaitlynn's stool.

She still sat there.

But wasn't alone.

Debbie squealed and her hands flew to her chest. "Ricky! Oh my gosh! What are you doing here?" Delight overruled the terror thumping in her heart as she stared at her brother standing next to Kaitlynn, placing candy on the cake.

"Not happy to see me?" He smiled.

"No—"

"No?"

"Well, yes, of course I am, but you scared the wits out of me.

I thought . . . " Tears fogged her eyes. Boy, those pregnancy emotions were working overtime today.

"Whoa, hey, I'm sorry. Next time I'll let you know I'm coming."

"I would greatly appreciate that." She limped toward him, her heartbeat slowing to normal.

"You okay?" His gaze went to her knee. "I heard you fall."

She looked down. No blood. Just wounded pride. "I'm fine." She stood straight and crossed her arms. "What are you doing here?"

"You made my favorite kind of cake." He arranged peanut butter cups on top of a train car. "I get this one."

"You'll share that one."

"Gee, do I have to?" He smiled his contagious smile, the one where his mouth lifted up more to the right, carving long dimples in his cheeks, the smile he shared with their dad and brother, the one that had made her high school and college friends swoon. His six-foot-two frame, farmer-sized shoulders, and nearly black hair probably had something to do with his appeal.

Personally, she never did understand the attraction. He was her brother, for heaven's sake.

"Yes. You have to share."

"No one's made me a train cake in years." His smile dipped a bit; his voice wore a wistful tone.

So, he did miss home. A rare chink in his armor.

She stared square in his eyes. "You haven't been home for your birthday in years."

He looked down and continued to arrange candy on the train.

"Come home this year." She rested a hand on his forearm. "I'll make you a cake."

"Better yet." He peered up. "You come to New York. You, Jerry, Kaitlynn. Make the cake there."

"You know we can't afford it."

"You don't have to. It's on me."

"Yeah, right." She huffed through her nose. "I'd love to. You know that, but you also know Jerry would never agree to it."

"Why not?"

"It has something to do with the male ego. The same something keeping you away on your birthday."

He laughed a dry laugh. "Well, maybe my friends back home don't lay guilt trips on me."

If he'd grow up, his family wouldn't be laying those guilt trips. "You and Marcus. I swear I could strangle you both."

"Start with him."

"Start with you coming home for your birthday. Do it for me, Mom, the kids. Yourself."

"I'll think about it."

"That's all I can ask. Now come here and give me a hug."

"That, I can do." His strong arms surrounded her in a bear-like grip. When he released her, she socked his upper arm.

He rubbed the spot and glared at her. "What did I do now?"

"That's for scaring the bejeebers out of me, for not telling me you were coming—"

"Jerry knew."

"—for staying away so long. I miss you."

"I've missed you, too."

"So, why are you here? I thought you were flying to London."

"Sunday."

"Sunday?"

"You think I'd miss my Katydid's birthday?" He ruffled Kaitlynn's hair then leaned over and blew a raspberry on her cheek. Kaitlynn giggled and Ricky showed his infectious grin. How could she stay mad? "Try and keep me away. Besides, I had to deliver my present."

Uh, oh. "Ricky Brooks . . . " His elaborate gifts scared her. The dollhouse he gave Kaitlynn for her second birthday took up half a wall in her bedroom, and Kaitlynn rarely played with dolls. Debbie scolded him for that last year. Why couldn't he learn his lesson?

"Don't worry. I okayed this with Jerry." He walked to the window above the stainless-steel sink and pointed out. "A little birdie told me my Katydid needed a new swing set."

"A new swing set?" Kaitlynn climbed off the stool and ran to her uncle.

No. Debbie's mouth widened into a grin as she glanced outside. A rented truck, filled with dark stained, pre-treated lumber, and a yellow plastic slide, sat in her driveway. "You didn't." *I'm so glad you did!*

"Sure did." Ricky swooped Kaitlynn up and pointed outside.

"It's broken." Her lower lip protruded out.

"Well, your mommy and I will have to fix it then, won't we?" He tickled his niece's stomach.

Kaitlynn giggled.

"You come alone?" Debbie searched the truck's cab, looking for his latest girlfriend, whoever that would be.

"Just me." He turned around, put Kaitlynn down then leaned his backside against the sink, crossing his arms.

Debbie mimicked his action, as she often did. "So, you'll stay the night?"

"Still have that lumpy sofa bed?"

"Ye-ah." Probably not good enough for him.

"I guess I'll just sleep on top then."

"Thanks," she said quietly. It was so good to have him here, all to herself.

"And tonight, I plan on spending time alone with my favorite niece, so I expect you and Jerry to go somewhere. Leave us alone."

"So the two of you can destroy the house."

"I always clean up my messes. Besides, I don't think we'll spend too much time indoors. First, I've been craving a Big Mac—"

"McDonald's?" Kaitlynn's eyes widened. Fast food was a rare treat. To go with her uncle would be extra special.

Ricky laughed and picked up his niece, who hugged his neck, squeezing as tight as her little arms allowed. "You betcha." He rubbed his nose against hers. "Then, how about we find some pretty rocks from the creek? Your mommy told me you're helping her with a project."

Kaitlynn's eyes grew wider as her head bobbed.

"And then, how about some popcorn and—"

"And JELL-O."

"JELL-O popcorn?" Wrinkling his nose, he glanced at Debbie.

Debbie giggled. "No, I promised her I'd make strawberry JELL-O for her party tomorrow, with bananas and apples. Her recipe. She likes that better than cake."

Ricky grinned. "Think I can handle it?"

"Well, if you can boil water, stir, and cut fruit, it might turn out okay. You don't have to worry about my cranky oven burning it either. Even I can make JELL-O."

"So, there's hope." He looked back at Kaitlynn. "Well, I might need some help. I'm not a very good cook."

"I know. Mommy told me."

Debbie clamped her hands over her mouth but couldn't suppress her giggle.

He shook his head. "Maybe when your mommy and daddy go away tonight, you can fill me in on all those other secrets your mommy tells you about me."

"I don't tell my daughter secrets. Just the truth."

"Mommy always tells the truth." Kaitlynn nodded emphatically.

"That's what I'm afraid of." Ricky raspberried Kaitlynn's cheek. "Okay, so when we're done making strawberry-apple-banana JELL-O, *then* I'll make popcorn for our date with Ariel"

"*The Little Mermaid?*"

"My favorite." Ricky nodded.

"Of course, it is." Debbie shook her head. "Spoiled little girl disobeys her dad, runs off to make a deal with a witch, ends up getting everything she wants, and everyone lives happily ever after." Yeah, she loved the cartoon too, even if the message irritated her.

Ricky quirked a smile. "Are you sure you're talking about *The Little Mermaid?*"

"What do you think?"

"I haven't found my princess yet." He patted Kaitlynn's bottom then lowered her to the ground, headfirst.

Okay. Sore subject. I should know better than that. "Did Jerry put you up to this?"

"Could be. He said something about you needing a break."

I need to give Jerry an extra-special hug tonight. "Well, I guess you can watch her, but you've got to promise to behave."

"Scout's honor."

"Our brother was the scout."

"Don't remind me."

They exchanged smiles. Boy it was good to have him home, teasing and laughing together. But her smile quickly flattened. "You can handle Kaitlynn's meds?"

"She on anything new?"

"Not really. Just the inhaler, if needed, or if it gets terribly bad, the nebulizer."

"Shouldn't be a problem. I've done it before. Just show me

where you keep everything before you leave."

"Thanks." What a novelty to go on a worry-free date.

"Will you sing me to sleep?" Kaitlynn tugged on her uncle's pant leg.

Ricky grinned and shook his head. "You don't know what you're asking, sweetie."

"Daddy always sings, or I can't sleep."

"It's true," Debbie said. "She doesn't care that we Brookses can't sing."

Kaitlynn nodded, being too agreeable, the stinker.

"When Jerry can't, I have to. She hasn't had a nightmare yet."

"So how can I refuse?" Ricky squatted to Kaitlynn's eye level. "What does your daddy sing?"

"He made a song special for me about his special girl."

"Is it okay if I sing another? I don't know that one."

"It's okay."

"Then I know just the one." He kissed her check before standing and ambling to the table. He placed another piece of candy on the cake, then popped a few in his mouth. "Well, that set won't get built with me standing here." The upward curve of his mouth, as he rubbed his hands together, told Debbie he was eager to get to work. "Got my tools yet?"

"The only ones I use. They're in the garage."

"Great. Of course, I'll need a little help putting it up."

That, she'd be more than willing to do.

Chapter Four

Fingers entwined together, Debbie walked with Jerry along the lake's shore, dangling her sandals in her other hand. She squeezed Jerry's hand, relishing his unusual public show of affection. Humming a soft tune, he squeezed back. This evening out seemed to be as beneficial for Jerry as it had been for her.

God offered his own display of affection as the sun burned low on the horizon, firing orange, red, and yellow flames across the sky, mirrored in the rippling lake below. Lilac's spring bloom, her favorite fragrance, perfumed the air. The water lapping onto her feet was still too chilled for swimming, but after a day of physical labor, its soothing coolness and the sand squishing between her toes had a massaging effect.

To think God loved them enough to paint this incredible gift.

She caressed her stomach. No matter what Monday's tests revealed, God loved this child too.

This was the perfect ending to a perfect day. She and Ricky hadn't finished building the playset before supper. It was too big. How typical of her brother to go overboard, but she wasn't complaining. Ricky and Marcus promised to work together tomorrow and finish it before Kaitlynn's party. The two of them getting along would be a gift to the entire family.

But tonight, her brothers' feud wasn't her concern.

She leaned into Jerry's shoulder, and he continued humming. Crickets strummed, enhancing Jerry's beautiful tenor. This alone time with him was more important than anything. To think they were on an actual date with no worries about Kaitlynn, no time constraints, or even money concerns as Ricky had paid for supper. The miracle was, Jerry had accepted. Even unease over the new baby was set aside.

Delicious freedom. If only for one night.

"Care for some more?" Jerry held up his A&W Root Beer float. Hard ice cream. Not that fake, creamy stuff.

"Please." She sipped the delectable treat through a straw until only ice cream remained. Heaven on earth. She looked behind her. The public beach was over a football field's length away. Plenty of space for privacy.

"Let's sit." She tugged on Jerry's hand, pulling him down on the sand so they could fully enjoy the evening's color demonstration.

"Thank you for today," she whispered, not wanting to distract from the view.

"You're very welcome." Jerry inched closer, wrapped his arm around her back, and kissed her cheek. "Ricky surprise you?"

"Surprise? Huh!" She dug her toes into the sand. "Scared me out of my wits. He came in when I was in the basement. I had visions of Kaitlynn's picture and name being broadcasted via AMBER Alert." She kissed Jerry's cheek. "But, yes. It was a good surprise."

He smiled, highlighting the cute creases by his green eyes.

Debbie lifted his hand, her thumb caressing her love into it. "Today's been wonderful."

"I knew you needed your brother." His smile lifted into a grin. "Tonight, I'd rather concentrate on you."

He kissed her again, surprising and pleasing her. She could

count the number of Jerry's public displays of affection, on her thumbs. According to him, teachers needed to set the proper example and be discreet about such matters. Discretion was good, but this bold behavior—bold for Jerry, anyway—was downright sexy.

Resting her head on his shoulder, she glanced out over the water. Far to the south, dark clouds encroached on the sunset. They were no threat, but added to the kaleidoscope of color stretched before them. God was so good.

Jerry shifted closer, leaving no space between them. He pulled her chin toward him and pressed his hand into the small of her back, drawing her closer. Completely disregarding his PDA rule, he kissed her on the lips.

She kissed him back, enjoying where his concentration was heading. Together, they would weather Monday's threatening storm.

JERRY CLOSED HIS EYES as Debbie's lips melded with his. Kissing in public wasn't normally his style, but tonight he didn't care. And, if any of his students spotted him, well, good for them. They could learn a few things about the blessings of marriage. He couldn't think of a better way to communicate his feelings.

Debbie's eager response showed she shared the sentiment.

The tranquil evening almost chased Monday's impending storm from his thoughts.

He dug his heels into the sand as Debbie pulled away and rested her forehead against his.

"What are you doing?" she asked in a breathy whisper barely heard above the waves lapping against the shore.

He grinned. "Did you know you taste like a root beer float?"

"Oh, you." She swatted his arm.

"Hey, I'm just kissing my wife." Loving her . . . cherishing her . . . wanting her . . . What had he done to be blessed with Debbie after messing up with Francine the first time around?

Debbie giggled. "I think 'making out' is more descriptive."

"Ya think?" Why hadn't he taken Ricky up on his hotel offer? For once, couldn't he forget his stupid pride?

"I think." She giggled again and splayed her fingers over his chest. "I have an idea."

"Oh yeah?"

"Um, hmmm. I think we need to call Ricky and ask him to take Kaitlynn to Mom's for the night. What do you think?"

"Hmmm, let me think . . . " He kissed her again, tasting root beer, ice cream, and love. An intoxicating blend.

She pulled away, her eyes reflecting the sunset, and took Jerry's cellphone from his belt. "You call."

His gaze focused on dark clouds swelling above whitecaps as he dialed and waited for an answer. Spring's resurrection frequently ushered in turbulent weather, but the forecaster claimed these storms would remain to the south. If only that were true. Experience had taught him, swirling winds have a way of fooling even the educated. Of sneaking up on a person, blowing and beating them, leaving behind permanent scars.

"Hello."

"Hey, Rick? I've got a favor to ask."

"Shoot."

"Could you bring Kaitlynn to Grandma's tonight? Debbie and I—"

"Say no more. Her bag's already packed."

"Thanks. We owe you big time." Jerry snapped his phone shut then helped Debbie stand.

Come Monday, he and Debbie would know for certain if the clouds' threat was false, or if they would have to look for a rainbow at the storm's end.

Three nights and two full days until then. He wasn't going to waste the time worrying.

Chapter Five

*D*ebbie wiped the perspiration from her forehead as she knelt next to her mom and pulled a dandelion from between the white alyssum. Nothing hindered the sun in the northwest angle of her yard. Her Son garden should thrive.

"This is quite the undertaking." Mom untangled a weed hiding in the strawberry bushes.

"If Dad could farm five hundred acres—"

"That's not what I'm talking about." Mom glanced back at their family gathered around Kaitlynn's swing, completed just this morning by two uncommonly cooperative brothers. "With the baby coming, are you sure you can handle our anniversary?"

"It's no big deal." Not at all. Combine her brothers getting along with last night's romantic evening with Jerry, and this was turning into one of the best weekends she could remember. She wasn't going to spoil it with worry, and planning an anniversary party was the least of her concerns. "You deserve a party. I mean, having put up with Dad for forty years, you've earned a medal, don't you think?"

Her mom laughed. "Maybe he's the one who deserves a medal."

"Seriously. We've got the church fellowship hall booked, and Ricky's promised to pay for it all. That was my biggest concern."

"You'll tell me if it gets to be too much?"

"Mom, please." She plopped down and stared outward at the five blue spruce pines towering like sentinels across the backyard as if guarding it from the farmer's growling machinery beyond. Her mom worried just as much as Jerry. Thank goodness Debbie hadn't inherited that gene. She looked upward and breathed in the fragrance from the lilac bushes, their branches bowed with purple blossoms, fencing in the western yard with natural privacy. A perfect place for her to talk to God when life got too tough. "This party's for you to celebrate, not work. And I will have help. Speaking of which, the guys are inside waiting for me to discuss plans. Hope they haven't spilled too much blood."

Marlene yanked another dandelion before its roots choked the healthy plants. "They survived this morning."

"As long as they avoid talking anything personal, they're fine." Debbie stood and wiped her hands on her jeans. "But I'll go referee just in case."

Without looking to see the disappointment she knew darkened her mother's face, Debbie slow-jogged to the house. She entered the kitchen through the garage door, and listened. No fighting. Just the TV baseball announcer. Thank you, God, for small miracles.

Enjoying her temporary moment of freedom, she rested her backside against the sink, closed her eyes and smiled.

But the smile quickly receded. Everyone was so happy about the baby announcement. Would they show the same enthusiasm come Monday? Would they, once again, question her wisdom in marrying Jerry?

"Something wrong?" Ricky's voice made her jump.

With her heart pounding in her throat, she glared at him. "Jeepers. You gotta quit scaring me!"

"Sorry." Ricky crossed his arms below his chest and leaned

against the cupboard across from her. His eyes studied hers. "You seem a little down this weekend."

"Do I?" How could he tell what she was feeling? Unlike him, she didn't wear her emotions where everyone could see.

"Is it the pregnancy?"

"It has to be. I feel like crying half the time, and you know I don't cry." Which was true, but thoughts of Monday's meeting with the doctor clung to her like weeds in her garden. If Jerry knew her concerns, he'd be completely stressed out. She couldn't do that to him.

Still, she needed to tell someone. Not her mom. She'd worry too. But Ricky? He would listen, hug her, probably even cry with her. "Can we—"

"What are you two up to?" Marcus walked between them to a fridge barely new enough to be white.

Ricky glared at Marcus. "Talking."

Marcus pulled out a can of Pepsi and held it up. "Don't let me interrupt."

"You already have." Ricky's jaw set as Marcus returned to the living room. "The man's got great timing," he mumbled.

Keeping a sigh to herself, Debbie kicked at the cracking linoleum. She should be used to these ageless squabbles by now. This definitely wasn't the right time or place for that quiet talk. Maybe if Ricky would stay for a bit once everyone left, then . . .

He rested his hand on her arm. "What were you going to tell me?"

"Ah, it's nothing. Like you said, it's the pregnancy hormones. My emotions are all over the place."

"You sure?"

"Positive." Positive that was all she would tell him at the moment.

His eyes squinted, but he left it alone.

"Come on." She nodded toward the living room. "Let's go watch the game."

He cuffed her wrist. "You'll tell me if something's wrong?"

"Of course." She painted on a smile. "Everything's fine." So, why were tears fogging her eyes? She shook off his hand and led him to the living room. Let the ballgame take her mind off things.

With Marcus sprawled on the couch, she sat in the padded rocking chair and propped her legs on the accompanying footstool.

Ricky chose the recliner, but didn't recline.

She focused on the game, but felt her brother's gaze. Maybe if she changed the subject, he'd forget his suspicions. "Staying the night again?"

"Can't." He sighed. "I've got a room by the airport. The flight's early morning. I don't want to add three hours to the trip tomorrow."

Marcus sat up and stared at his brother. "Is that the only reason? You don't have someone waiting for you?"

Here we go.

Debbie reached for the remote and muted the television volume. "Hey, can we talk about the anniversary?"

Ricky's eyes met his brother's, ignoring her. "Of course. Patrice. She spent the day at the Mall of America." He leaned toward Marcus, his lips tipped upward, and his eyebrows flitted up then down. "Tonight, she gets to spend the evening with me. Lucky woman." Ricky sat back in his chair and raised the footrest, wearing the smug smile of a victor.

What? Yesterday, he said he'd come alone. Was the lie to her or Marcus? Half the time, she wondered if what Ricky said was true or if he made things up to goad his brother. How could Ricky have such disrespect for women? He hadn't been raised that way, but then, he'd forgone many of the principles their parents taught, crossing lines that led to greater worldly success and away from his once-strong faith.

Reroute the topic again to something safe. "What are you doing in London?"

Ricky's smug countenance disappeared, and he gave her a genuine smile. Jekyll and Hyde. Argumentative with Marcus one second, and her charming brother the next. It would take weeks—months—of therapy to figure him out.

"London?" Marcus raised his eyebrows.

Maybe there was no such thing as a safe topic.

"Isn't that someone else's territory? I think I met the guy in New York once, didn't I? You introduced him as a good friend."

Ricky's eyes narrowed, and his jaw shifted.

"Ah, I thought so. I remember you joking that the guy better watch his back. You wanted his area." Marcus wore the sneer of an ungracious champion. "What did you do?"

"Look." Ricky raised his hands, palms upward. "The guy made a mistake. I caught it. They gave me his region. End of story."

"I'm more interested in the story's filler. Did he make the mistake, or did it miraculously appear?"

Debbie turned up the TV volume as the Twins first baseman circled the diamond with a homerun. "That had to go four hundred feet!"

"I don't like what you're insinuating."

She spoke louder. "We're up now, four to three."

"Really." Marcus glared at his brother. "Maybe I'm not insinuating. Maybe I'm downright accusing."

"Marcus!"

Both brothers stared at her.

"Stop." She raised her hands, pressing her palms outward. "Stop it," she said softly, briefly closing her eyes before connecting them with Marcus, then Ricky.

"Tell her, Rick." Marcus nodded in her direction.

Her gaze shifted toward Ricky.

"It's Richard," he said flatly.

Oh, boy. Debbie closed her eyes and slunk down in her chair. With him stressing his given name, the one all his New York associates knew him by, all semblance of peace for the weekend was lost. Maybe he should just leave.

She squeezed her head between her hands. But they never had time to discuss the anniversary. They didn't take time to sit and talk, just the two of them.

"Tell Debbie you didn't finagle your way into that job." Marcus pointed a finger in her direction, but his gaze fired at Ricky. "You wanted it. Now you've got it. How convenient."

"I didn't cheat." Ricky's jaw clenched, and his eyes darted.

"Yeah, right." A sneer filled Marcus' voice.

Ricky, what have you done? She focused on the threadbare carpet, avoiding her brothers. They were both beyond her help.

"Like I said, when I studied the reports, I noticed areas that could be improved on, bring in a greater profit—"

"So, it was already profitable. Just not enough for you."

"No." Ricky rolled his eyes. "Yes. It was already profitable, but the potential was far greater. I simply pointed it out to management."

"You couldn't point it out to your *friend*? You couldn't have helped him?"

"That's not how things work."

"Course not." Marcus laughed wryly. "You saw the opportunity and grabbed it regardless of who stood in the way. Let me ask you, how is that friendship now?"

Ricky's cheeks drew in.

"Just as I thought." Marcus snorted.

"Believe what you want." Ricky thumped the recliner's

footrest back in place. "You always do." He stood and stomped toward the kitchen, stopping beneath the arch separating the rooms. His shoulders heaved before he turned and glared at Marcus, then his eyes softened for her. "Sorry, Debs. It's time to go. I'll tell everyone goodbye."

She turned away and listened to the screen door open then settle into place. Every time he dared visit, the pattern repeated. These visits would most likely end abruptly someday. Probably soon.

Marcus sat loudly silent.

Bowing her head, she steepled her hands over her face. *One . . . two . . . three . . .* Do not cry.

When would resentment stop dividing her brothers, stretching her affections in opposing directions? She lowered her hands, folded them in her lap, and glowered at Marcus.

He stared at the television.

"Why do you do that?" She kept her pitch low, forcing him to listen.

"I can't help it." His eyes blinked rapidly as he clenched and unclenched his fists. "He gets under my skin, you know. You heard what he said about that woman. About his job. He's gonna get himself in trouble someday, and who's gonna be there to help him?"

"We will." She pressed a finger to her chest.

He laughed sarcastically. "Don't be so sure. You think he'd even want our help?"

"He wants our love. Our acceptance."

"Well, I for one can't accept who he's become."

"He talks like that to get your goat."

"But he's talking the truth."

"You should ignore it."

"Should I? Someone has to hold him accountable."

She slumped in her chair. "You don't think he did something illegal, do you?"

"Illegal?" He chuckled. "Nah. He's too smart for that. But conniving? Underhanded? Absolutely. There's no doubt in my mind. Look at his track record. How many times has he miraculously"—Marcus made the quotation sign with his fingers—"uncovered someone else's screw up? How many times has someone else's mistake propelled him up that corporate ladder? A few too many times for my comfort."

Debbie lowered her head. As much as she didn't want to believe it, Ricky's career ascension did occur awfully quickly, especially for someone raised in a Minnesota hick town.

"Listen." Marcus leaned over and rested a hand on her shoulder. "I know you don't like to hear it, but your brother isn't some saintly knight on a steed."

She lifted her chin. "Neither are you."

"I don't claim to be."

"Neither does Ricky."

"I just don't want him taking you down with him when he falls."

"Don't be so sure he's going to fall." Debbie shrugged off her brother's hand and stood.

"Don't be so sure he won't."

She marched away, slamming the door good and loud on her way out. She'd plan the anniversary party on her own, thank you very much. Who needed their kind of help anyway?

Chapter Six

Debbie wrapped her arms around Kaitlynn, watching storm clouds billow in the west, as the family hugged Ricky goodbye. Sometime in the last hour, the wind had shifted direction ushering out May's warmth, replacing it with a chill that seeped into her bones. Last night, the storm had bypassed to the south. Today, it looked as if it would hit dead on. Ricky's excuse for leaving so soon.

The family knew the truth.

Holding back her own tears, she watched the unhappy goodbye scene.

Her dad held out his hand.

Ricky stared, then grasped it, pulling his dad into a hug. "Sorry, I had so little time."

They slapped each other's back then let go.

"I reckon your mom and I'll just have to fly out there."

"I'd like that."

"I don't suppose you found a church—"

"Dad."

"—and a godly woman."

"You never let up, do you?"

"Not as long as we're related."

"Tell you what." Ricky chuckled. "When I find her, you'll be the first to know."

Debbie hugged Kaitlynn tighter. At least Ricky and their dad would depart on a positive note, with no tears shed. Outwardly anyway.

The tears clouding their mother's eyes weren't held back, and the hug Ricky gave her lasted a full ten seconds.

He wiped his eyes as she released her grip.

"Behave yourself now."

"Always." The moisture in his eyes muted the twinkle.

"And hurry home again."

He scratched the back of his neck. "As soon as the job lets me."

In other words, not for a very long time.

Their mom kissed Ricky on the cheek, took their dad's hand and walked away.

Debbie looked back and watched her mom lean into her dad. A funeral was less somber than this goodbye. It just seemed like this parting was permanent.

"It's time," Debbie said more to herself than Jerry as she grasped his hand and stepped forward.

Ricky reached for Kaitlynn, and Debbie eagerly handed her over. Perhaps it was wrong to use her daughter as a device to coax her brother back home, but she'd do anything to keep him returning.

He sniffled and wiped his eyes as Kaitlynn squeezed her arms around his neck. Clinging equally hard, he shifted her to his hip.

Jerry gripped Ricky's hand, his eyes boring into Ricky's with the controlled anger he'd mastered in his classroom, obviously unhappy that Ricky, once again, had let Debbie down.

After several quiet seconds, Jerry released the grasp, but not his stare. "You'll be back."

"I don't know." Ricky's voice wavered, and his glassy eyes gazed heavenward.

"The baby's due around Thanksgiving." Jerry smiled slightly. "You'll be back then."

Ricky focused on Debbie's stomach and chuckled. "I wouldn't miss it."

Thank you, God.

"But don't forget. You can come see me, too." Ricky's eyes fixed on Jerry, then her.

What she'd give to take him up on his offer.

Jerry nodded. "We'll think about it."

For five seconds, maybe, then his answer would be the same as always. No doubt about it.

"We appreciate you coming." Jerry stuck a hand in his front pocket. "For giving us a night out last night, for taking Kaitlynn to Grandma's. We needed the time alone."

"You deserved it, and I got to spend time with my girl." Ricky tickled Kaitlynn's tummy.

Her giggle made them all smile.

"Take care now." Jerry reached for Kaitlynn. "Tell Uncle Ricky goodbye."

Kaitlynn hugged Ricky's neck. "I love you!"

"Love you too, Katydid, and happy birthday again. You're getting to be such a big girl."

"I know."

Grinning, he rubbed his nose against Kaitlynn's then handed her to Jerry. "Man, I'm gonna miss that girl." His voice hung low as Jerry carried her toward the backyard.

Finally, a few seconds alone. Debbie leaned against Ricky's rental truck, gazing at her daughter. "She had fun last night."

"I did too." A true smile glistened in Ricky's voice. "She's a great kid. You're a good mommy. Oh, and congratulations again."

Debbie caressed her stomach. "Thanks."

He crossed his arms over his chest. "If I'd have known you were pregnant, you wouldn't have been helping me yesterday."

"Which is exactly why I didn't tell you."

"So, you'll be fine?"

"I come from hardy stock, remember?"

"True." He uncrossed his arms and aimed his gaze at her stomach. "I wish . . . " A sigh blew from his mouth.

"You'll be a good daddy someday." And he would, if he'd ever settle down.

He laughed dryly, shaking his head. "First, I have to meet someone who'd be a good mommy."

"Patrice maybe?" That was one way to flush out the truth.

"Patrice?" His gaze darted away.

"Yeah, you know. You said she spent the day at the Mall . . . "

Although his lips smiled, his eyes didn't shine. "Oh, yeah. Figment of my imagination."

Yeah right. "Come on. You know you can't lie to me."

He lifted his eyes to hers. "Seriously. I'm spending the night alone."

She stood quiet for a second studying his face, her mouth scrunching to the side. Why didn't she believe him? Well, no sense nagging. Like it would do any good anyway.

"Why'd you lie to Marcus?"

He scowled, and his eyes darkened. "Can't disappoint my little brother now, can I?"

Debbie combed her fingers through her bangs and over the top of her head. "I wish you would—"

"Stop. Just stop. Okay?" He shook his head. "It's not happening. I tried today, really, I did, and look what happened. You think I want to fly out here to pick a fight?" His shoulders heaved. "It's not meant to be."

"Ricky . . . " She kicked at the asphalt drive. *Please God, don't let me lose him.*

Ricky pulled up her chin.

Her eyes closed, blocking in the tears.

"Listen," he said softly. "Come see me. Just you."

If only she could. To experience freedom like her brother, without familial restrictions, and have no responsibilities. To lean on someone else for once. Even for a couple days. Nothing sounded sweeter.

Nasty tears escaped as she opened her eyes. "We can't afford—"

"I told you, I'd take care of it."

"Then you talk to my husband."

"When is Jerry going to learn to accept help?"

"If you grew up on welfare, you wouldn't be so willing to accept handouts either."

Ricky sighed. "I guess I can't blame him, but I'm not giving up. Someday he'll give in."

"If you say so." If Ricky wanted to ram his head into a brick wall, then so be it.

"And I don't want any arguments about letting me pay for Mom and Dad's anniversary. It's the least I can do with you planning the whole thing."

"Thanks." Even Jerry was grateful for that assistance.

Ricky squeezed her with a bear hug, followed by a kiss on the cheek. "Take care of yourself and my little niece or nephew. I'll call when I get back home. Probably a week from Sunday."

God, let me have good news to give him then. "I love you."

"Yeah, you, too." He winked as he opened the truck door then stepped up into the driver's seat.

Hugging herself, tears flowed freely as she watched him back from her driveway and accelerate down the pothole-ridden street.

Please, God, don't let him get hurt. As a therapist, she learned most human growth occurred after stumbling over, or falling into, potholes. Pain was inevitable.

It was the depth of Ricky's potholes that scared her.

RICKY DROVE TWO BLOCKS then checked his rearview mirror. The family was out of sight but would never leave his mind. He did love them. Really, he did.

And, he was going to be an uncle again. He grinned just thinking about it. Welcoming a new baby into the Brooks family was always a joyous occasion. Nothing was sweeter than holding a newborn, and nothing more humbling, reminding him that there were still things over which he had no control. An occasion in which he and Marcus always managed to put aside their differences and share the rare cigar with Jerry and their dad, ignoring their wives' agitation with the male bonding ritual. He wouldn't miss a birth for anything.

If only his family would . . .

Sighing, he retrieved his Bluetooth from the glove compartment and curved it over his ear. He pulled the BlackBerry off his belt and dialed the familiar number. It rang twice before he heard her voice mingled among many other voices in the background.

"Hey, it's me, Rick . . . " He rolled his eyes. "Richard." Less than thirty hours around the family, and he already resorted to old ways.

"Hi darlin'." A smile rang in her voice. The woman did have a great smile.

"How's shopping?"

"Better in Manhattan."

More expensive there, too.

"Are you heading back?" A sultry eagerness lilted her tone.

Maybe he should rethink this. With what he had to say, it would probably end their relationship before it had time to start. He tried visualizing her in the silky white negligee, the one leaving little to the imagination, the one she wore the other night. Instead, he saw Debbie's doubting eyes.

"Uh, no, actually." His family-induced conscience won this time. "I'm not going to make it back tonight." Plenty of other airport hotels would have a vacancy. "We'll have to hook up when I get back in town." Her focused breathing told him that wouldn't happen. "I am sorry. I feel bad for dragging you with me."

Her silence roared above the throngs at the mall.

Blinking, he fought the urge to change his mind, tell her he'd be back tonight, and they would . . . He blew out a breath. *Not tonight.* Tonight, he just wanted to have a drink or two, or whatever it took to crowd God's voice from his head.

Oh, like that would be real smart.

Ten plus hours on an airplane with a hangover wasn't something he'd wish on his worst . . . on Marcus. Well, maybe . . . His mouth tipped slightly.

"I mean it. I'm sorry." He steered onto the freeway entrance. "Hope you don't get too lonely, tonight."

"Huh. No fear of that." The woman was definitely miffed. "I discovered last night that Minneapolis has a great night life, that you're not the only interesting farm boy around."

His fingers choked the steering wheel. Maybe he should find a hotel with a masseuse to rub out his anger-tightened muscles. "Patri-ice . . . " Irritation rolled from his throat.

"Hey, don't get mad at me. You're the one who brought me here and dumped me off all alone in fly-over country. A woman's got to make do, you know."

Fine. If she wanted to be that way, let her. "Have a big time." He struck the *end* button, turned the phone off, and threw the headset on the passenger seat, accompanied by a curse. Why did doing the right thing hurt so badly? Sure, he hated disappointing Patrice, but disappointing Debbie was much worse.

DEBBIE WIPED HER NOSE and eyes with the back of her hand before turning toward the house. After everyone hugged their goodbyes, they'd returned to the backyard. Hopefully, they would stay there. She strode to the house needing to stabilize her emotions before facing the family. With the garage door open, she cut through to the kitchen.

Bracing herself against the cupboard, she closed her eyes and inhaled a cleansing breath then grabbed a tissue. Mumbled voices hummed through the silence as she dabbed at her eyes.

She peeked into the living room. Marcus and Janet. Marcus was leaning over, resting his elbows on his knees.

Janet kneaded Marcus' back. "Did you tell him?"

Tell who, what? Debbie stepped backward, keeping her brother and sister-in-law visible as her ears homed in on the conversation.

"No," Marcus said softly.

"Why not?"

"There wasn't time."

Janet pulled her hands away and fisted them on her hips. "Oh? Really? There was no time this morning when you two were working together?"

Marcus glanced over his shoulder. "The subject never came up."

"And how did you expect the subject to 'come up'?"

He shrugged and looked at the floor. "Who knows? Maybe he'll have an announcement of his own someday."

Janet swatted his back. "So you can rub that into his face too?"

Marcus raised his head and stared at his wife. "How can you, of all people, defend him? After what he did to you?"

"Don't even go there, Marcus. That was a long time ago and your imagination is making it out to be worse—"

Debbie cleared her throat, guilt winning out.

Janet and Marcus peered up.

"Sorry, guys." Debbie's face burned. "I didn't mean to eavesdrop."

Janet smiled in her typical effervescent way. She was cute with her heart-shaped face and chin length blonde curls. At only five foot two, Janet stood nearly a foot shorter than Marcus, but her spunky attitude more than made up for her lack of height. She was bubbly and outspoken and fit right into the Brooks family. It wasn't a shock that both Ricky and Marcus had dated her.

"That's okay, sweetie." Janet waved Debbie in.

Debbie slumped in the recliner and raised the footrest. Already, her ankles experienced the watery swell from pregnancy. It felt wonderful being off her feet.

"You sure you're feeling all right?" Janet asked.

"Tired. Bloated." It was all Debbie dared admit.

Janet nodded toward Marcus. "I suppose you're wondering what we were talking about."

Sure, she was curious, but that didn't give her the right to know. "It's none of my business."

"Maybe, but I'm dying to tell someone."

"I thought we were going to wait." Marcus sat up, narrowing his eyes.

"Let me tell Debbie, please?"

Marcus rolled his eyes before kissing his wife. "Go ahead." He shot Debbie a stern glare. "You've got to promise to keep it a secret. That means from the family."

Debbie drew an X across her heart. "I promise."

Janet bit into her lower lip, looking very much like a schoolgirl hiding a juicy secret. "We're pregnant."

"What?" Debbie's mouth hung open.

Janet nodded, grinning.

"You're not kidding!"

"Nope. Not at all." Janet grasped Marcus' hand, exchanging a gentle squeeze. "It's a bit unexpected, but hey, could you think of a better surprise?"

A major surprise at that. "Nothing better than more babies." But Debbie doubted she'd want the same kind of surprise eight years down the road. "Josh'll be nine next month, right?" Her training taught that sibling rivalry wouldn't be much of a problem. In theory. Unlike the constant bickering between Nathan and Joshua. Or Ricky and Marcus. Big age differences almost made it easier for siblings.

"Yep. I think he'll like not being my baby anymore."

"Probably." As for Marcus and Janet, it would be like starting over again. No thank you. And as sick as Janet had been with the boys? This wasn't going to be a picnic for her. "So, this is why I haven't seen you for so long. You've been sick, haven't you? Just like with the boys."

"Terribly. It's getting better. Today's been a good day."

"Wow," Debbie said the exclamation quietly. Two new babies. Her mom would be in Grandma Heaven. "No one else knows?"

"You're the first," Janet said. "This was your weekend. And Kaitlynn's. We didn't want to intrude on it."

"Thanks. I appreciate it."

"Of course, Marcus was supposed to tell Ricky . . . "

"Ah, yes, that's where I came in. I understand now."

"Um, hmmm. Now, he's gonna have to give your brother a call before we tell the family. It wouldn't be fair to let Ricky find out from someone else."

"Not that he'll care." Marcus frowned.

"You know he'll care," Debbie said. "Look how much he loves the boys and Kaitlynn. How excited he was for us. If you let it, this could help heal your relationship."

"That's exactly what I told him." Janet bumped her shoulder into her husband's arm. "But you've got one stubborn brother."

"Two, you mean." Debbie smiled weakly.

Janet kissed her husband's cheek. "Ain't that the truth?"

Marcus rolled his eyes.

"Seriously, Marcus, tell him." Debbie pointed to the phone on Marcus' belt. "Call him right now on his cell. Don't let him leave the country angry. He might surprise you."

"That's what I'm afraid of," Marcus mumbled. "I'll think about it."

"He'll do it." Janet grabbed Marcus' phone, dialed, and handed it over.

Marcus listened for a second then snapped the phone shut. "Got his stupid voicemail."

Chapter Seven

*D*ebbie clutched Jerry's trembling hand and led him into Dr. Haugman's office as thunder drummed outside.

"Please have a seat." Dr. Haugman sat in her leather chair and gestured to the cushioned seats facing her desk.

Although his face showed a smile, Jerry's grip tightened as they sat.

Debbie focused on the line of framed diplomas and credentials interspersed among greenery on the credenza beyond the doctor. Family portraits bookended the diplomas.

The somber-faced physician folded her hands on a manila file. "Thank you for coming in today." She took in a deep breath then flipped open the file. "I realize none of this is new to you."

Biting into her lower lip, Debbie peered at Jerry.

The edge of his pinched mouth twitched, and lightning flashed.

"Your baby has the extra twenty-first chromosome."

Debbie closed her eyes and covered Jerry's shaking hand with hers. "Trisomy 21?" she whispered as thunder chased the lightning.

The doctor nodded. "Yes. Your daughter has Down syndrome."

DEBBIE SAT ALONE ON the deck of the tree house, hemmed in

by a railing constructed of sturdy tree branches, blending in with the forest surroundings. Marcus called it the tree house on steroids, built in the very same oak she had climbed as a child. The same tree that held the house where she hid after her grandmother died. Twenty years ago. How things had changed since then.

She crossed her hands over her stomach, cradling her infant. Some things never changed. This tree house still sufficed nicely as a quiet getaway, a place drawing her nearer to God. She breathed in the damp air as her eyes turned upward. Starlight couldn't penetrate the muddy clouds, but stars shone there. Steady. Strong.

She needed to be steady for Kaitlynn. For Jerry. Now wasn't the time to show need, to be weak. The stars weren't weak. They always hung in the sky; during the day, the sun shone too brightly to see them. Sometimes at night, clouds obscured them. Sometimes like tonight. But the stars never left. They were right where God placed them.

Be steady. Strong. Breathe. It was the diagnosis they expected. The baby they had prayed for and rejoiced over when God answered their prayers with a yes!—their baby, their precious little girl, had Down syndrome.

Earlier in the afternoon, they had both sat quietly, listening to the doctor's encouraging words following her diagnosis. Words Jerry was too familiar with. Children with Down syndrome are mainstreamed into school. Adults with Down syndrome frequently live independent lives. Their little girl would grow up, get a job, and probably have her own place. The doctor's pronouncement didn't have the same effect now that it once might have.

Debbie had squeezed Jerry's hand and smiled. See, no reason for concern.

He returned the smile, but the quiver in his lip betrayed his feelings as the doctor laid out the litany of complications: hearing loss, eye disorders, Leukemia, thyroid disorders. Congenital heart disease. Jerry released her hand and cracked his knuckles. Although the risks of mortality from heart failure were far lower than they once had been, Jerry still worried.

He had every right.

A single raindrop landed on her sandaled foot, returning her thoughts to the present. That drop would be the first of many. She peered up at clouds dark and burdened with their weight, a burden about to be released. Minutes from now, she and Jerry would be releasing their own burden to her family.

With this pregnancy already making her weepy, she feared breaking down in front of the family. So, she'd come out here alone, in between periodic raindrops, to pray for strength, to pray for calm amidst the brewing storm.

More and thicker drops fell, providing sweet background music to her supplication. She flattened her back against the tree house wall, letting its three-foot overhang absorb much of the drizzle. Her legs stretched out, catching the soothing coolness on her swollen calves and ankles.

Crackling branches interrupted the prayer. "Debbie?" Concern laced Jerry's voice.

She sighed. "Come on up." Her quiet time was done, but that was okay. Time alone with Jerry was equally important.

He climbed up the seven boards to the deck, sat quietly next to her, and handed her a melted Hershey bar sandwiched between two peanut butter cookies.

"You shouldn't have." There was nothing better than chocolate and peanut butter to ease one's apprehensions. A glimmer of a smile touched his face as she swallowed a bite. Heaven. "Thank you."

"You're welcome." He grasped her open hand. His thumb rubbed back and forth, chafing her skin, proving his anxiety, confirming that she needed to remain strong. "Marcus and family just arrived. They all seem to be pretty worried. I told them not to be. Not that it helped."

"Well, then, I suppose we should go alleviate their worry." No sense in putting it off any longer.

He nodded and climbed back down.

Debbie took one more glance at the sky, at the thunderheads boiling up in the distance, and followed Jerry.

"HE'S DONE IT AGAIN." Debbie heard Marcus complain as she and Jerry walked through the farmhouse door, stepping into the enclosed porch. Behind them, the rain came down in sheets. They had made it just in time to avoid getting drenched by the showers. Just in time to get drenched with more complaints. With Marcus, it was always about someone else.

"Who's done what again?" She stopped in the doorway leading into the kitchen and wiped the moisture from her arms. Her parents sat with Marcus and Janet at the oak kitchen table. Each had a white Corelle cup, filled with coffee, set in front of them. Jerry's hand braced her shoulder, lightly pressing her forward.

Marcus peered up, wearing that familiar sneer. "Guess." He took a sip of coffee.

Sighing, Debbie sat next to her mother, crossways from her brother. Jerry settled in across from her. She rubbed her arms, wiping away the raindrops' chill. How could she steer clear of Marcus' latest tirade?

"Let me get you a hot chocolate." Her mother, Marlene, stood and hurried to the stove. "Warm those bones a bit." Even her mother didn't want to hear Marcus' latest grievance. Why couldn't her brothers see the pain they caused?

"Thanks," Debbie said, hoping to avoid an argument. "You want some too, Jer?"

"Coffee. Thanks. I'll be right back." He stood and jogged to the stairs. Perhaps he was trying to escape too. Not that she blamed him.

Her mother set a cup of hot cocoa in front of her. An inverted whipped cream tornado covered the top.

"You know my friend, Fred Beam?" Marcus curved his hands around his cup.

Debbie's shoulders hunched. Her brother wasn't taking the hint.

Marcus spooned sugar into his coffee. "He runs that small machine shop on the edge of town."

She sipped a taste of her cocoa, testing the temperature. Just right. She took a longer gulp, feeling the hot liquid warm the insides of her body as she considered Marcus' friend. The only thing she ever heard Marcus say about the man was that he clearly didn't belong in business.

Something soft and warm draped over her shoulders.

Jerry smiled as he found his way to his chair.

She mouthed "thank you" then slipped on one of Ricky's old maroon and gold sweatshirts.

"I asked Ricky for a favor." Marcus took a long gulp of coffee. "Actually, Fred asked for it. Said he wanted someone to tell him what he was doing wrong, said he'd pay Ricky whatever his going rate was for a consultation."

"Is this something we need to know?" Her dad, Bernie, plunked his coffee cup on the table, sloshing black liquid over the top.

"Would you rather hear it from me or the town gossip? Word is going to get around about this, and it's not the least bit flattering to your son."

He wouldn't even acknowledge that they were brothers. Debbie shook her head and glanced at her dad.

His left elbow rested on the table, fingers pressing into his forehead. Lifting his head, his hand made a small wave. "Go ahead."

Marcus leaned into the back of his chair. "I thought this would be a way to get in Rick's good graces. Maybe find a way to get along, and then he goes and pulls a stunt like this."

"Marcus." Debbie crossed her arms below her chest. "Enough editorializing."

His hands shot up. "Fine." He raised his coffee cup, stared into it, and set it down again. "Ricky did the job all right. Took my friend's money and told him to shut the place down. It wasn't worth saving."

"Maybe it wasn't," Bernie said. "You've constantly complained about Fred having no head for business."

"Exactly. That's why I asked Ricky for his help. Thought maybe he could teach Fred a thing or two. No, instead, he says close it down. Doesn't care about the two other guys who lost full-time jobs because of it. Ricky took the easy way out, Dad. Cost three people their livelihood. Got your son a new addition to that expensive wardrobe of his."

Debbie glanced at Jerry.

His head was bowed toward the coffee cup clasped between his hands. He'd often said that the playground squabbles between his students made more sense than the bickering between her brothers. His students had an excuse: they were kids.

But Debbie wouldn't give up hope. Someday her brothers would reconcile. They just had to, and since Ricky wasn't here to speak for himself, it was up to her. "Did you ever consider that you don't have all the facts? That maybe what Ricky recommended was the best thing?"

Marcus laughed. "For all of two seconds. But I know him. I know that the only person he thinks of is himself. All this did was solidify my opinion."

"I think you're wrong." Debbie lifted her chin.

"I think it's time we put this conversation aside." Her dad pushed his chair away from the table. "As Debbie said, we don't have all the facts. I'd hoped we'd trained you well enough not to gossip."

"Fine." Marcus stood. He carried his coffee cup to the sink, rinsed it out and placed it in the dishwasher before sitting again. The sneer had vacated his face. "Hey, I'm sorry, Debs, Jerry. Talk about being selfish. We came here for you guys."

It's about time. "Thanks." She stood, keeping the warm cup between her hands. "Can we go sit in the front room? I'd like to put my legs up." She didn't wait for an answer as she led the way. The light was off in the room, but a flash of lightning showed it was empty. No children.

"Where's Kaitlynn?"

"Downstairs with the boys." Janet stopped close behind Debbie as someone flipped the light on. "We sent them away with popcorn and a movie. Nathan'll keep an eye on her."

"Good." Kaitlynn was too little to understand her parents' concerns. This discussion was best left for adults.

A low roll of thunder escorted the rest of the family in.

Chapter Eight

"*I* t's a girl."

Jerry forced a smile with Debbie's announcement as she cuddled next to him on the loveseat, her legs resting on an ottoman. He studied the family's faces. Like him, they all wore a pretend smile. Clearly, they knew this gathering wasn't called solely to disclose the gender of the baby.

He wanted to be happy. He wanted to wear a smile like the one Debbie wore. Yes, her joy was sincere, and he wanted to share in her joy. It was important to demonstrate that this wasn't going to get him down, but the turbulence in his stomach, and the pain throbbing in his arm, equaled the storm raging outside. He squeezed Debbie's hand, letting her know he was ready for the rest, although it wasn't true.

She squeezed back. "A few weeks ago, we had an amniocentesis."

In a flash of lightning, the family's false smiles disappeared completely.

"You didn't tell us." Her mother sat up straight.

"We didn't want to worry you," Debbie said.

True, his wife would rather keep the concerns all to herself.

"I'm your mother. It's my job to worry with you."

Debbie shrugged.

Typical Debbie. She was so good at letting Jesus carry her

burdens. Too bad Jerry couldn't do the same.

Marlene settled back into the couch, a shroud of disappointment clouding her face.

Debbie took in a breath as she caressed her stomach. "Our little girl has Down syndrome."

What was left of the smiles turned into frowns. Their bodies seemed to seek refuge in the cushions surrounding them.

A peel of thunder shook the room. Jerry felt his chest constrict, and he grasped Debbie's hand tighter. He couldn't let this happen. Not again. Breathe. Inhale. Exhale. In. Out.

Quiet overtook the room as his chest pain slowly subsided. Feeling the family's eyes on him, he glanced around the room.

"Are you all right?" Marlene leaned toward him.

He nodded. The truth would be revealed if he spoke. They all knew what happened before and how he'd reacted to it, how he'd let his former family down. Having a past burdened with baggage, Jerry hadn't pleased Debbie's family when she started dating him.

Over time though, he had won them over. Now to make sure he didn't affirm their original reservations.

"It's okay," Debbie said, accompanied by the wind howling around the old house and whistling nervously through its cracks.

Jerry looked at the Berber carpet and shook his head. His wife, the one who deserved to be comforted, was doing the comforting.

"The possibilities for a person with Down syndrome to live a relatively normal life are steadily increasing." A genuine smile lit Debbie's voice. "I feel blessed that God chose us as her parents. You know, God doesn't make mistakes. We've even decided on a name."

Nodding, he looked up. Well, Debbie had decided. He hadn't argued. Who was he to disagree when this was his fault? The lights flickered off then on again. There were upturns in the family's mouths. She'd succeeded in lifting their darkness. He draped his arm over his wife's shoulders. He didn't deserve her.

"What is her name?" Marlene asked softly.

"Lilly." Debbie suggested naming the baby right away as if the name would make their child more real. More lovable. "Like my favorite flower. But spelled L-i-l-l-y. I think of the time God spent creating all the different kinds of lilies around the world. How he makes the lilies grow again every year, even after a harsh winter. How much more care will he have spent on this baby?" Debbie stroked her stomach and squeezed his hand again, then gazed straight into his eyes. "God's got a special plan for her. I know it."

His Adam's apple bobbed. He was intimately familiar with the words from the Psalm saying no one's an accident, we're all wondrously made. Now to convince his heart of it.

"Have you told Ricky yet?" Bernie asked.

"I'll call him when he gets home from London." Debbie said. "He'll be back Sunday, I think, and I feel better telling him without an ocean between us."

"You seem to be handling the news well." Janet looked at Jerry.

Janet clearly couldn't read him very well. He raised his arm to his forehead and dried it. How could one perspire and shake at the same time?

Debbie shrugged and raised her hand. "Do I?" She stole his answer, rescuing him.

"You always do," Marcus said.

That is so true.

Debbie shrugged again. "She's my baby girl. I'm gonna love her no matter what. But that doesn't mean I won't want all of your support, that there won't be times I'll be angry. I only hope you all understand if I explode once in a while."

Marcus chuckled and sat up straight. "To be honest, I'd like to be around to see you explode. Record it on the calendar. Call the newspaper . . . "

"Cut it out." Debbie chuckled

The rest of the family smiled too. Leave it to Marcus to provide levity for the moment.

"You know you can count on us." Marcus got serious again. "I'm speaking for your brother, too."

"I know. We'll be fine." Debbie embraced her stomach. "She'll be fine."

I'll be fine. The lights flickered again. Hurried footsteps pattered on the basement stairs. Had to be Kaitlynn. She didn't like thunderstorms. Truth be told, Jerry didn't either. He glanced at the doorway as Kaitlynn ran through it, and straight to him, desiring his courage. A daddy's courage. Feeling woefully inadequate to offer it, he held her tight, needing her love right back. *I'll be fine.*

The lightning flashed again, this time taking the house lights with it, leaving them in pitch darkness, hiding his fear.

Chapter Nine

Jerry lifted his sleeping daughter from her car seat and pressed her head against his shoulder. She snuggled in close, her feathery breath tickling his neck as he carried her through the house to her bedroom where glow-in-the-dark stars speckled her ceiling.

When he attempted to lay her down, her pudgy hands reached up and squeezed his cheeks, forcing a pucker.

Chuckling softly, he kissed her.

"Sing, Daddy." Her hands remained on his cheeks.

Warmth coursed through his body as he drew her in tight, accepting her innocent love. What a blessing it was that she'd never see the scarring on his cheek as a defect, that she could cradle his cheek with such tenderness. To her, the deep-pink waves and sharp ridges were simply part of Daddy, and that was all that mattered. Other children, and even adults, weren't as kind. How often had he endured the stares and the rude comments because he was different? It would be the same for his new baby.

If she lived long enough.

He closed his eyes and drew in a breath. Kaitlynn's strawberry-scented hair filled his senses. Children were blessings. All of them. He swayed as he sang. "You're my precious girl, created in love. You're a special child, a gift from Heaven above. When you are sad, I'll sing you a song. When you are glad, I'll laugh right along. When you are weak, I'll carry you. I'll be your strength. I'll walk with you."

Kaitlynn's arms became limp as Jerry finished his song, his voice thick.

He laid her down, tucked the covers beneath her chin, and left a kiss on her cheek before dragging his arm over his eyes. *Dear God, please help me be the man, the father, Kaitlynn believes me to be.* He walked from the room, his feet barely lifting off the floor.

It was time for a quiet talk with his wife.

DEBBIE PUT THE CARPENTER'S square in the corner of the boards she'd just nailed together, then tested the other three angles. Perfect. Just like Ricky would do it. She hung the square on her pegboard wall above her garage workbench as the door to the house opened.

"She stay asleep?" Debbie asked.

Jerry stepped into the garage and leaned against the Escort's hood. He stretched his arms out in front and cracked his knuckles. "I had to sing to her."

"Of course." Debbie sat in a folding chair and pointed to the one open next to her. "How are you doing?"

He pulled his wallet from his back pocket, opened it, and handed it to Debbie. A picture of a round-faced newborn, with teardrop eyes, graced the middle. "He would be ten now."

A lump rose in her throat. "Lilly will be fine."

"That's what they said about Christopher. Heart surgery would make it all better."

"I know, but—"

"I don't care if the statistics say less than three percent die from heart complications. Christopher beat the odds. Who says this baby won't beat them too?" He grabbed his billfold and snapped it shut. "I can't go through it again."

With misty eyes, he leaned forward and picked a pebble of granite off her workbench. "Can you imagine the power it took to break this?"

It was just like him to avoid the subject. Debbie stood and walked to her husband. She clasped the hand holding the stone between hers, closing his fingers around it. "Even granite needs a solid foundation, or it will crack. A cord of three strands is stronger than granite."

He jerked his hand away and hurled the stone onto her bench. It skittered across the top, pinging against an empty Pepsi can. "Funny, I believed that too, until Francine walked out on me."

"Ah, Jerry, we've had this discussion before. You know I would never do that."

"Right now, I don't really know anything." He shuffled back into the house, his shoulders hunched beneath the weight he insisted on carrying. The door slammed behind him.

Debbie blinked, and her mouth hung open. How dare he insinuate that she would leave him? Hadn't they discussed, *ad nauseam*, the possibility of having another Down syndrome child before they got engaged? Before trying for Kaitlynn, and now Lilly? She squeezed her eyes shut and drew in a deep breath. He was just reacting to today. He didn't mean anything, he's just hurting. She blew out her breath. *So am I.* But it wouldn't do any good to let him know that.

She slid open the top drawer of the dresser-sized tool chest tucked beneath her bench and reached in back, her fingers searching. She grasped a candy bar and pulled it out. Didn't matter if it was Milky Way or Snickers. Either one would do the trick. She twisted the top of the wrapper, but it refused to tear.

As she scanned her bench for scissors, a chuckle escaped her throat. Chocolate would make her feel better, for all of ten seconds, and leave a permanent impression on her thighs. Already had. Shaking her head, she threw the bar back into the drawer and slammed it shut.

Tomorrow, she'd remove the temptation from the drawer. Tonight, she'd talk to God.

She slumped into her chair and raised her chin, eyes searching upward. *Help him, please?* More words refused to come. She lowered her head, picked up the stone Jerry had thrown, and rolled it between her fingers.

Wouldn't it be nice, just once, to be like Ricky? Freewheeling around the world. No responsibilities to anyone but himself. Right, and face the fallout later. No. She had to remain staid and strong. For Jerry. For Kaitlynn. Debbie caressed her stomach. For Lilly.

Ignoring the dampness in her eyes, she returned the granite piece to the bench and picked up her hammer again. Time to pound some more nails.

JERRY STOPPED IN HIS bedroom doorway and massaged his left arm. It was happening all over again. Well, this time he planned to stop it. This time, he'd be the man his wife needed him to be.

He stood straight, turned around and strode back to the garage. The slam of a hammer meeting wood greeted him as he opened the door. He cleared his throat. "Debbie?"

She gasped, and the hammer bounced from the bench to the concrete with an echoing thud. Her hands covered her heart as she spun around. Her puffy red eyes opened wide and her cheeks were mottled and damp. "Jeepers, you nearly gave me a heart attack."

Moisture coated his palms as he walked toward her. Why was he so good at hurting those he loved? He was no different from his father.

He stopped within a foot of her, keeping his arms at his side. With the way he'd just acted, he'd lost the right to touch her. "Sweetheart, I'm sorry."

She closed her eyes, but tears seeped from beneath her lids. "You don't—"

"Yes, I do." He wiped his hands on his pants, then cautiously reached up to caress her arm. "I trust you. I do."

Her gaze met his, her lips hinting at a smile. "You're stuck with me."

He raised a hand to his mouth but was too late to cover his grin. Only Debbie could make him smile with turbulence still churning in his stomach. "I'll hold you to that."

Taking her hand, he guided her to the concrete steps leading into the house. He sat, pulling her down next to him. His thumb stroked the back of her hand. "Before we left your folks', Marcus invited me to a men's retreat. Not this weekend, but the one after. I told him I'd think about it, but planned on saying no. It's not fair to leave you alone—"

"Go." She squeezed his hand. "I'd love you to have time for yourself. You know me. I'll be fine."

He sighed. "Yeah, I know. I'll call Marcus tomorrow. Probably be good for me too. Sometimes, it's hard for me to believe that God doesn't leave us. I mean, I just don't see him in this. I can't feel him, hear him. Nothing."

Debbie clasped her hand over their folded hands. "I know what you mean."

"You do?" No way. She never doubted.

"I've told you how I felt after Grandma Brooks died, when I thought for sure God had abandoned me."

Jerry nodded.

"And it was Ricky who took me for that walk, in his own quiet way showing me how to see God, how to feel him, hear him, even taste and smell him."

"I have a hard time seeing Ricky with that kind of faith."

"I know. It's hard to believe, isn't it? But, someday, he'll return to it. Once God gets a hold of us, he doesn't let go. Just like he'll never let go of you."

How Jerry wished his heart believed that.

"I think maybe it's time to start a new family tradition." Debbie slapped her thigh. "Starting tomorrow, when you get home from work, I think we need to take that same God walk Ricky took me on, at least once a week."

The redness had fled Debbie's eyes, replaced now with a sparkle. *God, I love her so much. Please don't let me hurt her.*

"I think that's a very good idea." He leaned in and kissed her, sealing their deal.

Chapter Ten

*D*ebbie rose to her knees, dry grass crunching beneath her. The storms this past weekend had provided scant nourishment for the parched ground.

"Blue-eyed duck. Green-eyed duck." Kaitlynn circled the Bible study group—four moms, six children among them—pulling everyone's head back to study their eyes.

"Gray-eyed duck. Brown-eyed duck."

Get ready to run. It seemed kids always chose their own mom in this game of Gray Duck. Minnesota's answer to Duck, Duck, Goose. Kaitlynn paused and squinted when she pulled the next head back. Debbie sat silent, eager to hear Kaitlynn's description.

"Funny-eyed duck."

Okay, not terribly creative, but accurate. That mother had one brown eye and a blue one so, to a preschooler, it must look quite funny. Kaitlynn pulled back the head of the child sitting next to Debbie.

"Green-eyed duck."

Debbie raised one knee, resting on the other as Kaitlynn's pudgy hands pulled her head back.

"Gray duck!" Kaitlynn let go and started running, giggling all the way.

Debbie stood and chased her daughter, stretching her arms and legs forward in slow motion. Once Kaitlynn reached the opposite side of the circle, Debbie let loose, pursuing as quickly as her pregnant body allowed.

Kaitlynn ignored Debbie's vacated space and coughed as she began circling a second time. She stopped running and coughed again, a deep, guttural rasp that sounded like a seal barking. A wheeze clawed from her throat as she attempted to draw oxygen into tightening lungs.

Cringing, Debbie ran to her Bible bag, where she always kept Kaitlynn's albuterol inhaler and a bottle of water. She hurried back to the group, set Kaitlynn on her lap, and hugged her close as the toddler gasped medicine through a plastic accordion-like tube.

Debbie inhaled exaggerated breaths as Kaitlynn held up her fingers counting, with coughs interrupting each inhale. Once they reached ten, Kaitlynn yanked the tube from her mouth, but the cough persisted, adding bloom to already rosy cheeks. The angel's kiss between her brows—her birthmark—mottled a deep red.

Debbie hugged and kissed Kaitlynn then realized how quiet her group had become. The game had come to a full stop, with the kids holding wide-eyed stares toward Kaitlynn.

Ignoring Kaitlynn's ongoing cough, Debbie gulped in one more deep breath and smiled. "Kaitlynn'll be okay." Her quaking hands belied the calm she tried to display for the children. Nothing was more unnerving than these unpredictable and uncontrollable episodes. "She's got something called asthma that sometimes makes it hard for her to breathe. She takes a special medicine to make the cough go away. She'll be better soon. Why don't you keep playing?"

"Good idea," another mom said, thankfully taking the hint.

It was important to get the children's minds back on the game. They had never experienced one of Kaitlynn's attacks before, as they were rare. Still it had to be frightening for them to watch. Debbie carried Kaitlynn to a nearby bench, cuddled her on her lap, and sang the ABC's, with Kaitlynn periodically joining in. Sometimes music helped get Kaitlynn's mind off the coughing, or maybe it was Debbie's way of getting her own mind off the painful sound.

"Okay, one more time, precious." Debbie offered the inhaler again.

As Kaitlynn breathed and counted, Debbie pulled a Berenstain Bears book from her bag, another ploy to divert Kaitlynn's attention.

It was a good fifteen minutes before Kaitlynn breathed easy again. Before they both breathed easy.

Debbie kissed Kaitlynn's cheek and whispered, "Are you ready, precious?"

Kaitlynn nodded and slid off Debbie's lap but didn't run back to the other children. A life lesson learned early. Instead, she stayed close to Debbie's side, clinging to her hand. If only adults would remember to cling to God's hand when life threw its own coughing fit. Why did adults insist on going through hardships on their own?

The kids had scampered to the primary-colored, plastic playground equipment with its maze of tunnels, slides, and bridges, while the mothers remained in a circle. Debbie sat on the edge of the blanket, keeping Kaitlynn on her lap. Debbie wasn't ready for a repeat of the coughing fit. Her friends' conversation quieted as they looked at her with concern. What an odd sensation. Normally, she was the comforter.

"Is she okay?" Val laid a warm hand on Debbie's arm.

Debbie forced a smile. "She'll be fine."

Val winced as Kaitlynn coughed. "Are you sure?"

Debbie nodded, and her smile became genuine. Perhaps Val would help Debbie through this pregnancy. Perhaps this group would, for once, listen to her concerns. Perhaps she could become the counselee instead of the counselor. What a novelty that would be. "Thank you for—"

"Honey," Marsha interrupted, talking as much with her hands as she did with her mouth. She was famous for cutting in, for making her issues more important or sensational than anyone else's. Every small group has the "extra care required" member. Marsha aptly fit the description. "I don't know how you do it. Nothing ever seems to faze you."

Oh, it fazed her all right. It just did no good to telegraph those fears to her daughter. It was important to maintain a calm demeanor to keep Kaitlynn relaxed. "I wouldn't say—"

"Now, take me." Marsha broke in again, clearly oblivious to anyone but herself.

Debbie slouched as Marsha droned on about her bounty of issues. Debbie's window to voice her concerns closed as abruptly as it opened. Keeping a sigh to herself, she assumed the all-too-familiar role of listener.

Minutes later, the group began to break up. Debbie supposed Val and Connie, the wonder mother who had three children ages four and under, were as tired of listening to Marsha as she was. The last thing they wanted to hear was more complaints.

Debbie glanced at her watch as the mothers and children strolled away. Not even eleven yet. Kaitlynn needed at least another hour of exercise and fresh air before returning home if she was to take a decent nap in the afternoon.

Perhaps a little quiet time wasn't such a bad idea. Debbie stood, gathered her bag, and clasped Kaitlynn's hand. Usually, her daughter would be running ahead, leading the way. Today she was content to walk beside her mother.

They followed a narrow dirt path, created by foot traffic, with roots bulging above the trail's surface. Debbie held back branches so they wouldn't slap her or Kaitlynn. Soon, the park disappeared from sight as nature took over. Lilac fragrance clung to the air. A chorus of birds twittered and tweeted to an unknown melody. Rabbits, squirrels, and gophers scampered out of view. Up ahead, the faint trickle of water underscored nature's song as it swept over the rocks and dips attempting to stop it. But, like life, the water kept flowing, those impediments giving the creek its unique character.

The gray-blue waters of Granite Creek, the slender stream meandering on the edge of town, so named because of the area's generous harvest of igneous rock, peeked between the branches then fully came into view. Kaitlynn released Debbie's hand, kicked off her flip-flops and aimed for the water that had slowed to a mere dribble. A month ago, winter's melt had filled the winding, rock-laden channel, enough to create a swift current. Even with this past weekend's storms, the dry spring had taken the current elsewhere. As a mother of a curious child, Debbie was perfectly fine with that.

She sat on the grassy bank as Kaitlynn searched beneath the waters, sorting through the rocks, finding treasure only a mother could appreciate. Debbie stored the gems in a lunch baggie. Most would be added to the rock garden surrounding their house. A deeper purpose awaited the genuine pieces of granite.

As the sun climbed higher in the sky, Debbie looked at her watch again. Thirty more minutes to kill, and a damp child who needed drying off. "What do you say we swing for a bit, precious?" The rushing air should take the moisture away.

"Yeah!" Kaitlynn jumped up and bolted back down the path. Debbie puffed after her. By the time she reached the park,

Kaitlynn had pulled herself up on the highest swing, kicking her legs, making the swing rock. "Hurry, Mommy!"

Debbie quickened her steps, but the pregnancy already deprived her of wind. "I'll be right there, precious."

"Push me, Mommy."

"Okay." Debbie stopped behind the swing and grabbed onto the chains.

"Underdog!" Kaitlynn hollered.

"Underdog?" Now where had Kaitlynn come up with that?

"Like Uncle Ricky does."

Of course. She should have known. "Okay. What exactly is an underdog?"

"Go underneath me."

Underneath? Debbie grasped the chains, thinking. Finally, the answer became clear. She'd done it before but never applied a name to it. "Okay. We'll see if I can do it as good as Uncle Ricky." Debbie gripped the swing's chains then stepped back, pulling the swing along with her. When she'd gone as far as she could reach, Debbie ran forward, ducking beneath the seat as the ride sailed high, then let go. She curved her hand over her stomach. Underdog was not a pregnancy-friendly game. Still, Kaitlynn wore a full-toothed smile as her swing continued on its pendulum. How could she not accommodate her daughter?

"Pump, honey."

But for some reason, Kaitlynn wasn't trying today, and the swing quickly slowed to a gentle rock.

"Why didn't you pump?"

"Do underdog again."

"Didn't I do it good enough?"

Kaitlynn shook her head.

"No?" Debbie secured her hands on her hips. "Okay, little miss, what did I do wrong?"

"Say 'underdog,' like Uncle Ricky."

"Say 'underdog'?"

Kaitlynn nodded.

Debbie peered up, scrunching her lips, then shook her head. In the few short hours of his visit, her brother had completely spoiled her daughter. "Okay. I'll try to do it like Uncle Ricky, but I don't think I'll be as good. He's always the best at giving underdogs, you know."

"I know." The stinker was a little too agreeable.

Debbie pulled the swing back again, this time yelling "underdog" as she ducked beneath Kaitlynn's legs. She must have done it right this time because Kaitlynn giggled and began waving her legs. Attaining the perfect rhythm was still a ways off, but if she kept at it, the motion would slowly become natural. It would be one more piece of independence for Kaitlynn. And for herself. That freedom would make them both happy.

Debbie gave two more underdogs before Kaitlynn said she wanted to play on the jungle gym. As Kaitlynn ran toward the set, Debbie massaged her belly. Next time, Jerry would have to take over underdog duty.

She followed Kaitlynn to the plastic maze and spotted another child playing. An unfamiliar, towheaded little girl, who looked to be close to Kaitlynn's age. In this small town, it was unusual not to know everyone. A man, with hair as dark as the girl's was blonde, stood at the end of a slide as the child glided down. He caught the girl and swung her in the air, emphasizing broad shoulders he probably earned tossing hay bales, as so many did in this rural farm area. Debbie hurried to introduce herself.

He set the girl down and turned as Debbie approached. "Your daughter?" He pointed at Kaitlynn.

Debbie nodded. "All mine. And yours?"

"Yep." He smiled. "Looks like they're about the same age.

Amelia's three and a half."

"Kaitlynn turned three this weekend." Debbie maintained close watch as the girls played together as if they'd known each other for years. "Are you visiting?"

"Visiting?"

"It's a small town. I pretty much know everyone in it and recognize a stranger."

He gave his head a sideways nod before offering his hand. "I hope to remedy that. I'm Lee Aldrich."

Debbie accepted it. "Debbie Verhoeven."

"Actually, we're probably Granite Creek's newest residents. Moved in this weekend. It's our first opportunity to check out the park. It's quite a setup for this little town."

"It is, but still, it's not used much. People's lives are too busy, I guess. Personally, I prefer a more laid-back lifestyle."

"I agree. Now, Amelia's mother, she'd say something altogether different. For Elise, sitting still is akin to torture."

"I've got a couple of brothers like that."

Lee smiled then gestured toward a nearby bench.

Debbie led the way.

"So, what do you do when you're not playing at the park?" Lee sat next to her.

"What do I do?"

He rubbed his forehead. "I guess that was pretty vague. Do you stay at home with Kaitlynn? Do you have a career?"

Ahh, the dreaded question. Does she answer *I'm a full-time mom* and draw a blank stare or the placating *That's really a hard job* delivered with a lack of sincerity? That happened more than she could count on her fingers and toes put together. But, embarrassing or not, truth was always best. She nodded in Kaitlynn's direction. "Right now, she's my career."

"Good for you." He smiled. "So, you're a member of that rare breed of women who are, unfortunately, becoming extinct."

Debbie shrugged. "I guess. I hadn't ever thought of it that way. But it's true, isn't it?"

"Well, I for one applaud you. It's not an easy job, and it's quite misunderstood."

"Or maybe people understand it all too well. It's very challenging, and there's a lot of sacrifice that goes into the job. Most people aren't willing to make the sacrifice. I can't say I blame them." Someday she'd return to the therapist's chair, where she made a difference in people's lives, where she contributed to family finances instead of draining them. But for now, she was where God wanted her, as difficult as it was. "And what do you do, when not playing with your daughter?"

"Once upon a time, I was an electrician."

"Once upon a time?"

"You see, I'm an even rarer breed. I'm the stay-at-home dad."

"Really?" Very rare. She'd never met a full-time father before. "That must come with unique challenges, even in our supposedly liberated society."

"I admit, it does, but it hasn't been as awkward as I thought it would be. Most people are impressed with what I do. My former colleagues gave me the most grief. At first, when people asked me what I did, I gave them the line that I'm the CHO, Chief Home Officer, for a small company whose purpose was to train future leaders."

Debbie grinned. "I like that. I'll have to remember that one. I've gotten so when someone looks at me with glazed eyes and asks, 'What do you do all day?' I tell them, 'I sit and watch *Star Trek* and eat bon bons.'"

"*Star Trek*?"

"You seriously don't expect me to say *Oprah*?"

He laughed.

She laughed with him. "I know I shouldn't respond like that, but I love to see the look on people's faces. It works better than trying to explain away the mundane tasks that never seem to get done. What's funny is that if I'd say I'm a childcare worker or even a nanny, people would applaud me, but when I say I'm a full-time mom, they think I'm lazy. Tell me, what's the difference?"

"The difference is the one-on-one attention you can give your daughter. She gets the benefit of the hugs and kisses—"

"And the yelling and impatience and expecting her to behave older than she is."

"That too."

Debbie's stomach rumbled. She glanced at her watch again. Twelve thirty already? It was time to head back, eat, then get Kaitlynn's nap in, maybe a quick nap for herself. But she'd thoroughly enjoyed this adult conversation. Someone actually listened and understood her. "I need to get going." Debbie extended her hand. "It's been a pleasure talking with you, Lee."

He accepted her hand with a firm shake. "I'm certain I'll run into you again."

"I look forward to it." Debbie stood. "Kaitlynn. Time to go, precious."

"Do I have to?"

Debbie cuffed her hands on her hips and said nothing. It was good that Kaitlynn found a new friend, but Debbie didn't allow back talk.

Kaitlynn looked at her mom and opened her mouth then shut it, sucking her lips inward, then slid through the curving tunnel. Keeping her head down, she walked slowly toward her mommy, dredging a path through the sand.

Debbie patted her daughter's head. "You can play with Amelia some other time."

Kaitlynn stuck out her lower lip. "Okay, Mommy."

"You know," Debbie glanced at Lee again, "you'd be more than welcome to join my Bible study group. Right now, it's a group of four women, all stay-at-home moms, who usually meet Monday morning. I was busy this week, so we switched to Wednesday." If only her group had allowed her to tell them the reason for the change.

"Bible study?" His lips curved down. "I think I'll pass on that one. We're not too into religion."

"You don't have to be. You're welcome any time. We'd welcome a new perspective."

"I appreciate the offer. I'll think about it."

"Please do." Debbie took Kaitlynn's hand and turned away, then twisted toward Lee one more time. "We look forward to seeing you again. And welcome to Granite Creek." She jotted a mental note, *Create a welcome basket for Lee's family*. It was important for this family to feel welcome.

She grinned as she walked toward home. It sure felt wonderful to have a grown-up conversation for once. Hopefully, there'd be many more to come.

Chapter Eleven

*F*riday already. Debbie stared at her bedroom ceiling and yawned. Nearly two weeks had passed since the doctor appointment, two quick weeks, but the coming weekend was going to be a long one. With Jerry leaving for his men's retreat following work, she wouldn't get the break she looked forward to when the weekend arrived. But it was just as well.

Jerry needed this conference more than she needed an hour or two to herself. Maybe it would restore his confidence, his faith. She rolled over and breathed in the woodsy remnants of Jerry's *Halston* cologne. Hopefully, it would linger until Sunday. There would be no sheets washed this weekend.

She threw off the wedding ring quilt her mom had made, slid her legs off the bed, and shuffled to her oak veneer dresser. Too bad she couldn't go with Jerry. Women's retreats never had anything meaty like pro athlete speakers or seminars discussing the latest garage gadget.

No, they'd rather focus on scrapbooking, or makeup, or the latest cooking craze. Puhlease. Sure, that was fine for most women. It just wasn't her. She glanced in the mirror hanging above her dresser and frowned. Sometimes it would be nice to be typical.

From a drawer, she took out faded jean shorts and a red T-shirt advertising her church's VBS program. Maybe she should call her mom and invite herself out to the farm for the weekend. Have her dad help with Kaitlynn's ceramic project. Mom would pamper them, and give her some time off. Maybe even provide an opportunity to catch a chick flick with Val or Janet.

A smile crept to her lips. Yep, that was exactly what she'd do. She sat on the edge of the bed and pulled on her shorts, then stood up, sucking in her stomach as she tugged on the zipper. No use. This baby was growing way too fast. Back to polyester. Yuck. She folded the jeans and tucked them in the bottom of the drawer, then chose navy shorts. They had enough stretch to last the summer.

It would be nice if she had a little extra cash to purchase some new maternity clothes, something that wouldn't embarrass her in public. *Such is life.* If Jerry got the principal job, then maybe . . .

But, even if Jerry did get the job, his increased compensation would be eaten up by baby expenses. Yikes, she was complaining again. It was definitely time to call her mom.

She walked from the bedroom and found Jerry sitting by the kitchen table reading the daily paper. A cup of black coffee and an empty cereal bowl sat on the table next to a hand-sized, wire-bound book containing a daily Bible verse. Needing to keep Christ at the center of the marriage, he rarely left for work without them sharing the verse.

"Morning, hon." Before sitting, she leaned over and kissed him on the cheek.

He folded the paper and laid it on the table. "Sleep well?"

"Um, hmm, but this baby's draining me. I swear I could sleep all day."

"You'll be all right this weekend, won't you?"

"I'll be fine. I was even thinking of going to the farm. Keep Mom and Dad company for a bit."

"I'd like that." He picked up his coffee cup but didn't drink. Instead, he smiled. "Actually, I think that would be a great idea"

Her stomach fluttered. She'd seen precious little of his smile this past week. Maybe he was finally warming up to the idea of having a child with Down syndrome. The retreat, led by a man—a husband and father—who had defeated his own Goliath, would only help.

"Okay then, I'll give Mom a call now and let her know." She stood, grabbed the cordless phone, and it rang in her hands. Had to be Mom. No one else would call this early. She punched the answer button. "Hello."

"Hey, Debs."

"Ricky! You're home?" She leaned against the cupboard and grinned at her husband.

He set his coffee cup down, smiling back.

"Got in yesterday," Ricky said. "Had an unbelievable trip."

"Really? Tell me about it."

"Well, other than saving the company a few mil, there's not much to tell."

"A few million?"

Jerry's eyebrows rose.

"Give or take."

"I suppose that's cause for celebration."

"I think so. Come on out tonight. We'll celebrate together."

She laughed. Oh, if only she could, nothing would be more fun, and she'd be able to tell him about Lilly in person. No *I'm sorry* delivered over the phone could replace a sympathizing hug.

"I'm serious. Have Jerry watch Katydid for the weekend. Come on out. We'll catch a show, a hot dog, some good conversation—"

"Whoa, whoa, whoa. You're not kidding, are you?"

"I'm dead serious."

"You're making this awfully difficult to turn down."

Jerry's raised eyebrows furrowed.

"Then don't," Ricky said.

She grinned at her husband. If only she could convince Jerry to let her go. But it would take more than getting Jerry to agree. Who would stay with Kaitlynn?

"You don't understand. I'd love to come, but Jerry's gone this weekend. I have to watch Kaitlynn."

"What about Mom or Janet?"

Jerry suspended his coffee cup in the air, watching her, his tented brows revealing confusion.

"Can you hold a second, Rick?"

"No problem. If he says 'no' let me talk."

"Like that would do any good."

"It's worth a try."

"One sec, okay?" She held the handset against her hip and sat next to Jerry.

"Okay, what's up?" Suspicion reigned in his eyes and the downward arc of his mouth.

"Ricky wants me to come visit." She bit into her lower lip and held her breath. No way would Jerry agree.

But his lips slowly curved up, and his eyes brightened. "I figured as much." He sipped his coffee.

"And?" Raising her eyebrows, she nodded at the phone.

"How about next weekend? I'll be home then."

"Really?" He didn't just say yes, did he?

"It'd be good for you." A full-fledged smile took over his face as he set his coffee cup on the table.

Shoot. Now she felt like crying. "Thanks, hon." She closed her eyes and kissed him on the lips before lifting the receiver. "How about next weekend? Jerry will be home."

Debbie tapped her fingers on the table. *Please, oh please, say yes*. She visualized him studying his calendar.

"Sorry, Debs, I can't."

"Oh." Stupid tears threatened again.

"I'm really sorry. And my weekends are pretty full for the next month or two. I'm doing a lot of consulting outside the company this summer and, unfortunately, that fills most of my weekends. The only reason this one's open is because I got home earlier than expected."

"Well, it was worth a shot." She held the handset away from her face, dragged her arm across her eyes and looked at Jerry. "He's busy."

"Oh," Jerry said quietly. He stared blankly at the window above the kitchen table and scratched the back of his neck. "Well, then." He turned to her and smiled. "Call someone to watch Kaitlynn. My mom. Your mom. Janet. Someone. You're always helping everyone else; maybe it's time they help you."

Ricky yelled through the phone. "Listen to your husband."

She raised the receiver, seizing the moment before Jerry changed his mind. "Okay. I will. You're gonna have to give me a few minutes to make some phone calls."

"Fine. Make it quick, though, so I can find a flight for you. Might have to bring you first class."

"I might have to suffer through it. You at work?"

"Home."

"Okay. I'll call you right back." She clicked the *end* key and couldn't contain a smile. *Thank you, God*. The praise floated upward as she leaned over and kissed Jerry. "You don't know how much this means to me," she whispered, keeping her face close to his. Her husband looked very sexy at the moment.

He returned her kiss, gently stroking her face with his thumb. "Like I said, it's your turn to have a break." He finished his coffee and stood up. "Time for me to head out. I'm meeting with some parents this morning. Their son's been acting out lately, and I figure they should know what's going on."

"You're a great teacher, you know that?" That concern for his students' entire well-being was what drew her to him in the first place. Before she quit her job, she'd counseled more of his students' families than she could remember.

He leaned over and kissed her. "You're just saying that because it's true."

"I see you're taking lessons in humility from my brothers."

A grin sparked his eyes. "Go make your phone calls then call me, let me know when you're leaving. I don't need the car this weekend so you can take it to the airport. I'll walk to work. It'll do me some good."

"I love you, you know."

He backed out the door, smiling like he hadn't smiled in weeks.

AS HE WAITED FOR Debbie's call, Richard studied the calendar on his kitchen wall. The Disney film monthly was a prized possession, an annual Christmas gift from Kaitlynn. It didn't matter that the women he brought to his high-rise apartment questioned his sanity when they saw it prominently displayed on his wall. Little did they know, it also served as a litmus test. If they didn't appreciate his occasional childlike nature, well then, they weren't worth dating. Unfortunately, far too few appreciated his taste for the simple.

The phone on his belt chirped out a toddler's tune he'd downloaded when babysitting Kaitlynn. It always made the people around him smile. Why change it? He glanced at the caller I.D., knowing it wouldn't be Debbie. She didn't like bothering him away from home, so she and the rest of their family usually called his landline.

The I.D. read "ACM Technologies." His work had no trouble contacting him at all hours, on any phone. This was probably his assistant calling about some urgent project that needed to be completed yesterday. Well, tough. Whatever they wanted could wait. He clipped the phone back to his belt. This weekend was devoted solely to his sister.

Come Monday, he'd be aching to dive back into his job.

Maybe someday, he'd disengage himself from the corporate world, return to Minnesota, and find a woman worth making a home for. They'd raise a family, he might even return to church. Yeah, no doubt about it, he'd return to church. He even smiled thinking of it. His family would be pleased.

Someday.

But someday was in the future. For now, he needed to concentrate on the present. He looked back at the calendar. Nearly every day was filled. He flipped the pages to November. Debbie's baby was due early November, Janet's in December. Stuck smack in between their due dates was his parents' anniversary celebration. With the babies and the anniversary, he'd have to sacrifice going home for the holidays.

Perhaps this year, he'd find a church here. There were plenty of churches in the city. He'd just never attended. Besides, it was important to fulfill his church CEO—Christmas, Easter Only—obligation.

He ambled to the cupboard, slid his chrome toaster away from the wall, and popped in two slices of wheat bread. Perhaps guilt prompted his invitation to Debbie. He needed the time alone with his sister after stomping away like a spoiled brat two weekends ago. One would think that at thirty-five he'd have outgrown that phase. Sometimes Marcus was too right-on with his accusations.

Richard removed grape jelly and the butter dish from his fridge. Real butter. Spread all the way to the edges. Absolutely no cutting corners. No matter what Marcus assumed, Richard wasn't one for cutting corners. His executive status was achieved through hard work, skill, and a touch of luck. Ethics weren't worth sacrificing, either, but Marcus would never believe that so why bother trying to convince him?

He finished his sandwich and stared at the silent phone. *Come on, Debbie, call.* He hated quiet moments like this when his mind was allowed to ruminate, and guilt saturated his conscience.

God lived in quiet moments.

Reaching up, he hit the power button on the radio attached beneath a cabinet, sending talk show host white noise into the air.

Even that didn't blot out God's voice.

He grabbed the phone and squeezed it in his palm as he stared down at it, willing it to ring. Being alone this weekend wasn't an option.

If not Debbie, then there were equally satisfying ways to fill his time. So what if his family wouldn't approve? He scrolled through the contacts on his cell, and the doorbell rang.

Who in the world could that be? He strode to his door and glanced through the peephole. A bewildered smile crept to his face.

If for some reason Debbie couldn't make it, spending an afternoon with Patrice might make him forget all about his family and the guilt that came with them.

WHISTLING, JERRY WALKED DOWN a sidewalk that was heaving and fractured with age. For once, he'd actually let go of his pride and accepted an offer from his wealthy brother-in-law. Perhaps he'd done it out of guilt for leaving Debbie alone when she had already spent her entire week without another adult around. Regardless of his motives, it was the right thing to do. This weekend they'd both be able to leave their fears and frustrations behind and begin the coming week with a fresh outlook.

He pinched a white lilac blossom off a bush as he passed by. The scent would add an aromatic touch to his classroom . . . and it would remind him of Debbie. He was sure going to miss her. Maybe today he'd be able to forget about that smiling family tucked away in his desk drawer. Maybe this weekend's events would give him the strength he needed to support his wife. After all, as a man he was technically supposed to act as head of the family, especially in spiritual matters. So far, he'd failed.

According to Marcus, that was what this retreat was all about: relying on God's strength to conquer life's giants so a husband/father could be the spiritual rock a family needed. Right now, Debbie was definitely the spiritual leader securing their family's foundation. It was time he took his rightful place in that position.

He glanced at his watch then lengthened his stride. It was important to be in the classroom when Debbie called to relay the details. A thought stopped him. With this morning's fuss, they'd forgotten to read their verse of the day. He glanced at his watch again and frowned. Not enough time to return home. She could read it to him over the phone. He'd take the lead and remind her, take his first steps in assuming his rightful place in their marriage. No matter what happened with this baby, he'd be ready because God would be first in their lives.

"Okay God." He spoke aloud, not caring if passersby thought him loony. So what? "I want to be the man you created me to be." Remaining in prayer, he hastened to his job.

Not more than ten minutes later, he walked into his

classroom. He set his briefcase on the floor next to his desk and propped the lilac up in his pencil jar just as the phone rang. Smiling, he reclined in his chair. Although he knew it was Debbie relaying her good news, he answered professionally anyway. "Mr. Verhoeven."

"Hi, hon." Debbie's voice was soft, lacking its usual passion.

He slumped in his chair. No good news was associated with that tone.

Chapter Twelve

*J*erry ran a hand over his head. "There's no one?"

"Afraid not."

A foul word flitted through his thoughts. Failure hadn't been a consideration. "Honey, I'm so sorry."

"Hey, such is life."

Just like that, she covered her dejection and sounded ready to move on, but he knew her well enough to know her disappointment was only cloaked.

"Like I said earlier, I might spend the weekend on the farm; give Mom a hand with the boys."

"Oh, so she's watching Nate and Josh."

"Yep. I understand why she doesn't want to take on Kaitlynn too."

True, the boys were a handful. Still, it was frustrating. "And Mom?"

"She's got plans, is all she said."

"Of course," he said softly, drumming his fingers on his desk. His mom rarely babysat. Not that she didn't love Kaitlynn, but watching the toddler for a weekend was probably asking too much. Still, for once someone should come through for his wife. "Listen, hon. Give me a few minutes to think. There's got to be some way, someone who'll help you out."

She just sighed.

He picked up a pencil and tapped it on his desk. "I don't know who, at the moment, but I'll come up with someone."

"Really, it's okay. It's not like I'd had the weekend planned for weeks. I'm fine with it."

Well, I'm not. "Give me a few minutes to think, and I'll call you back."

"Whatever. I'll talk to you later."

The phone quieted. So, she didn't believe him. Well, he was going to come through for her. It was time he stopped letting people down.

He returned the handset to the cradle as a knock sounded on his door. Vince's parents. Standing, he pointed to the table Vince normally sat at. "Please, come have a seat." The couple walked into the room, gaits stiff and shoulders slunk, keeping an obvious physical distance from each other. Before sitting, they added an additional foot of space between the chairs. Looked like letting loved ones down was common, but at least these two came together and without argument. There was still hope for them.

He sat across from the broken family and laid Vince's file on the table. If he didn't want his family to become like this family, he needed to set the example.

His shoulders lifted as an idea came to him. Why hadn't he thought of it earlier? As soon as this conference ended, he'd give Debbie the good news.

"ONE MOMENT." RICHARD CALLED through the door. It took a good ten seconds to unlock the redundancy of chains and deadbolts before opening the door for Patrice. Judging by her come-hither smile, he assumed he'd been forgiven for stranding her in Minneapolis.

The bottle-blonde glided into his apartment, clutching a

plastic bag advertising the Museum of Modern Art, and pressed her collagened lips to his cheek. She brushed past him as if her being here was the most natural thing in the world—forgetting that their last words to each other had been laced with arsenic— and laid her Coach purse on his kitchen's granite countertop.

Scratching the back of his neck, he shut the door. "How'd you get in?"

"That Raymond is such a sweetheart."

"Raymond?"

"That dear security guard. He waved me right on in."

Dear, sweet, security Raymond needed a talking-to. Richard crossed his arms, remaining by the door. He should be thrilled that she was here, but the wrenching in his gut said otherwise. "I thought we were through."

"Oh, darlin'." The bag she carried dropped to the floor. She bent over, revealing a medically-enhanced chest uncontained by a scoop-neck sweater, and retrieved her purchase. "You can't believe I was serious about not seeing you again."

He shook his head, unimpressed with her blatant flirt. "Sounded serious enough to me."

She sashayed toward him, with an exaggerated sway in hips that must have been poured into her short silk skirt, and handed him the museum bag. "My olive branch." She batted her eyes.

Oh brother. It was a wonder those broom-like lashes didn't lift her off the ground.

He peeked into the bag and frowned. "I need this because?"

"Oh, please." She gave her hand a flip then pulled a calendar from the museum bag, opened it to June, and covered Kaitlynn's Disney calendar. "There now. I've been wanting to do that for weeks."

His jaw clenched as he walked over, jerked the calendar off the hook, and thrust it into her hands. "No one messes with my calendar." Maybe abandoning Patrice in Minneapolis had been the right thing to do. Too bad she hadn't stayed there. "What are you doing here?"

She curved a finger topped with an acrylic nail, down his chest, then pressed her obese lips onto his. "What do you think?"

After this stunt, that was the last thing on his mind. He backed away, barricading his chest with his arms. Why hadn't he seen her artifice before? "Could it have anything to do with the nice little bonus I'll be getting?"

Her lip protruded out more. How was that even possible? "Darlin', I don't need your money."

Sure, you don't.

Like a walking mannequin, she strode across his Brazilian cherry floors into the living room. She settled onto his brown leather couch and propped her legs on the coffee table, inching her skirt higher. "Come now, we mustn't let a minor disagreement get in the way of . . . " She patted the spot next to her. " . . . us."

"There is no 'us.'"

"That could always change."

Not in this lifetime. She needed to leave. Now. For good. A smile pulled on his lips. There was a sure-fire way to guarantee she'd never return.

Smiling the smile no woman could say *no* to, he approached her and held out his hand. "Are we talking a permanent change?"

Her eyes widened and her mouth opened, but nothing came out.

Gotcha. He tugged on her hand, prompting her to stand, and then led her to the wall fashioned in Minnesota cabin style. Resting one hand on the knothole pine, he flipped a switch, turning on an electric fireplace he'd framed in with field rock hauled from the farm. Unfortunately, the cabinesque touch hadn't helped turn this apartment into a home.

He clutched the mantel carved from barn wood. "This is what I want to give you."

"Wood?" Her hand hung in his, limp as a filleted walleye.

He released the mantel then waved in a sweeping motion toward the wall. "No, all of this." He pointed to the painting created by a Minnesota artist, that hung above the fireplace, and then wrapped his arms around her. "Can't you just see us nestled together in that log cabin?" His stomach roiled with the thought.

Oh, he could definitely imagine himself in a cabin like the one from the picture. A cabin embraced by waves of snow, with smoke spiraling from its stone chimney, and a frozen-over lake reflecting sunlight into the thick pine trees surrounding it. But with Patrice? Not in this millennium, or the next.

She wrenched her hand from his. "Surely, you're kidding."

"Oh, not at all." Bracing his hand in the small of her back, he gently guided her to the couch. He pulled her onto his lap and whispered into her ear. "Someday we'll have that cabin, or one like it, anyway. Nothing smells better than icy air blended with smoke from burning wood." He closed his eyes, letting his imagination transport him into the picture as he'd done so many times before. "I can just hear the crack of a branch breaking beneath the snow's weight, and winter's wind whistling through the pines."

Truth was, he could feel the snow crunching beneath his Sorel boots, and crisp air chapping his cheeks.

A peaceful scene inhabited by God. He'd return home to that. Someday.

But only with the right person. Patrice attempted to stand, but he gripped her tighter. A few more details to certify he'd never have to deal with her again. "Can't you just see us playing fetch with our dog?"

"Please tell me you want a Pomeranian."

He laughed. "Sorry, no ankle-biters for me. Gotta have a big dog. Probably a German Shepherd to guard the kids."

Her voice pitched high. "Children?"

"At least five." Actually, two would be ideal, but a little exaggeration didn't hurt.

Again, she struggled to stand.

This time he freed her. "What? Did I say something wrong?"

She pulled on her skirt's hem and hiked up the sweater's neckline. "You think you're clever, don't you?"

"As a matter of fact—"

"Say no more." She strode to the kitchen, the sway gone from her hips, and grabbed her purse and the calendar. "You're a real piece of work."

"Why thank you." Grinning, he saw her out the door, made sure every lock was secured, then turned back to the picture. So, Patrice thought he'd been playing her. Truth was, he did want that cabin and would have it. Someday.

But the present was where he had to live. He was only beginning to make his mark in this city and wouldn't leave until he'd carved a permanent impression. That couldn't be achieved with a family stealing away precious time. A sacrifice, albeit, but a worthy one. As long as he saw his niece and nephews now and then, that need for family would be fulfilled. Until he made his mark, this rustic wall would have to suffice as his taste of Minnesota. As his taste of home.

Having Debbie visit wouldn't hurt either. Tired of waiting for her call, he walked to the kitchen and poured a glass of orange juice made from a can. As he sipped, his home phone rang. He grabbed the cordless and glanced at the caller I.D. *Finally*.

"Debbie?"

"Hey, Rick." Defeat dampened her voice.

Oh, no. "Don't tell me . . . "

"There's no one." She sniffled.

She's crying? He pulled a high-backed stool cushioned in brown leather from beneath his breakfast bar and sat hard.

Maybe he should fly out there.

Maybe he was crazy for even considering it. "No one? Mom?"

"She's watching Nate and Josh."

Okay, so that eliminated Janet. "Why can't she watch Kaitlynn too?"

"You know how Mom is, and I don't blame her. The boys are a handful for her. She doesn't think she could take on Kaitlynn too."

"But Kaitlynn's so easy." Richard combed his fingers through his hair. "What about Jerry's mom?"

"She's got plans."

"Can't anyone change their plans for you for once?" He deliberately raised his voice.

Debbie sighed.

He rubbed the back of his neck trying to think of other options. With Kaitlynn's asthma, Debbie wouldn't leave her with just anyone for the weekend. Kaitlynn could fly out too, but then that would mean no Broadway show or shopping for a new maternity wardrobe and baby wants. Not necessities. This was supposed to be a pleasure trip, one in which he'd be able to spoil his little sister. Bringing Kaitlynn, as much as he enjoyed seeing his niece, wouldn't give Debbie the break she needed. It wouldn't give them uninterrupted time to talk.

He could save his company millions of dollars but had no solution for this life problem. Pathetic. "I'm sorry," he mumbled.

"Another time, I guess. I do appreciate your offer."

Come on, Debbie. Get mad, would ya? As long as she let things wash off her, people would continue to take advantage of her kindness. She was too good.

"Another time." He rested his forehead on his knuckles.

"Now that we know Jerry might agree to it." A smile rang in her voice, that frustrating, uniquely Debbie tone, the upbeat, *c'est la vie*, attitude.

He balled a fist, restraining a frustrated retort. "As soon as I get another free weekend, you're coming." It was about time someone returned her goodness. Might as well be him.

"I'll be there."

Yeah. Right. He frowned. She'd probably always have some excuse.

"But until then, can you do something for me?"

"Sure." He sat up straight. "What do you need?"

"Walk me over to your big window."

"Okay." Curious, he slid from the stool, carrying the phone and juice into his living room to the window opening up an entire wall to the outside world. "I'm there."

"Great. Now, since I can't be there to take in the view myself, will you describe it for me?"

Okay, now it made sense. When Debbie had visited before Kaitlynn was born, she fell in love with the panoramic view of Manhattan from his Brooklyn Heights apartment. Nighttime was especially grand when the Brooklyn Bridge and the city lit up, proclaiming they had no intentions of sleeping. This was better than living in Manhattan.

"Well, the Empire State Building's spire is poking at some clouds."

"Sweet." Debbie had loved staring at the cloud-seeking buildings, where people lived crammed like hens in a chicken coop and called it home.

So unlike the farm.

How ironic that it was acceptable—even expected—for humans to live, almost literally, one on top of another, consuming as little acreage as possible. It was quite another story for animals. Funny how humans realized the value of space for animals but chose to encage themselves. Just as he had done. For the most part, he even enjoyed it.

"The bridge is loaded with traffic and joggers and cyclists and mommies pushing strollers."

"You can actually see the people?"

"Well, not really, but I know those little dots below are buying ice cream and eating the world's finest hot dogs."

"Oh, that sounds like heaven. What else do you see?"

He scanned the horizon, peering through hovering smog. "The sky's a pale blue, streaked with cotton clouds, and it's kissing the river." A scene clearly painted by God's hand.

She giggled. "And you're a poet too. Thanks. You've just made my day."

And, you've just made mine. How did she do that when she was the one who'd been let down? "Soon, we'll get you here so you can see it for yourself."

"I can't wait." Genuine enthusiasm rang from her voice.

"Me neither. Now, give Katydid a hug for me."

"I will. I love ya."

"Yeah. Me too." He held the phone to his ear until it buzzed, then lowered it to his side, keeping his gaze on the horizon. How had God become lost in such wonder? Like his sister, the world beyond his window was real, not like the Florida juice squeezed out of a can, not imaginary like the scene created in the cabin painting, definitely not like Patrice, who long ago discarded the person God made her to be.

It took Debbie to remind him of the value of authenticity, of not surrendering to the world.

He raised his glass, touching it to the window. His way of giving thanks. Granted, serene moments like this were occurring with decreasing frequency—times like this when he toasted the One who gave him the gift, the One who ultimately brought him from his lowly beginnings on a farm to become a king among men in the world's most powerful city. Not so unlike that shepherd boy, David, some three thousand years ago, who became king over a whole nation; a man who found his purest delight in serving God.

Okay, so that was a major difference. Maybe Richard once felt that delight in God, but somewhere along the way, God had gotten lost. Still, Richard frequently heard God's call. God refused to let him go.

Would God always have that hold over him? Would he ever be free of God's censure? Did he want to be free?

Richard pulled himself from the view and strode to his den. Mahogany bookshelves lined three of the walls. Nearly all the shelves were full, organized using the Dewey Decimal system. Not a single Bible or even New Testament among the leather-bound tomes. How telling was that?

As a teen, as a youth leader, he'd loved the Psalms, appreciating the author's emotionally honest words. Words befitting the whole spectrum of feelings from joy to sadness, trust to doubt, courage to fear, love to hate, companionship to loneliness. Those passions lived on the pages. He ached to read them now, but wasn't able.

Well, that could change easily enough. Maybe that was what this apartment required to become his home. His favorite bookstore was only a couple of blocks away. Fresh air would do him some good too.

He returned to the kitchen, snatched his keys and wallet from the kitchen counter, and headed for the door.

It was time to answer God's call, restore authenticity into his life. He wasn't going to wait any longer for *someday* to arrive.

Chapter Thirteen

"Thank you both, again, for coming." Jerry handed Vince's parents a business card from a counseling center in Brainerd, the one where he'd met Debbie six years ago. "I'm pleased that you're willing to look to other avenues for help. I've recommended this service to a number of other families. Few have been disappointed."

The dad held the card, rubbing his thumb across the front, and nodded. "We appreciate you going the extra mile with Vincent." He exchanged a glance with Vince's mom. No smiles, but no animosity either. "Maybe it's time we do the same."

Jerry shook their hands and offered an encouraging smile as they walked from the room. The couple still kept the distance between them, yet appeared to walk with looser gaits as if the world's troubles weren't quite as heavy as before.

As soon as they disappeared through the doorway, Jerry glanced at the circular clock hung above the whiteboard then hurried back to his desk. Not even thirty minutes had passed. He picked up his phone and dialed. The chime of the morning bell and the arrival of his students would probably interrupt mid-call. Let them.

The phone rang twice before Debbie answered. "Hello." Her voice sounded cheerful.

He'd give her reason to be happy, so she didn't have to fake it for his sake. "Hi hon."

"Jerry."

Kaitlynn babbled in the background. That girl loved to hear herself talk. He loved to hear it too.

"I've been thinking." He pulled the lilac from the pencil holder and breathed in its spring bouquet.

"About?"

"About you going to see Rick. I think you should still go." He returned the lilac to its makeshift vase.

"Jerry, you know I—"

"Just listen a second, okay?"

"I'm listening."

He picked up a pencil and tapped it against his desk to the beat of "Don't Worry, Be Happy." "Here's what we're going to do. Bring Kaitlynn in to me. It's a family emergency—"

"It is not—"

"Yes. It is." He dropped the pencil and sat up. "You need this break, and I intend to give it to you. Bring her in to me. I'll stay home—"

"But you need this weekend."

"And you don't?"

"But you need time away."

"Deborah." Finally, silence answered. He smiled. Yes, this was definitely the right decision. "I'm staying home. You're going to New York. End of story. Call your brother."

He heard her take a breath, and then her voice came out soft. "Thanks, hon. I owe you. I love you."

The first bell of the school day buzzed as he returned his love.

RICHARD'S HOME PHONE RANG as he loosened the final deadbolt. He turned and stared at it for a second. *Leave now. Let it ring.* He drew the door open and stepped into the hallway. The call went to the answering machine as he began pulling his door shut, and his boss's voice boomed out.

Ignore it. Go, now. Get your book. Call Entenza when you get home. Richard pulled the door another inch and grimaced. If the CEO was calling his home line, it must be important.

Grumbling, he shoved the door open and hurried to the phone. "Sorry, Mr. Entenza. I was out the door when the phone rang."

"You'll be glad you answered."

I seriously doubt it. Richard leaned against his counter and rested his forehead on his fingers. "What can I help you with, sir?"

"First of all, I'd like to commend you on the exemplary work you performed in London this past week. We've always known their profitability should be greater than what we were seeing."

A smile tugged at his lips. Compliments were not thrown out carelessly by Entenza. "Thank you. I appreciate—"

"Enough schmoozing. Let me get to the point. I'd like you to join me on my boat this weekend."

Richard stood up straight, his smile growing. His boss's boat? The seventy-four-foot Viking Yacht? That was a privilege reserved for company VPs. Yes, he was close to achieving the title, and that was his ultimate goal, but it hadn't come to fruition yet. Or maybe . . . His smile became a full-fledged grin. "I'd be honored to join you."

Yet, for some reason, his heart didn't feel the honor. It should, if the invitation meant what he believed it did. Instead, he felt a pesky itch to tell his boss *no.* Yeah, right. And kill his career in the process. No one told Mr. Entenza *no.* To be perfectly honest, he didn't want to.

"Superb," Mr. Entenza said. "Is there anyone you wish to

bring along?"

"No one, sir." No one with whom he'd care to be shipborne for a weekend. A night, fine. But a whole weekend? That would put him over the edge.

"Too bad."

"I agree." Richard laughed.

The CEO laughed with him. "I'll have my chauffeur at your apartment in fifteen minutes. Don't be late. My boat won't wait."

Fifteen minutes? "I'll be ready."

"Oh, and leave your gadgets behind. This is a work-free weekend. No phones. No tablets, laptops. Not even watches."

Richard touched the phone on his belt. It was as much a part of him as his skin. "Sounds like a plan." Hopefully, his voice conveyed the confidence he didn't feel.

No goodbyes were exchanged as silence buzzed on the other end. Fifteen minutes. He hurried to his bathroom, brushed his teeth, and ran a comb through his hair. And then to the bedroom where he painfully removed his cell phone and Rolex before pulling his carryon from the walk-in closet. It took him less than five minutes to pack.

The phone rang again as he stepped out of his apartment. He pushed the door open and stared at the phone. Nope. Not again. He pulled the door shut, leaving civilization behind.

Chapter Fourteen

Standing beside her bed, Debbie arranged Kaitlynn's clothes in the overnight bag then zipped it closed. Only then did she allow herself another glance at the clock. Two hours had passed since she'd spoken with Ricky. Two hours of him not answering the phone, not even his cell. She could see one hour, maybe, but two? The only place he went without his cell was the shower.

Unless he was with someone. That wouldn't surprise her one bit.

She carried the luggage from her bedroom and peeked into Kaitlynn's room. Her daughter sat on the floor pushing a red tractor across orange shag carpet. "Precious, did you choose some toys to bring to Grandma's?"

"Uh-huh." She nodded and kept pushing the tractor.

"How about some books?"

"Grandma's got gooder books."

"Yep. You're right." The very books Debbie read as a child. She stepped into the room and rummaged through Kaitlynn's *Lightning McQueen* backpack. The coffee-can game, a couple of hand-sized plastic cars, UNO® cards, and a toddler-sized football. Not one ounce of frilly girl in her daughter. Just the way Debbie liked it.

"Looks good." She zipped the backpack. "Mommy needs to make a couple more phone calls, then we'll leave, okay? Daddy'll stop by Grandma's to kiss us goodbye."

"Okay, Mommy."

Dragging the wheeled carryon, she walked to the kitchen and vented a heavy sigh before picking up her phone. She'd give Ricky one more try. Recapturing her brother's description of his city view in her mind, she dialed his home. The window for flying to New York had closed, but his silence wasn't sitting well with her. Even if he'd found some new babe to go out with, he didn't typically ignore his phone. She bit into her lip as she counted the rings. At four, his voice spoke from the answering machine.

That left his cell. Her fingers tingled as she dialed. *Come on, Ricky, answer. Please.* She held her breath as the phone rang once, twice, three, then four times before his voicemail kicked on.

Breath rushed from her mouth as she put the phone down. *God, you know where he's at. He's okay. He's got to be. I'm leaving him in your hands.* Worrying never solved anyone's problems, which was why she seldom worried. This had to be another by-product of her pregnancy. Still, the nagging thought wouldn't leave her brain.

It was time to go to the farm. Maybe help their neighbors milk the cows. Anything to keep her mind off her brother doing who-knew-what in Manhattan.

THE WOODSY TOBACCO SCENT of recently smoked cigars greeted Richard as he circled down the yacht's spiral staircase into a salon clothed in teakwood. With legs still adjusting to the roll of the sea, he stumbled past an L-shaped leather sofa on his way to a breakfast bar fronting the galley.

"Gentlemen." Richard steadied a hand on a leather barstool

and nodded at the four other men crowding around the galley's granite-topped bar. Three vice-presidents. One CEO. And him. Very nice odds.

They each raised their glass, tipping it toward him.

One VP winked. "Welcome to the club."

So, it was really going to happen. "Glad to be here." Ecstatic, actually.

"What's your poison?" The CEO pulled a tulip-shaped tumbler from a cupboard also made of teak.

Richard eyed the bottles of rum, vodka, and whiskey overflowing on the galley's countertop. No beer in sight. Perhaps it was time for his taste buds to mature. "Give me a Jack, straight up."

"Smart choice." Entenza filled the clear glass with dark amber liquid and handed it over. "Hold off on taking that first drink. I've got an announcement I'm certain you'll want to hear with a clear mind."

Richard looked down to hide the grin growing on his face. He didn't want to appear too eager or excited.

Entenza came around the bar and cuffed a strong hand over Richard's shoulder. "Have a seat, son."

He gladly sat on one of the high-backed barstools. If he stood any longer, his knees would probably give out.

Keeping a lock on Richard's shoulder, Entenza raised his glass. "When an employee repeatedly discovers means of enhancing our profit margin, especially in this difficult market, I believe that service needs to be rewarded."

Whiskey leaped from the glass Richard held in his trembling hand. Man, he must look like a stargazed amateur.

Entenza laughed and slapped Richard on the back prompting more ale to splash. "We've all been in your shoes before. I'll make this as quick as possible so we can do some celebrating."

Perspiration beaded on Richard's forehead. This was the moment he'd been working toward ever since moving to New York. *God, please help me keep my cool.* The prayer slipped out without thought.

Entenza reached into his pants pocket and pulled out a set of keys. "An office just opened up on my floor."

An office seventy-two stories up, with two walls of windows framing Manhattan's skyline. An office vacated by a man who prioritized family over his career. No longer trying to hide his grin, Richard grasped onto the keys. Prioritizing work wouldn't be a problem for him.

The CEO stuck out his hand. "How does Vice President of Operations sound?"

Like heaven. Richard pocketed the keys and accepted his boss's hand. "I won't let you down, sir."

"I don't expect you will." Entenza raised his glass to eyelevel, tilting it toward Richard.

The other three Vice Presidents copied the gesture.

"To Richard Brooks. The youngest Vice President in the history of ACM Technologies."

"To Richard." The men echoed, then drank.

Richard inhaled his whiskey and grabbed a deck of cards and a cigar off the bar. It was time to show these men he'd earned that office, that he was a take-charge type of guy. "Let's get this party started."

Chapter Fifteen

"Can I offer you a hand with your luggage, sir?"

His head pounding, Richard squinted at the chauffeur as he opened Richard's door. The Sunday evening sun created a halo around the man's head. "I think I can handle it from here."

The driver had already surpassed his customary duties, performing them with a genuine smile. It was good to see a man satisfied in his career. In the corporate world, there was seldom satisfaction, maybe a moment of pleasure when the next level was conquered, but that glee was quickly swallowed up by the desire to reach an even higher status.

He hoped that wouldn't be the case for him with this promotion, that he'd finally found contentment. Like the chauffeur.

Richard pulled his wallet from his back pocket, removed two fifties, and offered them to the driver.

He shook his head. "Entenza takes good care of me." A wry smile appeared on his face. "Now it's time to take care of yourself. Go to bed, and sleep it off."

Richard nodded. The buzz, wobbles, and nausea were finally gone, but they'd been replaced with a headache he hadn't felt the likes of since college. But then, he hadn't partied this hard since college either.

Dragging his carryon behind him, he squeezed through the revolving doors of his apartment building. Richard nodded to the security officer before crossing the marbled floor to the elevator. Once inside, he pushed the button directing him to the top floor. As it began its ascent, he prayed his stomach would remain settled. Ah, but the minor discomfort was worth it. Few other small-town farm boys could lay claim to his achievements.

A bell dinged as the elevator jerked to a stop, propelling what little was left in his stomach into his throat. He covered his mouth and turned toward the back of the elevator to gag the acid back down as the doors slid open. Funny, he'd never noticed the elevator's rough stop before. The floor bounced as two chatting, giggling women stepped in wearing sequined black dresses that covered little more than what was necessary.

He kept his gaze downward, hoping to be invisible. Any other night, he'd be counting his blessings and turn on that Brooks charm.

Not tonight. His stomach lurched again as the elevator climbed. Not even a sexy smile would keep him from his ultimate goal. Bed. All by himself. The sledgehammer vibrating in his head would have to be slept away.

Tomorrow, he'd be ready to show his co-workers that he attained what they all desired, that this Midwest farm boy left in his wake so many others attempting to tread their way to the top. So what if he stepped on a few fingers along the way. One didn't achieve what he had by being meek. He felt some sadistic pleasure thinking of their envy.

That obnoxious elevator bell tolled again, reverberating in his head, signaling his exit. He felt his eyes roll toward each other as he followed the women out of the elevator. Good thing, they took their annoying hen-prattle in the opposite direction.

He shuffled down the hallway, working his way through the

pain pulsating in his brain. His fingers fumbled the keys as he attempted to find the keyhole; his shaking hands refused to steady.

Hopefully, business "meetings" would be far and few between. As someone who thrived on organization and control, he enjoyed the celebrations but hated the cost.

Finally, the key found its home. Richard pushed it in and turned the key before it could jiggle loose again. Shoving the door open, he gave himself a simple command: water, aspirin, sleep. His foggy gaze caught the light blinking on his answering machine as he closed the door behind him.

Tomorrow. He hauled his carryon to the bedroom before returning to his kitchen where the light continued to blink. The stupid thing wouldn't be ignored. He swallowed his aspirin, drowning it with water, then slumped onto his bar stool and hit the *play* button.

"Hey, Ricky, guess what. I can come!" Debbie's excited voice rang out. "Jerry's gonna stay home with Kaitlynn. Call me back. Let me know what I need to do. Can't wait to see you!"

Recorded seconds after he left on Friday. Most likely the call he'd ignored.

Two sledgehammers battered his brain as he leaned over, resting his head on crossed arms. If he had ignored the CEO's call on Friday, and gone to the bookstore as intended, he'd have spent the weekend with his sister. The promotion still would have come, without the extra gift of a hangover.

His family was probably worried sick. Life couldn't get better, could it? Ignoring the remaining messages, he walked to his bedroom and grabbed his BlackBerry from his bed. Debbie had left the same message there. And texts. She never texted. He scrolled through his e-mail. Another message from Debbie wondering where he was, and more from family all asking the same question. Wonderful.

The hammering increased. When would that aspirin kick in and work its numbing magic? Calls had to be made. Now. And, he needed to be pleasant. He'd call Debbie first, and she could relay the message to everyone else. Tomorrow, he'd talk to them. He checked the clock on his bed stand. Ten o'clock. Nine back home. Debbie would still be awake . . . maybe even worried. A thousand miles away, and he still couldn't escape their accusing tentacles.

He returned to the kitchen and poured more water, swallowing it in one gulp, hoping to chase the dry fibers mummifying his tongue. It didn't help. He picked up his cordless and walked to the living room, his feet scuffling over the hardwood, and fell into his recliner, hoping the soft leather would cushion his aching body. No such luck. Nothing felt comfortable. Ah, what did that matter, anyway?

Sighing, he hit the speed dial number for Debbie and raised the phone to his ear, then sighed again.

Dratted busy signal. Sleep would have to wait.

DEBBIE GLANCED AT THE digital clock on the lower right hand of her computer monitor. Bedtime. But how could she go to sleep when her brother was still lost? She clicked on her e-mail icon and leaned back in her chair, closing her eyes. Someday they'd be able to afford high-speed internet.

The door squeaked behind her, announcing Jerry's entry. She opened her eyes and looked back as his hands rounded over her shoulders.

"Anything yet?" His gaze met hers.

She watched the monitor, biting into the left side of her lower lip. The e-mail finally popped up. Nothing new. Where in the world was Ricky? "Not a peep from him."

Jerry patted her shoulders. "I'm sure he's fine."

"Oh, I know he's fine." She closed the browser then spun her swivel chair around to face Jerry. "I'm just teed off that he's ignoring us, for whatever reason."

He squatted to her eyelevel, his eyes perusing hers. "You sure you're okay?"

She shrugged and crossed her arms. "He's a big boy. He doesn't have to tell us where he's going. Probably at some Connecticut cabin with a new girlfriend. If I were him, I wouldn't answer the phone either."

"You're probably right."

"I just wish I hadn't said anything to Mom. You know how she worries. She told Janet, of course, so now Marcus is probably all riled up. Again." She uncrossed her arms and reached for Jerry's hands, allowing a slight smile. "Thanks for listening."

"That's one thing I learned this weekend. I need to be a better listener."

"You do fine."

"I can do better." He squeezed her hands as he stood, encouraging her to stand with him. "I learned something else this weekend."

Her smile grew as he drew her closer. "Oh yeah? What's that?"

He nodded toward their bedroom. "Why don't we go pray together, give Ricky over to God?"

Her lips parted, but nothing came out. Thank goodness, she didn't go to New York. Jerry had never initiated prayer before.

Keeping her hand in his, he led her out of the office, soon to be the nursery, and into their bedroom. Together, they knelt beside the bed.

"Dear Father, please—" The phone's ring interrupted his prayer.

Debbie glanced at Jerry, who nodded. Her fingers shivered as she clutched the handset. Okay, maybe she was a teensy-bit worried. She swallowed a breath, calming herself before answering. "Hello?"

"Hey, Debs—"

"Ricky! Oh my gosh! Are you okay?" She flopped back on her bottom.

Jerry's head bowed toward the bed. "Thank you, Lord," he whispered.

"Yeah. I'm fine. I didn't mean to worry you guys."

"Where've you been?"

"I was called away—"

"And you left without your phone?" An unusual edge hardened her voice. "Without telling anyone where you were going? I realize you're an adult, and you don't have to check in with us, but when I couldn't get a hold of you . . . " She sighed heavily, willing away tears.

Ricky sighed too. "It couldn't be helped. My boss called shortly after you said you couldn't come. He offered to take me out on the ocean. No electronics allowed. I had fifteen minutes to get ready."

"Oh," she said softly. "I'm sorry for jumping to conclusions. This pregnancy has my emotions out of—wait, what? Did you say your boss took you on his yacht?"

"Sure did."

If his boss invited him on the boat, that likely meant he'd gotten a promotion. A big one. Only bigwigs got boat invitations. "Does that mean what I think it does?"

"That your big brother is now a VP with ACM Technologies? You bet."

"Oh my gosh, that's amazing, Ricky!"

"What's amazing?" Jerry raised his palms upward.

She held up a finger to Jerry, then talked to Ricky. "I'm so happy for you!"

"I'm rather pleased myself." A yawn came through the phone. "But I'm also beat. Can we talk tomorrow?"

"No problem."

Jerry secured an arm around her shoulders. This past weekend really had been a blessing, for all of them.

"Would you mind calling the family?" Ricky asked. "Seems I worried everyone. Could you let them know I'm okay and that I've got news? I'll fill them in tomorrow."

"Really?" He had amazing news and still wanted to avoid the family? "Sorry. This is your mess, intentional or not."

"It was worth a try."

"Go make your calls. Get some sleep. Fill me in on the details tomorrow."

"Will do."

With a sigh, Debbie set the phone on the nightstand. Scrunching her lips, she sat next to Jerry on the floor. She was happy for Ricky. Really, she was, but his worldly successes never equated to returning to faith. In fact, they usually meant the opposite. And if she thought he had no time for her before, it was going to be worse now.

A tear leaked onto her cheek. Dratted pregnancy emotions.

Jerry wiped the tear away. "I thought he had good news."

"He did." She sniffled and once again knelt by the bed, folding her hands on the quilt. "Our first prayer tonight was answered, but I think we need to keep at it."

Jerry knelt beside her, curving one arm over her shoulders before wrapping his open hand over hers.

She smiled. Other prayers had been answered too.

Chapter Sixteen

*D*ebbie sat on the edge of the blanket, curving her hands over her expanding stomach, and watched her Monday morning group scatter. At their so-called Bible study this morning, the Bibles hadn't even been cracked open as Marsha dominated the conversation. Again. How their morning discussion had morphed into a discourse on pop culture was beyond her. Why even bother bringing her Bible?

To top the morning off, the women left still not knowing about Lilly.

Kaitlynn tugged on Debbie's shirtsleeve, regaining her mom's attention. "Can I go play?" Before Debbie could say *yes,* Kaitlynn was off running toward the climbing wall. Oh, to have that kind of energy. Debbie caressed her stomach. Apparently, this baby needed the energy more.

Ricky didn't know about Lilly, either. His phone call last night relayed good news. She wasn't about to dampen his spirit before beginning his first day as a Vice President. Tonight, she'd give him a call, lean on his broad shoulders for a moment, then go on with the life God planned for her and do it with joy.

She offered up a silent prayer that her brother would be thankful for his latest achievement. It didn't surprise her one bit. He never failed at anything. Now, if Jerry could find the same success in his first round of interviews next week, that would be worth celebrating.

"'Melia!" Kaitlynn's excited voice broke Debbie from her reverie.

She glanced up and smiled as Lee walked toward her, a dark green sports bag slung over his shoulder.

"Hi there." He gestured toward the blanket. "May I."

"Oh, please do. It's good to see you again." How nice it would be to talk with someone who wouldn't care what Barbara Walters wore on *The View*.

Lee dropped his bag on the blanket, then sat across from Debbie. "Are you here every Monday?" He looked toward the jungle gym.

"Most every day, if it's not too cold or rainy. Kaitlynn has too much energy to keep her indoors."

"I hear ya. We were getting settled in the house last week, so I didn't make it down until later in the day, but now I think we're all unpacked."

"I'm sure that's a relie—" Debbie jumped to her feet as Kaitlynn funneled handfuls of sand on the slide just as Amelia slid down. "Kaitlynn Nicole, what's the rule about slides?"

Kaitlynn spread her fingers, letting the remaining sand sift down, and lowered her head, sticking out her lower lip. "No throwing sand." She swished it onto the ground.

"Good job." Debbie crossed her arms. "And now what do you do?"

Keeping her head down, Kaitlynn waded through the sand toward her new friend. "I sorry 'Melia."

Amelia hugged Kaitlynn. "I 'give you."

Debbie bit into her cheeks, trying to maintain a stern face. "Very good, precious. Play nice now." She plopped back down and shook her head. "You would think that one day she'll remember the rule before I scold her about it. She's just like her uncle, always testing to see what she can get away with."

Lee laughed. "Amelia's the same way. Takes after her mother."

"Daddy, Daddy! Can we play catch?" Both girls ran toward the blanket. Amelia dug into the sports bag, pulled out a toddler-sized baseball glove, and slid it onto her right hand as if it were the most natural thing to do.

"How can I say no?" Lee reached into the bag, tugged out a red playground ball, and stood. "But I think we should use this one with Kaitlynn." He underhanded the ball to Amelia, and it bounced off her glove. She threw the glove at Lee as both girls gave chase, giggling as they ran.

With a little effort, Debbie got up and followed Lee, who jogged after the girls.

Amelia reached the ball first and grunted as she heaved it back toward her dad.

He caught the ball and fell to the ground with a theatrical flair. "Child, you have got some arm." He soft tossed it to Kaitlynn, standing just five feet away.

Debbie reached his side, panting. "She's a lefty, huh?"

"Sure is." Lee stood and wiped dirt and dead grass from the back of his jeans. "The minute I knew for sure, she had a ball in one hand and a glove on the other. If I have anything to say about it, she'll be the first female pro baseball player, the next Cy Young."

Kaitlynn threw the ball to Debbie. It arrived after the fifth hop.

Debbie scooped up the ball and bounced it to Amelia. "But Cy Young was right-handed."

Lee's brows knit together. "I can't believe you know that. Elise just asks, 'what's the difference?'"

"My husband, Jerry, would say the same thing, although he tries his best to fake interest."

Lee leapt up to catch Amelia's throw, and grinned. "I can see those dollar signs now." He soft tossed the ball to Kaitlynn.

It boomeranged off her fingers, flying several feet behind her. Both girls gave chase.

"I look at this as one more advantage of staying home with her. This way I can teach her the important things in life like how to figure out a batting average, and that Cy Young is one of the best *right*-handed pitchers of all time."

Debbie laughed, watching the girls fight over the ball. "I believe our daughters will get along perfectly." She nodded toward Amelia, who won the battle. "What does her mother do that allows you to stay home?"

"Elise is a pediatrician in Brainerd."

"Really. Well, good for her."

Amelia flung the ball over Debbie's head. Debbie didn't even try to reach the ball as the girls raced after it.

"Elise is an awfully good doctor too, which unfortunately means putting in a lot more hours than I like." Lee looked upward at geese flying in a "V" formation. His voice softened. "I guess that's why I decided to stay home. I wanted Amelia to have some constancy in her life."

"Sounds like you made the right decision."

"What about Kaitlynn's dad?"

"Jerry also works with kids. He's a fifth-grade teacher here in Granite Creek, who, next week, will begin the first round of interviews for the principal position."

The girls ran back, this time Kaitlynn was the victor. She threw the ball to Lee. Again, it dribbled on the ground. No baseball future for her daughter.

"Are you optimistic about Jerry's job?" Lee skyed the ball.

Kaitlynn's eyes grew round as she watched the ball sail straight up then rocket downward. The girls ran in opposite directions as the ball dropped and bounced another good ten feet before they chased after it.

Optimistic? "Cautiously." While other teachers told Jerry he was a shoo-in for the job, he maintained a healthy skepticism. "He's got the education, the experience, a solid reputation in dealing with students and their families, familiarity with the school and the school district, good rapport with the school board. But I think his best achievement has been making his classroom a welcoming place for special-needs students."

"Sounds like he'd make the perfect principal." Lee caught Amelia's throw in his gut and grunted loudly, prompting more giggles from the girls.

"That's what scares me. I'm afraid we're getting our hopes up too high. We really need Jerry to get the job. Supporting a family on a small-town teacher's salary isn't easy, and now with a new baby coming . . . "

He underhanded the ball to Kaitlynn, who caught it this time. "Atta girl."

Kaitlynn beamed with the praise and tossed the ball to Amelia without even one bounce.

Amelia threw the ball beyond her dad.

Lee dug his hands into his pockets, his eyes assuming a far-off glaze. "Too bad Elise isn't here to see this."

"Is there a problem?" Debbie eyed the girls as they kicked the ball, trying to keep it away from each other.

"Elise wasn't—isn't too happy about living with a man without a job."

"You're kidding, right?"

He laughed a dry laugh and brought his hand up to squeeze the back of his neck. "I embarrass her."

"Excuse me?" Debbie pointed to a bench and led the way.

"Well she hasn't exactly said that, but when you've known someone since grade school, you tend to know what they're thinking." He sucked in a breath, then blew it out as he sat next to Debbie. "At hospital functions, before I stopped working, she'd introduce me as an electrical engineer. Sounds more impressive than electrician. She has a lot of egos to impress working in the medical profession. Unfortunately, hers has grown right along with the others. She never used to be that way." He sighed again.

Debbie remained silent, experience having taught her that listening was one of the greatest forms of advice.

"Since I quit work, she's stopped asking me to join her for company parties."

"I'm sorry. I didn't realize—"

"Mommy! Mommy!" Kaitlynn and Amelia ran toward them, both wearing toothy smiles. "Can 'Melia come on our God walk tonight?"

Lee expelled his breath.

She glanced at him peripherally and could tell he was happy to avoid further discourse concerning his home life.

"God walk?" Lee asked.

"Mm, hmmm." Kaitlynn raised her arms and pointed fingers at the corners of both eyes. "I see God." She raised her fingers to her ears. "I hear God." And, to her nose. "I smell God." Then tented with her other fingers. "I feel God." And finally, to her mouth. "I taste God."

Debbie drew her daughter onto her lap, and gave her a tight squeeze. Kaitlynn had learned the game well, explaining it far better than Debbie could.

"I see." Lee smiled. "Are you going now?"

"Nope." Kaitlynn shook her head. "Not until tonight."

"We like to go out late, right before sunset." Debbie kissed Kaitlynn's flushed cheek. "It's past her bedtime, but it's how I first learned to play, and it's probably my favorite time."

"It's a family custom?"

Debbie bobbed her head from side to side. "Not really. I did it with my brother years ago. A few weeks ago, we decided it would make a good tradition."

"Sounds like there's a story behind it."

Kaitlynn plied Debbie's head toward her. "Mommy, can she come? Please?"

"Please, Daddy?" Amelia tugged on her daddy's arms.

"You two go play." Lee kissed Amelia's forehead. "Mrs. Verhoeven and I will discuss it."

"Okay." Amelia took off for the swing set with Kaitlynn running behind.

"She could stay overnight." Debbie watched the girls climb onto the highest swings. "Kaitlynn would love to have a sleepover. It would give you and your wife a night alone."

The muscles in Lee's cheeks tightened. "No. I don't think so, but I appreciate the offer." His head lowered again.

So, all was not well on his home front, but since he wasn't asking for her wisdom, she stayed silent. Personally, she didn't appreciate receiving unsolicited advice and therefore refrained from offering it to others.

Lee rubbed his hands over his thighs. "Tell me about this God walk."

She was happy to explain. Her friend clearly needed God's strength right now. "I guess Kaitlynn explained it the best. The three of us—me, Jerry, and Kaitlynn—take a walk, sometimes it's around town, other times just in our back yard—through my garden—reminding us God always walks with us. He gave us five senses through which we can know him, so our challenge is to find at least one thing through each of those senses that proves God."

Lee sat back on the bench, crossed his arms over his chest and stretched his legs out in front of him. "Okay, and just how do you *prove* God?" Cynicism chortled in his voice.

She nodded toward Kaitlynn. "She's probably the best example. Last week when we went out, she started pointing out different colors. She pulled a leaf and told me it's green, then picked a dandelion and said, 'It's yellow.' She pointed at the sunset and told us it was orange. I could go on with dozen more examples.

"As a mom, I patted myself on the back thinking I'd successfully taught her colors, but after a while I realized she was seeing more than colors. She was telling us *God is* because there are so many colors. In a child's innocence, that's proof enough of God. As an adult we need the more spectacular: the sunsets, waterfalls, rainbows. A child finds him in everything. She's teaching us to come to God as a child again."

Lee nodded politely as he stared out at the girls. At least he didn't argue. "Where'd you come up with the idea?"

She smiled, her memory sending her back over twenty years. Too bad Ricky wasn't here. It would be a good reminder for him as well, a reminder he needed right now. "Growing up, my grandparents lived on the farm with us. They had their own little house, but we saw them every day. I was Grandma Brooks' favorite. Probably because I was her only granddaughter. She died when I was ten, and I blamed God."

Debbie swallowed a yawn as the girls ran from the tunnels to the merry-go-round, where they took turns pushing each other. Kaitlynn would take a nice long nap this afternoon. Today, Debbie would join her.

"I started spending a lot of time away from the house, away

from people, most often in a tree house my brothers built. Well, my oldest brother, Ricky—he was probably fifteen at the time— he knew how much Grandma's death bothered me. One night he came out to the tree house to find me. How many fifteen-year-old brothers would give their kid sister the time of day?"

"I didn't want my kid sister anywhere near me."

"Exactly. That night was probably a defining moment in our relationship. He really earned my respect." Unfortunately, that respect was being whittled away. Tonight, when she called to tell him about Lilly, she'd remind him of that day twenty years ago. Maybe that would encourage him to seek God again, just as he had taught her.

"So, it's after nine that night when Ricky climbs up and sits with me. We just sat and talked for an hour or so: about Grandma, Grandpa, Mom and Dad, our brother Marcus. When it got around to God, I just got mad. How could God take Grandma away from me? I said I didn't believe in God anymore. Ricky didn't preach at me, trying to get me to believe, instead he took me for a walk, backpack in hand—after clearing it with Mom and Dad of course."

"They must have understood what your brother was doing."

"That and the fact that he'd always proven himself mature for his age. They trusted his judgment." Funny, how things change. In some ways, he seemed more mature then than now.

Debbie located Kaitlynn spinning on the merry-go-round. Good thing they hadn't eaten anything since breakfast.

"Well, Ricky took me to Grandma's garden and gave me a strawberry and kept one for himself. The taste of those berries was unreal. You know how the flavor bursts in your mouth and makes your eyes roll back in your head? Almost better than chocolate."

"Almost?"

"Nothing's better than chocolate." Boy, a candy bar would taste good right now. She glanced at her watch. No wonder. It was noon already. Time to finish the story and head home. Eat. Nap. "So, anyway, now we're out in the middle of the hay field, Ricky tells me to close my mouth and breathe in. I'm beginning to think he's a bit crazy but, because he's my older brother, I do as he says. I always did. But, when I breathed, I forgot about him. The smell of rain-freshened air was absolutely beautiful."

"I love that smell too. Especially in the spring."

The girls ran from the merry-go-round back to the slides and tunnels.

"But I still don't get what Ricky's trying to do. Just so happens, a cat meowed at my feet. She had the loudest meow you can imagine." Debbie looked upward, and her eyes flitted back and forth as the memory returned. "She was tortoiseshell-colored. Short hair. Whimple was her name. I know, goofy name. Blame my grandpa for that." She brought her head back down and smiled. It was so easy to get off track when remembering the details of those good times. "Sorry. I know I tend to get sidetracked."

"That's all right. I enjoy the little details. It shows it's an important memory."

"It is. Very important." Yes, she definitely needed to give Ricky a call. Repeat the story to him the same way she was telling it to Lee. Ricky would fill in the blanks and maybe, just maybe, remember the meaning behind the walk. "Anyway, Ricky told me to pick up the cat, so, of course, I did. I held her at my shoulder, feeling her rumbling purr down to my toes."

"I know what you mean. My grandparents farmed and had dozens of cats."

"Us too. My brothers were softies around them." Debbie watched Kaitlynn try to climb up through the sliding tunnel, but her feet kept slipping. "I carried the cat down by our lake where we had a fire pit. Ricky lit it up and laid out a couple blankets from his backpack close to the fire. He told me to lie on my back and keep my eyes open. After a rainy, cloudy day, I couldn't believe how clear the sky was. Not a single cloud. I don't remember if there was a moon or not, but I remember seeing the stars, really seeing them for the first time.

"For the longest time we just lay there, looking up, then I heard him say—I don't even think he was speaking to me, he spoke so soft. 'The heavens declare the glory of God; the skies proclaim the work of his hands.' Then he spoke louder. I knew he meant for me to hear this time. 'As long as I can see these stars, I'll know God exists. I'll know how much he loves us. I'll know he'll always walk with us.'

"That was it. It's all he had to say, but it was enough. I understood what he was trying to tell me, that God gave us our senses to experience him, to worship him, to remind us that even when things get bad, he's still there."

Lee nodded through a frown.

She sighed. Why didn't she just keep quiet? Let God do the talking as Ricky had so many years ago?

"Maybe, sometime, I'll take you up on the offer," Lee said quietly.

Debbie breathed a relieved sigh. "You're welcome anytime. I'd like you to meet Jerry. The two of you have a lot in common."

"I'd like that." He glanced at his watch and grimaced. "Past lunchtime. If I don't feed Amelia the right food at the right time, Elise has a fit."

"I don't think Jerry'd care if I fed Kaitlynn SpaghettiOs every day."

"Well, Elise ... " He shook his head and that glazed look returned.

Debbie laid a hand on his arm. "If you ever need a listening ear, I've been told I've got a good one."

"Maybe some time." His mouth curved into a sad smile as he stood. "Amelia. Time to go."

Amelia ran to him.

He raised his daughter and kissed her forehead before hugging her close. "Thanks for the talk, Debbie."

"Anytime." *Be with him, God. Lee and Ricky.* She watched Lee walk away, holding Amelia tight in his grip.

It was time to go home. Give her brother a call. Tell him to take a walk. Find those stars again.

Chapter Seventeen

Richard raised the champagne flute to his lips and gazed through his apartment window. No stars shone in Thursday's overcast sky, but that was okay. He sipped the golden bubbly and grinned. The lightless night didn't match his mood. Four days on the job, and he still rode the emotional high from his promotion. No matter what the dreary weather proclaimed, he couldn't foresee the thrill ending. This drug named "success" possessed far more power and endurance than any illicit street drug. His skyscraper view only added to the euphoria.

He'd risen above everyone—everything. From his high-rise, the stars glittered below. So what if their glow was man-made. Their fluorescent flame provided confirmation of what he'd attained, entirely on his own.

This view was what he had worked for, sacrificed for, and it was honestly earned, even if others at ACM Technologies thought otherwise. They were jealous, plain and simple. He was good at his job, and without family ties tethering him, he could pour his entire self into his career. Too many others fell back because they wouldn't make the same sacrifices.

He took another sip of the dry beverage. Several stories below, cars bustled over the streets, but the tree-filled park looked empty and quiet. Some evening, soon, he'd take a walk, grab a hot dog along the way, smother it with sauerkraut, onions, and mustard, and chase it with a Piña Colada.

If no one was around, he'd lie in the park's grass, damp with evening dew, breathe in its freshly cut scent that reminded him of mown hay fields, and gaze at the uncountable stars, just as he and Debbie had done back on the farm. He'd rather do it with her. Maybe in a few weeks, he'd have the opportunity.

He drained his glass then set it on the credenza below the window and picked up the portrait of his sister's family. Their Christmas card from last year showing a smiling, tightly woven unit unaware they were about to increase by one. Someday, he'd pose for the same type of photo, but to commit to a family now would be unfair to them. He would want to spend time, quantity time, not just quality, with them. Right now, that wasn't a possibility.

His high position was acquired without leaving a wife and children floundering in his wake. Having spent over ten years in New York City, he witnessed, more times than he dared count, the corporate world's brutal slaying of families. So, a choice had to be made. He studied the miniscule cars lighting the streets below and felt pride surge in his gut. Yes, he had made the right choice.

He set the portrait down, and left the view to listen to his answering machine. It played as he returned to the light show outside his window. A whispered curse blew over his lips.

"Hey Ricky." Debbie's voice filled the room. "I was so excited to hear your news last night. I'd love to hear more about it. Give me a call as soon as you can. Congrats again. Love ya."

He'd played the message before. Every night this week, as a matter of fact. Debbie recorded it on Monday night. Three days, and he still hadn't returned her call. But, how could he? There'd been no time. Proof that he wasn't ready for family life.

Chuckling to himself, he pulled the BlackBerry from his belt. He'd officially become a member of the Office on a Belt Club, as his brother disdainfully put it. Well, he'd earned his membership and wasn't going to be shy about displaying it either. He dialed his office and left a message for his assistant. "Verna, remind me to give Debbie a call. Thanks."

Leaving Verna in charge was a sure way to get him to call. She always assumed responsibility for penciling in those important non-work-related issues: anniversaries, birthdays, and now phone calls. Verna could take credit for keeping his family ties knotted, as loose as those knots were. If not for her nagging—yes, she nagged like a mother, and he loved her for it—his family ties would probably be permanently severed. In spite of their differences, Richard still knew the value of family, especially those nephews and the niece who always made him smile. He grinned, just thinking of them.

A hand caressed his back as he clipped his phone onto his belt, and her faint reflection smiled at him in the window, enhancing his city view. He smiled back.

"Still working?" A sultry voice accompanied the arms circling his waist, wrapping his senses with *Chanel's Allure Sensuelle*. His favorite woman's fragrance, with a name befitting its effect.

He took her hand and turned to admire her dressed in one of his long sleeve dress shirts, the indigo sateen top accented with narrow black stripes. Naturally, she chose one of the pricier ones. Not that he had many others anymore. He had given up shopping at regular department stores years ago. A wardrobe from those shops didn't fit the image he needed to fashion for his position. Besides, he didn't mind that she wore it. It made her all the more appealing . . . and helped sculpt his image.

That carefully sculpted image brought her here today. The right side of his mouth curved up as he scanned her body, letting her know he approved. "Work's all done." She made it easy to leave work behind. For the night anyway. Tomorrow morning, he'd be right back into it, smiling all the way.

"It's about time." Entwining her fingers with his, she led him toward his bedroom. Another benefit of his promotion; a perk he wasn't ready to sacrifice for family.

The grin remained intact on his face as he turned back one more time to glance out his window. Still overcast. It didn't matter.

Who needed a walk beneath the stars when he ruled above them?

Chapter Eighteen

With eyes pleading for sleep, Debbie watched the remaining minutes of some home design show demonstrating how to decorate on a budget. It didn't teach her anything new. Honestly, she could probably educate the hostess on a thing or five. Their whole house was furnished, painted, and papered on a small-town teacher's salary. Few household budgets were more meager than that.

She clicked off the television and glanced at the digital numbers on their DVD player. Eleven. Time to give her brother another try. She took the phone off the end table. Naturally, he'd called this morning when she was at the park. Since then, he'd been unreachable. What else was new? She dialed his home number. As it rang, she propped herself up on the sofa and secured the crocheted blanket under her arms. It rang two, then three times. *Come on, Ricky. It's midnight there. You should be home.*

Following the fourth ring, his recorded voice cheerfully asked her to leave a message with a promise to return the call as soon as possible. Who knew when that would be? Regardless, she'd leave a message tonight, tell him it was important. Maybe then, he'd make it a priority.

A tear trickled from her eye as the beep signaled it was time to talk. She whisked the tear away, but more followed. "Ricky," she sniffled, "this is Debbie. I . . . "

His receiver picked up, and she smiled.

"Listen, honey, this man's taken," a woman's voice said.

Her smile lapsed as her mouth fell open. *Richard* . . . She held her eyes shut, trying to force in the tears as her brother's agitated voice filled the background. "Natalie, give me the phone."

The woman talked over him. "You can just—"

Debbie's eyes widened and her jaw dropped further as the woman spewed words Debbie seldom heard and never wanted to hear again. Trembling, she pressed the End Call button. "Richard," she said under her breath, her heart quickening. What kind of woman was her brother with now? What kind of person could say those awful things? Clearly, Ricky would be no help tonight. Couldn't he behave? Just once?

She dried her cheeks and threw off the blanket. That big brother of hers was going to get a call bright and early tomorrow morning, and it wasn't going to be pleasant. She stood to return the phone to the kitchen when it rang in her hand. As much as she wanted to avoid answering, she couldn't, not if she wanted Kaitlynn to sleep. She pressed the Talk button and held the phone against her thigh. If she remained silent and hit End without speaking, that would give him the hint.

"Debbie?" His muffled voice held worry.

So what? He should be worried. Tears fogged her eyes again.

"Please, talk to me. What's wrong?"

Sniffling, she raised the phone to her ear. "I'll call you tomorrow. I didn't mean to interrupt."

"I'm sorry." He sighed. "Really I am. That was uncalled for. She isn't who I thought she . . . " He sighed again. "She's gone." A *boom*, probably a door slamming, reverberated in the background. "For good."

She shook her head. Did it even matter? Tomorrow night, there'd be someone new, someone equally crude, no doubt.

"Talk to me, Debs. You're scaring me."

Good. Maybe he needed the occasional scare. It would be good to make him wait until morning. "I need my sleep." As if she could sleep now. "I'll talk to you tomorrow."

"Come on. I said I'm sorry. What else do you want me to do?"

Fly home. Stay away from the city that's stealing your soul.

"Please? I know it's important. I heard you crying. You don't cry."

She sighed and turned back to the couch. May as well just tell him. Who knew when she'd reach him again? "I have some news."

His sigh echoed hers. "Do you want me to fly out?"

Yes, her heart said, but her voice answered differently. "No. That's not necessary." At least he was in the listening mood now. She needed to talk to him, someone for whom she didn't have to hold up a courageous front. "It's about . . . " Her throat clogged.

"Kaitlynn? Is she okay?"

Debbie shook her head and worked her voice through the tears. "No. No. Kaitlynn's fine."

"Oh, good."

Not so good. "It's the baby."

"The baby? What's wrong?"

Debbie wiped her cheeks. "She has Down syndrome."

Silence answered.

Her lips and chin shuddered. It must bother her more than she thought, more than she'd dare let Jerry see.

"Oh, Debbie. I'm so sorry."

The memory of the woman who answered the phone slipped away. Debbie was talking to her big brother, the one who protected her, the one who knew how to get inside her heart.

"Thanks," she mumbled.

"Are you doing okay? How's Jerry handling it? Do you want me there?"

She smiled through her tears. Marcus was so wrong. Ricky did care beyond himself. "We're fine, really." The tears dried as fast as they'd come. "This is the first time I've cried. I think I needed this."

"I wish I could do more."

Of course, he did. "You're listening. That's what I need more than anything." Knowing Ricky, he probably wanted to fix it, as he fixed everything else. But her baby didn't need fixing. Lilly was exactly who God created her to be.

"You can have more children, right?" His tone was soft and caring.

"What?" She had to have heard wrong.

"Ending this pregnancy won't prevent you from having more children, will it?"

Her heart quickened. "You're kidding right?" Ricky couldn't possibly mean that.

"No, I mean, with Jerry's past and all, God wouldn't want you to be burdened with a sick child, would he?"

She pinched her eyes shut, and her breath escaped in shortened waves. Marcus was right. He was so right.

"Debbie! Are you okay?" Urgency and worry imbedded his voice.

As if she cared anymore. *I'm fine, but you're not.* More tears streamed as she lowered the phone to her lap.

"Listen. I'll catch the next plane out. I'll be there in the morning."

A humorless laugh escaped her throat as she raised the phone, finding her voice. Anger overcame the tears. "Don't bother, *Richard*." She hoped the rage she felt came across.

"Marcus is right, you know. All you care about is taking the easy way out. If a business struggles, close it. If a baby isn't perfect, get rid of it. This is a human life we're talking about. A human. Life! She's not some inconvenience I can dispose of."

"I didn't mean—"

"Don't give me that. You meant every word."

"I'm flying out. We need to talk."

"What? And interrupt your precious business? I wouldn't dream of asking you to do that."

"I'll be there by noon."

A sardonic laugh leaped from her throat. "Don't bother coming. Don't ever bother. I don't want to see you." She punched *end* then whipped the phone onto the couch. At the moment, she couldn't care less if she ever saw her brother again.

She strode to the bedroom, told Jerry she'd be out in the garage, then hurried through the kitchen, stopping just long enough to grab a Nut Goodie bar from the cupboard before stomping into the garage. The woodworking part of her project was complete, but hand whipping a small batch of quick-setting concrete would be just as effective at calming her nerves.

RICHARD BREATHED AN EXPLETIVE as he pitched the phone onto his bed. With elbows resting on his thighs, he stared at his bare feet cushioned on the lamb's wool rug spread across the floor, and covered his face with his hands. They pressed inward, squeezing his skin until his fingers steepled at his forehead. "Dear God, what have I done?" With closed eyes, he raised his head upward, holding his hands in place. "What do I do now?"

He wasn't sure if it was a prayer he'd sent up or an expression of frustration, but an answer quickly came. He'd call back. Fly out tomorrow, just as he promised. Tell her, in person, that he was sorry. She'd have to forgive him.

Reaching for the phone, he leaned over onto his bed and became sickened by the lingering odor. That alluring fragrance had been used to disguise a skunk. How could he not have sniffed it before? He'd sleep on his couch tonight. Wash the bedding tomorrow. Get rid of every trace of that fetid weasel.

He retrieved the phone then hit Redial as he walked into his living room. The blinds remained open, but the overcast sky hid the stars' light, enveloping the room with blackness. He slumped into his leather recliner and drummed his fingers on its arm as he waited for someone to answer. Finally, he heard a click on the other end, followed by a pause of silence.

"Kaitlynn's asleep." Jerry's whispered voice bristled.

"Let me talk to Debbie."

"She doesn't want to talk to you."

"I don't care. I need to talk to her."

Jerry emitted an exasperated sigh.

"Please." He wasn't hanging up. Not until he spoke with his sister. "Listen, Jer." Richard sat up in his chair, planting bare feet on the hardwood. "I messed up. I know that. Let me talk to her."

A disdainful laugh echoed over the phone line. "I think you've done plenty of talking for the night. Go back to bed."

"Come on. This is my sister we're—"

"And she's my wife, who's been through the shredder recently, and now I have to try and piece things back together, no thanks to you."

Richard cursed. He didn't care what Jerry thought. "It's late. I'm tired. I wasn't thinking. I didn't mean anything."

"Not intentionally, maybe, but at least she knows the truth. She knows how you really feel."

"That's not true."

"Isn't it? Can you honestly tell me you don't think this baby's a mistake?"

Richard closed his eyes. There was no diplomatic answer. Considering the hardships a special-needs child brought to a family, but more so considering Jerry's background, that was exactly what he believed.

"Just as I thought."

"But I know . . . I should have known that isn't how you guys feel. Like I said, I'm tired, I wasn't thinking. Let me talk to her. Tell her I'm sorry."

"Not tonight."

"Fine. Then I'll see you tomorrow." He could catch a six a.m. flight out of JFK or LaGuardia, and be in Minneapolis shortly after eight. Be up to Debbie's before noon.

"No. Don't."

"And why not?" He'd never been angry with Jerry before, but then Jerry had never given him reason.

"She doesn't want to see you." Jerry's voice sounded apologetic.

"What?"

"She doesn't want to see you."

"I don't care! I'm coming."

"Please, Rick. I'm serious."

Richard rotated his knotted-up shoulders.

"She's upset," Jerry said.

"I realize that. That's why I need to see her, to set this straight."

"Think of it this way. You've just told a pregnant mother that her child is worthless."

Oh, man. He slumped into his chair and moaned. That was precisely what he'd done.

"Right now, you could apologize until the Vikings win the Championship, and it wouldn't matter."

"So, what do I do?"

"Give it a few days. Maybe a week or two. You know Debbie. By then it'll all be forgotten. You'll be back in her good graces."

"Okay." He didn't like the plan, but understood it and even agreed. "Please tell her I'm sorry, that I love her. Tell her I want to be there for her."

"I'll pass it on. And Ricky, she already knows."

"Thanks." Richard put the phone on his glass-topped coffee table then strode to the den, to his computer. May as well get some work done. There would be no sleeping tonight.

Chapter Nineteen

*D*ebbie opened the front door and breathed in late-June's showers drumming the parched ground. With the wet weather, they couldn't walk to the park, but a full day of steady precipitation would return green to a yard hijacked by dandelions. Kaitlynn said the yellow outdoor carpeting was beautiful. That must be why God created dandelions.

Kaitlynn joined Debbie at the door, peering through the screen. "Can we see 'Melia today?"

"Not today, precious. The park'll be all wet and muddy."

"But I like playing in the rain."

Debbie knelt to Kaitlynn's height. "Tell you what, if we can get our work done inside, and the thunder and lightning stay away, we'll play in the rain and jump in puddles and—"

"And have toothpick races?"

"Gotta have toothpick races." Debbie kissed Kaitlynn's forehead.

"Daddy too?"

A quick glance down the hallway confirmed the bedroom door was closed. "We'll see how Daddy's feeling when he wakes up." Sound sleep had eluded him this past week as he waited for final word on the principal position. Two other candidates had made the cut along with Jerry, and final interviews were held last week.

He was told then that the decision would be made this week. The anticipation was almost worse for him than meeting her family six years ago. Almost.

Debbie stood and patted Kaitlynn's head. "Now, go get your crayons and some paper so you can help me with Lilly's book."

"Okay." Kaitlynn galloped off to her bedroom singing *ta da dum, ta da dum, ta da dum dum dum,* just as Jerry taught her. At least she had the rhythm down, but that Brooks gift for singing off-key had been passed down, poor child.

Debbie walked to the kitchen table, patting her stomach. Maybe Lilly would inherit Jerry's on-key talent. She pulled Lilly's baby book from its box. Few things were more stress-inducing than scrapbooking, but recording the key events in Lilly's life shouldn't be too difficult. She paged to the twenty-first week marker.

Just over halfway there, more than halfway to seeing her daughter's beautiful face and stroking her cashmere skin. Even Jerry showed enthusiasm when they heard Lilly's heartbeat last week.

As Debbie recorded the rate, Kaitlynn returned with her box of crayons and a coloring book. Though only three, her daughter rarely colored out of the lines. That girl was too much like her Uncle Ricky. Debbie raked her teeth over her lower lip. No, Kaitlynn wasn't at all like Uncle Ricky. Her daughter had a heart. Debbie forced a smile, pushing thoughts of her brother away. The girl definitely took after her mother.

"Mommy, what are you coloring?"

Debbie showed Kaitlynn the shiny paper with lines peaking and dipping across it. "This shows Lilly's heartbeat."

As if hearing her name, movement tickled Debbie's stomach. She quickly brought her hand down, attempting to trace Lilly's activity.

Kaitlynn reached out. "Can I feel her heart?"

Debbie guided Kaitlynn's fingers to the motion. "This isn't Lilly's heart, but she's moving, and you know what?"

"What?" Kaitlynn's eyes brightened.

"I think God gave Lilly a feather because she's tickling my tummy."

Kaitlynn giggled. "Did God give me a feather too?"

"Nope." She beeped her daughter's nose. "He gave you a drum set. Your little arms were always moving to some beat, especially Daddy's singing."

"'Cause Daddy sings gooder than you."

Grinning, she poked Kaitlynn's nose again. "Much gooder than me." She pointed at the coloring book. "Why don't you color a picture to include in Lilly's book? Something to show how much you love her."

"Okay." Kaitlynn turned the pages, stopping at a swan. "See? Feathers for Lilly."

"Perfect, precious."

Crooking her tongue from the edge of her mouth, Kaitlynn focused on the bird. That would engage her for several minutes.

Debbie paged toward the front of the book. It was a good day to catch up. The phone rang as she penned *Bernard Brooks* on the maternal grandfather line. Nervous excitement built in her as she stood to answer it. *Please let it be the school superintendent relaying good news.*

Heaving a heavy sigh to steady her nerves, she carried the phone to the table and answered after the third ring. "Hello."

"Debbie?"

Her fingers gripped the receiver, knuckles whitening. Two and a half weeks had passed since they fought. She should have forgiven him by now, but anger still swelled in her belly. How could her brother hate his niece so much?

"This is Rich—"

"I know." She caressed her stomach. "What do you want?"

"To talk . . . apologize," he said softly. "I've got this weekend open. Could you fly out?"

He had to be kidding. "I'm busy."

"How about the following weekend?"

"Richard . . . " Her forgiveness could not be bought.

"Please." It sounded like a beggar's cry.

Kaitlynn held her green crayon in the air, her eyes round and sparkling. "Uncle Ricky?"

Inhaling a deep breath, Debbie stood and held the phone away from her ear, yet keeping it close enough for her brother to hear. "Sweetie, I need to take this call in my office. Stay here and color."

"But I wanna talk to Uncle Ricky."

Debbie shook her head. "Not today, precious. He's at work. This is going to be a short call."

She strode through the living room, closed and locked the front door, then hurried to the office, ignoring Ricky's pleas for her to say something.

She settled into the *faux*-leather office chair and reclined before speaking again. "You don't get it, do you?"

"Debbie—"

"I asked you not to call. If you fly out for Nathan's birthday party next month, fine. You should. Just don't expect me to set any time aside for you, and I'm certainly not coming to New York."

"I'm sorry, Debbie. How can I get you to understand?"

"Understand?" She sat upright. "Let me help you understand something. All this time I thought you were different. I believed you made your way in New York by taking the high road. I even defended you to Marcus when he told us about the friend you ripped off."

"What are you—?"

"Jerry and I heard Lilly's heartbeat the other day. Just a few minutes ago, I felt her move."

"You don't know how sorry—"

"Did you know that more than nine out of every ten fetuses diagnosed with Down syndrome are aborted?"

"No, I—"

"So, how does that make you any different from anyone else? You're just a carbon copy of the rest of the world. You're not the brother I grew up with anymore." She shook her head and thought she heard him sniffle. *God, why can't I forgive him?* She wiped her cheek. How could she love him, yet despise him so fiercely? "I know you're sorry. I just can't . . . "

"Can't what?"

Sighing, she reclined in her chair, slumping into it. "I'm done fighting, okay? I'm done trying to understand you. You used to care. You used to have standards. I'm done defending you. I'm done being blind to you, okay?" She forced down the softball in her throat. Why did recognizing the truth have to hurt so much?

"So, you've turned into a judge, too." A *bang* echoed from his end, as if he pounded something against his desk, followed by an obscenity he didn't even try to muffle. "I'm not good enough for you, either. Well, fine then. The family finally gets their wish. I'm done with all of you."

Silence screamed over the phone then became a whiny beep. Debbie bit into her lower lip. There would be no tears. Enough stress filled her life without having to babysit her older brother too.

It was time to finish the baby book, but she needed chocolate first. Sneak a bite without Kaitlynn seeing. Maybe do some work in the garage. Scrapbooking would only add to her stress.

Squaring her shoulders and raising her chin, she strode toward the kitchen, walking past her bedroom as the door opened.

Jerry, standing in the doorframe wearing only his farmer-plaid pajama pants, grasped her arm. "What's wrong?"

She jutted her chin higher and shook her head. "Nothing."

With his mouth scrunched to one side, he pinched her chin, bringing it downward, leveling her eyes with his. "Nothing?"

"Nope." Maybe Jerry should go into counseling too. In truth, wasn't that part of a teacher's or principal's job description?

"Ricky?"

Her head gave one slow nod. "Nothing I want to talk about right now with little ears in the kitchen hearing everything."

"But you promise to talk about it later?"

"I promise." The phone rang, rescuing her from further discussion.

Jerry squeezed her hand and snuck back into the bedroom to answer it. "Hello."

She sat next to him on the bed and watched his face brighten. "Yes, Mr. Brinkmeier."

Smiling, she clasped his hand. Finally, the school superintendent. It was about time they got some good news.

But the glow leaked from Jerry's eyes, and his mouth flat-lined. His fingers tightened around hers. "I see." He released her hand, cuffing his own, and cracked his knuckles. "I understand." The confusion glossing his eyes and reddening the ridges of his burn scar, said otherwise.

Please, God. Not this too. She circled her arm around his back as Lilly fluttered. How could they afford to feed another mouth, buy more diapers, and pay medical expenses that would certainly be higher than for the average child, on his current salary?

"I'm coming in this afternoon. Do some summer school prep.

Thank you, Mr. Brinkmeier." There was no gratitude in her husband's voice as he laid the phone on the bed. Heavy disappointment, maybe. A hint of anger, probably. Despondency, definitely.

She kept her arm around him, filing away her feud with Ricky. Jerry needed her strength more than Ricky needed a sister.

Chapter Twenty

With blisters forming on her hands, Debbie pulled the final weed from her garden and dropped it in the yard bag. She plopped on her bottom and, with the back of her arm, wiped sweat from her forehead. Heat and humidity were already invading on this sunny July morning, sapping her of strength. But too much work awaited. There was no time to be tired.

She watched Kaitlynn jump into the yellow plastic tube slide, reappearing at the bottom seconds later. Debbie removed her gloves and threw them on the ground and leaned back, supporting her weight on her arms, giving Lilly more space to move.

"Kaitlynn, Mommy can use your help for a bit, please."

"But Mommy—"

"No buts, young lady."

Her daughter's lower lip stuck out far enough to perch a bird as she stomped across the yard.

Debbie sucked in her cheeks, holding in a smile, and pointed at the narrow patch snaking through the garden, outlined with garden hoses. "You can put your rocks there and when you're done, you can have some strawberries." She leaned over, pinched one off, and handed it to Kaitlynn. "Here's one for energy."

Kaitlynn popped the berry into her mouth. "Tank you, Mommy."

"You're welcome." Debbie gestured to a bucket, loaded with common stones, set on the edge of the path. "There's a cup in there. Just fill it, then dump the rocks on the path, and you can tell everyone you made it."

"I do a good job."

"I know you will, precious." It was the perfect job for her daughter. Not a stone would dare cross the garden hose boundaries with Kaitlynn in charge.

Crossing her legs, she leaned back and watched her daughter dump stones between the white sweet alyssum, with its honey-like fragrance, bordering the front of the garden. Kaitlynn continued, spreading the stones on the path meandering among mouth-watering strawberries, then through Purple Emperor butterfly plants just beginning to flower. She poured a cupful of stones by one of the Stargazer lilies that dotted the garden with no apparent pattern, mimicking the stars in the sky. In a month, the buds would flower, their crimson and white petals opening to the heavens in worship.

The stone trail wandered between dusty pink Grandma's Blessings rose bushes and past Giant Sungold sunflowers, whose fuzzy pompom heads couldn't wait to cheer for the sunshine they would pursue through late summer and into fall. The path finally spilled into a pie-slice-shaped open space pointing north. So, the garden was unusual. It was turning out just as Debbie planned, even without a green thumb.

"I have berries, now?" Kaitlynn dropped her cup in the pail still more than half full.

Debbie's gaze followed the path, a trickle of rocks spotted the dirt from the alyssum to the open space. Well, it was a start. She held up her hand, spreading her fingers apart. "Five berries, okay?"

"Tank you, Mommy." Kaitlynn kneeled in the soil, oblivious to the dirt staining her knees. She picked the largest berry she could find and bit into it. Juice bled from the corners of her mouth and down her chin. The child would definitely need a bath before naptime.

A yawn forced Debbie's mouth open. Maybe she'd cuddle right next to Kaitlynn this afternoon. After that, she could begin work on her next project: preparing the nursery.

She leaned to her left to pluck a berry.

"Deborah." Jerry yelled behind her, a voice rife with frustration.

Now what? She stood, wiped her soiled hands on her shorts, and turned to Jerry, who was dressed in khaki slacks and a burgundy polo for his late morning class. "What's wrong hon?"

The scowl on his face and the slump in his shoulders matched his voice. "The stupid shower drain's clogged. I've just wasted the last fifteen minutes plunging. Can you call Marcus?"

"That bad, huh?" It had to be if he was asking for help.

He shook his head, his frown deepening, and his shoulders sagging further. A cloudy sadness clung to his eyes that had been there for a month, ever since the school board's rejection. "I hate to leave you with this. I know you had plans for the day."

"Plans that can be changed. I'll give him a call. See if he can help."

"And make sure you pay him."

Yeah, right. "He won't take anything."

"Pay him. Whatever we can afford."

Debbie held up her hands in surrender. "Whatever you say." It wasn't worth the battle. She'd rather fight with Marcus than give Jerry another thing to worry about. A clogged drain was just one more pebble building her husband's wall of perceived failures.

He checked his watch as he turned back toward the house. "I need to get going."

"Wait one second." She slow-jogged toward him then gave him a quick kiss, keeping dirty hands at her side. Anything to help brighten his day.

He smiled. It lasted for a millisecond, but it was definitely a smile.

Kaitlynn ran toward him. "Me too, kiss."

Debbie scooped Kaitlynn up before she reached her daddy and secured her arms. "Lips only. No hands."

Kaitlynn puckered her berry-stained lips and touched them to her daddy's, making a smacking sound as she pulled back.

This time Jerry's smile lasted a full five seconds, at least. "I love you, punkin."

Lilly awoke with a stretch. This little child seemed to move more when Jerry was around. Already, she loved her daddy.

Debbie grasped Jerry's hand, hoping to broaden his smile, and brought it to her stomach. "Lilly wants to say hello."

Jerry jerked his hand away and looked at the ground. "I need to go."

Lilly stretched again, seeming to beg for her daddy's attention.

But Debbie wasn't going to force him. She kissed Jerry, hoping to offer unspoken encouragement.

"I'll take care of the drain. We'll take a little walk tonight." Debbie pointed to Kaitlynn's path. "Your daughter made it all by herself."

Jerry beeped Kaitlynn's nose. "I can't wait until tonight." At least Kaitlynn could make him happy.

"I love you." Debbie kissed her husband again before he

turned and began his brisk walk to work.

DEBBIE WRINKLED HER NOSE as Marcus pulled the steel wire spring from her shower drain, dragging with it a nest-full of hair.

Smirking, he held it up. "I don't think I can blame Jerry for this clog."

She propped her hands on her hips. "Ha, ha, ha."

"You know—" Marcus swiped the goop into an ice cream bucket. "—a little Drano would have done the trick."

Debbie shook her head. "Not in this house."

"Why not?"

"I thought you knew."

"Knew what?" Marcus turned on the shower and rinsed off the snake and his hands.

She leaned against the bathroom's doorframe and smoothed her hand over her cheek. "That's how Jerry got his burn."

"Oh man, I'm sorry. I completely forgot."

"Don't worry about it. It's just one thing we'll never keep in our house."

Marcus dried his hands on a bathroom towel. "Does he ever hear from his dad?"

"Once or twice a year."

"What kind of man abandons his family?"

Debbie shrugged. "He can't seem to get over his guilt for leaving the Drano out. Jerry was only a toddler at the time. I counseled parents who abandoned their kids with much flimsier excuses."

Marcus coiled the snake, anger still tensing his cheeks. "Well, good thing Jerry's nothing like his dad."

"Yeah, good thing," she said softly before standing straight. She reached into her pocket and pulled out two twenties. "I know it's not much, but—"

Marcus stopped winding and stared at her, his brows nearly touching. "You're kidding, right?"

She held the money out. "Please take it. Jerry insists."

"Bull to that. This isn't charity."

"Yes, but you left your worksite, you—"

"I did a favor for my sister."

She breathed in, her shoulders rising with her breath, then blew it out as she stuffed the money back into her pocket. A smile tugged up her lips as she pulled out a quarter. "He didn't say how much."

Marcus snatched the quarter from her hand, but the frown remained. "He's gotta get over this."

"Yeah, well." As much as she agreed with Marcus, she also understood Jerry's hesitance.

She clapped her hands together, looking to change the subject. "How about I get you a cup of coffee and serve one of those donuts Janet sent with you?"

Marcus nodded and the tension eased from his brows. "That'd be great. I'll be done here in a second. Oh, and I left the stuff you asked for on your workbench. I can't wait to see what you're going to do with pizza boxes and window screen."

"You'll see soon enough." That project would start next week. "I'll go get your coffee ready."

She stepped out of the bathroom.

"Oh, Debbie?"

She leaned back and peered in. "Yes?"

"I wanted to ask you before I forget." He secured a hand over the sink's edge and leaned into it. "I got a strange call last night."

Limbs fluttered in Debbie's stomach as she stepped beneath the doorframe. "Oh?"

"From your brother."

Debbie looked down at her rounded belly and ran her hands over it.

"What's up with you two?"

"Nothing," she whispered, hoping Marcus didn't hear her voice shake. Biting into her lower lip, she glanced up.

His midnight-blue eyes pierced hers. "And you're a rotten liar." He crossed his arms. "What did he do now?"

Debbie stared at Marcus, her hands tracing Lilly's movement. "You asked earlier what kind of man abandons his family."

Marcus' eyes darkened, and the muscles in his cheeks strained.

What felt like an elbow or knee flitted beneath Debbie's hand.

Unconsciously, she caressed her belly where her beautiful daughter grew. "The kind of man who can't tolerate imperfection."

Chapter Twenty-one

*J*erry wished for the lilac's spring fragrance as he ambled past the bushes fencing in part of his front yard, but that scent had disappeared over a month ago, taking hope along with it. He turned onto the cracking sidewalk leading to the front door of their 1950s rambler. More maintenance for this old house. Next year, he'd ask Marcus for another favor. Make him accept more than a quarter.

Jerry circled his hand on the doorknob and heard music drift through open windows. Although July's oppressive heat and humidity warranted turning on the central air, foregoing air conditioning was just one more sacrifice they'd chosen to make. Even with Debbie's pregnancy overheating her body, they simply didn't have the money to spare.

Still, the song's words told him she wasn't complaining. Music was a great way to decipher Debbie's mood. When she wanted calm, there was nothing better than a string orchestra. The driving guitars of Skillet meant she was tired and needed energy. Casting Crowns suggested she desired moments of honest reflections. What he heard was the worshipful praise of Chris Tomlin. And, she was singing along. With the direction their lives were going, how could Debbie possibly be in the mood for praise?

Or, maybe that was what they both needed.

With his ears tuning into the praising words, Jerry entered his home, set his briefcase next to the closet, and smiled.

Kaitlynn sat in the middle of the living room floor, her legs V'd outwards, dropping orange juice lids through a rectangular hole in the plastic cover of a coffee can. Each tumbling lid clanked out a percussive underlayment to Debbie's discordant melody. With all the toys she'd gotten for her birthday, this homemade one from Aunt Janet was a favorite. Only the outdoor playset occupied more of her time.

"M." Kaitlynn inserted a lid decorated with an alphabet sticker through the opening, then finally looked up. "Daddy!" With eyes twinkling, she popped up and ran to him, holding her arms in the air.

He lifted her, swinging her above his head before cradling her against his body. "Hi, punkin." Her unconditional love was the perfect antidote for his melancholy. "Did you and Mommy have a good day?"

"Mm, hmmm. Uncle Marcus brung peanut butter cookies with chocolate stars. They're gooder than Mommy's."

Well, if Debbie had an oven from this century, maybe she could bake a decent cookie now and then. "You didn't tell your mommy that, did you?"

"Uh-huh. Always tell the truth, right Daddy?"

"That's my girl." He grinned and rubbed his nose against hers. "Now, where is your mommy?"

"She's in Lilly's room."

All his joy crashed to his stomach, and every cell in his body tingled. Why was it so hard to accept his new daughter? He loosened his grip on Kaitlynn, letting her slide down his legs to the floor.

She returned to her musical coffee can, dropping the lettered lids through the hole in the correct order. His little girl was too much like her uncle, an uncle who was sorely missed by not only his niece. Debbie had been less than honest about the hole piercing her heart from her brother's estrangement.

But who was Jerry to complain? Not once had he confessed his misgivings about having this child. He never would. What Debbie needed was his support, not his fears.

Maybe he'd encourage her to take the night off, catch a movie with Janet, so he could give that uncle a call, tell him about Kaitlynn's favorite toy, let Ricky know he was missed. Debbie would get over her anger soon. Judging by the joyful music coming from the back room, maybe that had already happened.

His ears protested, as he followed the off-key tune to the office, but his heart heard the beauty. Perhaps praise music was a good idea for today.

He hummed out harmony, his tension evaporating with each step. When he peeked in, what he saw drained the budding happiness from his body.

Praise music continued to rise from the portable CD player, mocking him.

"What are you doing?" He grasped the doorframe, bile inching up his throat.

Debbie peered up, gripping a Phillips head screwdriver. Her mouth hung open. She clearly had no clue what he was seeing.

"I asked . . . " He raised his voice and accented each word. "What. Are. You. Doing?"

She clamped her mouth shut and shrugged, her fingers white-knuckling the screwdriver. "What does it look like? I thought we needed something positive for the day."

With that all-too-familiar pain spreading across his chest, he clenched his eyes and fists, and snapped his knuckles one at a time. "You don't understand," he whispered, his eyes still closed.

He heard her stand, and then felt her hands grip his arms.

Her soothing counselor's voice broke through. "Help me understand."

He refused to succumb to it. Opening his eyes, he stared past his wife and nodded. "The crib."

"I wanted to put it up while I have the energy." Her voice remained soft.

She obviously didn't comprehend how it made him feel. This week of all weeks. Did she even consider the date?

He stared straight ahead, the pain from ten years ago returning, squeezing his heart. "It's empty." The words croaked from his throat before he hurried to the bathroom.

Chapter Twenty-two

*D*ebbie threw the screwdriver on the beige carpeting and chased after her husband. She should have anticipated his reaction. To Jerry, an empty crib meant one thing. Especially this time of year.

She stopped in the bathroom doorway and tented her hands over her lips as her husband knelt before the blue porcelain toilet, heaving. *Please, God, give me the right words.* Holding her breath, she walked forward, sat on the edge of the blue tub, and rested her palm on Jerry's shoulder, choking back her own reflex to purge her food.

"I'm sorry. I wasn't thinking."

Jerry answered with another surge.

"Daddy, are you okay?" Fear etched Kaitlynn's round eyes as she stood in the bathroom doorway hugging her toddler pillow.

Debbie floated her hand over Jerry's back. "Daddy's going to be fine. Why don't you go play some more?"

Biting into her lip, Kaitlynn walked into the bathroom and held out her pillow.

Jerry looked up, his face mottled with various shades of pink, and accepted Kaitlynn's offering. "Thanks, punkin, that'll make me feel much better."

"You know what, precious?" Gluing on a smile, Debbie took

Kaitlynn's hand and led her out. "Why don't we make some soup for your daddy?"

"With buttered crackers?"

"Can't have soup without buttered crackers."

"Me too?"

"That sounds like a terrific idea. All three of us can have soup with cracker sandwiches. Can you do me a favor and get a big can from the basement?"

"Okay, Mommy."

Debbie bent down and kissed Kaitlynn's forehead before her daughter ran toward the stairs. "Be careful on the steps. No running, now."

"I be good, Mommy."

Naturally. Debbie huffed out a breath and returned to the bathroom.

Jerry sat on the edge of the tub, wiping a towel over his face. "I'm sorry, hon."

"Me too." She sat next to him and curved her arm around his back, snuggling close, trying not to breathe the noxious scent.

"I just can't . . . " He threw the towel into the tub and stood. "I need to lie down."

"Go ahead. Kaitlynn and I'll bring in supper . . . " A tear burned down her cheek as Jerry strode to their bedroom and slammed the door.

Her entire body felt weighted with rocks as she lumbered to the nursery. She shut off the music then left the room, closing the door as noiselessly as possible. It would just have to remain shut for now. Maybe for another fourteen weeks.

NOON SUNLIGHT FILTERED THROUGH Debbie's kitchen curtains as she listened to the garage door meet concrete.

Kaitlynn sat up tall, craning her neck so she could watch out the window. "Daddy's bye-bye."

If she only knew. "To his afternoon class." Debbie followed her daughter's gaze and watched the Escort motor down the street, informing the entire neighborhood that the car needed a new muffler.

Jerry hadn't said a word this morning.

She prayed his silence confessed he wanted a restored heart.

If only she'd waited one more week to put up the crib.

The car turned a corner and disappeared from her view. The engine's roar faded and vanished. Her gaze shifted to the daily Bible reading on the table. It hadn't been touched for a month, not since Jerry was denied the promotion. His promise, following the men's retreat, that he would assume leadership in spiritual matters had languished far faster than the muffler's voice.

"I done, Mommy." Kaitlynn raised her plate off the table, proving it was empty.

"Good job, precious." Debbie reached for the Bible reading. May as well start reading them by herself. "Put it in the dishwasher, please. Then, it's naptime."

"'Melia doesn't take naps."

"But Kaitlynn does."

"'Melia's too old for naps."

"But Kaitlynn isn't."

"Okay." Pouting, Kaitlynn climbed off her stool, reached for her plate, and bumped it onto the floor. The "unbreakable" Corelle didn't break. It shattered. Into a zillion pieces.

Kaitlynn screamed, followed by a hacking cough, igniting the angel's kiss birthmark on her forehead.

Debbie hurried around the table, disregarding the shrapnel piercing her slippers, and picked up her daughter. She carried Kaitlynn to the living room and set her on the couch before retrieving the inhaler and a bottled water from the kitchen.

The cough deepened as Debbie rushed back. She scooped Kaitlynn up, and brought her daughter down on her lap, cuddling her to her chest as Kaitlynn breathed in her first puffs. Kaitlynn held up her fingers, counting off the seconds, then released the tube. Debbie wiped hair from her daughter's face and sang the ABCs before dispersing the second dose of medicine.

Thirty draining minutes later, Kaitlynn finally lay asleep on the couch, her breath easing into a natural rhythm.

Debbie covered her yawning mouth. A nap would be a good idea. She glanced at the carpet and the kitchen linoleum sprinkled with plate remnants, at her unusable slippers, then at the cordless phone lying on the end table next to the couch. Clean first, then make a few calls. Do some much-needed venting. She covered Kaitlynn with a *Dora the Explorer* blanket before bringing the phone with her into the kitchen.

After sweeping up the floor and tossing her slippers, she leaned against a cupboard and dialed the farm. No answer. She tried Janet. No one home there either. And, with the exception of Ricky, her family didn't believe in being tethered to cell phones. That left the women from her "Bible" study group. Nope. She wasn't even going to try. When was the last time they listened to anything she said? And Lee? Well, calling him was hardly appropriate. Besides, it had been a few weeks since she'd seen him at the park.

Of course, there was one other person.

Her shoulders tensed as she scrolled through the saved numbers until she found her brother's work extension. Had it really been a month since they talked? Perhaps it was time to offer forgiveness and ask for it in return.

Stress tingled in her finger as she hit the silver Talk button.

Hopefully, he'd want to speak to her.

Chapter Twenty-three

Richard slammed down his receiver and cursed. It was downright unreasonable for Entenza to expect him to skip out of an important meeting with clients, just for one of his gripe sessions. The verbal reprimand didn't surprise him, though. This entire week had been a disaster.

It didn't help that his research on Down syndrome, at the library last night, sat in his gut like day-old donuts. The library's resources backed up what he'd found online, but this McQuick, throwaway "civilization" he'd surrounded himself with had taught him otherwise.

How could he have been so wrong?

He deserved his sister's fury. He glanced at the phone, wanting to call her, but the reproof from his boss stopped him. At this moment, he was too upset to be decent to anyone. Even Debbie. Maybe later, once he had the presence of mind to offer a sincere apology.

Sure, he'd earned the scorn from Debbie, but from his CEO? If Entenza wanted a puppet Vice President, he'd have to go elsewhere for one. Richard wouldn't kowtow to anyone.

Between work and Debbie, he'd become one ornery businessman. His poor assistant endured the brunt of his poor attitude. Well, he wouldn't take it out on her anymore. His work here today was complete.

He punched the phone's button paging Verna.

"Yes, Mr. Brooks." Her cheery Southern accent sang over the intercom.

Usually he loved that tone, so different from the nasal New Yorkers. But today, even that grated on him. "Verna, just take messages for the rest of the day. I'm heading out."

"I'll do that. Now, you have a good afternoon."

Yeah, right. He reached down to his BlackBerry and shut it off, shutting himself off from the world. It was time to go home, throw in a movie racked with car crashes and fiery explosions, make popcorn drowned in butter and salt, and chase it with a six-pack. He'd begin next week with a clear head, ready to counter the disagreements and difficulties that stole this week.

He grabbed the Versace suit coat off the back of his chair and strode for the door. Once he exited this building, no one could bother him. His office phone rang as he pulled the door open. What part of "take messages" didn't Verna understand? He glared at her and made a slicing motion in front of his neck.

She looked back at him with those stern motherly eyes. "You will answer that phone, young man."

He opened his mouth to protest, but Verna's brows furrowed. Arguing would be pointless. With a bear-like growl, he threw his hands up in mock surrender and retreated to his office, forgetting to ask who or what was so dratted important. Terrific. Now he couldn't mentally prepare for the next onslaught.

He snatched the phone off the cradle. This caller would know right off, he was ticked. "Richard Brooks."

"Hi Ricky."

Debbie? His shoulders slumped. *Why now?* There was no way on earth he could sustain a civilized dialogue right now. Maybe later, after he'd downed a few Coronas.

"You there, Ricky?"

"Yeah, I'm here. What do you need? I was heading out."

"Oh, I'm sorry. I just wanted to talk."

"Well, you picked a heckuva time to want to talk." *Idiot.* He closed his eyes and shook his head. *She's extending the olive branch. Grasp it.*

"Well, forgive me." The disdain in her voice said she wasn't asking for forgiveness. "I thought, maybe . . . Ah, forget it. I was obviously wrong."

He slumped into his chair and massaged the headache burgeoning in his forehead. "Wait, I'm sorry."

"You seem to be saying that a lot lately."

"I know. I know." He combed his fingers through his hair. "I've had a really . . . " Debbie wouldn't appreciate the salty word that nearly eased off his tongue. If his mother heard his language now, he'd have the permanent taste of soap in his mouth. It was unsettling how the cursing he'd once scorned and preached against had become a natural part of his daily lexicon.

"I've had a bad day. Can I call you tonight? After I get home and have had some time to wind down?"

He heard her blow out a breath.

"Fine. I'll be home all night." Her voice came out flat, disinterested, but she wouldn't have called if she didn't need to talk, if she wasn't ready to listen.

"I'll call. I promise." He would be there for her, and make her realize he truly was sorry, that he not only understood her rage, but he absolutely agreed with it. "And, Debs, thanks for calling. It's good to hear from you. Really good." Better than good, actually.

"You too, Rick." The smile was back in her voice. "Oh, and Kaitlynn wanted me to tell you, you give the best underdogs."

He closed his eyes as they misted over. Who'd he been kidding to think he could give his family up? "Tell Katydid I love her."

"She loves you, too. We'll talk later."

"I promise."

He laid the phone back in its cradle then headed out his door for the second time.

Verna sat at her desk wearing a smug smile. "You two kiss and make up?"

"I hope so." He offered a slight smile. "Debbie wants to talk." The thought alone broadened his smile. He'd be able to tell her he was genuinely sorry about what he said, that he'd been plain ignorant, that he looked forward to Lilly's birth and to holding his precious niece. "I'm calling her tonight." He wouldn't fail again.

"When you're not so grumpy?"

Richard grinned. "Exactly." After working with him for ten years, Verna knew him too well. Including things he didn't want her to know. "That is precisely why I'm checking out for the day. I'll be back in on Monday, ready to go." He'd come in over the weekend too, as he always did. Get work done without the phone competing for his attention.

The stupid thing rang again.

"ACM Technologies, Richard Brooks' office. How may I help you?"

He shook his head and mouthed "no."

"One moment, please." Verna put the caller on hold and smiled. "Human resources."

His shoulders drooped. One lousy reprimand, and his promotion was on the line? "Tell them I'm gone." He might as well wait until Monday to get the news.

Verna pointed to the blinking line. "It's Ethan."

"Ethan? Why didn't you say so?" There was no one in the company Richard respected more, and who he could truly call a friend. "Tell him I'll get back to him in an hour or two."

Verna pointed to her phone with the red blinking square highlighting line two. The woman was as bad as his mother. Maybe that was why he enjoyed her so much.

He picked up Verna's receiver, and hit the blinking key. Escape would be quicker from here. "Ethan. How's it going?"

"Hey, Rich, heard you got the treatment today."

"The treatment?" Richard chuckled. He swore gossip traveled faster in the corporate world than it did at a women's scrapbooking outing. "Is that what you call a verbal whipping?"

Ethan laughed. "Hey, don't worry. It's just the boss blowing steam. Wants to let everyone know he is still The Boss and that he's got some good ideas. We've all learned to listen. Let him have his say, then go back to your job. Whatever you were doing, I wouldn't change a thing. By Monday, he won't remember what he was upset about. So, forget about it."

That was exactly what Richard hoped. "So that's why you called? To get the gossip firsthand?"

"Nah. I have a proposition. One I think you'll appreciate."

"Okay." Richard itched his chin. "What have you got?"

"An extra ticket to the game tonight. My daughter's sick so the wife has to stay home."

"Yanks and Boston?"

"The Sox," Ethan said. "Impossible tickets to get."

He stared at the Picasso print which hung above Verna's desk, ignoring her frown of disapproval. There was nothing like watching a game in New York. Especially Yankees versus the Red Sox. There would be no better way to wind down than to have a few brews and a brat with a friend at an outdoor stadium. A real baseball stadium. Beat the Teflon domed place he used to watch games at back in Minneapolis. Someday he had to go home and check out Minnesota's new baseball stadium.

"I'd love it, but I need to head home first." He couldn't stand to watch baseball in a suit. It was strictly a jeans, ball cap, and T-shirt event.

"Richard," Verna said with a quiet firmness.

He smiled at her. Didn't work.

Her eyes narrowed, and her lips stuck out.

What was her problem now?

"Works for me," Ethan said. "Come down to my office. I've got the ticket. I'll meet you at the game."

"Great. I'll be down in a minute." If Verna would let him know what he'd done wrong now, if she'd let him escape.

Verna's eyes scolded him as he returned the receiver to its home.

"Now what?"

"Don't you forget to call that little sister of yours."

He frowned, but Verna was right. If he didn't call Debbie tonight, she might never forgive him. "I won't. She's too important."

"Just you remember that."

"I will." No way would he forget something that important.

"CAN I GET YOU ANOTHER drink, gentlemen?" The waitress leaned over, the dipping neckline of her tight sweater revealing more than Richard wanted to see.

He glanced at his watch. Only one woman was on his mind this evening. He had fifteen minutes to spare, at the most, before catching a cab home. The call to Debbie required privacy.

"You got some babe waiting?" Ethan's words slurred.

"Not tonight." Richard looked upward at a ceiling tarnished from years of holding in cigarette smoke. An acrid aroma still stained the air, although smoking hadn't been allowed for years. Mistakes didn't easily relinquish their grasp on people's memories. "I need to make an important call to my sister."

Ethan raised his glass in salute. "That's what I always liked about you, Rich." His words blended together. "Your family is still priority. Just remember to keep it that way. Family is irreplaceable."

Richard touched his glass to Ethan's. "Can't argue with that."

"Gentlemen." The waitress pulled on the hem of her sweater, drawing the neckline lower yet. "Can I get ya somethin' or not?"

Not what you're selling. Richard pushed away his half-finished Corona. It was time to go home. "Bring us each a Coke."

Ethan downed his Guinness and slid the glass toward the waitress. "Make sure you mix a generous helping of rum with that Coke."

Richard locked eyes with his friend. "Skip the rum."

"What? Can't a guy have a few drinks?"

"You call three at the game and two at this dive a few?" Not even by Richard's standards was that a few. What was Ethan thinking? His wife would be furious.

The waitress cleared her throat. "Do ya want rum or not?"

"Not." Richard slapped a fifty on the table. "Just bring the drinks, and leave us alone."

Ethan slumped against the booth's angled wood back that reached several inches above his head. "I feel like I'm out with my mother."

"Your mother would've stopped you three drinks ago." Richard rested his elbows on the table and leaned toward his friend. "What's Linny going to think with you coming home three sheets to the wind?"

Ethan hiccupped through a laugh. "If Linny were home—"

"What?"

"—I'd be sleeping in the guest room."

"Where is she? Is your daughter okay?"

Ethan laughed again with tears clouding his eyes. "Turns out Tali was never sick. Linny just used the excuse so she could get out before I got home. She didn't expect me to stop at home before the game."

"She left?" The words croaked from Richard's throat. No way could it happen to Ethan. He loved his family. There had to be another explanation.

"Went home to Fargo. Fargo of all places." He grabbed Richard's half-drunk beer and downed it in one swallow.

"Man, I'm sorry."

"She said in North Dakota, husbands are married to their wives not their jobs. Said I can visit my girls anytime. Visit." He spat the word. "A dad's not supposed to *visit* his kids."

No, he's not. Richard leaned into the bench's unforgiving back. He glanced at his watch and rubbed his forehead as the server returned with their sodas. Even Debbie would agree with this decision. She just had to.

He pulled a twenty from his wallet and handed it to the waitress. "I'll take those rum and Cokes after all."

Chapter Twenty-four

The phone rang as Debbie touched the bottom step in the basement, a pound of frozen hamburger chilling her hands. She looked toward the door and shook her head. If the call were important, they'd leave a message. It rang only twice more as she climbed the stairs. Couldn't have been too vital.

"Hello." Kaitlynn's voice filtered through the open doorway.

Oh, that little stinker. She knew she wasn't supposed to answer the phone.

"Uncle Ricky?"

What? *He's only calling twelve hours late.* With anger straining her body, Debbie clutched the railing and stomped up the remaining stairs.

She stopped in the doorway, posed one hand on a hip, and stared at Kaitlynn, who was skipping around the kitchen.

Debbie bit into her cheeks and concentrated on breathing, trying to keep her fury in check.

"Can you come give me underdogs?" Kaitlynn's cherubic enthusiasm slightly softened Debbie's anger. "Mommy's not very good. She says Lilly's too big to do underdogs now."

Don't you dare get her hopes up! Debbie forced her lips into a smile and strode toward Kaitlynn, dropping the frozen meat with a clunk on the kitchen table.

"Yep." Kaitlynn stood still and smiled with a glow only her uncle could light. One a broken promise could snuff out for good. "Mommy's tummy's growing and growing. She says Lilly gets the hiccups. Sometimes I get hiccups, too, when Daddy tickles me too much."

A giggle escaped from Debbie's throat. She forced the smile down and reached for the phone. "Kaitlynn, say goodbye."

Kaitlynn smiled and skipped away, keeping the phone at her ear. "Daddy's with Aunt Francine."

"Kaitlynn."

"It's Christopher's birthday 'versary."

Debbie clenched her fists. Her daughter talked way too much. "Kaitlynn Nicole. It's time to say goodbye."

"It's Uncle Ricky. He called special to talk to me."

One, two, three. Debbie's fist tightened. "Oh, I'm sure he did. Say goodbye and give me the phone. Please."

"Bye-bye, Uncle Ricky. I love you." Kaitlynn's smile grew then she stroked her cheek. "Yep, and I rubbed it in, too. It'll be there forever."

Debbie grabbed the phone before Kaitlynn could say anything else. Those two conspirators could say goodbye for forever. "Why don't you go to your room and play for a bit? We'll play UNO® later."

"Okay, Mommy."

Debbie held the phone to her hip until Kaitlynn rounded the corner, leaving the kitchen. Debbie took in a deep breath and sat at the kitchen table. "Richard." If that was what he wanted to be called, so be it.

"Debbie, I'm sorry about—"

"There it is again. Boy, you're getting good at saying that."

"I mean it. Something came up last night. I didn't get home until—"

"Just stop, okay? I don't need to hear about your newest girlfriend."

"I wasn't—"

"I waited for you last night. I needed to talk to you, and you blew me off. I don't care who you spent the evening with. *I* needed you. You promised me you'd call. You promised."

"I know." His voice broke. "I'll come out there if you want."

That was the last thing she needed. "I don't want you to come."

"I can listen to you better if—"

"You want to listen?" Her tone rose. "You want to know what's bugging me?"

He sighed. "Yes. I do."

She stood, strode to the cupboard, and pulled out a dark chocolate bar. "Okay. Here's my life right now. First of all, Jerry didn't get the job, and we're doing our best to stay afloat."

"What? Why?"

"The superintendent said he was too valuable to the Special Education community. His leadership in the classroom was too vital to sacrifice. Jerry says that's a bunch of bull."

"No one told me."

"Well, you haven't exactly been returning our calls now, have you?" She ripped the candy bar wrapper.

Silence answered. At least he didn't express another meaningless apology.

"Then there's the issue with Lilly and now, with Christopher's birthday today, I don't think he can take much more."

"Sounds like you need some support."

"I do." She wiped her cheek. "Just not you." She bit off a chunk of chocolate.

"What? Why not?"

Well, here it goes. If he wanted to know the truth, she was

going to lay it on as thick as July's humidity. "I need someone who doesn't break promises. I need someone who's not too busy for me. I'm not going to get my hopes up with you again. Can you understand that? I've got enough to deal with, without your empty promises." She wiped away another tear. What she wouldn't give for one of his bear hugs.

"Debbie, I . . . "

She broke off another piece of chocolate and stuffed it in her mouth as she listened to his silence. Apparently, both of them had said enough.

"I understand." His voice teetered. "But I'm gonna make it up to you. I'm gonna be there when Lilly's born. Nothing will keep me away."

"Right." She backhanded more tears as the bar caught in her throat. That was as difficult to swallow as his promises.

"I will."

She choked down the bitter chocolate. Why didn't he just shut up? His vacant guarantee only made it worse. "Yeah, well, I gotta go." She hit *end* and threw the remainder of the candy bar into the garbage. Jutting her chin in the air, she strode to Kaitlynn's room. She'd promised Kaitlynn a game of UNO®. Someone needed to demonstrate that promises were made to be kept.

Chapter Twenty-five

A single blue jay flew over the country graveyard as Jerry dared to circle an arm around his ex-wife's trembling shoulders. He stared down at the granite grave marker softened by a rainbow assortment of geraniums. The flowers were Francine's touch, her way of adding life to unfathomable death.

She rested her head against his shoulder and sniffled.

At least he'd come prepared. He reached into his jeans pocket and pulled out several tissues.

Francine accepted them with silence.

Once upon a time, she would have poured out her feelings. So unlike Debbie. But he'd lost the right to be Francine's confidant.

He pulled his arm away and knelt by the stone engraved with Christopher's picture and words from the Psalmist. Taunting words. " . . . knit together in my mother's womb . . . fearfully and wonderfully made . . . All the days ordained for me were written in your book before one of them came to be."

All the days . . .

Days stolen by congenital heart disease caused by Down syndrome. A dawning life cheated by a ninety percent promise that surgery would be successful. It had never occurred to him that Christopher would be in the ten percent who didn't survive.

Jerry traced the outline of his son's face carved into the

tombstone and felt Francine kneel next to him.

Someone always has to beat the odds. There always have to be those who keep the odds below one hundred percent.

Why did it have to be Christopher?

Jerry reached into his pocket and pulled out another tissue. This time for himself.

Christopher wasn't the only one who needed his heart repaired, especially when the geneticist fingered the blame on Jerry. He reached up to his cheek, his fingertips tracing his scar's peaks and valleys.

Was he any better than his own father?

Jerry was responsible for his son's death. He carried the rare translocation chromosome that occurred in only three to four percent of all Down diagnoses, the only kind of Down syndrome that was inherited. He'd passed that uncommon gene on to his son.

Again, beating the odds.

He personally was responsible for the empty crib.

And now, he'd passed that chromosome on to his baby daughter because of his selfish desire to be a father again, perhaps to replace the son he'd lost. Who was to say that this child wouldn't beat the odds?

Just like Christopher had.

All the days . . . Jerry ran his hand over the carved Psalm. God's promise etched into granite. All one hundred twenty-four days, until the imperfections seized Christopher's heart.

Francine's body shuddered, and her sobs broke the stillness in the air as she gave freedom to her sentiments. Debbie would never do that. Every emotion Francine felt was projected for the world to see, passions that magnified with Christopher's death.

Jerry's emotions had shut down. How could he possibly love his new baby when Christopher, whom he'd loved fiercely, was stolen away? His goal then had been survival.

But Francine wanted to live, not just survive. The divorce papers—confirmation of wedding vows broken—hadn't fazed him. He got what he deserved.

He wiped his eyes and stood, thinking about the promise of life growing within Debbie. God never promised long life. Nothing frightened Jerry more than that.

Perhaps Ricky'd had the right idea all along.

What did that say about the kind of man—the kind of father— he was? Willing to sacrifice his child's life so the rest of them could have an easier future? What kind of teacher did that make him if he judged those with special needs as being hopeless? What kind of husband desired to steal away his wife's joy?

God, I desperately need your help.

Without sharing a word, Jerry squeezed Francine's hand and walked away, pausing at some other family's headstones. The couple had been together sixty-two years, far outliving two children who died in infancy.

He'd made a vow to Debbie, and to God, in front of a hundred-plus witnesses, to love through sickness. The same vow he'd made to Francine. With regret seizing his heart, he glanced back at Francine kneeling by Christopher's tombstone. *God, forgive me for not loving her through this.* She hadn't deserved to be abandoned.

He laid his hand on the couple's headstone. They never broke their promise.

His vow to love Debbie wasn't broken, but the fear of loving his child had rifted a paper-thin fissure in that love. If it wasn't mended soon . . .

He hurried to his car which was parked in a lot shared by the cemetery on the south and a baseball field to the north.

Life juxtaposed against death.

An idea brightened his spirit. He knew just what he needed to begin bonding that fracture back together.

DEBBIE KNELT IN THE grass next to a blacktop driveway that generated more heat than the mid-afternoon sun. With hands perspiring inside rubber gloves, she gave the concrete mix another stir. It still maintained its cake batter-like consistency, even after completing three other stepping-stones. The texture was perfect for the final stone.

She glanced at Kaitlynn, who looked beyond adorable wearing the over-sized safety goggles and rubber gloves as she laid fluorescent green stars on top of the last stone. Too bad, Debbie hadn't thought to bring out a camera. This was one of those endearing moments she never wanted to forget. If Jerry would ever get home . . .

Don't think, just work. "Okay, precious, time to add the JELL-O."

"Yippee!" Kaitlynn stood, wiped her gloves on worn jeans, and grabbed the package of instant-gelatin.

While Kaitlynn was turned, Debbie loosened a bottle of concrete dye and hid it strategically behind the pail of cement mix.

"Here, Mommy."

Debbie accepted the package from Kaitlynn, tore it open, and handed it back. "Now you get to make JELL-O cement."

"Can I eat it then?"

"Nope. This is just to look pretty."

"Okay." Kaitlynn dumped the strawberry mix into the concrete.

"Good job, sweetheart. Now, go ahead and finish putting on your stars. In five minutes you can add your fruit to this one." The clock hung above the workbench in the garage read one thirty. Jerry had been gone four hours already. He'd never spent that long at the cemetery before.

He'll be home soon. She wiped her arm across her forehead. The perspiration was probably as much from concern as from the heat. *Just keep busy.*

With Kaitlynn occupied, Debbie poured red dye over the JELL-O. She stirred it in, turning the gritty off-white mixture a dark red. Not exactly gelatin-colored, but good enough for Kaitlynn. She scooped the mix into her prepared mold—a medium-size pizza box coated with plastic wrap—until it was half-full. She laid a pre-cut piece of screen on top of the cement for reinforcement and capped it off with more cement. After smoothing the top with a school ruler, she tapped the sides of her makeshift mold with the back of an old serving spoon to remove air bubbles.

Done. Debbie sighed as she plopped down in the grass and pulled off the clammy gloves. She still needed to create two more stones, but that was a project for another day.

"I done, Mommy." Kaitlynn stood and applauded herself. "Can I add fruit now?"

Debbie craned her neck to view the stepping-stone with green stars marching in rows straight enough for the Army. "Good job, sweetie. Now go get your fruit. I think it's still on the kitchen table." Keeping the plastic play fruit inside was a good way to make the time go faster for her daughter. Gave her less down time. Debbie glanced at the clock. One thirty-four. Perfect.

In just another minute Kaitlynn would cap off this last stone with plastic banana and apple slices. The sun would take care of the drying, and a good three days from now, Debbie would seal the stones with an acrylic spray.

The door slammed as Kaitlynn ran out of the house. "Mommy, I got the . . . Daddy!"

Jerry? Debbie turned toward the street and released a relieved sigh. She remained seated, and studied him as he walked toward her. His shoulders weren't stooped, his gait was confident, and his eyes actually had a twinkle.

But that wasn't what had her confused. It was the two boxes he carried. One long and flat, the kind she saw in movies, that carried flowers. The other was jewelry-sized. A red bow garnished each.

Jerry never gave her flowers or jewelry. Truthfully, that didn't matter. That wasn't who she'd married. Besides, when did she ever wear jewelry anyway? And what would they have to sacrifice to pay for this gift?

He must have been talking to her brother.

Sure, turn this bright moment into a negative. How stupid could she be?

Kaitlynn, still wearing the gloves and bug-eyed goggles, crashed into his legs and hugged his knees. "I missed you, Daddy."

"Hey, punkin." He squatted and kissed her cheek. "I missed you too."

"Mommy and I are creating."

Jerry touched Kaitlynn's gloved hand clutching the plastic fruit. "I see that. Can you show me what you're doing?"

"Uh-huh." Kaitlynn grabbed his hand, and dragged him to the JELL-O stone where they knelt side-by-side. "This one's my favorite." She laid the fruit on top of the soft concrete and gave it a delicate push, just enough to imbed it. "But don't eat it, Daddy. It's yucky."

Eyes bright, he drew an X over his heart. "I promise."

Shoot. If this was how he acted after going to the cemetery, she was going to send him more often.

"And Daddy," Kaitlynn pulled on his arm and stood. "Come

see . . . Auntie Janet!"

Janet? Debbie looked toward the road as Janet's red Saturn pulled tight to the curb.

"I see Auntie Janet?" Kaitlynn tugged her hand away from Jerry and ran to her aunt, who'd come around the front of her car.

"I wonder what she wants." Jerry covered his mouth, clearly hiding his complicity in Janet's appearance.

"Yeah, I wonder." Debbie finally stood and walked to her husband. She reached for the gift boxes, but he pulled them away. "Okay, what's going on?"

"Why don't we go ask Janet?" Wearing a mischievous smile, he took her hand and led her to the curb.

Janet, disgustingly cute in the maternity top stretched over her belly, walked toward them, carting Kaitlynn on what was left of her hip.

There was nothing cute about Debbie's smock-like garage-sale top and her polyester Capris. Nothing cute at all.

"Auntie Janet wants me to come swimming at her house. Can I, can I?"

"She does, eh?" Debbie raised her brows and glanced between Jerry and Janet. "Why do I feel like this is some kind of conspiracy?"

Janet laid a hand over her heart and grinned. "Conspirator? *Moi*? Can't an auntie have a sleep-over with her favorite niece without it being suspect?"

"Sleepover?"

Jerry squeezed Debbie's hand then kissed her on the lips. "That's okay, isn't it?"

"I . . . " Debbie snickered. "Shoot, you've got me all flustered."

"Please, Mommy. I be good for Auntie Janet."

"Please, Debbie." Janet giggled. "I'll be very good with your daughter."

"Please, honey." Jerry set the boxes down and took both of her hands. His moist eyes locked with hers. "A night alone would be very good for the two of us."

It would be heavenly. She pointed at the gift boxes. "Any more surprises?"

"Is that a yes?" Jerry lifted her chin.

She wiped her hands on her grimy clothes and wrinkled her nose. "Will you let me shower first?"

He kissed her, grime and all, and winked. "As soon as we say goodbye."

Chapter Twenty-six

ebbie spritzed on citrus body splash before pulling her nicest maternity top over moist hair. She stared at the mirror above her dresser and bit into her lower lip. This secrecy was a rarity for Jerry. And one hundred percent romantic. He wasn't at all the gloomy person who left their house early this morning.

The door creaked open and Jerry walked in, still wearing his sexy smile. "You ready?" He stood behind her, wrapped his arms around what used to be her waist, and nuzzled her neck.

She turned in his arms and grinned. "I'm dying here. What's your surprise?"

He kissed her and took her hand. "Come with me."

Feeling giddy as a schoolgirl, she followed him into the living room and sat on the couch while he retrieved the mystery boxes from the kitchen.

He set them on her diminishing lap then sat tight next to her.

"Thank you." She said softly, fingering the bow on top of the flower box. "I can't remember the last time you brought me flowers."

He grimaced.

"Sorry." Her hand covered his. "I wasn't complaining. I don't mind. Really I don't."

"I know, but I still need to show you how important you are to me. I haven't done that. I'm so sorry for how I've been this summer, and these last two days . . . " He clutched at the left side of his chest. "I don't know what happened. I felt like I was losing Christopher all over again. I could literally feel his loss in my body."

Debbie laid her fingers over Jerry's mouth. "Honey, it's okay."

He grasped her hand and pulled it against his heart. "No. It's not. I was doing the same thing to you that I did to Francine, and what really bothers me is that I know I'm doing it, but I can't seem to stop it."

"When you numb yourself, it hurts less."

"And then I hurt you."

She looked down and blinked away tears.

"When I left the cemetery, it became clear to me that the choice was mine to make. I could numb myself and keep hurting those around me, or I could choose life and learn to live with a little pain."

"You know I'll help you."

"I do, and that's why I needed to make tonight special. Your family was eager to help out. I even called Ricky—"

"You didn't."

"—and asked him for advice on how to properly apologize to a beautiful woman."

"Jerry." Now, he was exaggerating.

He smiled. "Your brother said he always uses the universal language of women: flowers and jewelry."

"But—"

"Yeah, I know. He also said you speak a different dialect than most women." He took the jewelry box from her and pointed to the larger gift. "Why don't you open it?"

"What am I going to do with you?" She pulled the bow from

the box, raised the cover, and laughed. The gift was perfect. She lifted the construction-quality level from between its cushion of tissues. "I love it, but it had to cost—"

He put a finger to her lips. "When someone gives you a gift, you don't worry about the cost. Besides, when Marcus told me he just bought a new one, I couldn't tell him no."

"Is my whole family in on this?"

"You could say that." He ran his hand over the level. "This is to remind me how important it is for me to keep my emotions on an even keel. When foundations aren't level, they easily crack. I can't let that happen to our family."

Oooh, dratted pregnancy tears. "It won't." She fingered the moisture from her cheeks as he handed her the smaller box.

"Janet helped me with this."

"This is not necessary." Her fingers trembled as she removed the cover then pulled out a velvet box. "Jerry, what did you do?"

"Open it."

She eased up the cover. And laughed again as she pulled out two strips of paper made to look like tickets to a Twins game. For tonight. At six. Just an hour from now. The stadium was over two hours away. "I don't understand."

"Well, I figured going to the game was a bit out of our budget, but who says I can't bring the game to you?"

"What are you up to?"

"I've got hot dogs, popcorn, Coke, even nacho chips and cheese, if you want, so we can sit and watch the game together, pretend like we're really there. I'll even pretend to enjoy it."

"Can we pretend we're on the Kiss Cam?"

"That would be my favorite part." He put the gifts on the floor and gave her a G-rated kiss. "If we're on Kiss Cam, kids might be watching."

"Oh, you." She circled her arms around his back and pressed

her lips to his, taking the kiss well beyond family-friendly ratings, then leaned back. "Do you have plans for this next hour?"

He grinned. "Actually, I do." Jerry bent down and pulled a CD from beneath the tissue lining the large box. "Janet burned this for us. Said it's got some nice slow-dancing music."

"Dancing?" She crossed her hands over her pattering heart.

"A little in here." He stood, crossed the room, put the disc in the portable player, and nodded to the back rooms. His lips edged up and a mischievous gleam lit his eyes. "Maybe a little in there."

Her cheeks heated as he bowed and extended his hand. The keyboard introduction of a Chicago love song filled the air. She giggled as he pulled her in tight, snuggling Lilly between them, his fresh-shaven cheek brushed against hers. He sang along, his gentle voice embracing her fluttering heart. Oh, his steamy tenor could melt steel.

The song waned and a piano melody waltzed in, accompanied by strings then a haunting female voice. Jerry hummed sweet harmony as they swayed to the words of the lullaby.

Dampness, from tears that weren't hers, puddled on her cheek and his humming stopped. She drew Jerry in tighter still as a tremor crescendoed through his body and perspiration saturated his trembling hands.

He jerked away and grasped at his chest. His face was void of color.

He's having a heart attack! She pulled him to the couch, his body wooden, objecting to the movement. "Honey, sit. I'll call 911." *Please, God, please save my husband.*

Chapter Twenty-seven

*N*o." The plea creaked from her husband's throat. Debbie ran to the kitchen, ignoring him.

"Stop." He yelled from the living room.

With the phone in hand, she rushed back, hitting nine, then one. "I'm not going to watch you die."

"It's not . . . " Squeezing his head between his hands, he stood and strode to the CD player. "Not a heart attack." He punched at a button, but the music played on. "Make. It. Stop!" He picked up the player and threw it on the ground.

Debbie jumped as it bounced on the carpet. The lid flew off and Jerry collapsed on the rolling CD.

Still clasping the phone, Debbie knelt by her husband and drew his head to her chest, hoping he didn't feel the fear pulsing in her heart. "What is it then? Talk to me."

He wheezed as if grasping for air. Just like Kaitlynn. "Panic." Gritty breath. "Attack." Grating inhale. "I've . . . " Another gasping pant.

Okay, I know how to handle this. "Shhhh." She kept her arms around him, and sang the alphabet in her head. Four times through until his breath finally eased.

And her heart slowed to a mild jog.

He peered up at her with red veining his eyes. "That was the song—"

"Honey, it can wait."

"—I sang at night for Christopher." His words came out softer than a whisper. "I was singing it when he died."

JERRY WIPED THE PERSPIRATION from his forehead and forced himself to sit up. It was happening all over again.

"I'm sorry." Debbie massaged his shoulders. "I didn't know. Janet didn't—"

"There's no way you would have known." He folded his hands between his knees, trying to muffle the crack of his knuckles. The song had been forced from his mind years ago, and he had believed it would never haunt him again.

"You've had this before?"

Focusing his gaze on fingers aching to be cracked, he nodded once. "But it's been years."

"How can I help?" She kneaded the back of his head.

He shook her off. "Sorry. My hair hurts." In spite of the absurd truth in his statement, he forced his lips into a smile.

Debbie raised a hand to her mouth, clearly trying to cover her own smile. "What can I do?"

He pulled her hand from her mouth and kissed her lips, hoping to draw strength from her. "Just be you."

"That I can do." She glanced around and bit into her lower lip, obviously attempting to mask the fear evident in her glossy eyes. "How about I clean this up and you go rest?"

"Uh-uh." With a deep grunt, he stood. "I promised you a date tonight, and I fully intend to keep that promise." Watching a baseball game was safe. Nothing in it would remind him of Christopher.

"You sure?"

"Absolutely. I'm not going to let this anxiety control my life again." He picked up the gift box with the level and carried it to the kitchen. After stealing a quick glance over his shoulder, he ran his fingers over the level. He promised Debbie he'd keep his emotions on an even keel, that he'd be the husband she deserved. There was only one certain way to accomplish that.

Ignore his baby. At least until he could hold her in his arms and know she wasn't going to die on him too.

Chapter Twenty-eight

LATE AUGUST

Debbie took the bag filled with bread from the trunk of her car and handed it to Kaitlynn. With less than ten weeks until her due date, Kaitlynn's help was invaluable, even if it was just carrying in one bag of bread. And, as an added benefit, it kept Kaitlynn out of trouble while making her feel useful.

Now to come up with more projects that wouldn't require extra effort from Debbie. She was exhausted as it was.

She removed the insulated bag with frozen foods and left the rest. Jerry could bring it in when he got home. Hopefully, without grumbling.

"Can I help?" Lee's voice came from behind her as she tugged on the screen door leading to the house.

She made a slow turn toward him and grinned. "That would be heavenly." She tossed him the car keys. "My trunk is full." Now Jerry would have one less item to complain about, something he'd been doing an awful lot lately.

"'Melia!" The screen door slammed into Debbie as Kaitlynn pushed her way outside. "I miss you!" She ran to her friend and squeezed her with a hug. "We go play, Mommy?"

Debbie checked with Lee.

He nodded his approval, but that didn't disguise the worry lines by his eyes.

"Kaitlynn, why don't you show Amelia your new tractors? Mr. Aldrich will help me with groceries." And hopefully, he would be willing to share whatever was bothering him.

The girls ran into the house and down the basement stairs before Debbie was even inside the door. Oh, to have that kind of energy again.

Lee followed right behind her carrying four of the handled canvas bags. "Where would you like these?"

"On the table, please." Then she wouldn't have to do any extra bending.

By the time she had her frozen foods put away in the freezer, Lee had retrieved all her grocery bags from the car and set them on the table. But she wouldn't be putting them away soon. He was already seated, slumped down on a kitchen chair, his eyes glazed over.

She shoved the bags to the side and sat kitty-corner from him. "What's going on, Lee?" She kept her tone low. Though the girls were in the basement, their little ears seemed to have bionic hearing whenever they weren't supposed to hear something.

Lee's cheeks flexed. "Elise . . . "

"What about Elise? Is she okay?"

He laughed, but not from humor. "Oh, she's peachy."

"Then what's wrong?"

He looked out the window by the table and sighed. "She left us."

No. Debbie closed her eyes and sent up a silent prayer for help. "Lee, I'm so sorry." Her natural instinct was to take his hand, or touch his arm, but that would be inappropriate. A family member or a girlfriend? No problem. But a guy friend? No way. Instead, she folded her hands in what was left of her lap. "Do you want to talk about it?"

"No."

"That's fine." His answer didn't surprise her. It wasn't uncommon. But he wouldn't be here if he didn't want to talk. "What can I get you to drink?"

"Nothing."

She brought him a bottled water anyway. Her role right now was to sit still, be quiet, and wait until he was ready.

The wall clock ticked off the seconds as she listened to the girls laugh in the basement. Finally, Lee turned from the window. He rested an elbow on the table and scratched his nose, avoiding her gaze. "It happened over a month ago. We tucked Amelia in, then Elise went to our bedroom and started packing. I confronted her."

He took a draw from his water bottle then squinted at Debbie. "You know what her answer was?" He shook his head. "She said she needed a real man, one who wasn't lazy, who was willing to earn a paycheck. For all her talk about being progressive, you'd think she'd be the one applauding my decision to stay home with Amelia. You'd think a feminist would love the turnaround in roles, wouldn't you?" He took another sip.

Anger boiled in Debbie's gut. A woman deserting her husband was one thing, but abandoning her daughter? That was beyond Debbie's comprehension. She remained silent, afraid she'd spew something she'd regret. As a therapist, it was easy to listen to her clients without bias, and to offer equitable suggestions. But Lee was a friend, and this situation was too close for her to think or speak with impartiality.

"She packs up all her clothes, all her woman stuff, and then has the gall to ask me to take it to her car." He squeezed the bottle so tightly, water spurted from the top. He didn't seem to notice. "I said, 'Are you kidding me?' No way was I helping her leave. I sat on the bed watching her, trying to figure out what I did wrong."

This was where Debbie would normally draw family or a girlfriend into a hug. She never before realized how difficult it would be to comfort a male friend. Touch was so important to her, but here it would be crossing a line.

He covered his face with his hands, his breathing deep and purposeful. When he finally removed his hands, his chin twitched. "It's my fault. She never wanted to move, you know. We had a townhome in Brainerd for years. When my grandpa died last year, leaving his home to us, I thought Granite Creek was the perfect place for Amelia to grow up. She'd have her own yard to play in, with trees to climb. We were going to build a tree house. We could walk to the grocer down the street to get giant ice pops, and to the park where she could meet her best friend. To me it was heaven."

Debbie patted his hand, but left it at that. "I understand. I love the small town, but for my brother, it's torture."

"That's how it was for Elise." Lee moved the water bottle in figure eights. "She didn't want to move in the first place. I talked her into it. She didn't want me to quit my job. I argued it was for the best. Elise didn't agree, but I did it anyway. I was being selfish. I should have listened. She's done listening to me now."

"Mommy, Mommy, look!" The girls thundered up the stairs and appeared wearing superhero costumes. "I Spider-Man!" Kaitlynn held up her arms as if making muscles.

"I Iron Man!" Amelia mimicked Kaitlynn's muscle-making.

Debbie coughed down a chuckle. "You don't mean Spiderwoman and Iron Woman?"

"That's silly, Mommy." Kaitlynn rolled her eyes and ran back to the stairs with Amelia right on her heels.

Lee laughed through tear-fogged eyes. "How could a mom not

want to be around that?" He thrust a finger toward the stairway.

There was no answer to his question. Not a good one, anyway. How could a mom not revel in a daughter's joy? "Have you been in contact at all?"

"Only when I drop Amelia off at Elise's office for the weekend visit. Elise is too busy to make the thirty-minute drive to see her own daughter. If it was just me, I could go on. But she's abandoned her daughter. Cares more about her patients than Amelia." His murky eyes gazed toward the stairs.

"I'm sure that's not true." Lee needed some positive reinforcement. "Some people have to learn to make time for what's really important. Elise will figure it out."

He snorted. "I wouldn't count on it."

Debbie puffed out a breath. This was beyond what she could deal with as a friend. "Have you discussed seeing someone? I could recommend a good therapist, someone I used to work with."

"I've brought it up. She's not interested."

"Has she filed for divorce yet?"

"Ah, yes." Sarcasm coated his chuckle. "You see, that's where it gets easy for her. Elise and I were never married."

Chapter Twenty-nine

Not married? Debbie dropped her water bottle, and it rolled onto the floor. Thank goodness the cover was on tight. "But I thought . . . " How could she have missed that? Hadn't Lee referred to Elise as his wife? Hadn't Debbie specifically asked how his wife was doing? "I don't understand."

"I never said we were married. People make assumptions, and, to be honest, I guess I always felt married, so I don't make the correction. We didn't have the ceremony or the piece of paper. I didn't think it would matter. It never occurred to me that we wouldn't last, especially after she got pregnant. Now I'm realizing I made it easy for Elise to leave."

Debbie retrieved her water bottle. "I wouldn't give up on counseling." She'd helped many couples with a similar scenario. If only people would think of how their choices affected others. All too often, innocent children. "For the sake of Amelia, it's worth the effort."

"You and I know that, but . . . " He sipped his drink.

"Have you discussed what's going to happen to Amelia?"

"I've already talked to a lawyer. There's no way Elise is gonna get physical custody of our daughter, so I had to make the first move, even if it makes our separation seem more permanent. Sad thing is, I don't think Elise even cares."

Anger churned in Debbie's stomach. She pushed away from the table and grabbed the Tums bottle from the cupboard. How could a mother not care? But her counselor experience reminded her that happened often. How many times had she counseled couples where one chose their own needs above the family's? No wonder Jerry taught such difficult students.

She nodded toward the stairs. "How is Amelia handling this?"

Lee shrugged. "Better than you'd think. But then, Elise never was around much. It's just a little less now than before."

Acid clawed up Debbie's throat, and she chewed on a second Tums. Why did people like Elise have children? If Debbie ever saw Elise, she'd be tempted to say a few not-so-kind words. At least Ricky hadn't added "absentee father" to his list of indiscretions.

Not that she knew, anyway.

She banished that thought and focused on Lee. "Will you have to return to work?"

"Guess so." He downed the remainder of his water. "Kills me to do it, but what choice have I got? I own the house free and clear, but we still need to eat."

"Any job possibilities?"

"A few. With the economy the way it is, and construction season winding down, you never know. I've got decent references. I'm good at what I did. What I do."

"I'm sure you are." Debbie got up and pulled a small notebook and pen from a cupboard drawer. "My brother's a contractor." She sat and starting writing on the pad. "I hear he does pretty good work. I'll give you his name and number. You can tell him I referred you, but to be honest, he won't consider it a recommendation since I can't vouch for the quality of your work. What this will do is get your foot in the door so you can prove yourself." She tore off the slip of paper and handed it to Lee.

"Thanks." His brows furrowed as he stared at the paper. "Your brother is MarJan Homes?"

"My brother and his wife, actually."

"Really? Wow." He sat back in the chair. "I've never worked with him, but know a number of guys who have. The man likes a job done right the first time, from what I hear."

"Oh, yes." She smiled. "That would be Marcus, but I also know, if you do the job right, you'll be rewarded for it."

Lee pulled his wallet from his back pocket and folded the paper into it. "I appreciate it."

"Let me know how it goes. I'd be glad to help in any way I can. And if you need someone to watch Amelia when you work, I'm sure I'll be home, and you wouldn't have to worry about paying me until things get better."

The words slid out before she considered what she was saying. First of all, she was going to have a baby. Very soon. What made her even think she could take on another preschooler? Secondly, why did she offer to do it for free? Here, a job is almost laid in her lap, and she volunteers to do it gratis. She must be crazy.

"Let me think on it, okay?"

Me too. "That would be fine."

"The question now is, does my future involve Elise?"

"Do you want it to?"

"Of course, I do." His voice rose for the first time, and then softened. "Maybe at first, when we lived together it was to, well you know. There was a lot more lust involved than love, but that changed for me. Apparently, it didn't for her."

"Are you certain?"

"She left me, didn't she?"

"Maybe she's trying to get your attention. She might be testing you to see how hard you'll fight to get her back. You have to decide if you're willing to fight, if you're willing to make some sacrifices too."

"I am. I miss her so . . . " Tears finally broke free.

"Daddy, what's wrong?" Amazing how children could sense when they were needed.

Lee reached out and scooped his daughter onto his lap, grasping her in a tight hug. "I miss Mommy." His voice quivered.

"I do too, Daddy. Can we go see her today?"

"How about right now?" He peered up at Debbie.

She nodded.

Maybe it was time for Debbie to listen to her own advice and call her brother, fight for a relationship with him. She rubbed her hand across her stomach as Lilly stretched.

Or maybe not.

Chapter Thirty

SEPTEMBER

*J*erry ambled through the brick hallways he'd walked for the better part of eighteen years. Hallways that within an hour would echo with young lives. In past years, he had looked forward to hearing the laughter and the rattle and bang of metal lockers as students reunited with friends, classmates, and even teachers.

On the first day of school, everything always smelled fresh and disinfected. Graffiti was washed away or painted over. Even the cafeteria food tasted good.

There was always joy on the first day, and the thrill of hope, knowing he'd been given the immense responsibility of molding and teaching young lives, influencing them to be future leaders. A challenge he normally couldn't wait to face.

Not this year.

Today he couldn't force a smile as he turned the corner to his short hallway that led to the two fifth grade classrooms. He strode down the hall where the walls were an empty canvas awaiting children's artistry. Thanks to help from Debbie, and even Kaitlynn, student names were already posted on the front of pre-assigned lockers.

Before stepping into his classroom, he glanced in the other

fifth-grade room. The rookie teacher was already there, her face glowing with the *I can change the world* look so many new teachers wore. He'd stay away from her. A cynic's influence was the last thing she needed.

He reached his door, curved his fingers around the knob, and pushed it open. Heaving a sigh, he remained in the doorway of the room that had been his for the past three years. This year it would be home to twenty-six fifth graders: fifteen boys and eleven girls. In the mix, he'd have a number of children diagnosed with various special needs, plus two paraprofessionals to help. Smiling Harvey would be back, naturally. Jerry had always requested the special-needs students. Could he handle it again this year?

His lips dipped into a frown. If things had gone as planned, he would have been entering the principal's office instead. There he'd hoped to offer his support to a wider range of students, before they reached the fifth grade and were beyond help.

Well, no sense focusing on the *should-have-beens*. Still, anxiety, not joy, rolled in his stomach as he strode to his desk.

Teaching had finally become a job.

Eighteen years ago, when he accepted his first position, he told himself he wouldn't become one of those teachers who didn't know when to quit, who hung around merely because they achieved tenure, not because they had a passion for the work. He didn't want to be the teacher who lost their enthusiasm and ultimately their ability to be the best for the children. Back then, he swore he'd quit before that happened.

He set his briefcase on the desk and sat in his chair. Quitting now wasn't an option. Not with a family to support. Not with the baby . . .

Maybe he should listen to Debbie and pursue a different venue for his skills. The community college in Brainerd would provide a whole new challenge for him. There was always

Duluth. The larger city would have a greater range of education possibilities, possibly a principal's job. He'd even accept a vice-principal position. They could find a home with a view of Lake Superior. Debbie would be in heaven.

Yep. Exactly what he would do. He could start putting out feelers now and network at the conference coming up in October.

A flicker of hope stirred in his heart as he opened his briefcase and pulled out the picture of Kaitlynn. He smiled at his daughter's proud expression as she pumped on her swing. He put that picture on the corner of his desk then pulled out the family portrait, the stodgy one taken for the church directory before Christmas, when their baby was a dream but not a reality, when he still dared hope for a healthy child.

What good was hope anyway?

Debbie still held onto it, but she hadn't been through what he had. She hadn't lost what he'd lost. She'd never thrown away anyone precious to her.

Except Ricky.

At lunchtime he'd give that brother-in-law a call. Let him know how Debbie was doing. She couldn't lock her brother out for forever. Sure, he understood her anger, but what she didn't know—and would never know—was how he agreed with Ricky's point. They could try again. Next time have a healthy baby, one who would have a hope for a full future. Not just one hundred twenty-four days.

Jerry pulled out the other portrait.

"Hey, Jer, how ya doin'?"

The portrait slipped from his fingers and crashed on the floor, shredding the glass.

A curse slipped from Jerry's mouth.

"Hey, I'm sorry, you okay?"

Jerry glanced up at smiling Harvey, although the smile had

dipped somewhat.

"Just broken glass." On top of a broken family. The one who had beamed in the portrait with genuine smiles, deceived into thinking they had a future ahead of them.

"I'll call the custodian."

"I can handle it."

"Hey, no problem. Just checkin' in. Seein' if I could help in some way."

You've helped enough already. Jerry rubbed his head. Oh brother, this was not the way to begin a new school year. He forced a smile. "Thanks. Appreciate the offer. I just need a couple seconds alone, if you don't mind."

"Hey, not at all." Harvey rested his hand on the doorknob. "Wanted to let you know, too, that I'm glad to be back with ya this year. I know it's not what you wanted, and you'd have made a terrific principal, but no one's as gentle as you with our special kids. Parents know that. All the teachers know it. I guess the board knew it too."

Gee, that sure made him feel better. Not. "Thanks, Harv. See you in a moment."

Take the hint and leave.

Harvey nodded, and walked from the room, the grin intact on his face.

Still drove Jerry nuts.

With a sigh, he swept up the shards of glass, then stuffed the broken frame and portrait in his top drawer. Christopher couldn't be forgotten.

The first bell of the school year rang as Jerry closed the drawer. Swarms of students whisked through the hallways, their young voices ringing with hope.

Dear Lord, help me be the teacher these children need. Don't let me squash their hope. Like you've crushed mine.

Chapter Thirty-one

MID-OCTOBER

*D*ebbie squeezed an inch-wide fragment of granite into a sliver of an opening between other stones then stepped back to look. And grinned. The project she'd begun months ago in this garage, by embedding nail into oak, was finally nearing completion. A little grout would mortar the pieces together, and her garden bench would at last be complete.

"How's it going?" Jerry came up behind her and rested his hands on her hips, clearly avoiding her belly.

She forced a smile, so he wouldn't hear her disappointment. "I should finish it this weekend." Assuming she'd find time during Kaitlynn's naps.

"I don't have to go, you know," he whispered, nuzzling his face into her hair.

She took in a breath before turning around.

His hands sprung from her hips, and he backed away, clearing room for Lilly.

Again, she pried her lips upward. "You need to go." It would be good for him to go to the Minnesota Teachers Conference for a few days, maybe gain perspective on his attitude.

"No, I don't. Teachers miss it every year. Most think of the conference as a nice vacation. It wouldn't hurt me to miss one."

"Really? And what about making contacts, getting your name out to other school districts? I can't think of a better way to let people know you're looking."

He frowned. "I know. It's just timing. The baby could come any time now."

"Yeah, right. Kaitlynn was ten days late, remember?" Debbie massaged her stomach as Lilly stretched her limbs, responding as usual to her daddy's voice. "And this little one is far more complacent than Kaitlynn."

It amazed her how a baby's personality made itself known, even before birth. Kaitlynn had been in constant motion with little elbows and knees persistently jabbing, as if desperate to break free from her watery cell. Lilly's movements were slow, fluid, and rare. When she moved it seemed she made one yawning stretch, before settling back in comfort. This child was content right where she was. The chances of Lilly arriving twenty days early were slim to zilch.

"But it could happen."

"Sure, there's always that possibility. If it does, I know how to reach you."

"Who would support you until I can get home?"

With a shrug, Debbie turned and ran her hand across the granite-topped bench. His concern was logical. If Lilly decided to make an extra-early entrance, it would be difficult to find anyone to take her to the hospital. Teachers weren't the only ones who took advantage of the four-day weekend. Her parents had traveled to Duluth with Marcus and Janet. Jerry's mom was at her Florida home for the winter. Most of Debbie's friends were taking mini-vacations as well. Chances were she'd be making the twenty-minute drive to the Brainerd hospital all by herself.

"And Kaitlynn?" Jerry cuffed a hand over her shoulder.

I don't know. She continued examining her project while processing the names of everyone she knew in town.

"Well?" Jerry squeezed her shoulder.

"Don't worry." She certainly wasn't going to waste her time. Reality said Lilly would be late.

Lilly stretched again.

Wearing a sincere smile, Debbie curved a hand over her stomach, following Lilly's motion, and reached for Jerry's hand, still nestled on her shoulder.

He yanked it away.

Tears clouded her eyes. *God, he's got three weeks to accept this child. Please open his heart.*

"You're sure you'll be okay?"

Just hunky dory. "Sure. Fine." For another three to five weeks, anyway. Once Lilly arrived, he wouldn't be able to ignore her. "You know me. I'll get by."

He inhaled a deep breath. "Honey, I'm sorry."

Not sorry enough to touch his daughter. Resting arms on her belly, she turned to him, wearing her habitual phony smile. "Go. It's just two nights. I'll see you Friday." She kissed him, trying to convince him it didn't matter, even though it did.

He kissed her back and rested his forehead against hers. "Kaitlynn wants me to tuck her in."

"It's only seven."

"I know. She's gonna miss her daddy."

Lilly nudged Debbie's rib. Kaitlynn wasn't the only one who would miss her daddy.

"I'll miss you too." Jerry kissed her again before he headed into the house.

Clenching her fists, Debbie stared at her granite bench. The project could wait. She followed Jerry into the house, into Kaitlynn's room.

Genuine love sparkled in Jerry's eyes as he helped Kaitlynn dress in pink polyester-fleece footy pajamas. Then he picked her up and enveloped her in his arms.

Kaitlynn squeezed her arms and legs around him, clinging with a child's love.

His body began swaying to a silent tune before he sang along. "You're my precious girl, created in love. You're a special child, a gift from heaven above. When you are sad, I'll sing you a song. When you are glad, I'll laugh right along. When you are weak, I'll carry you. I'll be your strength. I'll walk with you."

Caressing her stomach, Debbie leaned against the doorway and closed her eyes, her thoughts reaching out to Lilly. *Someday, he'll sing that song for you.*

Chapter Thirty-two

*R*ichard knocked on Ethan's open door and stepped in without an invitation.

Keeping his fingers curved over the keyboard, Ethan looked away from his computer screen

"So, is it true?" Richard sat on the opposite side of Ethan's mahogany desk.

With a brow raised, Ethan reclined in his high-back leather chair and crossed his arms. "Is what true?"

"You're leaving."

Ethan combed his fingers through his hair and stared at the ceiling.

Grinning, Richard folded his hands on Ethan's desk and leaned forward. "Word has it you've given your resignation."

"Ten minutes." Ethan frowned. "Ten minutes ago, I talked to Entenza, and you already know. What? Is my room bugged or something?"

"Or something." Richard reclined in his chair. "I ran into the boss in the hallway. He knows you and I are close, and he wants me to talk you out of it. Any chance of that happening?"

Ethan shook his head. "Nope. Already accepted a position back at your old stomping grounds. A sporting goods distributor in Minneapolis."

"You're not kidding."

"Not one bit." Ethan stood, walked to his wall length window, and stared out. "With a name like Johnson, I figure I'll fit right in with all your Minnesota Scandinavians."

"The *Joysey* accent might give you away though. And you'll have to learn to say 'uffda' and eat tater tot hot dish and bars and lefse and—"

"Lutefisk." Ethan wrinkled his nose. "Linny's folks' church used to have a lutefisk supper every Christmas. I helped serve one year, and the smell alone made me sick for the next day and a half. I don't get it. What person in their right mind would eat rubbery fish soaked in lye?"

"Not this one. My parents' church did the same thing. People would drive hundreds of miles for it. Good thing we didn't have to go. Makes you question the sanity of Minnesotans, doesn't it?"

"Naw. After all, here I am with a career others would die for, and I'm giving it up. I'm halving my pay—probably halving my hours—and giving up this fifty-story window for a renovated ten-story warehouse building. Entenza says I'm crazy. Who knows? Maybe I am."

Richard joined his friend at the window. He loved the view and couldn't imagine giving it up. But if he had a wife and children? "You'll get your family back."

Ethan turned and smiled, sincerely this time.

Richard hadn't seen that smile for weeks. This was definitely the right decision for his friend.

"I've discovered no job is worth sacrificing my family. You're lucky in that respect. You don't have to make a choice."

"Not true. I made a conscious decision not to marry. Some days that's tough. You know those days when you really need someone to talk to." Someone who understood you better than anyone else. Someone like Debbie. "Right now, my career is what's important." Ethan's situation provided further proof that balancing a family and career involved too much compromise.

"Smart man. Entenza said he'd like to build the company out of men like you who avoid attachments."

"Words of wisdom spoken by a man who's had three wives."

"It's my goal to keep it at just one wife. I rather like the one I've got. I hope she learns to like me again."

"You're certain you're getting back together?"

Ethan turned and rested against the window frame. "We bought a house. Enough bedrooms so Linny and I each get our own room."

"Ouch."

"Tell me about it. But she's willing to work on it. She *wants* to work on it. Even has counseling sessions scheduled." Ethan walked to his desk, picked up an autographed baseball sitting on display, and tossed it from one hand to the other as he sank into his chair.

"You two'll be fine." Richard sat across from his friend. "When do you leave?"

"Two weeks and I'm done here. The following week I'm packing up and making the drive cross country."

"I'll be there to help. Just let me know when."

"I appreciate it." Ethan set the ball on its stand. "What do ya say we grab a bite tonight? I'm getting awful tired of salami sandwiches."

"I'd love to, but it's Wednesday. I've got a date with the soldiers' kids, and I've missed it too much lately."

"Aw, that's right." Ethan gazed at a picture frame on his desk and dabbed at his eyes. "Could you use another hand? I could use something to keep my mind off things."

"We'd be glad to have you." Richard glanced at his watch and slapped his thighs. "Well, I better get back at it. For the next couple of days, I get to woo a multi-million-dollar client. Me wooing. Ha! Isn't that a laugh? I told Entenza I fix, I don't woo. He says I do now." Richard stood, shaking his head. "So, today, I'm researching. Tomorrow and Friday, I get to spend every waking second with this person, telling them how great our company is and how terrific we'd work together. Lucky me."

Ethan's mouth tipped with a cynical smile. "The client wouldn't happen to be a young and attractive female, would it?"

Richard grinned. "If I'm lucky."

RICHARD TOWELED THE PERSPIRATION from his forehead then turned back to the church's basketball court, throwing his sweat-laden towel on the floor. Nothing like a game with a bunch of kids to really give him a workout.

He grinned as a teenage boy, probably a few years older than Marcus' son, Nathan, swooshed in a shot from the three-point line. "Way to go, Niemann," he yelled out, clapping. "Now get back and hustle on D. Next basket wins it."

His Army-Air Force team, ranging in age from seven to seventeen, their faces glistening with equal parts perspiration and glee, raced to the Navy-Marine end of the court.

Nothing felt better than bringing joy into a child's life . . . well, maybe seeing that joy on his nephews' or Kaitlynn's face. If Debbie didn't let him back . . .

He shook his head, tossing out the depressing thought, and focused on the game. A girl from the Navy-Marine team charged in for the layup. The ball circled the rim then flew out and bounced right toward Brittany who competed in a wheelchair. She reached for the ball, but her reaction was a half-second too slow as it bounded over her lap.

Scott Niemann grabbed the rebound and dribbled it back to Brittany. A full-toothed grin spread across her face as she clutched the ball to her chest and Scott wheeled her down court, popping a wheelie as they rolled, stopping just in front of the basket.

"You can do it, Britt." Scott patted her back.

"Go for it Britt," a Navy-Marine player yelled from mid-court. The rest of the players stood still, each shouting out their own encouragement.

Brittany raised her arms that crooked at odd angles, keeping the ball tethered to her fingers.

Do the right thing, guys. Richard held his breath.

Her grin growing, Brittany gave the ball a shove.

Scott grabbed it as it dribbled off her fingers, and he laid it in.

"Yes!" Richard pumped his fist and cheers erupted from the kids and the coaches.

Still grinning, Brittany high-fived Scott and said something in a garbled language.

"Yep." Scott patted her back. "You're the hero. Just like Dad."

Whew. Richard blew out a breath and plopped onto a folding chair. Brittany Niemann, even with all her struggles, had an uncanny ability to bring joy to whatever activity this group chose.

If her parents had chosen to do what he'd hinted to Debbie . . .

With the players still celebrating, Richard lowered his head and covered his face with his hands. How could he have been so stupid? No wonder Debbie hated him.

Well, that was going to change soon.

He jogged onto the court, joining his team in their victory celebration. After slapping backs and exchanging high-fives, he pointed to the gym door. "Go wash up. We've got make-your-own sundaes in the fellowship hall."

The kids ran from the gym, cheering louder than they had with Brittany's basket.

Richard stayed behind, his smile fading as silence settled

around him.

As much joy as these kids brought him, they still couldn't fill that Kaitlynn-sized hole in his heart.

Well, he'd dug that hole with a heart-piercing spade. It was up to him to fill it back up. Nothing, or no one, could keep him away when Lilly was born. Debbie would see he could keep his promises, but more so, she'd see how much he truly loved Lilly. Just as she was.

Reuniting with Debbie. Now, that will be a victory worth celebrating.

MORNING SUN FILTERED THROUGH the living room blinds as Debbie took a Precious Moments figurine from the curio shelf, emphasizing those blotches of proof that she hadn't dusted for weeks. Ricky would be appalled. Good thing he hadn't come around.

She set the statue on the couch, and her dust rag fell to the floor. Drat it all. Her lips scrunched as she stared at the cloth by her feet. May as well be in the next county. With a grunt, she squatted to retrieve it. Oh, big mistake. Now she had to stand back up. Using the couch's arm for leverage, she pulled herself up.

Just a few more weeks and she'd be able to bend again, to move without the extra effort. But for now, those few weeks looked infinitely long.

She reached for the next figurine, but her hand detoured to her stomach. Lilly was on the move again. This baby was certainly restless today after months of taking it easy. Maybe she missed hearing her daddy's voice. Debbie sure did.

With a sigh, she removed a final keepsake and stared at its depiction of a brother carrying his sister on his shoulders. She laughed at the irony of the words etched on the bottom of the birthday gift from Ricky. *I'll Never Let You Down*. Yeah. Right. One more broken promise heaped on a year dusted over with them.

She blew dust from the figurine. Dust motes flew at her face, and she sneezed.

Well, Ricky could still clear the dust off their relationship and redeem himself. Keeping one hand on Lilly, she wiped the curio clean. If he showed up for Lilly's birth—and that was a big "if"— that would prove his contrition. She'd have to forgive him. She cradled the statue next to her heart. *Please God, bring him home*.

Okay. No more thoughts about Ricky. He would not spoil her day.

She returned the mementos to the shelf then stood back and smiled. It looked nice. People would actually see her collection instead of the dust surrounding it. Maybe by the time Jerry got home tomorrow night, the house would be in order. A clean home would brighten both of their attitudes.

Jerry had told her not to worry about it. That was easy for him to say. He didn't have to look at the mess all day, and he'd done little to help. It seemed as if his class demanded more from him this year as he spent hours at night planning and correcting. Instead of slacking off, from not getting the promotion, he worked harder, leaving her alone more often. If he didn't care about the cluttered house, why should she?

Because she was paying for it now.

At least she felt energized today. She wasn't going to waste it. With Kaitlynn napping, the work should all get done.

She pressed a hand to her stomach again, and grimaced. Nature was calling. Again. Lilly left no room in Debbie's bladder for storage. If things kept up this way, she may as well spend the next three weeks sitting on the toilet. She waddled to the bathroom, practicing her Kegels along the way. It didn't stop the persistent drip.

She stepped in the bathroom and sighed. Another room neglected. She wouldn't be leaving any time soon.

After taking care of business, she squirted blue toilet bowl cleaner under the toilet's rim. She sprinkled baking soda into the sink, wiped it down with a wet rag then turned on the faucet to rinse. Stifling a curse, she crossed one leg over the other. Why was this being such a problem today? All she wanted to do was clean, but her body kept telling her to lie down. Nine in the morning, work was half done, and she was supposed to rest.

Fine. *I'm listening.* She threw the rag into the sink then shuffled to the bedroom, changed into a clean set of clothes, and lay down. It didn't stop the persistent drip. "Okay, God, what's going on here?"

It's time.

No. This was not what happens when water breaks. With Kaitlynn, it gushed out like a waterfall. This drip was plain annoying.

But it wouldn't hurt to talk to a nurse.

With a groan, she rolled onto her side and reached for the phone. Thank goodness Jerry had the foresight to program the doctor's number. A receptionist answered, then transferred her call to the nurses station. The minute she waited for a nurse to pick up seemed to last an eternity.

"Mrs. Verhoeven, this is Miriam, Dr. Drew's nurse. What seems to be the problem?"

Debbie hesitated one second. Certainly, the nurse would tell her this was not anything alarming. "I'm sure it's nothing, but I seem to be, uh, leaking. The baby's not due for another three weeks." After describing what she'd been experiencing, the nurse put her on hold.

It had to be nothing. *God, please, not now.*

The nurse interrupted the plea. "We'd like you to come in. Right away. It could be the onset of labor."

"I'll be there." With a sigh, she ended the call. Now, how to get there was the next question. Call Jerry, of course. But it could take him over three hours to get home. Find a ride first, then call Jerry so he wouldn't worry. She scrolled through the listings on the phone and tried several numbers with no luck. It was as if the rapture had occurred, and she was the only one left behind.

She closed her eyes and concentrated on breathing. *Okay. I can handle this.* Who else?

"Mommy." Kaitlynn crawled onto the bed. "Are you taking a nap?"

"No, precious." *What do I do with Kaitlynn?* Debbie snuggled her daughter. "Mommy has to find someone to take me to the hospital. Lilly wants to come see us early."

"Yippee! Then can I play with her?"

"No. Lilly won't be able to play for a long time. She'll be too little."

"Can I play with 'Melia then?"

Amelia . . . Lee! Debbie reached over, lifted her phone book off the nightstand, and dialed Lee's number.

"Hello."

Thank you, God. "Lee, hi this is Debbie. I hate to bother you, but I'm in a bit of a bind. I've got a huge favor to ask."

"Sure thing. What do you need?"

"It's . . . I'm . . . I think my water broke. Jerry's out of town. Everyone's out of town. I need a ride to the hospital."

Silence roared on his end. She was obviously asking too much. "You can drop me off at the door. I'm pre-registered so I shouldn't have any problems checking in. I just need a ride there."

"Of course, I'll help you and, no way am I going to drop you off. Amelia and I'll be right over."

Debbie breathed a relieved sigh. "Thanks, Lee. I really appreciate this."

"No problem."

"Thanks, God," she breathed out. Now for the most important call. Poor Jerry was going to be sick with worry. "God, give him peace," she prayed as she dialed his cell.

After six rings, he finally picked up. "Debbie? Sorry, hon, I had to get out of the room before answering. I got a pretty nasty stare from the presenter for interrupting."

"I understand." She pasted a smile on her face, hoping it would come through her words. "You'll never guess what happened."

JERRY JABBED THE *END* button. The walls around him drew in, and jelly filled his knees. He reached for the hallway wall behind him and lowered himself down. Leaning his back into the wall, he covered his face with trembling hands. *God, I'm not ready for this*. By now he should be ready and eager to walk the path God paved for him. But he wasn't. Not at all.

God, why now? Some kind of husband he was. He should have listened to his gut and stayed home.

"Hey, Jerry." A fellow teacher called out, concern tinged her voice. "Are you all right?"

Jerry removed his hands from his face and looked at the beige carpeting framed between his brown loafers. "My wife's gone into labor. I'm three hours away."

"And you're still sitting here?" Anger took place of the concern. "I recommend you get going. Now. This is no time to feel sorry for yourself."

"Yeah. You're right," he said softly. "Thanks." He didn't look at his colleague as he leapt to his feet and hurried down the chlorine-scented hallway to the elevator, his feet accelerating to a run as the urgency of the situation hit him. His toes tapped impatiently as he pushed the Up arrow and waited. One would think big-city elevators would go a little faster.

He clasped one hand into the other, cracking his knuckles. Finally, a *ding* sounded, and the doors opened. He stepped inside and, with clammy fingers, pressed the number ten. The elevator stopped at every floor along the way. The stairs would have been much faster.

A bell chimed, and the doors opened to his floor. He ran down the hallway to his room. It took him three tries with the key card before the door unlocked. He slammed the door open and grabbed his suitcase from the slatted metal shelf next to the entry. Having no concern for wrinkles, he threw everything into his suitcase, and then whipped out his cell phone. Before sitting behind the wheel of his car, he needed to make calls.

He left a message for Debbie's parents, and then dialed Ricky's cell number, praying his brother-in-law wouldn't break another promise.

"Jerry." Muted voices swelled in the background as Ricky answered.

"Debbie's gone into labor."

Ricky heaved a breath. "Nooo. It's too early, isn't it?"

"Three weeks, but the baby should be fine. Debbie's not worried."

Ricky's laugh lacked humor. "Of course not."

"Can you make it?"

"Jerry, I'd love to." He sighed. "You know that. But I'm in the middle of an urgent project. I can't leave. If I do," Ricky cursed, "I could lose my job."

"Hey, listen, I understand." But would Debbie?

"I can fly in tomorrow night. It could be late, but I need to be there, you know." He cursed again. "Man, she's gonna hate me. I'm letting her down again."

Jerry laughed nervously. "You're not the only one."

"What are you talking about? Did Marcus do something?"

"No. Not Marcus . . . me. I'm not even home. I'm in St. Paul. Debbie had to find someone else to bring her in."

"Oh, man."

"Yeah, tell me about it. So, I've got to get going. I'll see you tomorrow or Saturday. She'll understand." The lie came out too easy. Not everyone needed to feel lousy about the situation. "Just show up, and all will be forgotten."

"You're sure?"

"Go. Take care of business. We'll see you soon."

"Tell her I love her, okay?"

"She knows." Jerry closed his phone, grabbed his luggage, and strode to the door. Yes, Debbie knew her big brother loved her, but would it be enough

Chapter Thirty-three

His stomach churning, Richard stared blankly at his phone as he walked back to his client. Why now? He brushed a hand through his hair and down onto his neck to relax his tightening muscles. *It's the right decision.* What was one or two days anyway?

He ground his teeth as he spotted the client sitting alone in the booth, sipping her wine slowly. This client was too important to ACM to blow off. Besides, he'd like to know her better. Sure, she was pretty, but looks alone didn't make good companionship. This woman's sharp intellect, quick humor, and honest humility made her intriguing. To leave her now would ruin any chance with her or her business.

He tucked his phone back in the inside pocket of his jacket as he slid into the booth and smiled at the client. "Sorry, Heather. Family emergency."

"Oh?" She set her glass on the table, and folded her hands. Clearly conversation didn't have to center exclusively around her. Another unique and appealing attribute.

He sipped his wine, desiring something stronger to anesthetize his guilt, and raised his glass to toast Debbie. "My little sis is having a baby."

Heather clinked her glass against his.

Richard returned a strained smile. "Sometime today probably." *And you should be there.*

"Does she live around here?"

"Unfortunately, no." He drew a long sip and returned the empty stemware to the table keeping it in his hand. "Minnesota, two plus hours northwest of Minneapolis." If he left now, he could make it there before the baby arrived. "I'll fly out tomorrow when we're done." His mouth tipped in a genuine smile. "You can't keep me away from my nieces and nephews."

She smiled back—a sincere smile with no beguile—as the waiter delivered their meals. She'd ordered a steak, not a salad. No pretense there either. How often had he seen authenticity in the women he dated? Maybe back in Minnesota, but not since he took this job. Now, they all seemed to have ulterior motives.

Just like him.

He cut his rib eye into bite-size morsels, forked a piece, and brought it to his mouth. The meat was grilled to perfection, enough to lightly pink the center.

Heather copied his motion, but stopped her fork midway. "I'm impressed that ACM Technologies values families."

He choked and covered his mouth in time to prevent an embarrassing mishap. ACM values families? If that's what this woman wanted, then she better look somewhere else. For Richard to say anything further in support of ACM would be an outright lie, but today, that was what his job required, to convince her company to sign on with them regardless of the means. Which was why Entenza should have sent a salesman, not him.

Richard looked down at his steak so she wouldn't read the lie in his eyes. "Family has always been top priority for ACM—especially for me." He stuffed the steak into his mouth before another lie crept out.

DEBBIE HELD LEE'S HAND as he helped her out of his pickup. It was her fault Jerry wasn't here. He'd have stayed home if she'd asked. Why did she always have to be so brave? All that got her was a guilt-ridden husband. She'd have to do her best convincing to persuade him, he wasn't to blame. Besides, he'd be here in plenty of time to help her birth their daughter. He'd see for himself how lovable Lilly was.

She stood by Lee's truck, breathing in October's crisp air, as Lee unbuckled both girls from their booster seats. Their nonstop jabbering had offered a pleasant diversion during the ride into town.

Kaitlynn grasped Debbie's hand, then reached for Amelia, who already held Lee's hand. They headed toward the automatic doors, the girls skipping between the adults. A stranger would think they were the perfect little family.

The doors slid open and a man, with sea-blue eyes and short blond hair combed forward, stepped through the opening. His crisply pressed suit was tailored to emphasize broad shoulders and narrow hips. Displaying blinding white teeth, he smiled at their supposed family.

Amelia released Kaitlynn's hand and waved at him.

The stranger waved, but then his hand froze, and his brows rose above widened eyes. His over-white teeth disappeared behind pinched lips as his gaze roamed from Amelia to Lee then back to Amelia before he hurried past.

Lee turned toward the stranger then knelt to his daughter's level and rested his hands on her shoulders. "Amelia, do you know him?" He nodded toward the man.

"Um, hmmm. That's James. He stays at Mommy's house sometimes."

Debbie's stomach soured.

Color seeped from Lee's face.

"Are you okay, Daddy?" Amelia cocked her head to the side.

"I'm fine, sweetie." The tremor in his voice said otherwise. His Adam's apple fluctuated as he stood and took Amelia's hand. "Let's help Mrs. Verhoeven get checked in. Then we can go home."

Debbie rested a hand on Lee's arm. "If you want to go now, I understand."

"No." His jaw tightened, drawing his cheeks inward. "I'm going to make sure you're taken care of first. I follow through on my commitments."

Debbie nodded. The least she could do was allow him to finish his job. Taking the girls' hands again, they entered the hospital.

Lee strode to the waiting area, the girls in tow, as Debbie walked to the reception desk.

"Mommy!" Amelia's voice rang behind her.

Debbie turned as Amelia ran to a blonde-haired woman dressed in green scrubs. The woman scooped Amelia up and pulled her into a tight hug. But as she clung to Amelia, her eyes fired darts in Lee's direction.

Lee returned the look as he strode toward her.

"Kaitlynn, honey." Debbie held out her hand and wiggled her fingers. "Come by Mommy, okay?"

Kaitlynn ran over and took Debbie's hand. "That's 'Melia's mommy."

"Shhh." Debbie put a finger to her lips, bent down as far as she dared and whispered, "I know, sweetie. Let's let them have a family moment. You stay with me." She stood, trying to ignore the couple's vicious words, yet couldn't help but listen, and watch from her peripheral vision.

Everyone in the room probably heard the argument and felt the hurt in Lee's voice.

"Tomorrow's the day we agreed upon." Elise patted Amelia's head.

"I know that. I'm helping a friend."

Debbie stepped up in line and gave her name to the receptionist, her gaze drawn back to Lee.

Elise glanced over, and stared at Debbie's protruding stomach. "Friend?" She glared at Lee.

"Yes. Friend." Lee crossed his arms. "Her husband's out of town. She needed a ride."

"And Lee to the rescue. How sweet of you."

"Yes, actually, it is."

"Mrs. Verhoeven." The receptionist slipped a computer printout on the counter, drawing back Debbie's attention. "Can you confirm all this is correct?"

Debbie pried a smile for the receptionist, but the woman wasn't looking her way. The quarrel between Lee and Elise had stolen everyone's attention. Poor Lee. So, this was why he hesitated when she asked him for a ride. How could she not have considered that Elise might be here?

Her stomach tightened, forcing her focus back on her own situation. She read through the printout with ears trained on Lee's conversation.

"I thought there was still a chance for us." Lee's tone was hushed but pleading.

Guilt stabbed at Debbie's conscience as she peered over, becoming a voyeur into what should be an intimate discussion.

"I was willing to do whatever you wanted." He pointed toward the door. "Amelia greeted your *friend* on the way in."

Elise's face reddened, but she said nothing.

"Now, I understand the break-up had nothing to do with me." Anger smoldered in his tone.

Poor Amelia was literally pressed in the middle of the couple, still clinging to her mother, tears replacing her joy.

"Just how long have you and Mr. *GQ* been seeing each other?

I should have known that was the real issue."

"Well, at least he has a job."

Fury growled in Debbie's belly, coinciding with a faint contraction.

"Mrs. Verhoeven, you may have a seat." The receptionist intruded on the squabble again. "We'll have a wheelchair for you in a moment."

"Thank you." Debbie stepped away from the desk then sat with Kaitlynn cuddling quietly on what little lap Debbie had left.

The couple grew silent and stared each other down.

He broke off the stare first. His shoulders drooped, and his back hunched as he retreated one step. "I'll drop Amelia off here tomorrow." He kept his head down, defeat hushing his voice.

Elise held her chin up. "No. I'll pick her up. I don't need you coming around here anymore."

"Right." He reached for Amelia.

Tears streaked down the toddler's cheeks as the parents traded her off.

"Mommy loves you." Elise dried Amelia's cheeks with her thumbs then kissed her forehead. "I'll see you tomorrow." She half-jogged down a hallway.

Amelia turned her head and hid her eyes in Lee's shoulder.

Grasping Amelia in a hug, Lee sat next to Debbie, and lowered his face into Amelia's hair.

How could Elise give up such a treasure of a man?

Debbie placed a hand on Lee's arm. "You don't have to wait around for my sake. I'll be fine. Jerry'll be here soon, and I'm going to try to rest."

He raised his head, clamping his lips in a straight line. "I think that's for the best. I'm sorry."

"Oh, heavens, you've done me a tremendous favor. Please don't feel guilty."

"Well, can I at least take Kaitlynn with me? I don't think I'm going to be great company for Amelia right now."

"Are you sure?" She hated dumping another problem on Lee.

Kaitlynn tapped her hand on Debbie's shoulder. "Can I go with 'Melia?"

Lee nodded. "I'd like it."

"Then, I'd be grateful for the help."

"Debbie Verhoeven?" A young male orderly pushed a wheelchair into the room.

Debbie waved him over, set Kaitlynn down, and helped herself into the chair.

Not releasing his grasp on Amelia. Lee stood.

"Give Mommy a kiss." Debbie held her arms open.

Kaitlynn kissed Lilly then her mother.

"Now you behave for Mr. Aldrich. Grandma or Grandpa or someone will pick you up as soon as possible."

"I be good, Mommy."

"Of course, you will be." Debbie peered up at Lee.

False bravado filled Lee's stoic face. Tears would most likely come later.

"Thank you so much for bringing me. I'll have a relative pick Kaitlynn up as soon as possible."

"Don't worry about it. We'll plan for an overnight. After all, I've got the time, being I don't have a job."

"Lee . . ."

He waved his hand and turned to leave. "Keep us informed."

"I will. Thank you."

The orderly wheeled her away. Alone. No Jerry, no family. *It's okay.* At least her family was intact. She didn't need a bevy of supporters in order to have a baby. Lilly would arrive just fine, with or without them.

Chapter Thirty-four

The images from a hand-painted mural blurred as Jerry jogged down a hospital corridor, past the windowed nursery. He jerked to a stop and backpedaled to the window. Two infants slept there. Healthy. Normal. His child would be the exception. Again, he'd have to endure the placating tones of family and friends and strangers reminding him his daughter wasn't perfect. If they said nothing, maybe acceptance would come.

With a weighted sigh, he hurried to Debbie's birthing suite. He forced a smile, needing to show enthusiasm, not fear.

Her eyes were closed, and her lips curved upward in contentment. Man, he loved her. If only he could . . .

He swallowed a deep breath and walked to her bedside in a room that looked more like a classy hotel suite than a hospital, taking the patient's concentration away from the monitors and IV stands. *Please, God, let Debbie . . . and the baby, be healthy.*

Not caring if she awoke, he leaned over and kissed her. She needed to know he was here for her.

Her eyes fluttered open, and she smiled, but the smile turned into a grimace as she closed her eyes and bundled her fists.

He reached for a fist, embracing it with both hands, doing what little he could to guide her through the contraction.

Nothing could make a man feel more helpless than watching his wife suffer through labor.

Seconds later, she relaxed, and the smile returned. "I'm so glad you're here."

Keeping a hand in hers, he leaned over and kissed her again. "I love you, you know." No matter how the future played out for their baby. God had truly blessed him with a courageous and forgiving wife. *God, just give me an ounce of her courage.*

"I know." She squeezed his hand and turned away, looking straight ahead.

His gaze followed to where a clock hung from the wall opposite Debbie's bed. Only one o'clock?

A smirk infiltrated her smile. "Two and a half hours?"

"I guess I was a little heavy on the gas, and traffic was lighter than expected." He wouldn't tell her he'd taken the wrong exit coming out of St. Paul, adding an additional fifteen minutes to his drive time. He was fortunate not to have been stopped.

"I guess I'll forgive you." Pushing with her arms, she tried sitting up, then lowered herself back down. "Could you . . . ?"

His finger was already on the button, bringing the head of the bed upward. "Tell me when."

Once it reached about a forty-five-degree angle, she raised her hand.

He pulled a chair next to the bed—the chair that would fold out into a sleeper if he needed to rest—and took her hand again. "How's it going?"

"Slow. Like Kaitlynn. I think I've dilated to four centimeters. Whoopee." She twirled her finger close to her face. "Believe me, you haven't missed anything."

"I know, but I still feel bad for not being here."

"Hush." She touched her fingers to his lips. "You're here now."

He smiled half-heartedly. "Has anyone called?"

"I talked with Mom about thirty minutes ago. She was going to come home and watch Kaitlynn, but I told her not to worry. Kaitlynn's at Lee's. For the night, if necessary."

"I was wondering about that."

Debbie's grip tightened. Her breath deepened as she closed her eyes. Seconds later, it was over.

"You sure you don't want an epidural?" He hated seeing her in pain.

"Positive."

"It's up to you." Although, he'd feel much better if she'd take the numbing medication. Cracking his knuckles, he glanced at the phone. "No one else has called?"

She shook her head and shrugged. "Should I be expecting anyone?"

"Not really." He thought for sure Ricky would call, that her brother would personally tell her of his broken promise. Jerry wouldn't bring up the issue unless asked. No sense disappointing her.

That would surely come later.

AS THE CONTRACTION ROSE in her stomach and flowed around to her backside, Debbie focused on her husband's pale and weary face, and inhaled, one . . . two . . . three . . . Then she blew out a steady breath to a Michael Card lullaby swaying softly in the background, and Jerry humming perfect harmony.

Even with Jerry's soothing tenor, staying focused wasn't as easy as the Lamaze instructors made it sound. It had been a mere three and a half years since she'd delivered Kaitlynn. How could she have forgotten this part?

The wave of pain ebbed downward, but no longer left entirely. What in the world had convinced her that having another baby was a good idea? Why hadn't she listened to Jerry and had the epidural? Any sane woman would. But no, she had to be strong. How stupid could she be?

A knock sounded on the door, and a nurse walked in. After checking Debbie's vitals and dilation, she straightened. "You're almost there. Your little girl will arrive very soon." The nurse patted Debbie's shoulder. "You're doing well."

Easy for you to say.

"I'll be back to check on you shortly. Remember to buzz if you need me sooner."

"We will." Jerry squeezed Debbie's hand.

Soon wasn't anywhere soon enough. *God, now's a really good time for this baby to come.*

"More ice chips?" Jerry held up a plastic cup.

"Please," her voice squeaked out as another contraction built, seemingly right on top of the last one.

"Here. Let me help." He spooned a few chips into her mouth and dabbed perspiration from her forehead. "You know, you really are beautiful."

Oh, please. Why was it guys chose the absolutely wrong moments to be romantic? Rolling her eyes was too much work. A weak smile was all she could muster. How would she possibly find the energy to push Lilly out when the time came?

Her gaze met Jerry's as the contraction peaked and held, then subsided but didn't withdraw completely. The anxiety pinching his eyes wasn't helping her one tiny bit. With the exception of a few tender moments, he'd worn that dour expression since entering the room hours ago. At least, it seemed like hours ago. Well, she wasn't about to look at it any longer.

"Okay, what's eating you?" Her voice strained as her abdomen tightened.

"What?" He looked away.

Her short fingernails dug into his sweaty palm then gradually eased. "You . . . know . . . what . . . I'm . . . talking . . . about." Her words gasped out in between breaths, but doggone it, she was going to get them out. "There's something bothering you, and I want you to get it off your chest so you can do your job here." Nothing like being in labor to make her bold.

His wide eyes stared at her.

Her stare fought back and won as he released her hands and looked away.

"I didn't want to tell you." He looked down at fisted hands.

"Tell me what?" The contraction surged. Maybe an argument would help her focus elsewhere. Hopefully speed up the labor.

He picked up her hand and caressed it. "I talked to your brother earlier."

"Ricky?" She clamped her eyes shut as the pain rose, engulfing every cell in her body.

"He can't make it until tomorrow night."

She pried her eyes open.

A grimace wrinkled Jerry's face.

She laughed as the contraction cooled to a low burn. "Is that it? That's what's been bugging you this whole time?"

He nodded with hooded eyes.

"But he's coming," she whispered more to herself than Jerry and smiled through the pain. Even after she'd been so nasty to her brother, he was keeping his promise. *Thank you, God.*

"As soon as he can get here."

Her eyes moistened. "I don't care if he's not here today. All that matters is that he's coming, that hopefully he can forgive me."

"I wish I would have known that earlier." The familiar voice sounded from the doorway.

"Rick—" She peered up as the next wave pitched through her body. As much as she wanted to smile, she closed her eyes and concentrated on breathing instead. Warm hands surrounded her fist, guiding her through the contraction.

"I promised I'd be here." He spoke as the cramping eased.

She opened moist eyes and glanced up at her brother.

"No way was I breaking that promise."

"Thank you," she whispered as her body finally urged her to push.

Chapter Thirty-five

A three-quarter moon shone through the hospital window as Debbie traced Lilly's round and rosy face peeking out from her tightly-wrapped blanket. Her pink lips puckered like a fish, indicating contentment in her new world, just as she'd been in the womb.

An angel's kiss reddened her forehead between the eyebrows. Just like Kaitlynn. Lilly's eyes had the almond shape and tucks of skin they expected, and the bridge of her nose was wide. All tell-tale signs that the in-the-womb diagnosis had been correct. The doctor had since confirmed Down syndrome, but blood tests still had to be performed.

Debbie caressed Lilly's satin cheek. Her head turned and her tongue peeked out, seeking, hungry. The nurse should return soon with Lilly's first bottle.

What a blessing to know the diagnosis ahead of time. Debbie smoothed a kiss to Lilly's balled fist. Now, instead of being disappointed in Lilly's seeming imperfections, excitement surged in Debbie's heart. Just as it should. The imperfections the world saw, were wondrous character traits, chosen specifically by God. Friends and family could rejoice now, instead of offering sympathy for their disappointment.

She unwound the receiving blanket. Lilly's arms and legs

flung out, shocked by the chill of openness, but Debbie needed to explore every inch of her beautiful new daughter. She pressed her finger into Lilly's palm that displayed another tell-tale sign: the single palmar crease cutting straight across. Perfect, pudgy fingers, with dimples at the knuckles, closed around Debbie's finger.

Light footsteps were followed by a shadow creeping across Lilly's face.

Debbie looked up and smiled.

"She's beautiful." Ricky reached down and caressed his niece's cheek.

"Isn't she?" Debbie studied the miracle God had placed in her arms, and a tear tumbled down her cheek. Only moments before, she'd been happy that the pain was finally gone, with no rush of love for her daughter. But now, holding the cleaned, weighed, and measured infant, love filled her, permanently embedding itself in her heart. Lilly was perfect, just as God had formed her.

"And placid, like her mother." Ricky squeezed Debbie's arm.

She lightly brought her hand over the top of Lilly's head, taking care not to pressure the soft spot. "And she's got her father's hair." She smirked in Jerry's direction.

His eyes were closed, and a wet sheen glistened on his forehead. Poor guy. He'd had one tough day.

Ricky coughed, stifling a laugh.

Frowning, Jerry opened his eyes. "Ha. Ha."

She blew Jerry an air kiss. "I love you, hon."

"I can tell." A smile crinkled at the corners of his eyes as he closed them again, looking tired but content. Had he finally accepted their daughter?

"Can I hold her?" Ricky extended his arms. His words were beautiful music.

She shook her head. "Sorry, Daddy gets that privilege first." Debbie swaddled Lilly in the blanket and shifted toward her husband.

He frowned as his neck twisted slightly, as if he was going to shake his head "no," but he stopped it mid-motion. His lips rose forming a smile, but the joy didn't lift his cheeks or glow in his eyes.

Disappointment clotted Debbie's throat. *It hasn't changed.*

Even so, he reached for his daughter.

Debbie eagerly gave her up. At least he was trying. Maybe holding Lilly would break the barriers her husband had built.

A shiver coursed through her body. The temperature must have dropped ten degrees, and she was getting colder by the minute. Although it was mid-October, she hadn't felt chilled since last winter. But then again, her internal heater was gone. "Ricky, there should be another blanket in the wardrobe there. Could you get it for me, please?"

"Sure thing." He brought her a blanket and draped it over her lap and shoulders.

That helped the shakes a little anyway. Jerry's light humming warmed her even more. Let father and daughter bond so she could repair the fracture with Ricky.

As she turned to her brother, her gaze passed flower arrangements set on a shelf opposite her bed. One overflowed with purple flowers, another held a yellow tulip surrounded with baby's breath, and a third was graced with a single calla lily.

Ricky pointed to the tulip. "That one's for Katydid. It means 'there's sunshine in your smile.'"

"Oh, that is so precious. How perfect. Thank you for thinking of her."

"How could I not?" He fingered a white petal on the calla lily. "This one's for Lilly. It means magnificent beauty." Moisture glazed his eyes. "I truly mean that."

Nodding, Debbie bit into her trembling lip and fingered a tear from her cheek.

He picked up the larger arrangement, carried it over and placed the crystal vase in her hands. "Purple hyacinths."

She breathed in their fresh fragrance, effectively wiping away the antiseptic hospital smell. "They're lovely. Thank you."

"You're very welcome." He pulled a chair next to her bed and placed a hand on her arm. "They mean 'I'm sorry.'"

"Ricky." Her chin quivered as Jerry's music intermixed with Lilly's first pleas for nourishment. "You don't—"

"Hush, let me grovel here a bit." Ricky's lips leaned to one side. "It doesn't happen too often, so you better let me do it."

She nodded.

"As I was saying." He stroked a petal. "The purple hyacinth means I'm sorry." His gaze met hers.

A golf ball-sized lump clotted her throat.

"I was wrong. What I said, how I said it, what I believed. And I am so sorry. You've taught me a lesson about life I'll never forget. You've reminded me how very important you are to me, and I never want to let you down."

Debbie clutched the vase, struggling to keep her emotions intact. "I was wrong, too."

"No, you—"

"It's my turn." With Lilly's whimpers and Jerry's hums filling the background, Debbie set the arrangement on the table next to her bed, and took Ricky's hand. "I never should have shut you out. I don't know what got into me."

"You were a mother protecting her child."

"That and . . . " She bit into her lower lip. "Maybe it goes back to something Marcus said."

Ricky's eyes narrowed.

"He said I put you on a pedestal."

"Debbie—"

"Actually, what he said was that I looked at you as a saintly knight on a steed."

Ricky released her hand and crossed his arms. "Sounds like your brother."

"He's your brother, too."

"Right."

"Please behave." She touched his arm.

"Sorry."

"The thing is, Marcus was right. In a way, you've always been my hero. I've always looked up to you. I'm learning I expected too much, but you'd always been there for me. You always listened to me. I could always be honest with you. I could be real around you. Other than Jerry, I don't know who else I can say that about."

Jerry's humming stopped and Lilly protested. Jerry resumed his music.

Debbie ignored them, letting them get to know each other while she mended her relationship. Today was a magical day. God definitely was good.

"You demonstrated your faith to me." She grasped Ricky's hand. "I learned from you."

With a sigh, he leaned back and faced the ceiling.

She folded her hands over her flabby stomach—it would never be the same. The cost of new life. It was worth the price.

"Then you fell off the steed and showed that you were human after all." She squeezed Ricky's hand. "I didn't like seeing that empty saddle."

Shaking his head, he brought it down and cradled his face in his palms. His hands came together, steepling below his nose. "Sounds more like Humpty Dumpty to me."

She giggled. "I think you came back together just fine."

"I'm sorry I let you down."

"It wasn't all your fault. I brought a lot of this on myself.

That's what happens when we create idols. They can't help but let us down. I blamed you, but I guess I was really mad at myself."

"But that doesn't excuse what I said."

"You know what I care about? That look on your face when you saw Lilly for the first time, the yearning in your voice when you asked to hold her. You can't fake love."

"I do love her."

"You apologized. I forgave you. Can you accept that? If not, I won't let you hold her."

He grinned as Lilly's protests became sharper and more prolonged. "Then I guess I better accept it."

"Good. Now, if you'll forgive me—"

"Sounds like we have a hungry child, here." A nurse, wearing a smock covered in primary-colored cartoon characters, walked into the room carrying a small bottle of prepared formula. "You're certain this is the way you want to go?" The nurse held the bottle close to her chest, not attempting to hide her displeasure with Debbie's decision to bottle feed. But they didn't know the struggle she'd had with Kaitlynn. They didn't understand her need for Jerry to feed his child. It was worth the extra cost.

With a smile, Debbie reached for the bottle. "I have no doubt." She would not accept the guilt trip they freely offered.

The nurse's lips straight-lined as she hustled from the room.

Debbie took a breath then glanced at her brother frowning in the door's direction. Ever protective. But not perfect. She had to remember that.

She laid her hand on his arm, regaining his attention.

His glower turned into a smile. Man, she had missed that smile. It was her own fault she hadn't seen it. Why did it take having Lilly to figure that out? Well, it wouldn't happen again. "I'm so glad you're here." Her voice quivered. Darned emotions.

She bit into her lower lip as Ricky leaned over and hugged her. She had missed that, too.

Lilly's cry intruded, and Jerry's hum became a worded lullaby. What heavenly music. Lilly was breaking through.

Grinning, Ricky pointed at Lilly. "Sounds like someone else needs you right now."

Debbie squeezed his hand then let go. She turned to Jerry, eager to see the same smile he wore when he held Kaitlynn for the first time.

But the smile wasn't there. Jerry swayed as he sang, but he held Lilly loosely as if he'd never held a child before.

"Would you like to feed her?" Debbie offered him the bottle.

He stopped swaying and shook his head. "No. You go ahead." With no hesitation, he laid Lilly in Debbie's arms.

He just needs a little more time.

She prayed that was all he needed as she snuggled Lilly close to her breast and brought the bottle's nipple to Lilly's lips, barely perceiving the door opening and closing.

Lilly's head rooted back and forth a few times before her lips opened to accept the foreign object. It took a few more tear-filled moments from Lilly before she figured out the bottle's purpose and began to relax with her suckle. Lilly's first milestone achieved. Joyous warmth coursed through Debbie's veins. Other goals wouldn't be reached nearly as easily, and each one needed to be cherished.

Debbie looked up to Jerry to celebrate the accomplishment, but he was gone. She recalled hearing the door open and close. Where did he go? Why didn't he say he was leaving? She glanced at Ricky, who shrugged and smiled, but his wasn't a relaxed smile. His narrowed eyes gave away his true feelings. He was concerned.

And now, so was she.

Chapter Thirty-six

MID-NOVEMBER

Cradling wide-eyed Lilly in her left arm, Debbie walked past Kaitlynn's room and stopped. Jerry's sweet tenor embraced his evening lullaby, with love singing through each note. Lilly's head shifted toward the music, and her lips formed a satisfied smile. No one could convince Debbie that four-week-old babies didn't smile. This infant clearly loved her daddy's voice, even though he did what he could to avoid her.

Lilly's eyelids fluttered then remained closed. Contentment lingered on her face. The song's magic evidently worked for both of their daughters. Now, if Jerry would just recognize how much Lilly loved and needed him.

With a sigh, she carried the baby into the nursery, kissed her cheek, and laid her on her back, making certain the receiving blanket remained snug. She switched on the baby monitor, tiptoed from the room, and pulled the door slowly so it shut with a light click.

Debbie leaned against the closed door and smiled. Both girls asleep at the same time. And on a Friday night. Hallelujah. If she were lucky, she'd have three hours of blissful quiet. Fatigue tugged on her eyelids, but tonight there were more important things than sleep. Four weeks was long enough to ignore the T-Rex of a situation that had taken up residence with them.

Kaitlynn's door clicked shut, and Debbie found herself face to face with Jerry. A fine cul-de-sac of hair skirted his head making him look older than when he shaved it off in the morning, but he still looked fine. Tonight, there'd be no nagging. She'd focus solely on him, remind him how precious their relationship was. Then, maybe tomorrow, he'd be ready to discuss the dinosaur.

She stepped closer to him and unbuttoned his polo shirt. "I just love it when you sing to her."

A rare smile pulled up his lips and flickered in his eyes.

"I love it even more when you serenade me." She teased him with a quick kiss and stepped back.

A sheen of sweat glistened on his scalp. He wiped it away and glanced toward the living room. "Um, I was planning on reading the paper."

Okay. It's been so long, the guy's clueless. That would make tonight even more special. "Go ahead. I'm going to enjoy the quiet." And shortly, he would too. She kissed his cheek and sashayed into the bedroom without closing the door. Heavenly silence surrounded her, followed by what had to be Jerry's feet shuffling across the shag carpet, leading away from the bedroom, not into it. That was okay. It would give her time to get ready.

She dug her satin chemise and robe out from beneath the layers of pregnancy pajamas, then stole across the hallway, into the bathroom where she stripped off her jeans and sweatshirt—not exactly a romance-suggesting wardrobe. After freeing her hair from the elastic band, she combed life back into the strands, brushed her teeth, and spritzed vanilla body splash at the base of her neck. Jerry's favorite.

Whispering a prayer that it would fit, she slipped the chemise over her head and blew out a relieved sigh as it fluttered down to just above her knees. But then she glanced in the mirror and frowned. No cleavage in sight. Without breastfeeding, her breasts had quickly shrunk to their pitiful norm. Even worse was the obvious extra girth clinging below her waistline. How could she possibly look sexy to Jerry, especially if she continued to soothe stress by feeding it chocolate?

Well, after the anniversary party, only three terribly short weeks away, she would give up sweets. Until then, the added tension wouldn't be worth it. For tonight, hopefully darkness would conceal her post-birth body.

She ran a hand over her legs. Still smooth from this morning's shave. She was ready. With trembling hands, she put on her robe. Why did tonight feel like their wedding night? Had it really been that long?

Would Jerry still desire her?

Considering how cool he'd been to her since Lilly was born, that was the critical question.

God, please. The prayer blew over her lips as she walked from the bathroom to the living room, lifting her feet just enough to remain noiseless. Jerry sat in the rocker, with his back to her, his hands gripping the newspaper.

She cuffed her hands over his shoulders and squeezed.

He startled, then relaxed in the chair, letting the paper float to the floor, as she continued to knead his back . . . his shoulders . . . the nape of his neck. A low moan eased from his mouth as she massaged the smoothness of his head. "This is just what I needed."

"I know," she whispered in his ear as her fingers worked their way down to his back again. "This would be easier if you were lying on your stomach."

He looked back at her, and his gaze travelled down to her satin robe. His intense eyes met with hers. "You're ready?"

"Very." She nodded as her body responded to his searing gaze. "The doctor gave his okay."

With a sly grin, he got up, walked around the chair, and circled his arms around her back, pulling her tight against him. It had been so long.

"I need you." Her voice trembled as his lips traced the curvature of her neck, nudging the robe from her shoulders.

"Vanilla," he whispered as his hands caressed her back and worked their way beneath her robe and up her sides. "Are you still interested in that serenade?"

More than he knew. Breathing fast, she nodded, grasped his hand, and with her finger stroking his wedding ring, she led him back to their bedroom.

Tonight, they would share their love.

Tomorrow, they would address the dinosaur.

JERRY STRETCHED, AND HOODED his eyes, adjusting them to the sun filtering through the bedroom's vinyl mini blinds. Wearing a smile, he reached to his left, landing on empty sheets. He glanced at the clock, blinked, and looked at it again. Ten o'clock? So, she was up already and let him sleep. With a yawn, he sat up and grinned. Well, maybe he hadn't stopped grinning all night. He was one lucky man.

A knock sounded on the door before it opened a small crack. "Daddy's up!"

"Hey, punkin, come here." He patted the mattress. She jumped on and crawled on his lap. "How's my little princess?"

"Mommy made me waffles."

"Waffles, huh? With the toaster or the waffle maker?"

Her face scrunched up. "Mommy said she ironed them."

"Oh, she used the waffle *iron*."

"Uh-huh, and she gave me lots and lots of syrup."

He tickled her tummy. "Did you leave any for Daddy?"

"I ate 'em all gone."

"That she did." Debbie walked into the room carrying a breakfast tray loaded down with a plate of waffles, a tub of heated maple syrup, and a glass of orange juice. "So, these are hot off the iron."

"See, Daddy. Mommy ironed them."

He smiled at Debbie. "I like ironed waffles the best."

"Now, scoot, precious. Daddy needs room on his lap."

"I go watch cartoons?"

"Tell you what, how about I pop in a *VeggieTales* movie?"

"I love *VeggieTales*." Kaitlynn ran from the room.

"Hungry?" Debbie set the tray on Jerry's lap.

"Starving." He spread butter on the top waffle and drenched it with steaming syrup.

"Good. I'll get the DVD started for Kaitlynn, and maybe you could share some of your breakfast with me."

He forked a bite-size piece, raised it to his mouth and winked. "Is that all you want to share?"

"Jerry Verhoeven!" A grin flashed in her eyes as she leaned over and kissed him. "I'll remind you that little girls sometimes forget to knock. I'll be right back."

He put the waffle in his mouth and moaned. Nothing tasted better than homemade waffles. He washed it down with orange juice, cut off another piece, and glanced out the doorway. So, what was Debbie up to? Not that he was upset or anything. How could he possibly be bothered by last night's lovemaking?

And now, his favorite breakfast? In bed? His wife was clearly bribing him. He swallowed another bite. Bribery was good.

"Hey there, got a bite left for me?"

He stabbed a portion and raised it up, excess syrup dripping off its side. "This good enough?"

She sat beside him and let him feed her. "Mmm, mmm. You've got to admit, I iron my waffles very well."

He kissed syrup off her lower lip and waggled his brows. "One of your many talents."

"Oh, you." Giggling, she socked his bicep then linked her arm with his and leaned into his shoulder. "Thank you."

He bent over, placing the food tray on the floor, then cuddled against her. "Thank me for what?"

"For last night, this morning. It somehow doesn't matter that Lilly woke up twice last night. I needed you, and you were there."

"And you weren't sure I would be . . . " Gazing at his blanketed feet, he sighed. "Because I haven't been."

Silence answered him, affirming he was right. He hid his hands beneath the blanket, silently counting each knuckle as it cracked. "It's not intentional."

"I know, but it's still something we have to talk about, to work through. It's like we've got this dinosaur living in our house, and it's not that fuzzy purple one that sings about happy families. It's a Jurassic dinosaur, with massive sharp teeth, that's salivating to gobble our family up. I can't ignore it any longer."

"I know what you're saying, but I'm just . . . " Just what? Petrified? Scared to lose someone again? Afraid of pain? Terrified of dying?

She snuggled in closer, drawing her finger down his arm. "I've been doing some research lately. On panic disorder. It's been a long time since I've had to deal with it professionally, so I wanted to refresh my memory. What I do know is, in your case, the attacks are triggered by a major life stress."

"Christopher's death. I know all that." He flexed his fingers, chasing away a spreading numbness.

"And now Lilly's birth."

Closing his eyes, he swallowed what felt like a tennis ball-sized cactus scratching up his throat. Her finger, supposedly caressing his arm, sent waves of pain from his shoulder to his hands, so he slapped it away. But he grabbed her hand back. "I'm sorry. It . . . "

"It hurt." She sucked in her lips and closed her eyes, taking in deep breaths, and then turned to him, taking his hands in hers and peering directly in his eyes. "I'm trying to understand what you're going through. What it's like to feel a nonstop fear, to believe, without a doubt, that the worst thing will happen, to dread having more panic attacks. There are ways we can deal with this. Medications you can take. Therapists who—"

"Whoa, whoa, whoa." He jerked his hands away and raised them, palms outward. "This is what last night was all about? And this morning? I never looked at you as manipulative, but now—"

"Manipulative? If that's what you thought . . . " She turned her back to him and wiped her arm across her face.

He clenched his fists, willing away the crushing pain in his chest. More manipulation. Had to be. Debbie didn't cry. He curled his fingers around her arm. "Then look me in the eye and tell me it wasn't."

Her jaw was tense as she faced him again. Red veined her eyes and mottled her cheeks.

He crossed his arms. "The truth."

She stood up and lifted her chin. "The truth is, yes, I figured it would be easier to talk to you about this if we spent time focusing on you, if I could get you to relax—"

"I don't believe this." How could she use him like that? Balling a fist, he jumped out of bed and stared at the wall. Oh, how he wanted to propel that fist right through the drywall.

"Don't you dare walk away from me when I'm talking. I'm sick and tired of you turning away from all your problems." She sniffled. "If you can't believe that last night was about me loving you—" Her voice came out in a thunderous whisper. "—about me wanting to know if you loved me. Then I don't . . . "

Debbie plopped down on the side of the bed, resting her forehead on folded hands.

I've messed things up again, haven't I? Just like Francine. The pattern always repeated. His dad left. Christopher died. Francine walked out. Debbie . . . Everyone he loved. Pain shot through his chest and numbness tingled in his fingers. *Go to her.* Left leg, right leg. Left . . . Echoing the instructions in his head, he forced his legs to transport him around the bed. He knelt in front of Debbie and pulled her hands away from her face. "Please tell me you're not going to leave me."

He gasped as the ache knifing his chest seemed to twist deeper. Maybe death was finally coming for him. Maybe this time it was more than anxiety. Maybe that would be the best for all of them.

Debbie pulled his head to her chest, wrapping her arms around his neck and resting her head over his. "Just breathe, two . . . three . . . four. Exhale, two . . . three . . . four. Inhale."

But she hadn't answered his question. Like his dad, like Francine, she was going to leave. *Please, no.* Acid clawed at his throat. "I need you."

"And I need you." Her hands massaged his scalp. "Now breathe in and hold, two . . . three . . . four. Blow out, two . . . three . . . four. We're going to work through this together. Keep breathing. Relax. I'm afraid you're stuck with me."

Focusing on Debbie's heartbeat pumping against his cheek, he heeded her instructions. Inhale . . . . Exhale . . . Breathe in . . . Release.

Seconds. Minutes passed.

It didn't matter how much time elapsed as the knife receded from his chest, sensation returned to his fingers, and the burn in his throat cooled.

Kneading his shoulders, she whispered, "Is it over?"

He nodded. "Thank you." The words grated from his dry throat. "I love you."

Her breathing halted then she gasped in air as she pulled on his arms, encouraging him to sit by her. "I don't know how to convince you how much I love you. If last night wasn't enough . . . "

With his thumb, he wiped below her eyes. "It was. I'm sorry for doubting. I just can't stop . . . being terrified."

"And I'm working on understanding, but I'm too close to this situation. My perception is totally skewed. Will you talk to someone, please? I know a really good psychotherapist."

"We can't afford it." And would the school allow a crazy man to teach their students? Wasn't that what he'd be admitting by going to a therapist? No wonder he was turned down for the principal position. They'd made the right decision.

"Jer, our family can't afford not to."

He lay back on the bed and stared up at the ceiling as the baby whined over the monitor. Just terrific. "I'll think on it, okay?"

"Fine." Fatigue shadowed her eyes as she glanced at the monitor. "It's your decision. For now. But I need to reinforce to you, I will not . . . I won't ever leave you. And Lilly." She pointed toward the nursery. "She's fine. Her heart's healthy, and we're blessed with a happy girl who loves her father deeply, who desperately wants that love returned."

"I know. I know. That's what logic tells me, but I can't help it, that every time I look at her, all I see is an empty crib."

DEBBIE COVERED JERRY WITH a quilt, dried her eyes, and hurried from the room. It was apparent Jerry had no intention of getting professional help.

Lilly's squawks became adamant. "God, I can't take this right now." She balled her fists and clamped her teeth together to stop her jaw from trembling. If she didn't get rid of the tension, Lilly would sense it.

The Hershey bars stashed behind her rarely-used cookbooks called out. Today, she wasn't going to ignore them. After the anniversary party was over, once she had one less stressor to deal with, then she'd deal with Jerry, and maybe then, she could give up chocolate.

Chapter Thirty-seven

DECEMBER

The snowmobile's motor roared as Debbie squeezed the throttle, propelling the Polaris over the snow's fresh powder. December's windy chill bit into her face, but she didn't mind. Winter's invigorating scent slipped past her nostrils, filling her lungs. Nothing smelled better than this. Nothing felt better. Out here under the cloudless blue sky, crossing acres of open and hilly snow-covered fields, she was free—for the first time since Lilly was born.

The engine sputtered, and its soothing roar became an undulating whine. *Not now!* Marcus said his machine was in prime condition. The whine grew as she turned the sled in a large arc, aiming for her brother's home. He wouldn't be happy if he had to come way out here to retrieve it, even if it wasn't her fault.

She compressed the throttle, but gas didn't seem to reach the engine. Her shoulders tensed as she gave up and released the throttle. The snowmobile slowed, then stopped, and slowly sunk into the powder, but the engine's whine continued. So much for a relaxing afternoon.

"Mommy." The voice was faint as the motor sustained its noisy protest.

Huh? Kaitlynn? What was she doing out here?

Debbie removed the key, but the engine droned on.

"Mommy!" The voice was louder, closer.

A headache blossomed, and Debbie's shoulder throbbed. Why? Was she going crazy?

She raised her leg over the sled's seat and lowered herself into the snow as she glanced around the open field.

Kaitlynn's voice became insistent.

The engine wouldn't shut off.

Debbie kicked at the machine, knocking her backward on her pulsing shoulder. Snow flew into her face, clouding her vision. She blinked and brought her arm up to wipe the moisture from her eyes.

The haze cleared away and Kaitlynn appeared above her, shaking Debbie's shoulder. "Mommy. Lilly's mad."

Debbie blinked several times as the dream faded away, the bed of snow became her couch, and reality set in. How could she have fallen asleep? There was no time to nap. She squinted at the DVD player's clock and moaned. Four thirty. She'd wasted two whole hours. Two hours she could have used to pay bills, clean house, make the grocery list for the anniversary party on Saturday, call the photographer and confirm their appointment for Friday night.

The party wasn't even three days away, and she'd completed zilch this week. Lilly's hungry cries told Debbie that nothing else, including a nourishing supper her family deserved, would get accomplished in the next hour either.

"Thanks for waking me, precious." Debbie pulled herself up. A dull headache formed above her eyes as her body made its appeal for more rest. Lilly's hungry cries needed to be fed first.

"Can I watch a movie?" Kaitlynn patted Debbie's leg. "I be good now."

She nodded and sighed. Kaitlynn was spending far too much time in front of the television, but Lilly demanded so much time that Debbie had little energy left for Kaitlynn. Maybe, if Kaitlynn had been watching TV instead of being bored in her bedroom, Debbie wouldn't have spent half the afternoon cleaning, wasting more precious time.

Hopefully once the anniversary party was over . . . How sad that she dreaded this upcoming celebration. Honoring forty years of marriage should be a joyous event. It probably would be for everyone else, but for her, it was work.

Lilly's cries became adamant.

Fighting lightheadedness, Debbie shuffled to the refrigerator. At least she'd had the forethought to mix a pitcher of formula earlier. She dispensed four ounces into a bottle. Lilly wasn't a big eater yet, and they couldn't afford to waste any. Formula must cost more per ounce than gold, and they'd long ago used up all the freebies given to them by the hospital and sent in the mail.

Debbie microwaved the bottle for a few seconds. How things had changed; with Kaitlynn, using the microwave to heat formula was a definite no-no. Now, it was a means to give her a few extra seconds in the day. She removed the bottle and swished the liquid around, dispersing the heat.

Needing a caffeine jolt, she set the bottle on the cupboard and took a half-empty bottle of Pepsi from the fridge.

Her head pounded as she hurried to Lilly and picked her up from her crib. The poor child's face was bright pink from her crying; the angel's kiss, crimson. Debbie cradled Lilly tight against her body.

The infant took a breather, rooting toward Debbie's breast, and resumed her protest. Shoot, the bottle was still on the counter. Debbie robotically returned to the kitchen, retrieved the bottle, tested the formula on her wrist, and brought the bottle to

Lilly's mouth.

Lilly sucked, let go and cried, sucked, then let go again, voicing her dissatisfaction in having to wait so long for food. Her cries lessened as Debbie carried her into the living room where Kaitlynn watched a *VeggieTales* movie. At least it was good TV.

Debbie sat in her padded rocking chair and brought her feet up on the rocking stool in front. A smile tugged at her lips as they relaxed together.

This was Lilly's favorite spot. How different she was from Kaitlynn, who'd been born with an independent streak. She liked being held long enough to finish her bottle, and then squawk to be put down, to roam free. Lilly was most content when wrapped and held tightly.

Debbie kissed Lilly's forehead. She loved cuddling her daughter, just not eight hours a day.

With Lilly calm and Kaitlynn occupied, Debbie jotted a to-do list in her head. Feed Lilly. Make supper—yippee—probably hot dogs and macaroni and cheese . . . again. But what else did she have time for? Well, it would have to do for today. Tomorrow morning, if she remembered early enough, she'd throw some chicken and veggies in her slow cooker. At least then they'd have a more substantial meal.

Okay, what else? Grocery shopping for home and for the party. Order the cake from Sam's Club. Do that all tonight after supper, so Jerry could watch the girls. She wouldn't let him say no. How pathetic that she actually looked forward to grocery shopping.

Tomorrow, Amelia was coming over, which was actually a good situation. When Amelia was around, Kaitlynn didn't need Debbie to keep her occupied. The two would go off and play and only be heard from at mealtime.

Lilly released the nipple and took a breath.

Debbie raised the baby to her shoulder and searched the floor for a burp rag. It had run off, apparently. Amazing how things like that grew legs when she wasn't looking. Aw, what did she care anyway? The T-shirt she wore wasn't something she'd wear out of the house. So what if it got spewed on?

She circled her palm on Lilly's back, giving it periodic taps. The burp came out long and juicy, and seeped into Debbie's skin. Add "take a shower" to her to-do list.

Debbie lowered Lilly to her other arm and offered the bottle. She closed her eyes, relaxing again with Lilly, and continued with her list. Tomorrow, after preparing the chicken, she'd call the photographer, and then bake about eight dozen buns. *God, please let my oven work tomorrow.*

Friday would be the tough day. After cutting the veggies, she'd have to prepare the girls and herself for the family portrait. Yes, the picture would be taken in the hayloft at her parents' farm, and they would all be in jeans, thank goodness. She'd need to do her makeup. Makeup? What was that? Would she even remember how? Then to style her hair and Kaitlynn's, if her daughter allowed her. Kaitlynn hated having her hair combed and wasn't fond of bows or ponytails. At least Lilly—or Jerry— didn't have any hair to worry about.

Debbie rubbed a hand across Lilly's head. A fine texture was beginning to grow. If Lilly was anything like Kaitlynn, she wouldn't need her first haircut until she was two. Hooray for bald babies.

Saturday would be the big day: prepare the roast and the ham, bring everything to church, and decorate the fellowship hall. Thank goodness Janet was handling the salad and baking the bars and would be there to offer decorating advice. With her baby due any day, she'd most likely be too exhausted to do much else.

Lilly stopped sucking and looked perfectly content in Debbie's arms. Time to prepare supper. Not willing to invoke Lilly's ire, Debbie held her and headed for the stairs just as she heard the garage door lift.

Yeah. *Thank you, God.* In just a short while, she'd relish a few hours of freedom at the grocery store. It wasn't a snowmobile ride, but two hours without being needed sounded like absolute heaven.

JERRY LET THE CAR IDLE in the garage for a few seconds as he wound down from the exasperating student-parent conference. When would parents realize that respect had to be taught and modeled at home in order to have any success with it at school? He wasn't hired to parent his students. Still, that couple tonight blamed him for their precious son's troublemaking.

Sighing, he removed the key from the ignition, closed his eyes, and leaned his head back. In the past, theirs was the exact type of family he'd have sent to Debbie for counseling. Sure, he still recommended Debbie's old employer to families desperate for help, but no one else had Debbie's patient ear or achieved the same success.

Was he selfish for taking her from her career? Yes, the decision for her to stay home was a mutual one. It still didn't seem fair. Maybe she should return to work.

Yeah, right. Then in a few years, they'd be the ones going to counseling.

An image of their too-quiet, tension-filled supper last night flitted through his head. Maybe he should see a therapist. If they had extra money, he'd consider it.

He stepped out of the car, lugging a briefcase bulging with papers to correct by tomorrow morning. With visions of comfort food in his head, an old-fashioned meat and potatoes meal, he walked into the house.

He entered the kitchen and breathed in . . . hoping. Nothing. He glanced at the stove. No pots or frying pans. No heated oven. No slow cooker. His gaze rested on the cupboard, and he moaned. Not again. Sure, in college macaroni and cheese was a staple, but now? He lifted his briefcase to set it on the table, but bills and bookwork occupied nearly every inch of its surface.

The daily Bible calendar sat there too. He picked it up and groaned. A page hadn't been turned in over a month. Some spiritual leader he made. He put the book down and pulled out a chair, resting his briefcase there as he listened for Debbie.

No television. No radio. No baby crying. Not even Kaitlynn running to hug his knees.

Where were they?

Clumping feet sounded on the basement stairs. That answered that question.

Debbie stepped through the basement door carrying the baby.

Always holding the baby.

He wouldn't recognize them apart anymore.

Debbie cradled the infant in one arm and held a package of frozen hotdogs in the other hand.

He forced a smile, hoping to veil his dissatisfaction. He was hungry for a roast or a steak, not mystery meat.

"I thought I heard you come in." Her gaze shifted to the clock. "You're late."

Apparently not late enough, if he had to wait for supper. He kicked at the linoleum. Man, what was his problem? Maybe if he helped once in a while, he might get his comfort food.

Hiding his guilt, he glanced at the floor. "Yeah, I had a conference with some parents tonight."

"Oh." She shifted the baby to her other hip. "Is there a problem?"

"You could say that." He rested his hand on the back of a chair, taking care not to look at the child. Shadows hovered beneath Debbie's eyes. Her hair was pulled into a tight, unflattering, ponytail. If she'd lost any weight following the pregnancy, he couldn't tell. If anything, her face appeared plumper than ever. The T-shirt stretched over her stomach and hips was thinning and yellowed with spit up, and belonged in the trash.

He dug his fingers into the back of the chair. Was he doing this to her? A knot tied in his throat, and he cleared it. "They've got a son who insists on disrupting the classroom. I finally had enough and called the parents. It was easy to see where the kid gets his behavior from. All they do is mollycoddle him and contradict each other."

At least they spoke to each other.

"I'm sorry, hon." She squeezed past him to the stove.

Neither of them attempted to offer a kiss in greeting. When had that stopped?

Before Kaitlynn was born, they agreed that the husband-wife relationship needed to come first. When Kaitlynn would beat Debbie to him, he made a point to say, "Mommy first." Apparently, not anymore. *Reach out. Touch her. Let her know she's loved.* His arms refused to obey.

Keeping the baby balanced in the crook of one arm, Debbie squatted next to the stove, slid open the storage drawer at its bottom, and pulled out two stainless steel kettles. *Go help her. Take your daughter.* His feet remained rooted to the floor. Funny how Debbie had stopped offering the infant to him. Of course, he always had an excuse to refuse her offer.

With some effort, Debbie stood, keeping the pans' black handles in one hand. She brought the kettles to the sink, filled them halfway with water, and then, one at a time, returned them to the stove. He supposed a mother could get used to doing three things at once, especially when all the husband did was stand and watch.

She turned to him, eyes narrowed in worry. "Is there a problem?"

"Uh, no." He nodded toward the open basement door. "Kaitlynn downstairs?"

A slight smile hinted on Debbie's lips. "Riding her trike. I never thought I'd be grateful for an unfinished basement. For the moment, she's occupied."

Debbie walked to the basement door and shut it. "She's discovered that having a baby sister isn't near as much fun as she imagined. She thought she'd have a built-in playmate. Instead she got this doll-sized troublemaker who steals all her mommy's attention. She learned that coloring on her wall will get Mommy's attention back."

"No." His shoulders sagged.

"Oh, yes. Your *perfect* little daughter has shown signs of rebellion."

His perfect daughter.

"I told her you'd talk with her when you got home. That's why she's still downstairs. She's avoiding you."

"So, I get to be the bad guy?"

"You *and* me. I made her wash the walls. Of course, I had a bigger mess to clean up after she was done cleaning, but I don't think she'll do it again." Debbie pulled out a chair and plopped down. Her back hunched as her eyes surveyed the mess covering the table. She motioned to another chair. "Can we talk for a second?"

He scratched his head and shrugged. This wasn't going to be good. "Sure." He pulled out a chair, set his attaché on the floor, and sat down.

Debbie rested her hand, palm up, on the table.

This would be a good time to take her hand in his and demonstrate his support. He folded his hands in his lap. "What's wrong? Is this about Kaitlynn?"

She shook her head. "I need you to watch the girls for me tonight."

"Debbie, I can't—"

Her eyes grew wide, and her face flushed with anger. "Can't?" The baby squawked. "And why not?" Debbie put a finger to the infant's lips, letting her suck.

He kicked at his briefcase. "Homework."

"Homework!" She slid her chair from the table and strode to the stove. "Since when do your kids have so much homework?"

"It's these new testing rules."

"Right," she mumbled. "I need two hours, Jer. Just two hours to get groceries. Chances are Lilly will sleep the whole time I'm gone, and you can put in a video for Kaitlynn. You'll be done correcting before I even get home."

He picked up his briefcase and set it in his lap. *She's right. Help her out.* Pain stabbed his chest at the thought. "Not tonight, Deb. I can't babysit with—"

"Babysit?" She ripped open the box of macaroni and cheese, yanked out the powdered cheese packet, sending noodles flying, and dumped the remaining noodles into boiling water. Accomplished with one hand. "You don't *babysit* your own children."

He gripped the handle on his briefcase and stood. "Semantics," he mumbled.

She tore the plastic casing surrounding the hot dogs and dumped the wieners into the pan. Water splashed across the stove and dripped onto a floor already stained with spilled food.

"Can't you go tomorrow?"

"No! Tomorrow's my day for baking." Debbie retrieved a washcloth from the sink and wiped off the stove, then she grabbed a paper towel and dried the floor. "Besides that, Lee's going back to work. I promised to watch Amelia."

"Oh." *It wouldn't hurt you to care for your daughters.*

"All I'm asking for is two hours." She yanked a wooden spoon from the homemade utensil jar on the counter and stirred the noodles, her knuckles whitening on the spoon. "Two hours so I can get ready for Mom and Dad's anniversary party. Two hours to get away by myself and have a moment to breathe."

His grip tightened on the attaché handle. Two hours. That was nothing. But the mere thought made his heart gallop, and his arm numb. He couldn't. Not yet.

"Not tonight." He hurried from the kitchen before she could say anything to make him feel guiltier than he already felt.

Chapter Thirty-eight

"Hi, Lee." Debbie greeted her friend with a weary smile as Amelia sat on the floor to remove snow-covered boots, creating muddy puddles. One more thing to clean today. Someday, she would get sleep again. Someday.

"You look exhausted." Lee straightened Amelia's boots. "Are you sure you can watch Amelia?"

She made herself smile. "Amelia's no trouble. She actually makes my job easier. Jerry calls it subtraction by addition."

"Is there another problem?"

Yes, but nothing she'd share with Lee. "I'm finding out that two times the kids means more than twice the work."

Amelia tugged on Debbie's T-shirt. Another shirt worthy of the garbage. What did it matter anyway? Taking three kids out in public in December in Minnesota was something only a masochist would do.

"Is Katy up?" Amelia kept tugging.

Debbie knelt to Amelia's eyelevel. "Not yet, sweetie, but you can go in the basement and play there. She'll be awake soon."

"Okay." Without protest, Amelia ran to the basement.

"She's a good kid, Lee."

Lee gave a halfway smile. "Yeah, she's not too bad." His mouth straightened. "I hope my being away for work doesn't hurt that."

"She'll be fine. You've provided a good foundation. That's what she needs most." That was what they all needed most. Frowning, Debbie glanced at the Bible verse on the table. Her foundation had never been weaker.

"What about you?"

"Pardon me?"

"Will you be fine?" Lee put a hand on her arm, and his eyes probed hers.

Debbie shuddered and looked away. Jerry hadn't made that simple gesture in weeks. Not a kiss. Not a touch. Not even a "How was your day?" It was becoming clear why Francine abandoned him. Debbie sucked in a breath. She wasn't anything like Francine.

"Really, I'm just tired. Lilly demands a lot of attention, and now Kaitlynn does too. It's nothing that every other mother hasn't gone through. Right now, the girls are still sleeping, and I need to get everything done before they wake. When Lilly's up, she begs to be held, and I haven't had the patience to let her cry herself out. Maybe after this weekend. I think I'll deal better with everything once this party's over."

"If you need someone . . . " His hand remained on her arm . . . and unexpected warmth tingled through her veins.

She yanked her arm away and hid it behind her back.

"I think you could use a break."

She shrugged. Sure, she could, but that would come after this weekend. Then, maybe, her mom would watch the girls for a few hours. And Jerry would provide the tingling warmth instead.

"You know." Lee slid his winter gloves on. "Sunday night after the Vikings game, I'm staying at The Century in Minneapolis." His eyes locked with hers. "Maybe that wouldn't be a bad idea for you, too."

A smile pulled at her lips. At least he noticed her. Maybe it wouldn't be such a bad—

Her eyes widened, and her breath quickened. *Oh, God, forgive me.* "Just because Jerry and I are going through a rough patch doesn't mean—"

"Whoa." He raised his hands and smiled. "That's not what I meant. I'm just saying it would be good for you to get away, meet a friend for a drink. That's all."

And she knew exactly what that kind of "innocent" meeting could lead to, planned or not. She inhaled a breath and held it, calming her heart. So-called innocent dinners frequently opened doors to marital problems. She and Jerry had enough already. "You should get going."

"I'll see you tonight."

She nodded as Lee pulled the door closed behind him. By the time he returned, Jerry would be home. Thank goodness. She massaged her temples. Lee was too good a friend to lose, but if that happened again, she would have no choice. The fact that his touch felt so good, and that she'd given a millisecond of a thought to his proposal, chilled her.

She rubbed her arms. Well, there was no sense worrying about that now. No harm had come of it. Her goal, at the moment, was to make it through the day without cracking. She could get a good start while her girls slept, beginning with chicken in the slow cooker. Nothing tasted better than slow-cooked meals. Just throw all the ingredients together and forget about it. By suppertime, the meat would be falling-apart good.

But that was the second item on the list. First, she needed to make the call to the photographer.

She placed the call, confirmed pictures for tomorrow night, and smiled.

One task done.

Now to tackle supper. She dragged her slow cooker from the

corner of the counter and turned it on high. After laying out the chicken breasts and seasoning them, she added water, bullion, and the vegetables she cut last night.

Yes! She pumped her fist. Item number two off her to-do list, and it was only eight. Maybe she'd make it through the day after all.

Lilly should sleep another hour. Kaitlynn, maybe another two. Plenty of time to bake the ready-to-bake dinner rolls. If she got them done, she might even sneak in a nap this afternoon. She smiled. Two smiles in one morning. Yep, it was going to be a good day.

She pulled out four cookie trays and laid them side by side on her cupboard and began spacing the rolls.

The phone rang as she finished the first sheet. Now, who in the world would be calling so early? Had to be Mom. She answered after the second ring. "Hello."

"Hey, Debs."

"Marcus, hi. How's it going?"

"Uh, we've been better, I guess."

Oh, no. Not the baby. Debbie pulled a chair from the kitchen table and sat. "What's wrong? Is Janet okay?"

"It's Janet's mom, Joanna. We brought her to the hospital last night."

Oh, no. Debbie clasped a hand over her chest. "What happened?"

"The doctors say it's her gall bladder. It's got to come out."

"What exactly does that mean? Is—"

"It's a common surgery. Sounds like they can remove it using laparoscopic surgery and avoid major cutting, unless it's worse than they're anticipating."

"I'm sorry." Debbie slumped in her chair. "How's Joanna doing? How's Janet?"

Marcus laughed dryly. "Joanna's in pain, but her spirits are high. She's telling the doctors to hurry and get it over with so she can hold the new grandchild."

"Sounds like a grandma."

"Doesn't it though? Now, Janet's a basket case. With the baby due any time, I'm a little concerned."

"Will surgery be today?"

"Yeah. They're prepping her right now."

"Is there anything I can do for you? Watch the boys, maybe?"

"We can use prayers."

"Of course."

"Mom's already got the boys. We dropped them off last night on the way to the hospital. But I do have a favor to ask."

"Sure. Anything."

Marcus exhaled loudly. "It's the seven-layer bars."

Debbie closed her eyes. Not the bars. Not more baking. Anything but that.

"Janet was going to make them today."

Debbie sighed then wished she could take it back. How could she complain when Janet's mom was sick? Talk about selfish.

"Or maybe I'll go to Sam's and pick some up." Marcus apparently got the gist of her moan.

"No, you don't have to. Dad loves Janet's bars. It wouldn't be the same without them. If you've got the recipe you can—"

"Already done. And we've got the ingredients too."

Thank you, God, for small favors.

"I'll run it all over as soon as we hang up."

"I'd appreciate it."

"Hey, we appreciate you helping out. I know you've ended up doing the brunt of the work with this party, and I feel bad dumping more on you."

Que sera sera. "That's what family's for, right? You guys

would do the same for me."

"In a heartbeat."

"Tell Janet we're praying for her and Joanna, okay."

"I will. And thanks."

"Not a problem." Okay, that was a little lie, but he didn't need to know. "We'll see you shortly."

"Yeah. Bye."

"Bye." Debbie closed her eyes and sighed again. Her throat constricted as tears threatened. No, she would not cry. Janet needed her help, and she'd bake those bars with a smile. She brought the to-do list up in her mind and slotted "bake bars" before "take a nap." That little item would have to wait until next week.

Chapter Thirty-nine

*D*ebbie sat up straight, leaned forward slightly getting rid of any hint of a double chin, and smiled. She tried to think happy thoughts so it would show in her eyes. Lilly wasn't crying. That definitely was a happy thought. The flash brightened the hayloft, leaving dark spots floating in front of her eyes.

Lilly jerked and Debbie pulled her in close, giving comfort before the baby complained.

"Wonderful." The perky blonde photographer flashed her own photogenic smile. The woman was pretty enough to be permanently in front of the camera, instead of behind it. "That should do it. Now if someone would kindly help me lug this equipment back down, I'd be more than grateful."

The photographer looked straight at Ricky and stuck out her lower lip. Puhlease. What was it women saw in him, anyway?

"Be more than glad to." Ricky stood and wiped the hay from the back of his Levi's. Debbie rolled her eyes as he swaggered forward.

He rested his hand on her camera case. "But I'm afraid it's going to cost you."

The woman's returned smile affirmed she'd be more than willing to pay his price.

Marcus mumbled behind Debbie. "The man can't take a two-minute break to be with his family."

"Tell me about it." Debbie hoped to have a few minutes tonight alone with her brother. Apparently, he had other priorities. What should she expect?

At least she had no more work for the night. She could go home, get a good night's rest, and, in the morning, Ricky would help set up for the party. Assuming he was around to help.

The family headed for the opening in the loft's floor, their feet dragging a path through the brittle hay. Keeping Lilly tucked in her arm, she sat on a bale, closed her eyes, and shut out the inane conversations going on around her. She rocked Lilly as the voices faded. As long as Lilly was content, Debbie would enjoy the calm and banish any niggling thoughts about her crumbling marriage.

"Deborah?"

She glanced at her mother in the loft exit.

"Why don't you hand Lilly down to me? I need some Grandma time with that precious granddaughter."

Thank you, God. "Gladly." Too bad Jerry hadn't taken the initiative to help, but he and Kaitlynn were long gone. He was probably the first one to leave.

Next week.

She carried Lilly to Grandma. *Next week we need to get back on track.* Kneeling, she handed Lilly down the hole. "She's got a bottle in the fridge. Thanks, Mom."

"No problem at all." Her mother cradled Lilly in her favorite position. It was just like a grandma to instinctively know that.

Debbie returned to the bales, sat, and closed her eyes, shutting out any thoughts. She inhaled a deep breath and let it pass, whistling slowly through her teeth. Her shoulders relaxed for the first time all day, and she tuned her ears in to the glorious sound around her.

Silence.

Silence probably wasn't what God had in mind when he said, "make a joyful noise," but to her it was the most joyous noise ever. She reclined against a bale. *One more day, one more day, then I'm done.*

But there was so much left to do.

Her shoulders tensed again. Her chin trembled, and her throat tightened. No! No crying now.

But maybe it was okay here. Maybe a good cry was exactly the medicine she needed. No one would see her. No one would know how poorly she was handling life. Moisture seeped onto her cheek, and she wiped it away.

"Debbie?"

Ricky? Shoot! He was supposed to be gone. Debbie kept her eyes closed and raised her arm to dry her eyes.

"You okay?" His voice was closer, but still distant.

Keeping her eyes closed, barricading the wetness, she bit into her lip and balled her fists as she turned to face him. She nodded several times quickly. Too quick. She opened her eyes and looked, through tear-filled fog, at her brother standing by the wall closest to the loft entrance. Maybe he wouldn't see her tears from that far off.

He stuffed his hands into his front pockets, and his gaze remained on her. "Do you need some time alone?"

Yes, she wanted time alone, but she also needed time with her brother. She breathed out and patted the spot next to her. "I'd like time alone, but I'd rather have a few minutes with you. I assumed you were leaving."

Frowning, he narrowed the space between them. "Well, let's just say I figured I should spend this weekend with the family." He sat next to her. "I'm glad I stayed."

"Me too." She wrapped her arm around her brother's back and leaned in to his shoulder.

He curved his arm around her.

For several minutes, neither of them said anything. The still conversation told Debbie how much respect her older brother had for her, how he knew her and understood her. How could she have stayed angry with him for so long?

She looked up at the rafters where a thick rope once hung. "Remember how we used to play up here?"

"Those were good times, weren't they?"

The best. "I remember building hay forts and having Nerf wars—"

"And swinging from end to end—"

"And playing tackle football. People couldn't believe that I played tackle football with my big older brothers and cousins. They all thought you were taking advantage of me."

"They had no clue how tough you are."

"Real tough." She frowned.

"You are. With everything. Always have been. Except for my mess-up this summer, nothing seems to faze you. Take this party, for instance. How you could organize this bash with a new baby, and without Janet's help, is amazing. You've done a great job, Debs."

"Thanks," she mumbled and blinked away encroaching tears. Why did his compliment make her want to cry again? She didn't feel tough at all. "I'm glad Joanna's okay."

"Yeah. Sounds like the surgery went well. Janet says she'll be home in a day or two."

"I'm glad you're home this weekend."

"You know I wouldn't miss this."

"But I didn't think you'd ever miss Thanksgiving, either."

Ricky's chest rose against her shoulder. "I didn't have much choice, knowing I'd be gone this weekend. My work won't go away if I'm not there, and now that Entenza's got me working with this new client . . . " He shook his head.

"The new client. Is that the one you were working with when you came for Lilly's birth?"

"The same. I thought that stunt would cost me my job, but you know what happened? This client was so impressed that I—that the corporation—would put family first, she decided we were the right company to handle her product. So, of course, Entenza's jumped on the family bandwagon and has been implementing family-friendly policies to ensure we don't lose the client. That'll last until people start taking advantage—well, I guess that's already happening, unfortunately. After Christmas it'll be work as usual."

"And you get a bonus out of the deal?"

"A nice little chunk, yeah." He grinned.

"I remember you telling me how impressed you were with her."

His grin flattened as he laughed. "Yeah. Was going to ask her out too, but then her, um" —He cleared his throat—"girlfriend showed up when I was about to ask her."

Debbie wrinkled her nose. "Sorry, Rick."

He shrugged. "I'm beginning to think I should give up."

"Like you could do that."

He chuckled. "It's a thought."

"When are you going back?"

"Sunday after church."

Her eyes widened. "Church?"

"Yeah, yeah, I know. Don't make anything of it. I promised Mom, that's all. Probably the best anniversary present I could give her."

Debbie laughed. "Probably. You'll be staying with them tomorrow night?"

"Right. Thanks for lending out your couch again." He rubbed his back and neck.

"Sorry. Someday, we'll get a new one."

"Hey, I'm just kidding."

"I know. I'm glad you're staying with us and not in town."

"Me too."

A comfortable silence surrounded them again. She hadn't felt this at peace for months.

"Are you happy, Debbie?"

Or she thought she was at peace. She should have known the question was coming. Tears grouped behind her closed eyelids, and her throat filled. She nodded, and then shook her head.

"Is that a yes or a no?" A smile filled his voice.

"It's an 'I don't know.' It's an 'I'm tired.' It's an 'I'm wishing I could be more like you.'"

Ricky laughed. "Oh, you better not let your brother hear that."

She opened her eyes and fingered away the moisture. "Well, it's true. Do you know how I've envied you? How I've wished, just for once, that I could let loose like you do? But no. I've always got to be Miss Perfect. Miss Reliable. Miss Steady and Strong."

"Don't forget peacemaker."

"And people pleaser." Oh, please. She slouched on the bale. So how come she couldn't make peace with her own family? Please her own husband? What kind of therapist was she anyway?

Ricky squeezed her shoulders. "That wasn't an insult. There's nothing wrong with—"

"Isn't there? I mean, look at you. Marcus thinks you're a—"

"A screwup. Yeah, I know."

"Well, those weren't my exact words."

"I'd say mine are more accurate."

"But you're not. I look at you and your life. You're having a ball. You've got the job of your dreams, you're not tied down to anyone or anything, you don't care what others think of you. Do you know what I'd give to have that kind of freedom? Just once, I'd like to have fun too. Just once I'd like to know what it's like not to have everyone expect me to be perfect all the time. It's too much pressure."

"I suppose Marcus and I shoulder the blame for much of that." Ricky rubbed his chin. "If we would try to get along, you wouldn't have to be the go-between. Still, no one expects you to be perfect."

"Oh, really?" She angled her face toward the timbered rafters and shook her head. "Do you know what the most rebellious thing I ever did in college was?"

He nudged her ankle with his foot. "The tattoo?"

"I love my tattoo, and look at the brouhaha I caused with that."

"That was pretty funny. I thought Mom and Dad were going to have a coronary. Marcus accused me of luring you to the dark side. All over one little lily we need a magnifying glass to see."

"So, you see what pressure I'm under. After that, I never dared step out of line. No one even knows that I TP'd the resident director's car. Whoopdy-doo."

His cheeks were sucked in as if trying to prevent a smile. Oh, yes, he was far too amused.

She'd heard stories about his escapades in college. Many of them made her blush. She didn't want that, did she? "Oh, and guess what I did on my twenty-first birthday?"

"I'm guessing you didn't chug twenty-one shots of tequila."

"Not even one. Nope. Not Miss Perfect. I ordered root beer while my friends got wasted, and I was the designated driver."

Ricky laughed out loud.

"See? Even you think that's pretty lame. I'm pathetic."

He squeezed her shoulders. "No, you're not. It's who you are. It's why we love you. You, my little sister, have set the example for me. I'd say that's admirable. Besides, you've one-upped me. Even I don't have a tattoo."

"Yeah, well . . . " It didn't make her feel any better. "Maybe I'm tired of being crammed into this perfect Debbie mold. Maybe, for once, I want to experience life outside this confining box." Oh, what she'd give to rebel. And maybe—just maybe Jerry would finally start seeing her again.

"Sounds like you need a break."

"Ya think?" Well, at least Ricky noticed. That was more than she could say for her husband.

"My offer's still open to come visit. Let Jerry watch the girls for the weekend—"

She laughed, hoping to stave off the tears. "Well that, you see, is the problem." She pulled her arm from her brother's back and stood. "I'll be lucky if Jerry's even around to watch the girls." Digging her fingernails into her palms, she strode to the other side of the loft.

She'd blown it now. Nobody was supposed to know that was what she feared. Nobody was supposed to know she was a failure.

The hay crunched behind her, before Ricky wrapped his arm around her shoulders. "I'm listening."

Well, I'm not speaking.

"Talk to me, Debbie."

She shook her head. "I can't. Please go."

He remained at her side.

Don't let him see you cry. Her body pulsed from the strain of holding in tears.

He kissed her cheek and squeezed her shoulders. "I'll be here when you're ready."

She nodded as his arm pulled away, and didn't move until she heard him land on the floor below.

At last, she could cry.

Chapter Forty

Debbie sat on a metal folding chair in the church basement and rested her feet on another as she watched her parents thank and hug the final departing guests.

Thank goodness, the party was over, and it had gone well. Maybe she wasn't such a failure. It had even been a good day. This morning, Jerry and Ricky had helped set up while Janet watched Lilly and Kaitlynn. Once guests arrived for the open house, Lilly was no longer a concern. Everyone begged to hold the newborn. She had never considered that the party would have built-in babysitters.

Even now, Lilly slept in a crib in the nursery. The baby monitor sat delightfully soundless on the table next to Debbie, and Kaitlynn had challenged Uncle Ricky to a duel of UNO®. From the way Ricky protested, Debbie could tell her daughter was winning again. She closed her eyes, and she actually felt . . . content.

A hand squeezed her shoulder. She opened her eyes as Marcus sat next to her.

"You did a great job, Debs."

"Thanks, I appreciate it."

"And thanks again for helping us at the last minute. I sure hated doing that to you."

Debbie waved her hand. "The bars even turned out good. Only a few got burnt."

"They were exactly like Janet's."

"Well, maybe not, but I'll accept the compliment anyway."

With a flushed face, Janet waddled over, her hand pressing into her lower back, and stopped next to her husband. "I'm ready, hon."

Marcus' mouth twitched. "Uh, yeah." He got up. "We've gotta get going. Janet's been having contractions all afternoon."

"What? And you haven't said anything?"

"They've been pretty far apart most of the day." Janet took deep breaths between words. "It's just been in the last half hour that they've become steady."

"Oh my gosh, then you better go!" Debbie grinned. She was going to be an auntie again!

"I hate to leave you ... " Marcus glanced around the fellowship hall cluttered with dirty plates, silverware, and leftover food, although there wasn't much of that.

"Don't even think about it." The mess didn't bother Debbie. It was all disposable. Not a big deal. "The boys'll help us clean up. We'll keep an eye on them. Now, go." She literally pushed her brother's back to get him moving.

"Thanks, Debs."

Still smiling, she watched the couple go to her parents and inform them they were about to get another anniversary present. Hugs were shared before the two took off.

"What was that about?" Jerry wrapped his arm around her shoulders. Even Jerry had been more nurturing today. Yes, this was a good day. Last night must have been a PMS moment or something. Today, she felt no depression whatsoever.

"You're about to become an uncle again."

"Really?"

"Yep. We can take care of things here, then go to the hospital, if that's okay with you."

"Sure thing." He kissed her lips. "I do love you, you know."

Her cheeks heated. When was the last time he made her blush? "Yeah, I know."

He kissed her again. "Why don't you have a seat for a second, I'll go coordinate our workers, okay?"

"Thanks, hon." She gladly obeyed him and sat back in the folding chair. Her eyes automatically closed, and her body slowly unwound.

It seemed only a second later when she felt someone shaking her shoulder. She opened her eyes and blinked. A hazy figure of Jerry stood in front of her.

"Hon, I'm gonna need your help."

Debbie blinked her eyes into focus and looked around the room. The tables remained up and were filled with the dirty dinnerware, but no one else was around. "Where is everyone?"

He smiled. "I sent them away."

"You did what?" Just like that, her good mood was stolen. How dare he? "Excuse me. We have all this help around and you send them away? Do you think I like to clean?" What was Jerry thinking? The anger and fear she felt last night resurrected.

He sat in the chair opposite her, smiling apologetically. "I'm sorry. I know you've worked hard on all this, and I know I haven't been there to help." He balled a hand and wrapped the other around it, cracking his knuckles. "Your brother and I had a little talk last night. He wasn't too pleased that I made his baby sister cry."

Tears glistened in Jerry's eyes. "I'm sorry, Debbie. Really, I am. I sent everyone to the hospital, so I'd have some time alone with you. Rick took Kaitlynn and the boys. I know it's not terribly romantic, but I wanted to grab the moment and talk."

"And Lilly?"

"Uh, she's still napping."

"Oh." She wanted to be mad. At Jerry for sending everyone away. At Ricky for spilling her secret. But she couldn't. To Jerry this was romance, and she'd grasp onto whatever she could get.

He pulled his chair close until their knees mingled. Taking both of her hands in his, he leaned in. "When's the last time we've had time alone?"

Forever. She leaned forward to meet him.

He pressed his lips to hers in a soft lingering kiss, and then rested his forehead against hers. "I'm so sorry."

Moisture from his eyes melded with her tears. He kissed them away, his tender lips caressing her cheek, her chin . . . her mouth. Mint flavored his probing kiss as he wrapped his arms around her back, pulling her tight against him.

It's been so long . . . With her heart pumping faster than it had for weeks, she pulled back and bit into her lower lip. "We are in a church, you know."

He grinned.

And what a gorgeous grin it was. Of course, this solitary moment didn't automatically make everything better, but it was a start, and she'd encourage it.

"Yeah, well, I don't think God minds one bit that I'm kissing my wife in his house. As a matter of fact, I think he's probably saying, 'It's about time.'"

Debbie laughed as Jerry leaned in again. She savored his kiss until the monitor squawked.

He stiffened and pulled away. His gaze settled on the monitor announcing Lilly's unmistakable newborn rasp. "I guess that's it."

"Yeah, I guess." They had a few moments anyway. It was better than nothing. And maybe this was the perfect time for father and daughter to bond. "Tell you what, I'll go get Lilly and change her. Then, you can feed her while I clean."

He stood quickly, knocking his folding chair over with an echoing clatter. "No. I should be the one to clean." He picked up the chair. "You go ahead, relax and feed her. It shouldn't take me too long to straighten the room. Once we're done, we can go see that new baby."

Her shoulders drooped. Why waste her time fighting? Fearful of doing or saying something that definitely would not be acceptable in God's house, or any house for that matter, she strode to the nursery.

Next week.

She picked up Lilly and snuggled her.

Next week, I won't be so easy on him.

THE WAITING ROOM WAS crowded with Brooks family members, and Debbie found several volunteers to hold a sleeping Lilly. Debbie eagerly handed the baby off to Grandpa Bernie then headed for Janet's birthing suite. Jerry followed close behind, but he'd never felt so distant.

This had to change, or she'd crack for sure, but now wasn't the time to address those changes.

She walked into Janet's room that overflowed with flower arrangements, balloons, and stuffed animals and eyed the newborn cradled in Marcus' arms. A perfectly healthy little girl with a head full of dark, wavy hair. A beautiful blend of mother and father. A mixture of pride and humility emanated from Marcus' bright eyes and crooked smile.

So, that was what a new father's face should look like.

Debbie heaved in a breath and smiled at the proud papa. "She's absolutely beautiful."

He grinned. "Some surprise, huh? A year ago, Janet and I

thought we were done. I was perfectly happy with that. God's amazing, isn't he?"

Debbie ran a thumb over the newborn's velvety cheek. "Amazing," she whispered so Marcus and Janet wouldn't hear her envy.

Jerry's hand rested in the small of her back as he too reached out to caress his niece. "Have you named her?"

"Jaclyn Marlene." Janet sat up and crossed her arms over her midsection. "Honey, can you get me a blanket please?"

"Sure thing." Marcus extended his arms, offering his daughter. "Would you like to hold her?"

Jerry's hand left Debbie's back. "I'd love to." He reached out, accepting Jaclyn.

What? Debbie's gaze whipped to her husband, but his eyes were focused on the perfect child. *How dare he?* She cleared her throat. "I need to use the restroom." With fists scrunched in tight balls, she strode from the room, not caring about making a scene. She hurried past her family in the waiting room, avoiding their stares, and aimed for the chapel. Not that she was in the mood to have a conversation with God, but the room would likely be quiet, if not empty.

She quickly found the chapel, and it was unoccupied, thank goodness. It would be so easy to curl up in a pew and fall asleep, shutting out her worries. Maybe she'd wake up to a doting husband willing to make some changes. Hah! Like that would happen.

But it had to happen. He ... they both needed to make changes. Marital problems were rarely a one-spouse issue, and as much as she wanted to blame their discord solely on Jerry, she couldn't. She was just as culpable as he was. Now to let him—

"Debbie?" Jerry's voice came from behind her. He sat beside her in the pew, and she blinked away tears she hadn't realized she cried. "What did I do now?"

Say what? She opened her mouth to punch him with all the things he'd done wrong, but held back. If she did that, he'd close himself off again. This discussion had to be about them, not him.

A wet sheen clouded his green eyes as she took his hand. "I'm scared." Her voice trembled. "I feel like we're sitting on opposite sides of this rock that's fractured in the middle. I'm afraid to lay more problems on you, because you're dealing with so much already, and one more thing might make you crack. But if I keep holding everything in, I'm the one who's going to crack."

He wiped a tear from her cheek. "Do you think it could be post-partum depression?"

Her eyes grew wide and her mouth fell open. He had to be kidding. Scathing, cutting words flew through her mind and wanted to fly from her mouth, but she managed to restrain them.

She did, however, tug her hand away from his. "Yes, that's a possibility." And it was. "But that's only part of the problem. You . . . we." She pointed to him then herself and gathered her thoughts. As a counselor, what would she recommend? "We have a problem. You and I. Not just me, not just you, but we, and we need to talk with a professional."

He shifted on the pew, his gaze looking everywhere but at her. "I don't know."

"I do know." She took his hand again. "Think about how we met. I was impressed with this teacher who cared so much about his students that he went way out of his way to research counseling centers to recommend to broken families. I knew if you cared that much for your students, that you'd do that much more for your own family, and Jerry, we're a very broken family."

He sighed. "I know."

Yes! Admitting there was a problem was half the battle.

"Have you looked at our finances lately? Even if I thought it would help, we can't afford it."

Argh! Did defeat have to follow every won battle? "We can't afford not to, Jer. There are programs—"

"Absolutely no charity."

"Fine. Then we go to Mom and Dad. Or Ricky'd help us in a heartbeat."

"I'm not airing our problems in front of your family."

"Is your pride more important than our survival?" She sniffled, and tears dripped down her cheeks. "I love you, Jerry, but I don't know that you love our family enough. Kaitlynn. Lilly. I don't know that you love me enough to fight for us."

Facing the crucifix and the front of the chapel, he shook his head. "Of course, I love you."

His body language contradicted his words, and that scared her more than the rest of this conversation. It took two to fight for a marriage, and right now she was the only one willing to go into battle. But she was willing and determined to win this war, even if that meant doing something she swore she'd never do. She prayed it wouldn't come to that.

Chapter Forty-one

*D*ebbie slapped the snooze button on the clock radio. It felt as if she'd just fallen asleep. That wasn't too far from the truth as Lilly woke up twice during the night. Probably too much excitement from the day before. But she slept now. Had been for two hours. If they didn't have to get ready for church, Debbie would sleep along with Lilly.

With a groan, Debbie sat up, stretched, and hustled to the shower. One hour to prepare herself and the girls for church didn't allow time for dawdling. The steam rolled around her, loosening muscles, hopefully washing off the anger her heart had stored since yesterday. Effective today, Jerry was no longer going to get a pass for stepping out on his family.

A knock on the bathroom door said her time was up. Much too soon. She dried off quickly and opened the door.

Jerry stood there, his mouth tight, and his scar flaming pink. "Thanks for leaving me some time."

"It's not that late . . . " She glanced at the bathroom clock. Thirty minutes? "I'm sorry. I didn't realize . . . "

"Well, you better get the girls going."

"Would it have hurt you to get them up?"

He raised his hands, palms toward her. "Let's not argue now."

"Right. Let's save it for after church." She slammed the door on the way out then cringed, listening for Lilly. Silence, thank goodness.

She slid on jeans and a Walmart sweater, rebelling against her parents' teaching of bringing your best before God. Tough. Ricky would laugh at that definition of rebellion. Well, for her, it was.

That left her with twenty-five minutes to eat breakfast and get the girls ready. It could be done. She'd done it before. Two minutes later, she'd downed a granola bar and a glass of orange juice.

Kaitlynn walked into the kitchen as Debbie put her glass in the dishwasher.

"Morning, precious." Debbie kissed her daughter on the top of her head.

"Morning, Mommy. I hungry." Kaitlynn crawled up on the fold-out stool that served as her table chair.

"One second. I'll get you some cereal."

"Can I have Lucky Charms?"

"Sure." There would go her Mother-of-the-Year award for feeding her child sugar. Hah, like she'd ever be a candidate anyway. Maybe Janet, but never her. Debbie poured cereal into a melamine bowl with Junior Asparagus painted in the bottom, and topped the cereal with one-percent milk.

"Grape juice?"

"Hm, hmmm." Kaitlynn nodded and stuffed a spoonful of cereal in her mouth. The marshmallows disappeared faster than the other pieces.

With a sigh, Debbie retrieved the grape juice from the fridge. Most other mornings, Debbie would have told Kaitlynn to eat both. Not today. She handed Kaitlynn her juice in a glass colored with Laura the Carrot's smiling face.

"Thanks, Mommy."

"You're welcome, precious." Her daughter was polite. At least

Debbie was doing something right. "You finish up, then have Daddy help you get dressed and brush your teeth, okay? I'll get Lilly up."

"I want you to help me."

"Sweetheart, not this morning. Please let Daddy help."

Kaitlynn slammed her spoon on the table. "I don't want Daddy's help."

Debbie fisted her hands on her hips. "Kaitlynn Nicole, you will not argue with me."

"But I want you!" Kaitlynn's arms flung upwards and came down simultaneously. One hit the cereal bowl, catapulting milk and cereal through the air. Her other arm toppled the glass, and grape juice streaked across the table. It cascaded over the table's edge, onto Kaitlynn's lap, and smattered onto the floor. Kaitlynn screamed and began crying.

With tension snaking through her arms like an electric current, Debbie jerked out a chair, sat, and crossed her fingers behind her head, pulling it downward. *Please, make her stop.* One . . . two . . . three . . .

Kaitlynn's cries became shrill.

"What's going on in . . . " Jerry said from behind her.

Lilly's cries added to the dissonant choir.

Debbie kept her head down. Eleven . . . twelve . . . thirteen . . .

"Kaitlynn Nicole." Jerry raised his voice. "That's enough."

Like yelling will really help. Sixteen . . . seventeen . . . eighteen . . .

Kaitlynn's chair clattered. "Don't hold me, Daddy!" Her cries turned into a seal's cough.

"C'mon, Deb, help me out here."

God, I can't handle this!

"Where's her inhaler, Debbie?"

He doesn't know? She raised her head. "Where it's been for the past two years." She shoved away from the table, stomped to the cupboard next to the fridge, and grabbed it off the top shelf. "Here." She thrust it into Jerry's hand. Let him deal with this for once. She returned to the chair, rested her elbows on the tabletop, and covered her ears again.

Lilly's cry grew shrill.

"I ... " Cough. " ... want ... " Cough. " ... Mommy." Kaitlynn's bark crescendoed as she wriggled out of Jerry's arms.

Heaving a sigh, Debbie's shoulders drooped. "It's okay, Jer. I'll take care of her."

"And what about the baby?"

"What about *Lilly*?" Debbie emphasized their daughter's name, as Kaitlynn crawled onto her lap. She hated yelling, but doggone it, she'd had enough.

Jerry held his hands out for Kaitlynn. "Kaitlynn, Daddy's helping today. Mommy'll take care of Lilly."

Her cough persisting, Kaitlynn clung to Debbie's shoulders.

"Let go, precious." Nothing would get accomplished with the girls upset. May as well get them calm, and then have the tired heart-to-broken-heart talk.

Crying and coughing harder, Kaitlynn shook her head.

"Now!" Jerry yelled.

Lilly's cry pierced through Debbie's head and heart.

If only she could join in. "Stop!" She heard herself scream as every cell in her body tingled.

"Sweetheart." Jerry laid his hand over hers, his voice saccharine. "Why don't you calm down?"

Calm down . . . Calm down? Right. Maybe his students bought that soothing voice, but not her. No way. How was she supposed to relax when everyone fought against her? If only she could run away for once, leave behind responsibilities.

Be like Ricky.

A laugh rose in her throat as an idea popped in her head. It was the perfect solution. "Fine." Her stress began easing away. "I'll take care of Lilly." She smiled, her syrupy voice matching his.

He raised his hands in the air. "What do you want me to do?"

"Take care of your daughter." Even with the racket her girls made, calm flowed through her body. Holding Kaitlynn, she stood and faced Jerry.

He opened his mouth and shut it.

"Precious," Debbie said firmly. "Go to your daddy."

Kaitlynn slid from Debbie's arms to Jerry's. Her chest heaving for breath amidst the tears, she pressed her face into her father's chest. For once, Jerry would have to handle it.

"You get the baby." Jerry carried Kaitlynn to the bathroom.

The baby . . . "Her name is Lilly!"

Debbie allowed Lilly to cry on as she picked up the phone and dialed 411. She had information dial the requested number for her as she wrote it down. Once that call was completed, she glanced at the clock. Church started five minutes ago. God understood she had to save her family today. Wasn't that an act of worship in itself?

She swallowed a deep breath before retrieving a pre-made bottle from the fridge. After microwaving it, she rescued Lilly, trying to ignore Kaitlynn's hack.

Within a few minutes of feeding, Lilly was content, and Kaitlynn's rasps decreased. Debbie raised Lilly to her shoulder, not even bothering to look for a burp rag. What difference did it make, anyway? Lilly released a juicy air bubble. Debbie kissed her daughter's cheek and lowered her to the other arm.

Lilly attacked the bottle.

Debbie couldn't remember her being so hungry before. She must have gotten in good exercise with her cry.

Gradually, the noise quieted, and Debbie closed her eyes, relaxing. If only it would last. It did, for maybe three more seconds, when Kaitlynn tugged on her arm.

"Mommy, I hungry yet." Debbie glanced at her daughter. The poor thing's face was scarlet, and still damp from tears. She breathed in and said as calmly as possible, "Ask your daddy politely. He'll help you."

"I sorry, Mommy."

Debbie kissed Kaitlynn's forehead. "I forgive you, precious. Now, go let Daddy help."

"Okay, Mommy."

Keeping her head down, Kaitlynn shuffled to the kitchen.

Debbie gritted her teeth. The strain between her and Jerry now affected Kaitlynn. It made sense, of course. This was what happened when two parents couldn't get along. Well, starting today, Jerry should learn his lesson.

A whistle came from the bottle as Lilly sucked air. She actually finished an entire bottle.

Debbie raised Lilly to her shoulder, patted her back, and was rewarded with a healthy burp.

It was time to restore her family.

She carried Lilly into the kitchen. Fear and anger clutched her throat, just thinking about what she had to do.

The Sunday paper was spread in front of Jerry, but his eyes were closed.

Kaitlynn sat across from him, her gaze fixed on her cereal bowl.

Don't back down. Debbie swallowed a breath, gathering strength. "Jerry."

"Yes." He didn't flinch a muscle.

"Look at me please."

His shoulders rose and fell before he raised his head. His face was red, too. Yes, she knew he loved her, and he obviously felt bad for this morning, but it wasn't enough. Their family needed more. She drew Lilly away from her chest and held her out toward Jerry.

He frowned.

"She's your daughter." Her gaze locked with his. "Take her."

Fear replaced the frown. "Debbie . . . "

"Take her." *No* wasn't an option.

His Adam's apple dipped as he reached for his daughter.

Lilly remained quiet, making the transfer easier than Debbie hoped.

He held his daughter loosely. Last night he'd cradled Marcus and Janet's baby girl.

"Precious." Debbie offered her hand to Kaitlynn. "Mommy'd like to talk with you for a moment, okay?"

With her lower lip still pushing outward, Kaitlynn slid off her stool and grasped Debbie's hand. They walked to Kaitlynn's bedroom. Debbie sat on the edge of the bed and pulled Kaitlynn onto her lap. This little talk was not going to be easy, but it was necessary not to scare her daughter. As for Jerry, perhaps what he needed most was a true scare.

"PRECIOUS, DO YOU UNDERSTAND what Mommy's going to do?" Probably not completely, but hopefully their little discussion helped alleviate some of Kaitlynn's fear.

Tears still trickled down Kaitlynn's cheeks. "I 'stand, Mommy."

God, why is this so dratted hard? Debbie kissed Kaitlynn's forehead and patted her bottom. "Okay, then, why don't you go finish eating breakfast? I'll be out in a minute. I love you, precious."

"Love you too, Mommy." With her lower lip trembling, Kaitlynn walked from the room, her feet clearing a path through the shag.

Don't back down now. Everything was going to be fine. Keeping silent, Debbie walked from Kaitlynn's bedroom to hers. She changed her spit-upon shirt, and packed a small suitcase. That done, she retrieved her winter coat from the living room closet, and grabbed her purse and keys off the kitchen counter. Her family hadn't moved, but their fear tingled the air.

"What are you doing?" Jerry tried to sound stern as he stared at her suitcase, but the quiver in his voice said he was frightened. Which was exactly what she wanted.

Debbie stood by the door leading to the garage. "I want you to know that I do love you. I don't feel it at the moment, but I do love you."

Jerry jumped up and stepped toward her. "Honey, I don't understand."

Honey? She reached behind her back, found the doorknob, and squeezed her fingers around it. This was the right thing to do. Her only option at the moment.

Just say the words.

She inhaled a deep breath and gazed into his misty eyes.

No backing down. Just say it.

"I'm leaving."

Chapter Forty-two

*J*erry's face paled. "You're what?"

"I'm leaving." There. She'd said it again. The very words she'd promised Jerry and all her friends and family she'd never utter.

But some promises weren't meant to be kept.

He clutched Lilly tighter as she whimpered, and he grabbed the back of a chair. "You can't." His whisper sounded like it passed over sandpaper.

Okay. He's adequately scared.

Ignoring Kaitlynn's sniffles, she handed Jerry a piece of paper with a hotel name and phone number written on it. "I'll be staying here, and I don't know when I'll be back." That wasn't quite true, she did know, but revealing her plans wouldn't scare Jerry enough.

He stared at the paper and crumpled it in his hand. Hugging Lilly to his chest, he stepped toward Debbie. "You're kidding me, right?"

"Oh, I'm dead serious." She backed into the door, keeping her hand on the knob, afraid if she let go, she wouldn't have the guts to go through with this.

He cuffed his hand over his smooth head and sighed loudly. "What about school?"

"I guess that's something you'll have to figure out, won't you?" She twisted the knob and turned toward the door. "I'm taking your car, by the way."

"Please, stay." He rested his hand on her arm. "Let's talk this over."

She released the knob and spun around, glaring. "Yeah, right. Like we tried three weeks ago? And yesterday? Last night? Like that did any good."

"Mommy, don't go, please." Kaitlynn sniffled and tears washed blotchy cheeks.

Debbie squeezed her eyes closed. She didn't want to scare Kaitlynn, but if she stayed in this house one more second, she'd surely lose her sanity. Inhaling a deep breath, she opened her eyes. "Precious, we talked about this. Mommy needs a little vacation, remember? Daddy'll be here all day and night." Debbie kissed and hugged her daughter. "I love you, precious." Kaitlynn grabbed on tight, but Debbie gently removed her arms and looked into her eyes. "I'll see you soon. I promise."

"I miss you, Mommy." Tears coursed down Kaitlynn's cheeks.

Maybe this wasn't such a good idea. But what else would catch Jerry's attention enough for him to act? "And I'll miss you, too. But you and Daddy will have lots of fun together."

Heaving labored breaths, Jerry touched Debbie's cheek. "Please."

Don't look at him. If she didn't take advantage of this opportunity now, she'd never have the courage to do it again. Without meeting Jerry's eyes, she kissed Lilly. "I love you so much, my calla Lilly."

Holding in her own tears, she turned to the door, curved her hand over the knob, and then turned back, still avoiding Jerry's eyes. "We'll talk when I'm ready. And then we're going to make an appointment with a therapist. Until then, I'm taking some time off."

"But I don't know how to—"

"You're a teacher. Learn."

She twisted the knob, opened the door, and left her family behind.

Finally, she'd get a true taste of freedom and hopefully save her family in the process.

WITH THAT FAMILIAR KNIFE cutting into his chest, Jerry stared at the door, waiting for Debbie to come to her senses, but his heart said she wouldn't. A similar scene had played out before. Nearly nine years ago. And just like then, he didn't know how to fix it.

Kaitlynn sniffled, her face flattened to the window, watching her mother desert them. She seemed to be handling it far better than he.

The pain in his chest sharpened, and he struggled to breathe. What would Debbie tell him to do right now? He slid out a chair, sat, and brought the baby to his knife-pierced heart. Breathe. That was it. In and hold. Out and hold. Inhale. Exhale.

Pray.

Pray?

How had he forgotten the most obvious solution? Jesus, please . . .

Excruciating minutes ticked past, and the pain slowly receded. After what felt like hours, he looked at the baby cradled in the crook of his arm. Her wide eyes stared up at him, seeming to see right through him into his heart.

So much like Debbie's eyes.

And like Debbie—or like how Debbie normally was—Lilly was content. How could that be when she didn't even know him? When he didn't know her? When he was scared to know her?

He ran his thumb over her cheek, and his mouth curled up. There was nothing like baby skin. Oh, Debbie was crafty. She knew precisely what this would do to his heart.

Kaitlynn still stood at the window, but her sniffles had subsided.

"Kaitlynn, come give Daddy a hug."

She turned around and looked down. "I don't want Mommy to go on a 'cation."

"I know. I don't either, but Mommy needs it. It will make her happy again. You'll see her again soon." Please God, please bring her home soon.

His first wife had never returned.

"Today, it's you, me and . . . " He looked down at the infant—his daughter. " . . . and Lilly." A name he'd never uttered before, afraid that by doing so, he would claim her.

And could lose her.

"We're gonna have a fun time today. Just the three of us. Why don't you go downstairs and ride your trike?" He stroked Lilly's cheek. "We'll be down in a second, and you can show me how good a rider you are."

She sniffled. "Okay, Daddy."

"That's my girl." He slumped in his chair as she walked down the stairs. Now what? He grabbed the phone off the counter, and dialed his in-laws' number. The answering machine picked up, as expected. They were most likely at church, right where his family would have been if he'd only opened his heart and eyes to see what he'd been doing to the people he loved most. Oh, he dreaded facing Debbie's family, but it was time to talk with a friend. "Hey, Rick, this is Jerry. Would you mind stopping in on your way to the airport? I need to talk."

JERRY WIPED HIS MOIST hands on his jeans, then opened the

door to see his brother-in-law. "Thanks for coming."

Ricky brushed past him. "What's going on?"

"Uncle Ricky!" Kaitlynn ran in from the living room.

"Hey Katydid." Ricky scooped his niece up and drew her into a hug.

"Mommy's taking a 'cation."

Thanks, Kaitlynn. Jerry kneaded the back of his neck.

"What?" Ricky pulled back, his dark eyes glaring at Jerry.

"Kaitlynn, Uncle Ricky and I need some time to talk. Can you go in your room to play?"

"But I—"

"No buts, young lady. And be quiet. Lilly's sleeping."

"Okay, Daddy."

"Have a seat." Jerry pulled out a kitchen chair. "Can I get you a drink? Coffee? Water?"

"I'll take a pop, if you've got one. Leaded. Yesterday was a long one."

Jerry pulled two Pepsi bottles from the fridge and sat down. He squeezed the bottle between his hands. "I guess Kaitlynn let it slip."

"Debbie's taking a vacation? What's that about?"

"She needed a break and took it."

"What aren't you telling me?" Ricky's voice rose.

Jerry stared down at the pop bottle strangled between his fingers. "She walked out on me."

"What?" Ricky slammed his closed pop bottle on the table.

"Keep it down. Lilly just went to sleep."

"What did you do?" Ricky lowered his voice, but anger came through clear as thunder.

Jerry sighed, scratched his head, and relayed the morning's events. "So, what do I do now?"

"Isn't it obvious? You go after her."

"No. That's the last thing she'd want."

"Are you kidding me? She's begging you to love her."

"And I'm going to love her by giving her some freedom. That's the one thing she's complained about since Lilly was born. She doesn't get a break."

"Is that true?"

"We've got an infant and a toddler. Ask your mom how much of a break she got when all of you were little."

"But she doesn't want a break from you."

"Oh, I think she does. Right now, I'm the last person she wants to see." Jerry took a drink. "I've been absent from her life for a long time."

"That's what I thought." Ricky fingered his bottle. "We've all let her down, haven't we?"

Jerry backhanded dampness from his eyes. "I need to make this right, but I don't know how. It's killing me, letting her go. I have visions of Francine running out on me. Letting Debbie have this time away is the one thing I know I need to do, but it scares me to death." He stared down at his knuckles, cracking them one at a time, and whispered, "What if she doesn't return?"

"She will." But the quiet way Ricky spoke didn't fill Jerry with confidence.

He drew his arm over his eyes and sniffled. "What do I do?"

Ricky sighed. "You won't like this."

"Doesn't matter. I'm not giving up on our marriage. I love her."

Silence, then another sigh. "Call Mom and Dad."

Jerry groaned. Ricky was right, but Jerry hated the idea of airing his marital problems out in front of the whole Brooks clan. "I don't know."

"I think you'll find my family loves to help lost sheep. I should know."

As much as Jerry hated the idea, he still nodded. "Maybe it's time we learned to lean on others."

He'd do anything to bring Debbie back home. And keep her there.

Chapter Forty-three

Grinning, Debbie dropped the shopping bags on the king-sized bed. She certainly didn't need a bed that large, but it was all the hotel had available. Aw shucks. She'd have to suffer through it. She glided to the window overlooking Nicollet Mall. Just like she'd have to suffer through admiring the view of downtown Minneapolis with the Holidazzle floats, covered in bright Christmas lights, just beginning their procession down the Mall. She couldn't hear the music, but still enjoyed this unique visual perspective. She could see why Lee had chosen this hotel.

Would she see him?

A flutter winged through her belly. She hugged herself, hoping to eradicate the wayward feelings, and stared out the window.

I wish you were here, Jerry. A few years back, the two of them had taken in the parade from street level. They'd huddled together beneath a blanket, sipping hot cocoa to keep warm in sub-freezing temperatures made colder by wind whipping between the buildings. Now that was romance.

Next year, maybe. With the girls. They'd love it. They'd love Macy's animatronic holiday exhibit too. The Santa at the end of the show could have passed for the real thing. Maybe they should make a trip down here yet this winter, create some positive memories for this Christmas.

Maybe.

If her running away would finally scrape the rust from Jerry's heart.

She remained at the window until the parade marched out of sight, and then she turned her attention to the bags on the bed. A pinch of guilt niggled at her as she sat among the purchases. Never had she spent so much money at one time. But Christmas shopping was done now, and all in one day.

She withdrew items from the bags, refreshing her memory. Yes, she'd gone slightly overboard with her gifts to Kaitlynn and Lilly. Maybe she should return some. Jerry was going to have a fit when he saw the toys and clothes. She withdrew tiny jeans with the *Hello Kitty* emblem on the back pocket. Rebellion surged in her heart, just as it had when she got the tattoo. Didn't she deserve to have what she wanted for once? So what if Jerry threw a fit? She wasn't returning a thing.

Especially not her black pantsuit. She pulled the jacket, skirt, and pants from the Macy's bag, along with a red scalloped shell. She'd actually left the department feeling good about herself. Ricky might even approve of this purchase. She looked at the tag and winced. At half price, this outfit cost her at least four times what she usually spent on herself.

But this was a practical purchase. Not a luxury. She needed something dressy for church, for Christmas. Something that would last, that she'd like herself in. She folded the suit and set it beside the bag. At this price, it would have to last several Christmases.

Beneath the suit were the girls' matching Christmas dresses: red crushed velvet with soft lace around the necklines and hems. White lace tights matched the lace on the dresses perfectly. Shiny patent leather Mary Janes, with polished silver buckles, completed the ensemble. Total extravagance.

Another pang of guilt. But why should she feel guilty? She'd always been frugal. Always. What was wrong with going overboard for once in her lifetime? Even Ricky would approve. Wouldn't he?

Nope. No doubting. She reached into the bag one more time and pulled out the final indulgence. Godiva chocolate. Jerry probably had to work nearly two hours to pay for this one pound of candy. She ran her fingernail under the lid breaking the seal, and raised the cover. An intoxicating aroma of chocolate escaped into the room.

Her stomach growled, demanding to be filled. She hadn't eaten since this morning, but she ignored her stomach's plea for the truffle. Save it for later. It would be the perfect thing to top off the evening. After supper, of course. She'd return to the room to watch a movie of her choice: a grown-up movie—not a cartoon, not an adventure, maybe a chick-flick. Life couldn't get better than good chocolate with a movie.

But for now, it was time to find real food. The bar downstairs served a full menu along with its drinks. The Sunday night football game should be showing. It wasn't any fun to watch a game by herself. She'd go down and sit among strangers and root for whomever her gut told her to cheer for. Jerry didn't like football, but he usually suffered through it for her sake. Tonight, she'd enjoy it without him.

From another handled bag, she picked up the shirt she'd purchased for the night. It didn't scream "Mom," but wasn't too young, either. Debbie slipped off her faded maroon and gold sweatshirt. Yes, she deserved to treat herself to something new. Something nice.

She pulled the blouse over her head and dared to look in the mirror. Her reflection smiled back. When was the last time that had happened? The lady at the makeup counter had given her wonderful tips on how to accentuate her positive features without appearing phony. For once, she looked in-style, wearing the silky top. The V-neckline created the illusion of a long, slender neck. Material hung loosely from the empire waist, helping to conceal her post-pregnancy stomach.

She raised her arm and pinched the tag off, then stole a quick glance at the price. Another clearance rack item, thank goodness. Full price was downright scary. The clearance price was bad enough.

So now a quick brush of her hair, and she was ready. To think she'd gotten dressed in a matter of minutes without a single interruption. This must be heaven, and she didn't plan to return to earth until tomorrow. By then, she'd be prepared to calmly talk to Jerry. She prayed he'd finally listen.

JERRY TOOK LEFTOVER BEEF and gravy out of the fridge. Good thing he had extras from the party, or he'd be eating macaroni and cheese again. Spending all day placating both girls left little time to do much else, and he still had homework to correct.

No wonder Debbie had begged for a break.

But that still didn't excuse her for walking out on him like this. Or did it?

He spooned beef and gravy on a plate and placed it in the microwave, then pulled a bowl of pre-cut vegetables from the fridge and put them on the table. Thank God for leftovers. Never again would he complain about a meal. Now, if he and Kaitlynn could eat before Lilly awoke, he'd be satisfied.

He tugged open the basement door. "Kaitlynn. Supper."

"Coming, Daddy."

He kneeled at the top of the stairs and held his arms open as she ran up.

With a bright smile, she accepted his hug.

He picked her up and kissed her cheek. "I love you, punkin."

"I love you too, Daddy." She returned the kiss.

At least Kaitlynn had forgiven him. Now to convince Debbie that he was eager to work out their differences.

He set Kaitlynn on her stool, put two slices of bread in the toaster, then sat next to her. The day calendar on the table glared at him. October. Had it really been that long since they'd turned the pages? Since before Lilly was born? No wonder they were in trouble. He picked up the calendar and tore off the pages, the days they'd neglected. He couldn't recapture what he'd missed. From here on in, he was moving forward. No more looking back. No more living out his losses. Starting now.

He glanced down at the verse for today. "Do nothing out of selfish ambition or vain conceit . . . " Philippians 2:3.

Had he been selfish? He excused himself from the table and plucked his Webster's Dictionary from the shelf below the television, from right next to where the family Bible lay frosted with dust. They used the dictionary too often to collect dust.

He stuck his finger in at the "S," flipped it open and paged to his word. "**self-ish** (sel'fish) *adj*. 1 Too much concerned with one's own welfare or interests and having little or no concern for others; self-centered."

No one had ever accused him of being selfish. He snapped the book shut. No one but God. And now his favorite tool, the dictionary.

Perhaps he'd confused the word with "conceit." No, he wasn't conceited, but selfish? Letting his pride convince him not to seek professional help? That was something to think on. To pray about.

He put the dictionary away then sat in the recliner. His briefcase stood next to it. Inside were dozens of papers awaiting correction, homework he'd given for the sake of keeping the students busywork that would give him an excuse to avoid his family in the evening and on weekends. The decision hadn't been a conscious one, but it was still a choice.

How was he any different from his dad? The man who'd physically abandoned a wife and child so he wouldn't have to face his mistake.

Emotional abandonment was just as bad.

Was Jerry any different than the self-centered, disrespectful students who filled his classroom? How could he expect them to act any different when he modeled the very behavior he resented? No wonder teaching had become a chore.

He glanced at the kitchen table where Kaitlynn sat patiently. He'd never seen her so still, but then her mother had never left her before. Amazing how fear will change a person.

Could God take away his fear and restore him? His marriage? His family? There was one way to find out. He returned to the table and sat in his chair then held out his hand for Kaitlynn.

She eagerly accepted it.

"I pray, Daddy."

He nodded and smiled. "Go ahead."

"Dear Jesus, please be with Mommy on her 'cation. I miss her, and Lilly misses her, and Daddy misses her, and thank you for our food. Amen."

Not a thread of selfishness in her honest prayer.

"Amen," Jerry repeated with a smile that dulled as Lilly announced she was awake. He gazed down at the warm food on the platter and shook his head. *So, this is how Debbie must feel.* Before getting the baby, he filled Kaitlynn's plate with beef and corn, cutting the meat into bite-sized pieces. Then, he prepared Lilly's bottle and hurried to stop the grating cries.

He massaged the ache numbing his arm as he entered her room. Would accepting this child always be so difficult?

Her arms and legs flailed, kicking the blankets away from

pudgy legs still enclosed in fleece footy pajamas. He hadn't bothered to dress her for the day. How did Debbie do it all?

With the exercise Lilly got from this cry, she certainly wouldn't be cold, but he wrapped her in a receiving blanket before lifting her from the crib. Pain shot through his heart as he pulled the infant close to his chest. *Please God, not now.*

Her sobs immediately eased up. She trusted him? Why? He'd given her no reason.

The pain in his chest ebbed away as he returned to the kitchen and removed cold toast from the toaster. As long as she was quiet, he'd hold her and eat. It usually worked for Debbie. Balancing Lilly, he tried buttering the toast then threw the knife down. Only Debbie could do three things at once. He carried the bread to the table and smothered it with beef and gravy then stuffed a bite into his mouth.

As he chewed, he glanced down at Lilly. It was amazing how two daughters could be so different. When Kaitlynn was a newborn, she rarely wanted to be held. This child clearly loved the intimacy inherent in the Brooks gene.

He cut off another piece and brought it to his mouth, but his appetite vanished.

He'd deprived his daughter.

Of his touch

And his love.

"Lilly," he said the name softly, laying claim to her. Nausea coated his stomach, and he dropped his fork on the plate. In his fear and selfishness, he'd deprived Lilly, and Debbie, of the very thing they needed most. Worst of all, with Lilly it had been intentional.

He wrapped both arms around his daughter. *My daughter.* Flesh of his flesh. *Lilly.* Loving her was absolutely worth the risk of getting hurt.

Chapter Forty-four

"Thank you." Debbie accepted the menu from the hostess, who was dressed all in black, with the exception of a red tie. "Thank you." What luscious freedom this was to sit at a table with no screaming children and no growling husband. And to be surrounded by flat-screen televisions broadcasting football and basketball games. Pure heaven. She'd pass on basketball, but football? Sweet. Now this was living, Ricky Brooks style. No wonder he seldom returned home to Hicksville, Minnesota.

She looked down at the menu and grimaced at the prices. Too bad she didn't have just a smidgen of her brother's bank account to go with this one day of freedom. Yikes. She could treat her whole family to an evening out at Dairy Queen on what this place charged for one entrée.

"Can I bring you something to drink?"

Debbie startled at the server, also dressed in black with a touch of red. "A Pepsi, please." *Pepsi?* How lame was that? Wasn't today about letting go of the Debbie everyone knew? About living for once? "No. Wait."

"Care for something else?"

Biting into her lower lip, she picked up the drink menu and glanced through it. What was it Janet loved? Something mild. A strawberry something or other. "What is that strawberry drink?"

"A daiquiri?"

Strawberry daiquiri? That must be it. Say yes before exposing her naiveté. "Yes. I'll have a strawberry daiquiri instead of Pepsi."

"Our specialty is a chocolate covered strawberry daiquiri, or we have a chocolate-strawberry-caramel swirl that's unbelievable."

Chocolate, caramel, and strawberry. Her mouth watered just thinking of it. It had to be delicious. "Oh, that sounds heavenly. I'll try the swirl."

"Would you care for an appetizer to go with that? I highly recommend the crab dip."

Debbie wrinkled her nose. No seafood. She preferred her dad's fresh water sunnies or walleyes. "No, I think I better stick with just the entrée."

"Certainly. I'll bring your drink right out."

She grinned like a twenty-one-year-old anticipating her first adult beverage. How pathetic that at the age of thirty, she'd never finished a mixed drink. She'd tasted them before, but had sworn off alcohol. How many families had she counseled because of alcohol problems?

But what was one drink? That never hurt anyone, and wine flowed throughout the Bible. Besides, she wasn't driving anywhere. It was about time she grew up.

She studied the menu again. The drink most likely wasn't cheap, and she'd blown enough money today. Best to go with the old stand-by.

The server returned carrying a funnel-shaped glass that looked like a piece of artwork. The funnel swirled to a narrow stem perched on a circular base, and a chipped-ice design etched the crystal. The flute alone was beautiful, and the Christmas-red drink, with twirls of dark chocolate and brown caramel on top, looked delectable. A chocolate-dipped strawberry garnished the glass's rim, which was coated in bitter chocolate. If it tasted as good as it looked, she'd be in paradise.

"Are you ready to order?"

Debbie nodded. "I'll have a cheeseburger. Cheddar. Medium rare." She fingered her glass. A hamburger would probably spoil its taste, and she wanted to savor every drop. It would be a very long time before she'd have another. Save it for very special occasions.

"Can you bring the burger after halftime?" She wasn't even that hungry. Probably because she'd escaped the stress for the day. If only she could do that at home, she might be losing baby weight instead of gaining more.

"Certainly. Would you care for a salad?"

Salad? She wrinkled her nose again. During her pregnancy, she lived on limp greens. The thought of more curdled her stomach. Besides, this was a vacation. May as well eat dangerously. "No salad, but I'll have waffle fries." Tomorrow, after downing the box of Godiva tonight, she'd finally start that diet.

The server smiled and left without writing anything down. How was that possible?

Debbie's gaze fell to her drink and apprehension stirred in her gut. How silly was that? She swallowed a breath and blew it back out. It was time to grow up. She raised the glass to her lips and downed a healthy sip. Her body froze, and her eyes crossed. This was mild?

Slow down, girl. She raised her glass and took a little sip, swishing the liquid in her mouth before letting it burn down her throat. *Whoa.* She shook her head again. If this was mild, what was a strong drink like?

But it did taste good.

Leaning back in her chair, she turned her attention to the football game. San Diego was kicking Dallas. She loved watching Dallas lose. Apparently, so did many of the bar patrons as a cheer rose up when Dallas fumbled the ball on their own five-yard line. She cheered along and smiled. Being bold felt good. She downed a healthy sip this time. Oh, this was delicious.

By the time the San Diego entered the end zone, right before halftime, her glass was empty.

The server picked up her glass almost as soon as Debbie put it down. "Would you care for another?"

Debbie looked at the empty goblet and smiled. "Sure, why not?" Why not shed every remnant of naïveté and be a real human being for once? She giggled and covered her mouth. Where had that come from?

Within a few minutes, the server returned and put the daiquiri on a square napkin advertising the eating establishment. "Your food will be up shortly."

"Not a problem. I've got lots of time." Lots of time, all to herself, with no one crying or whining or complaining or begging to be waited on. Instead, she was the one being served. Life couldn't get sweeter. She should have done this ages ago.

Debbie lifted the drink from the napkin. This time it flowed down smooth and easy. All these years she'd cheated herself by becoming a Puritanical prude. Jerry would slip into teacher mode and call that a redundancy. Alliteration, too. That's what she got for marrying a teacher.

A teacher she missed terribly.

Sucking on tingling lips, she set the glass on the table and stared down at it, rotating the stem between her fingers, watching what was left of the liquid splash up along the sides like a lava lamp.

A cheer resounded in the bar. She glanced at the television

and blinked a couple times before it came into focus. Halftime was over? Already?

With her napkin, she patted away the prickle stinging her lips as a San Diego player streaked for the sidelines only to be tackled after five yards, a kick-off return that left his team in an eighty-five-yard hole.

Like the hole her marriage was in.

Tomorrow, she and Jerry would begin their upward climb.

Today, she sat in a bar, alone, drinking. Could she fall any lower?

No, she would not let tonight become a downer. It had been too good of a day for that.

The server set the cheeseburger and waffle fries in front of her.

"Would you care for anything else? Another drink perhaps?"

Debbie glanced at her drink and grimaced. It was nearly empty. She hadn't drunk that much, had she?

"I'll have water, please." The bill would be bad enough as it was.

She cut the burger in half and took a bite. It felt awkward going over tingling lips, but it tasted pretty good. It had better at this price.

A flash of heat coursed through her body. She picked up her cloth napkin and fanned herself. They should turn down the heat in this room. She downed her daiquiri hoping the frozen drink would cool her down, but her body temperature only increased, along with her heart rate.

"May I buy you another?"

Debbie shook her head, startled by the familiar male voice. She blinked her gaze into focus. "Lee! I wondered if I'd run into you." She gestured to an open chair. "Please, join me."

"I'd love to." He sat across from her. "You changed your mind.

You should have called and let me know you were coming. I'd have met you earlier."

"Well, it was a spur-of-the-moment thing. I decided you were right, and I've had a marvelous day." She giggled.

"Good evening, sir." The server returned. "May I get you a drink?"

"Sure. Bring me a martini and refresh whatever my lady friend is having. Oh, and I'll take an order of chicken tenders with barbeque sauce."

"Right away."

Lee reclined in his chair, crossing his arms below his chest. "You look different today."

Her face heated even more. "A good different?"

"Absolutely. It looks like your day off is agreeing with you."

"It is. I've needed this for so long."

"Everyone deserves a break once in a while. Even moms and dads."

"I hear ya. I didn't realize how much I needed one." A giggle rose in her throat. She covered her mouth, but the laugh still escaped as their drinks arrived. Debbie raised her glass. "I discovered a new favorite today."

He clinked his drink against hers. "To freedom."

"To freedom." She took a long sip this time.

Fanning herself, she put her glass down, trying to center it on the moving napkin. "You think they could turn the heat down a bit." Her stomach churned.

Lee rested his elbows on the table and his chin on his hands. He nodded toward her plate. "It might help if you eat some of your burger."

She blinked, and his dark hair and broad shoulders came into focus. "Oh. Right." She looked down at her meal, and her stomach flip-flopped. One would think she'd be hungry after not eating all day. She picked up the burger and took a small bite. It was missing something. She put it down and lifted the bun. No ketchup. She squeezed a dollop on her burger and tasted it. Much better. She chased that with another sip of her drink.

Heat flashed throughout her body, and her heart rate quickened. She wiped her forehead. "Lee, did she bring me water?"

He put the glass in her hand. "Are you okay?"

"I don't know." She took a long sip then placed the glass back on the table and watched it teeter before regaining its balance.

Oh, no. She'd done it, hadn't she? With her stomach churning, she pushed her plate aside, and laid her head on her arms. How could she be so stupid? Seconds later, she felt Lee's hand on her back.

"Here, have some more water."

Groaning, she raised her head.

He handed her two glasses. No make that one.

She reached for it and missed.

Lee shoved it in her hand.

I am so stupid. She dabbed her napkin in the water and wiped it over her face as Lee returned to his seat.

"I'm shorry, Lee." She giggled then her lip quivered. Oh, man, what was wrong with her?

Through her cloudy gaze, she saw Lee smile.

"You don't drink, do you?"

"N-never." She giggled again and shook her head. Oh, big mistake. How could she be euphoric and depressed at the same time? She laid her head back onto her arms.

"I think it's time to get you to your room."

"But my bill?" That Jerry would never forgive her for.

"I'll take care of it for now." He waved for the server.

"No—"

"Consider it my treat for watching Amelia."

She nodded, and a tear trickled down her cheek.

After paying, Lee rounded the table and assisted her up. He braced his arm around her back, and she leaned into him.

Jerry, I need you. I'm so sorry.

"What's your room number?"

What was it? Six something. Yeah. "It's room six, uh, six-thirteen, I think."

She let him lead her away, wanting to forget all about this night.

DEBBIE ROLLED ONTO HER side, curled into the fetal position, and moaned. Nature called her to the bathroom, but then she'd have to move again, and that was the last thing she wanted to do. She needed a drink—water—badly, as shreds of cotton floated around her mouth, embalming her tongue, coating her throat. Then, again, getting a drink involved moving. She tried to open her eyes but the pulsating pressure in her head and in the back of her neck stopped her. Her whole body shook.

Moving deliberately, she crossed her arms in front of her, wrapping her hands over her shoulders to stop the chill, and realized she was dressed only in her underwear. Even under the covers, she felt naked and exposed. Where were her pajamas?

And, where was she? This wasn't her bed. It wasn't home. That much was certain. A faint hum of voices sounded in the background. The stench of vomit penetrated her nostrils. Wherever it was, she shouldn't be here, and she needed to go home.

She needed her girls.

She needed Jerry.

Lifting a single eyelid, she peeked through her lashes. Why had no one told her that eyelashes felt pain? Moving her head in the slightest of motions, she scanned what was in front of her. A wall. A drab, beige-papered wall with an orchid print centered on it.

Nature's call urged again. Wherever the bathroom was, she better find it in a hurry. She began uncurling her legs. They didn't break off. Good sign. She tugged up the second eyelid.

"You okay?" A deep voice spoke in front of her, echoing in her head as if he'd yelled. She rotated her neck, turning in the direction of the voice. Her eyes still refused to focus, but she saw his outline sitting at the foot of her bed.

Dark hair and broad shoulders wrapped tightly in a T-shirt.

Oh, dear God, what have I done? Her supplication reached upward as incomplete obscure images from the day before splashed through her brain.

Meeting Lee in the bar.

Him escorting her to her room.

Removing her clothes . . .

Her heart thumped rapidly.

No. Please, no.

All she wanted was a day away, one day to shed her Minnesota-nice image, to live a day unplanned and uncontrolled.

Oh, she shed that image, all right. Rather, she shredded it, into a million, unfixable pieces.

Her eyes struggled to focus on the figure in front of her, the man who clearly wasn't her balding, slight-shouldered husband.

Would she ever be able to return home?

Chapter Forty-five

 *J*erry pushed an arm into his coat sleeve and looked up at the clock. Seven fifteen in the morning. Would he get there too late? His mother-in-law stood in his home's entryway, bending down to remove her boots. "Kaitlynn's a late sleeper." He slipped his other arm into the jacket. "Lilly, now I'd expect her up most anytime. I've got formula mixed in the fridge. I don't know if Debbie'll be happy or jealous to know her daughter slept at least five hours. Lilly's never slept that long before."

Five whole hours, and he felt like a walking zombie. No wonder Debbie begged for a break, and she'd endured over six weeks with lack of sleep. He had one night. Look at the measures she took to get a few hours to herself.

Well, it worked. She certainly grabbed his attention. His and the rest of her family. He didn't know who her family was more upset with. Him or Debbie. Marcus would probably find some reason to blame Ricky.

"Thanks again, Mom, for watching the girls." Jerry clasped the doorknob. Marcus would be wrong. Ricky bore no fault in this mess. In fact, Ricky had been right. Jerry should have followed Debbie. He never should have let Debbie go off on her own in the first place, especially in her frame of mind. She'd needed him, but he hadn't been man enough to go after her.

Could he undo the harm he created through his fear and self-centeredness?

Marlene smiled and hugged him. It wasn't her usual bright, affirming smile. This one uncovered her concern. "I wish Debbie would have told us how she was feeling."

His problems had affected the whole family. "Well, you know how she is. She wouldn't ask for help if she was gonna fall off a cliff. She'd either figure her way out of it or fall."

Wasn't that what happened yesterday? But did she fall, or did she dive? He'd find out soon enough.

"And so, we don't offer help, either? I should have known. She's my daughter."

"Yeah, well, don't be too hard on yourself." He crunched his knuckles in his palm. Was this how normally obedient children felt when sent to face their school principal? He hadn't just let Debbie or his girls down; he'd proven to his in-laws he was exactly the man they presumed him to be in the beginning. It was time to show them, he didn't intend to keep playing that role.

"I'm the one who created this problem in the first place. I can assure you, I will make it up to your daughter. I never meant to hurt her."

Marlene's smile showed assurance. She placed her hand on Jerry's arm, much in the same way Debbie did when offering support. "We trust you to do what's best."

"Thanks, Mom." They'd trusted him before, too. Now he needed to re-earn that trust.

DEBBIE'S BREATH QUICKENED AS she pulled the blankets over her head, and vomit climbed up her throat. There was a familiar feeling. She vaguely remembered filling the ice bucket last night while he held it for her.

A hand tugged at the top edge of the blanket.

"It's okay," he said softly.

She squeezed her eyes shut as the voice played in her head, and warm relief coursed through her veins.

Thank you, Jesus!

She edged the blanket past her chin and blinked him into focus. "Ricky." She tried to smile, but that hurt too.

He sat next to her, taking care not to bounce too much, and rested the back of his hand on her forehead. "No fever."

"Do fevers usually come with a hangover?"

He grinned. "Not usually."

"Oh."

"So, you're feeling it this morning."

"I'm feeling every molecule in my body, and every one of them is screaming 'ouch.'"

"Well, this should help a bit." He handed her a glass of water and a couple of aspirin. "But not much considering you're not used to it."

She secured the blanket around her upper body and sat up, accepting the medicine.

While she gulped it down, he tucked pillows behind her back.

"Why would anyone want to get used to it?" This would never happen again.

His smile turned wry as he massaged the back of his neck. "Good question."

She closed her eyes, trying to will the ache away. Tears gathered beneath her lids, it hurt so badly. Thinking about telling Jerry made it throb more. What would he think of her when she confessed?

Ricky worked his arm around her back, and he tucked her head against his shoulder. "It's okay," he said softly.

"No, it's not." She shook her head, and then regretted the action. "It wasn't supposed to happen."

"I'm sure not." He caressed her arm. "But judging by the amount of food left on your plate, I gather you hardly touched your meal."

"You saw my plate?"

"Yep, and from what your friend tells me . . . By the way, I meant to tell you, this guy friend of yours . . . "

Guy friend. She groaned and covered her face with her hands. That rendezvous last night never should have happened. No, she hadn't planned it, not consciously anyway, but she hadn't discouraged it either.

"When, I came into the bar last night and saw you leave your table, leaning on him, well, let's just say my intentions toward him were not kind. But he recognized me, from when I picked up Kaitlynn after you had Lilly, and waved me over. He explained what happened. I have to admit, I found myself respecting the man."

"Really?" And here she had thought Lee had taken advantage of her. How low could she get? She owed Lee a huge apology. Some Christian witness she turned out to be.

"He's the one who reminded me to eat, I mean, I hadn't eaten all day. I suppose that had something to do with how I'm feeling." Man, she was stupid.

Ricky chuckled. "Oh, that definitely had something to do with it."

"Still, it's a mild drink—"

"Mild? Sweetheart, I tried some of what you were drinking, and let me tell you, it's not what I'd call mild."

"But it's what Janet likes. She says there's hardly any alcohol in it."

"What you had was not a Margarita."

"No. It was a daiquiri."

He chuckled again. "That explains a lot. Janet likes

strawberry Margaritas, not daiquiris."

"What's the difference?"

"A little bit of tequila, and a whole lot of rum, and the bartender didn't skimp on the rum."

"Oh," she said, more to herself. and pulled the covers up over her head. "I am so stupid."

He pulled the covers back down. "You are far from stupid. Maybe a bit naïve—"

"Just a bit?"

"Okay, very naïve, but that's nothing to be embarrassed about. If I met a woman with half your naiveté, I'd be happy."

"Like that makes me feel any better." She pulled the blanket back over her head and felt nature's call again. It wouldn't be ignored any longer. She slowly rolled the blanket down, keeping her gaze on the blanket's edge, heat rising in her cheeks. "Uh, Ricky, where'd my clothes go?"

Please, don't let his answer embarrass us both.

He walked to the entryway and returned with a plush, white robe. "I'm having the hotel clean them. You got a little sick on them last night."

Her shoulders sagged as she backed into the pillow. "You didn't . . . "

He handed her the robe. "Nah. I hid in the bathroom."

Thank God. At least she had some remnant of dignity left.

"You'll feel better if you shower. I'll run down and get us some breakfast."

"Then we can talk?"

"That's why I'm here."

DEBBIE COMBED HER FINGERS through her wet hair, pulled it back for a ponytail, and then released it. Even that hurt. Blinking, she stared into the bathroom mirror. The bright lights made her tender eyes water. There would be no makeup today. No fancy clothes. No more hiding from who she was. Yesterday had been an escape into vanity. Today she suffered the punishment for that escape.

She opened the bathroom door and peeked out. The television was tuned to ESPN, talking football. The clock read nine seventeen. Only forty-three minutes left until checkout. Nearly time to go home and face Jerry, but first she'd cherish the few moments with her brother.

He sat reading a newspaper by a round table tucked in the corner of the room, with his hand curved around a bottle of Pepsi. On the table was a bottle of 7UP and chocolate covered old-fashioned donuts. Her favorite. Not now, though. Nothing appealed now. Maybe later. But the 7UP would probably go down well.

She rested on the edge of her bed and downed several ounces.

Ricky peered up as she settled.

Her gaze avoided his as she squeezed the bottle. "Thanks, again, Ricky."

"I've always told you I'm here for you."

"Yeah, I know." She shook her head, and her eyes crossed. Sudden movements were not good. "But why are you here? Weren't you flying home yesterday? Don't you work today?"

He laid the newspaper flat on the table, and turned his chair toward her. "I never made it home."

"I don't understand. How did you even know where I was?"

"Well, you've got a husband, who loves you very much by the way, who asked me to stop by your house before I left for the airport. He told me about your, uh," he cleared his throat. "Your conversation yesterday morning. Let's just say, I wasn't too happy with him for letting you go. I told him to follow you. He said *no*. That it wasn't what you'd want." Frowning, Ricky scratched the tip of his nose.

Debbie brought the blanket over her lap and fiddled with the edge. "He's right, you know. I wanted nothing to do with him yesterday. I needed time for myself. He needed to get to know his daughter." She sighed. "Today, he won't want to have anything to do with me."

Ricky smiled. "I think you'd be surprised. Jerry understands more than you think."

"I sure hope so."

"He does." Ricky took her hand. "But he didn't react the way I wanted him to. I'm not saying whether that's right or wrong. It's not what I would have done."

"It's not what you did."

"Yeah, well, it took me a while to make the right decision, too. I got to the airport, checked in, went through security then, when my flight was boarding, I decided I couldn't go home. I caught the light-rail to downtown."

"Does Jerry know you're here?"

"He does now."

"What else does he know?" Her stomach churned again.

"I couldn't lie to him, Debbie."

"No. I suppose not." She sighed and wiped her eyes. How could she do this to her family? "I'm a terrible mom."

"Debbie—"

"A terrible wife—"

"Would you stop that?" He dropped her hand, stood, and walked to the window.

Debbie stared at his back. "Kaitlynn was coughing just before I left yesterday. What kind of mom does that? I didn't even call to see if she was all right." When had she become such a despicable person?

Ricky turned around and crossed his arms. "Isn't Jerry

capable of taking care of her?"

Debbie shrugged. "I guess."

"And you left the number where you could be reached?"

She shrugged again.

"Has Jerry been around every time Kaitlynn's had an attack?"

Debbie shook her head.

"You don't have to take on everything." He sat and took her hand again. "Kaitlynn's fine."

"Are you sure?"

He nodded. "Lilly is too. Jerry's a big boy. He can handle it on his own."

"I guess I need to learn that."

"I guess you do."

She bit into her lower lip and peered at the corner of the room, opposite the table. "I have a little more confessing to do." She folded her hands between her knees and nodded toward the bags lined neatly against the wall. Ricky must have done that for her too. "I went a tad overboard, yesterday."

All the guilt she'd shoved down yesterday clawed its way to the surface. "I'm gonna have to spend the afternoon returning things."

He glanced at the bags, then back at her. "Why?"

"Why? Because we can't afford it, that's why. I put everything on plastic. I don't know what I was thinking. I mean, I don't do that."

"Don't return it."

"You don't understand, do you? As it is, we'll have to dip into our savings to pay for this stupid stunt. Christmas is going to be meager this year."

"No, I mean, let me cover it. The whole weekend. Consider it an early Christmas gift."

"I can't let you do that. This is my mistake. I need to face the consequences."

"Aren't you already?"

"Sure, but there's more."

Ricky dropped her hand. "I know I've been poor about going to church, but I still remember the Bible talking about pride, that it leads to destruction."

"Yes, but—"

"But nothing." His voice rose. "It's about time you learn to accept help."

Great, now she'd made him angry. She lay down and closed her eyes. Why was it easier to punish herself than to accept his offer? "Can I think about it?"

"As long as the answer turns out to be yes."

"You're impossible."

"Love you too."

A knock sounded on the door. Must be maid service. Well, it was almost time to check out.

"I'll get it." Grinning, Ricky walked to the door.

If she felt better, she'd have whipped a pillow at him, but her reactions were far too slow.

She sat up and threw the blanket off. It was time to return home and plead for forgiveness.

Chapter Forty-six

*J*erry rubbed his palms on his jeans while waiting for the door to open. If Debbie answered, what would he tell her? Would she slam the door on him? Would she talk? Would she listen?

The door opened and Jerry looked up at Ricky's scowling face. A scowl Jerry had put there personally. It felt as if he were going on a first date again and was meeting the father for the first time.

Jerry held out the keys to the minivan. "Third floor. D12."

Ricky nodded but said nothing as he accepted the keys, grabbed his carryon from inside the door, and walked down the hallway.

Inhaling a deep breath, Jerry stepped into the room and wheeled his suitcase behind him. Straight ahead was a wall lined with shopping bags from stores they couldn't afford to walk into, much less purchase from. Ricky had warned him, but it was still a surprise. It was so un-Debbie-like.

He stepped past the bathroom into the sleeping area.

Debbie sat on the edge of the bed with her back to him. Her head was lowered, and her shoulders hunched. She always carried her tall frame with confidence.

God, help me restore that confidence.

He walked to the end of the bed, leaned over, and touched her arm. "Debbie?"

She startled as she looked up. Her shoulders straightened, and she smiled, then she looked away, but not before he noticed the shame pervading her bloodshot eyes and blotchy cheeks. This wasn't his Debbie at all.

But was he the same man she'd married? The one who confessed his sins when they began dating and assured her it wouldn't happen again?

Clearly, he'd been wrong. The stranger his wife had become was his creation. Now it was up to him to repair what he'd altered.

He laid the suitcase at the foot of the bed, and sat next to Debbie, leaving a good foot between them. His fingers ached to be cracked so he cuffed his hands over his knees. "I'm sorry, honey."

Turning, she scanned the room. "Where's Ricky?"

"He's giving us some space."

"Oh." Her shoulders drooped. "I'm the one who's sorry. I don't know what got into me."

He tightened the grip on his knees. "I think I do."

Her shoulders lifted and fell with her deep breath. "Yeah, well . . . "

"Sweetheart, let me do the talking here for a bit, okay?"

She nodded, keeping her head down.

Contrition time. "I asked for this. You taking off like that made me realize I was doing it all over again. I was letting fear control me, and I locked you out."

"But that's not what upset me. Lilly's your daughter, Jerry, and you wouldn't even recognize her. It was like she wasn't even there."

"Because if I acknowledged that she was there . . . " His voice broke. "I might love her, and I can't bear to lose another child I loved."

"But she's fine. Her heart's fine."

"I know. My brain knows. But ... " He massaged the ache budding in his chest.

"But what?"

Breathe in. "Christopher wasn't supposed to die." Exhale. He sniffled, and Debbie pulled away. Would she never understand? Disappointed, he glanced at her.

But she smiled, handing him a handful of tissues, and leaned into his side as he wiped his nose. "I'm listening."

Lord, please help her understand. "I didn't have the will to take down the crib after Christopher died. If I did, it would have acknowledged that Christopher was gone." He brushed a tissue over his eyes. "I couldn't deal with his loss, and Francine couldn't handle my retreat. She lost two people when he died. I lost the two people I loved more than anything, and I literally felt the hurt in my body."

Like now, as a sharp pain seared his chest. Just breathe. Blow out. Inhale.

He rubbed his arm, hoping to restore feeling. "I'm terrified of going through pain again. My heart tells me that if I love Lilly, she'll leave. She'll be just like Christopher. Those thoughts aren't rational, but something inside of me keeps saying if I love her, she'll die."

"That's what panic disorder does. Which is why you need to get professional help, and that means you need to see someone other than me." Debbie placed her hand on his arm.

Oh, how he missed that. "I'm realizing that. Your walking out forced me to hold Lilly and to care for her. How could I not love her now?" He dried his cheek. "And I love you, too. I do. You're right about needing help. I want to do whatever it takes. Just your breathing technique has made it better, but if there's more I can do, I'm going to do it. Take meds. Even go see a therapist.

You're way too important for me." He put his arm around her back and pulled her close, breathing in her minty shampoo.

"Thank you." She kissed his cheek. "And I'll be right beside you." Her fingers dug into his arm. "It's my turn to confess. I really messed up, Jerry."

"It's about time." Rubbing his chin, he glanced at the packages in the corner. He'd driven her to this. "It's hard to measure up to you when you're perfect all the time."

"I'm not perfect."

"But you try to be."

"We all do."

"But you forget about grace, especially for yourself."

She nodded at her purchases. "I think that's what Ricky was trying to teach me."

"Your brother's smart."

"I know."

His gaze lifted to Debbie's mouth. When was the last time he'd kissed her? A kiss demonstrating his love.

But she needed more than a kiss. More than physical intimacy. "I brought something with me." He leaned over, zipped open his carryon, and pulled out their daily Bible reading and the family Bible, now dust-free. "I've been leaning on you to keep me strong. No wonder you snapped." He flipped open the Bible reading. "I've let our foundation crumble. It's time I assumed the spiritual leadership God commands me to take. "

She hugged him, her tears dampening his cheeks, then pulled away and glanced toward the bed stand. "I've got to check out."

His lips curled into a smile. He'd have a hard time paying Ricky back for this favor. "Not until tomorrow morning."

"What? What about Ricky? The girls? Your job?"

Jerry placed a finger over her mouth. "Ricky's gone. He's bringing your van back home—"

"Ricky's driving the Mommy van?"

Grinning, Jerry nodded. Too bad he didn't have a picture of Ricky in it. "He's going to help your mom watch the girls tonight. He decided to take advantage of the new family-friendly policies at work and take a few more days off."

"But we can't afford it."

"When we get home, we'll tell your brother thank you."

Chapter Forty-seven

*D*ebbie stepped from the garage into the house and Kaitlynn tackled her with a knee hug. Oh, what a glorious feeling. She swooped her daughter up and kissed her nose. "I missed you, precious." She didn't think she could miss her daughter so much, but she wouldn't trade the past thirty-two hours with Jerry for anything. They'd talked and argued and cried and loved each other enough to agree to talk to a marriage therapist, on top of him seeing a psychotherapist. Their family was far too important not to make every possible effort to become healthy.

"Six o'clock. It's about time you got home." Ricky stood in the archway, looking so natural cradling Lilly in his arm. "How a small body can create such a noxious odor is beyond me." He wrinkled his nose, but his eyes and mouth smiled.

Please God, give Ricky his own child to love. And a wife first, of course.

Debbie passed Kaitlynn off to Jerry, who'd come in behind her, and reached for Lilly.

"She slept six hours last night."

"Six?" Debbie stared down at her peaceful daughter. "No way." Ricky grinned.

"That is so not fair."

He shrugged. "Mom stayed overnight, but then she had to go

to coffee with Dad this morning." He tousled Kaitlynn's hair. "We've had a good day. Katydid even likes my mac-e-cheese and tuna combination."

"It was yummy, but Uncle Ricky made a mess."

Ricky tickled her tummy. "Hey, squirt, you're not supposed to say anything."

"A mess, huh?" Debbie smiled and kissed Lilly's cheek. Oh, she'd missed that too.

"The kettle boiled over. You know you should never leave me alone in the kitchen."

She laughed. Her brother was the only person who could make her look like a gourmet chef. "I bet the stove's cleaner now than when I left."

"Could be."

Kaitlynn wiggled out of her daddy's arms and clung to Ricky's leg. "And I beat Uncle Ricky in UNO®."

"Yeah, the little stinker beats me every time." He patted the top of her head.

She giggled. "I'm not a stinker. You said Lilly is."

Everyone chuckled.

"Katydid also introduced me to *The Incredibles* last night. That mom was amazing." Ricky's face turned serious. "Reminded me of someone else I know."

Debbie rolled her eyes. She had a long way to go before she could be compared to that elastic mother who held her family together. "Thanks for your help."

"I enjoyed it. The girls and I had lots of fun, but I'm afraid I've had all the fun my job will allow for a while."

"You gotta go?"

"The boss isn't happy but hey, I had other priorities." He glanced at his watch. "Dad'll be here within the hour to pick me up. I think he's looking forward to some father-son time."

"Are you?"

"Sure. Why not?" His frown said otherwise. Ricky looked at Jerry. "But, before Dad gets here, would you mind if I take a walk with your wife?"

"Go ahead. The girls and I need to get reacquainted." Jerry reached for Lilly. "Come to Daddy."

Debbie couldn't contain a smile as she handed over their daughter. Wariness still rested in his eyes, and it would take a while for his emotions to catch up with his actions, but at least he was willing to work at it. She couldn't ask for more than that.

Kaitlynn tugged on her uncle's pant leg. "Can I come, too?"

"Not this time, Katydid." Ricky patted her head and sat down to put his boots on.

Debbie placed her shoes in the box by the door, and put on her boots. Old ones, of course. Moon boots from the eighties. So what if they were out of style. They were tall and warm and, in Minnesota, that was what mattered. She pulled her gloves from her jacket pocket and led her brother into the garage. "I have something to show you."

As the door closed behind them, she pointed at the completed granite project still sitting beneath her workbench. "What do you think?"

He removed his gloves and ran his hand over the top where a cross, formed of the darker stones, stood out against lighter shades of granite. "You did this?"

"All by myself." And plenty of whispers from God.

"It's beautiful. I never realized you had 'artist' in you."

"I didn't either. Mom must be rubbing off on me."

"Well, you can't ask for a better influence."

"I agree." With Christ back at the center of her marriage, no doubt she and Jerry would be celebrating forty years together someday too. She kicked at one of the wooden legs supporting her project. "Would you mind helping me bring it outside?"

"Sure." He grunted as he hefted an end. "Whoa, this thing's heavy."

"Which is why it's still sitting here." She grabbed a flashlight off the workbench, stuffed it in her jacket pocket, then hoisted her end and let Ricky back out of the garage into the backyard.

The sun had disappeared long ago. Clouds hid the heavens, but the snowflakes wafting down looked like millions of floating stars.

Closing her eyes, Debbie breathed in and listened. She loved the peace, the silence of this small town where you had to strain to hear man-made sounds. As much as she'd wanted to emulate her older brother, after a day of experiencing the supposed freedom of his lifestyle, she wouldn't relinquish the serenity of small-town life for the chaos of the city. If that was freedom, she'd rather be caged. *Please God, let Ricky see past the clouds. Help him to see your stars again.*

Her muscles began to squawk, and she glanced ahead. Just a few more yards to go. She could do it. Her muscles squealed louder. Well, maybe she should listen. "Mind if we rest for a second?"

"No problem."

They set the project on the ground and sat side by side on it. His hand rested on her arm. "Will you and Jerry be okay?"

Her mouth tipped into a half smile. "Yeah, we'll be fine. We did a lot of talking the past few days." And a lot of making up, too. Ricky didn't need to know that intimate detail. She bent down, gathered a handful of snow, and sat back up, patting the snow into a tight ball. "In the long run, I'm sure this'll make our marriage stronger." She placed the snowball next to her on the bench where, left unattended, it would eventually fall apart or melt. Her marriage was too important to be ignored. "Bet you never figured I'd be the one in our family who was totally screwed up."

Chuckling, he patted her shoulder. "Or maybe you're the only one who'll admit to it."

"True. Now, if I could get you and Marcus in to see a counselor, we'd be a happy family again."

His laugh was sarcastic. "If he trusted me, I might consider it."

"Maybe you need to give him reason to trust."

He pulled his hand from her arm and crossed his arms over his chest. "I didn't accept any payment from Marcus' friend. That's what I wanted to tell you tonight." His jaw shifted. "I know what Marcus is saying, that I came in here and cost people their jobs, but the business was dead already. I couldn't revive it if I ran it myself. Especially in this economy." His eyes bore into hers. "What was I supposed to do? Lie to the guy? What would Marcus have said if his friend had gone into bankruptcy? This way his friend could get out and save face. I even offered to write recommendations for the employees."

"I knew that." At least she wanted to believe it at the time. Now there was no doubt. She'd have to let Marcus know. Ricky would never tell him. The truth wouldn't bring her brothers together, but Marcus should know it. Maybe the next time a rumor spread, Marcus would be more discerning.

Ricky shook his head. "I knew I shouldn't have taken the job. Thought maybe I'd get back in your brother's graces. It was a lose-lose situation."

"Someday, you guys'll work it out."

"I want to. Really, I do. I know what it does to Mom. Dad." He sighed. "Janet."

"You."

Someday, they'd all come together. In the process, she hoped he wouldn't hurt himself too badly falling off his horse again.

Yes, he'd fall again, like they all did. Like she did. But next time, after spending much more time on her knees, she'd be prepared to help him up.

She clapped her hands on her thighs. "Ready?"

"If you are."

Together, they hoisted the project, and she nodded to the corner of the yard. "Just beyond the garden, we can put it down."

They walked past where the sunflowers had stood only a few months ago, to the pie-shaped open space pointing north. "Right here." They settled it so its top corners kissed the white-flaked grass.

"A bench, huh?" Ricky shook out his muscles. "Couldn't be a better place for it."

"Well . . . " Debbie switched on the flashlight and shone it on the granite. "That was my intention."

"Not anymore?"

"Here, let me show you something first." She led him around to the front of the garden, to Kaitlynn's walking path, and aimed her flashlight's beam on the stepping-stones Kaitlynn had decorated. "Remember when you took me for that walk years ago, after Grandma died?"

"Yeah . . . "

"We do that now. As a family. Or at least we did . . . " It was time to renew the tradition. She shone the light on the stepping-stone topped with green stars.

"Kaitlynn decorated these. Each step represents one of our senses as Kaitlynn understands it." Debbie turned off the flashlight and the stars glowed.

"Kaitlynn thought of this?"

"Yep. She wanted it to be like your place. You keep telling her you see stars twinkling below and above."

"Wow," he said under his breath.

Debbie turned on the flashlight and highlighted the next stone covered in orange juice lids.

"Taste?"

Debbie laughed. "You'd think so, wouldn't you?"

"No?"

"They make music. It's percussion."

He chuckled. "Makes sense."

"Absolutely. Now this one." Debbie trained the light on a stone imprinted with Kaitlynn's and Lilly's hands touching.

"This one I understand." Ricky knelt and fingered the impression. "You sure you want this outside? This is quite the keepsake."

"I made two."

"I should have known that."

Debbie smiled and skimmed the beam along to the red step with fruit embedded in it.

"Now this one's taste, right?"

"Yep. JELL-O. Her favorite dessert." She floated the light to a stone covered in yellow tulip and white calla lily petals. "And I think you'll find this one quite special."

Again, Ricky knelt and touched the stone. "Are these the flowers I gave the girls?" His voice choked.

"Um, hmmm. We had another stone made up with just lilies before you gave them the flowers. Kaitlynn insisted we make a new one for her path."

Ricky clasped his hands in back of his head and heaved a sigh. "She's one special girl, isn't she?"

"She is. Kids can be so much wiser than adults."

"Tell me about it." Ricky stood and stepped over the stone, not on it, then stopped. "Six?"

"Of course." Debbie grinned.

"Interesting." With eyebrows raised, he knelt by the final step.

"An inhaler?"

Debbie squatted next to him and rubbed her hand over the plastic case that had once held Kaitlynn's medicine. "Oh, there are six senses, but this one, most of us take for granted. Have a guess?"

She tented her hands beneath her chin as he stared down.

"Breath?"

"You've got it." She fingered the inhaler. "For someone with asthma, and even for people like Jerry who suffer panic attacks, breathing isn't so natural. For them, getting air into their lungs is an experience just like touch and taste are for us."

"Kaitlynn came up with this?"

"Need you ask?"

"Wow."

"If you think about it, Christians have this sixth sense, the breath of God—his Holy Spirit—moving in us."

He puffed out air then pointed at the granite bench they'd carried from the garage. "Now you'll explain?"

"Right up until yesterday, it was meant to be a bench." *Give me the words, Lord, to help him see you again.* She knelt in front of it, clasping her hands over the inlaid cross. "God had other plans."

Ricky squatted next to her. "An altar."

"Um, hmmm. A place where I can come and bow before God and lay everything at his feet. Just like we're doing now." She passed her hand over the granite fragments she'd grouted together. "Looking back on these past months, I've learned how easy it is for granite to break apart. When the foundation's uneven, it's easy for rock to chip."

"Yeah, so?"

"My foundation, my faith. I didn't lean on it. In my quest to be self-sufficient, to never ask for help, my foundation became rocky. Every little thing that happened over this past year has been slowly chipping away at me. I couldn't take the pressure anymore, and I finally cracked. But Jesus mortars all our broken pieces together. From now on, when I want to use my hammer to pound out frustrations, I have to remember that a certain carpenter promised to carry the load for me. I don't have to do it alone."

"And it's our fault for not seeing this in you. Always wedging you between me and Marcus, asking you to stanch our bleeding relationship. You put on this stoic mask to show us how strong you are. It's our fault for not seeing that you're as human as the rest of us."

Debbie crossed her arms.

He pried them apart. "It's okay to ask for help."

"I know." She sighed. "But I hate being needy, especially when I can do it on my own."

"Just because you can, doesn't mean you should." Ricky curved an arm around her shoulders. "It's okay for Spock to show her human side once in a while."

A giggle bubbled out.

"And, as you full well know, the rest of us are all too human. Jerry's not always going to be perfect. The girls are going to drive you nuts. I won't always be around."

She peered up at him, sensing an emptiness in his words, something deeper in his statement, and it scared her.

He looked outward. "But, as you say, there is someone who's always there, someone to walk with you, to be strong for you."

God, he's remembering. "Are you saying that for yourself as well?"

Ricky shook his head and stuffed his gloved hands into his coat pockets. "It's different for me." Frowning, he gazed upward. "God and I haven't been on speaking terms for a while."

"You could change that, you know."

"Tonight isn't about me." Bitterness infused his voice. "Sorry." He inhaled a deep breath then forced it back out. "You said yourself that things are going well for me and they are. I love my life. I don't want to change it. I'm asking you to respect that."

"But . . . "

Give him to me. Let me carry him. God's voice spoke to her heart.

Biting into her lower lip, she stared at the snowflake stars and dried her eyes. Lord, he's all yours.

She pursed her lips in a half-hearted smile and rested a hand on Ricky's arm. "I'll respect that."

"I know your faith is important to you. You need God." He nodded upward. "I guess I wanted to remind you."

This time her smile was genuine. "And I thank you for that reminder. But I'm not going to stop praying for you."

Ricky stood. His breathing was pronounced as if he were holding back tears. "I wouldn't want you to." He offered his hand. "Shall we go?"

With a nod, she stood and looped her arm around his. They walked back on Kaitlynn's path where sunflowers once glowed, and butterfly flowers once robed themselves in regal purple. Past rose bushes formerly laden with thorns, and strawberry bushes that bore heart-shaped, blood-red berries in summer's heat. They walked past the row where bleach-white alyssum used to release a honey-like fragrance.

Always stepping *over*, not *on* Kaitlynn's stepping-stones . . . those individual steps that could slowly pull Ricky away from the heavenly Father, or draw him closer.

It was his path to choose.

It was her job to pray.

DEBBIE THUMBED TEARS FROM her cheeks as she stood by the kitchen window watching her brother get in the car with her father. Father and son would have some necessary alone time together. Shoot, she was going to miss him.

A lullaby drifted from a back room. Kaitlynn must have asked for more music. Jerry always obliged, even though he and Uncle Ricky had serenaded her earlier, with Jerry grimacing as he tried, unsuccessfully, to hold Ricky on-key.

Kaitlynn loved it. The poor child was probably as tone deaf as the rest of the Brooks family. Hopefully, Lilly would inherit the Verhoeven music gene.

Her dad's Oldsmobile rounded the corner and disappeared. Why did it feel like Ricky had turned a corner in his life, taking those steps further away from his faith?

Well, he was in God's hands. Ricky had to learn this lesson on his own. She prayed the lesson wouldn't hurt too badly.

Jerry's soft melody lured her from the window, easing her hurt. It drew her through the living room to Kaitlynn's bedroom. She opened the door and peered in. Kaitlynn lay in bed, sound asleep. No sign of Jerry.

Her brows furrowed as the song summoned her to the nursery. She stopped in the doorway and covered her mouth, hoping Jerry didn't hear her gasp.

Tears followed the gasp as she listened to the wondrous symphony of father singing to, and dancing with, his daughter.

"You're my precious girl, created in love. You're a special child, a gift from heaven above. When you are sad, I'll sing you a song. When you are glad, I'll laugh right along. When you are weak, I'll carry you. I'll be your strength. I'll walk with you."

Debbie glanced up at the ceiling, imagining the stars God placed above, and gave thanks, hearing God's voice in Jerry's words, singing just for her.

"He gives strength to the weary

and increases the power of the weak . . .

but those who hope in the Lord will renew their strength.

They will soar on wings like eagles,

they will run and not grow weary,

they will walk and not be faint."

(Isaiah 40:29, 31)

Additional Books

IN THE COMING HOME SERIES

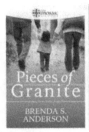    

Chain of Mercy

Memory Box Secrets

Hungry for Home

Coming Home, a short story

A Christmas Homecoming, a short story

(Coming Soon!)

Dear Reader,

Thank you for joining me on this novel journey. We live in a world where self-reliance and self-sufficiency are lauded, as they should be. Readers love stories about strong women, and I do as well. The problem comes when that self-sufficiency, that strength, takes the place of our reliance on God. The saying "God doesn't give us more than we can handle" sounds good, but I disagree with it. As Debbie and Jerry learned, God continually gives us more than we can handle on our own, and that forces us to rely on Him. When we don't, when Christ isn't our firm foundation, then our lives will crumble. But isn't it marvelous that He is our foundation!

I hope you will continue to follow Debbie and the Brooks family in the remaining three books in the Coming Home series. CHAIN OF MERCY is about Richard's return-to-faith story, a journey of forgiveness. You'll find the first chapter at the end of this book. Books three and four in the series are also available, as well as a Coming Home Series short story. Debbie also makes an appearance in A BEAUTIFUL MESS.

If you enjoyed PIECES OF GRANITE, I'd be grateful if you spread the word and posted a review on popular book review sites.

Again, thank you for taking this journey with me!

Blessings,
Brenda

Acknowledgements

As a fan of roller coasters, I should certainly appreciate this writing journey ride with its ups and downs and sharp twists and dark tunnels! But no ride is fun when you go it alone, and I certainly haven't been alone.

Shortly after I completed *Pieces of Granite*, I was assigned to a critique group within ACFW (American Christian Fiction Writers) along with Lorna Seilstad, Shannon Taylor Vannatter, and Jerri Ledford. This group was a true blessing from God. I learned more from them about the writing craft than any other class I've taken or book I've read. With their generous help, my writing matured into something worth publishing. But best of all, I've gained life-long friends.

Speaking of critique partners and friends, I have to thank Stephanie Prichard who never lets me get away with misplaced commas and overused words, and makes certain that all my scenes have a purpose.

And Stacy Monson—this has been a wild ride, hasn't it? Although I think we'd both appreciate fewer hills. Thank you for listening to my praises and my gripes over Caribou hot chocolate. You help keep me sane.

My dear crazy-for-Jesus friend, Kelly Jo Yaksich, your energy and enthusiasm are contagious, and I love how you live your life full-out as a demonstration of Jesus' love. You set the bar very high, my friend! Thank you for joining me on this ride. I'm blessed by your support and encouragement and prayers.

To my first readers Debbie Berglund, Lisa Laudenslager, and Sandy Pippo. You're very courageous to read those first ugly drafts, and I'm grateful for your encouragement and prayers.

To Lisa Miller – Thank you for helping me understand the

triumphs and the trials of being a parent of a child with Down syndrome, and for showing me what a true blessing your beautiful daughter is.

Thank you, Ashley Weis, for giving me this opportunity to get my stories out there. I am forever grateful. And thank you George Weis for creating beautiful covers that immediately grab the reader's attention!

To my large, terrific Bryant family: know that the feuding brothers in this book were not modeled after you. Rather, you all show the beauty of growing up in a large family.

And that family extends to my in-laws and their extended family, all who have welcomed me and have offered amazing encouragement on this writing journey.

Sarah, Bryan, and Brandon—being your mom has been an awesome privilege. It's a joy watching you grow up into caring, Christ-loving adults. I can't wait to see what you all do with the artsy gifts God gave you!

Dear Marvin, you believe in me when I have little faith in myself. I love your passionate enthusiasm for my stories. You are a blessing!

And to the One who gave me this gift and won't let it sit unused. It's a tremendous privilege to write for You, and all glory goes to You!

ABOUT THE AUTHOR

 **Brenda S. Anderson** writes gritty and authentic, life-affirming fiction. She is a member of the American Christian Fiction Writers, and is Past-President of the ACFW Minnesota chapter, MN-NICE, the 2016 ACFW Chapter of the Year. When not reading or writing, she enjoys music, theater, roller coasters, and baseball, and she loves watching movies with her family. She resides in the Minneapolis, Minnesota area with her husband of 30-plus years and one sassy cat.

LET'S CONNECT

Visit Brenda online at www.BrendaAndersonBooks.com and on Facebook, Goodreads, Instagram, and BookBub.

For news and encouragement about upcoming books, contests, giveaways, and other activities, sign up for Brenda's bi-monthly newsletter: http://brendaandersonbooks.com/subscribe/.

If you enjoyed *Pieces of Granite*, please consider leaving a review. Your words bring hope and encouragement to the author, as well as other readers.

Other Books

BY BRENDA S. ANDERSON

The Potter's House Books

Where the Heart Is Series

Find all of Brenda S. Anderson's books at:

www.BrendaAndersonBooks.com/books

Coming soon to

THE MOSAIC COLLECTION

A Star Will Rise:
A Mosaic Christmas Anthology
Coming November 4, 2020

Take a peek inside

CHAIN OF MERCY

Book 1 in the *Coming Home Series*
by *Brenda S. Anderson*

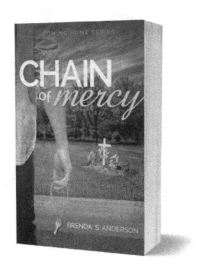

Chapter One

"The good news is that the company only lost a million this quarter." Richard Brooks smirked at his assistant and slapped the quarterly report down on her desk.

"That's the good news?" Verna stopped typing and turned to him, propping a hand on her hip, her Southern accent always a welcome sound in this sea of nasal New Yorkers. "Young man, in my day people didn't make a million dollars, much less lose it. Now, tell me, if that's the good news, what's the bad?"

He stared at the Picasso print above Verna's desk. Reminded him of his life. "It looks like we're going to have no choice but to close the Phoenix plant." How had he missed the unmistakable signs of its mismanagement? Now, because of his lack of foresight, hundreds of people would lose their jobs. In all his years in New York City, he'd never made such a costly blunder.

"Goodness. And you're blaming yourself. I can see it in those beautiful blues of yours."

"I should have seen it coming months ago. All the signs were there."

"It just so happens you've had a few other things on your mind lately."

The muscles in his cheeks tightened. "I'm not paid to think of other things."

"You stop putting yourself down. It's time I see that gorgeous

1

smile again."

He chuckled. "Happy?" Only Verna could make him smile under these circumstances.

"That's more like it. Now for my good news." She handed him several pink message slips. "Your wonderful family is sending you love and birthday greetings. There were two very disappointed little ladies by the names of Katydid and Lillykins who couldn't wait to talk to you."

"I missed their call?" He peeked at his watch. Not enough time to call them back now, but definitely later. They always brightened his day, and today he could use some sunshine.

"They called about ten minutes ago and told me to make sure I gave you this." Verna reached beneath her desk and pulled out a shoe-sized box covered in Little Mermaid wrapping paper and what looked like an entire roll of tape.

His Katydid's work most likely. He accepted the box and shook it. A slight rattling. They probably used an overabundance of tissue paper too. He tore at the paper, revealing a shoebox. He lifted the cover and grinned. Just what he expected. Nestled among balled tissue paper were several plastic toys from kid's meals. He pulled out a Spider-Man figurine and moved its arms. This one he'd center on his desk.

"Those darling girls love you, you know."

"Not as much as I love them." He replaced the toy and covered the box. They'd be perfect additions to his shelves back home. He'd keep his favorites on his desk here at work. His colleagues could scoff all they wanted.

"Then when are you going to take a weekend off and go see them?"

Oh boy. Here it comes. "I saw them at Thanksgiving."

"Which was seven weeks ago."

He massaged the back of his neck. "It's not like Minnesota is right next door."

Verna poised her hands on her hips. "And it's not like your bank account doesn't have a few dollars, not to mention frequent flier miles to spare for plane tickets."

"And when do I have spare time to fly out there?"

"I'm very glad you asked." She struck a key on her keyboard, and turned the monitor toward him. With a pen, she pointed at the screen.

His schedule. Crafty woman. She aimed her pen toward three open days in the coming week. "And you're booked on Delta's six a.m. flight."

"Fine. I should know better than to argue with you." He shook his head. What a blessing this woman had been to him. If not for her mothering, his life would be in even worse shape than it was now. "Verna, you're something else."

"You just remember that."

"You won't let me forget."

She resumed typing on her keyboard. "Speaking of not forgetting, the board meeting's about to begin, and you have the privilege of explaining that little million-dollar loss."

Yeah. He scratched his head. Not something he looked forward to. Especially since that loss never should have happened. He carried the shoebox into his office, set it on his desk, then walked to his wall-sized window and stared out at Manhattan's skyline. If only he could turn back the clock. Make the right choice this time. Then he wouldn't have been distracted from doing his job. None of this should have happened.

One reckless decision devastated so many lives.

With a sigh, he snatched his Versace suit coat from the back of his leather chair, slipped it on, grabbed his briefcase, and headed for the conference room. He had fifteen short minutes to come up with a viable explanation for the company's doldrums.

Keeping his head down, avoiding eye contact, he walked down ACM Technologies' carpeted aisle. He'd heard enough of his co-workers' sneers these past seven plus months to last until the next century. And now, this company loss heaped on top of all his other problems. Just what his life needed.

He rounded a corner and strode past his CEO's assistant, praying she wouldn't notice him. Only a few more steps to the safety of the conference room.

"Hey, Richie."

He stopped and pinched the bridge of his nose before looking back at her. "Patrice."

She tucked a bra strap back into a skin-tight sweater that dipped way too low to be professional. "You got a minute, darlin'?"

"Sorry." Not for her. Hard to believe he once dated the woman. His standards once dipped as low as her sweater, but not anymore. Never again.

He nodded toward the conference room. "I've got a meeting."

"Oh, well it's busy." She waved fingers with half-inch long red nails. "They're not ready for—"

"They? Who's they?" He looked down the hall at the room reserved for board members only. The doors were closed. His heart rate accelerated as he glanced at his watch. Still ten minutes early. "What's going on, Patrice?"

"A board meeting. Mr. Entenza asked that you wait here." She pointed to a visitor's chair. "Can I get you some coffee?"

"Whoa. Back up. A board meeting? I'm a member of the board."

"I know, Richie, they—"

"It's Richard." He stared at the room's closed door and panic tingled through his body. This couldn't be happening. He was too valuable to the company. The failings of these past seven months were his first blip in four years as a vice president. No one could match his record for saving the company money.

He wiped perspiration from his forehead and squinted at Patrice. "How long did they say they'd be?"

"Oh, a few more minutes."

Good. Enough time to gather his wits and steel himself against the accusations he knew were coming. To prove they needed him.

"I haven't seen Marissa around lately."

His jaw tightened, and he glanced at his watch again. The board's accusations would be more pleasant than Patrice's inquiry.

"Did she quit or something?"

Or something. "She's at the White Plains office."

"You break up? I mean, if you did, I just broke it off with—"

He glared at the assistant, praying daggers would shoot from his eyes. "Yeah. We broke up." Marissa had single-handedly destroyed his personal life. Now, it looked like he was about to lose his career. All because of her.

"You don't need to get testy about it."

Testy? Patrice was lucky he didn't hit women. He glanced toward the conference room and dragged his arm across his forehead. No more waiting. He'd barge in there and show them he wouldn't be walked on.

He strode down the hallway and tugged open the heavy wood door. Eight other men sat around the mahogany table, relaxing in their plush seats. Each one looked up at him, surprise written on some of their faces, but scorn on the others. Or, was it gloating?

"Gentlemen." He rolled out his padded leather chair and laid his briefcase on the table. "I apologize for being late. My memo told me two o'clock."

The CEO, Montegue Entenza, leaned back in his chair and rested hands on his ample stomach. "Actually, Richard, your memo was correct."

Richard's stomach twisted, but he tried to hold his poker face. Don't let these men see his fear. He sat, folded his hands on the table, and looked around trying to connect with each man, but most looked away. Cowards. He glared at Entenza. "Please enlighten me."

"The facts are right there in your quarterly report. I don't take kindly to losing money."

"Come on, every business on Wall Street is losing money right now. Besides, most of that loss comes from the Phoenix plant. Once we close that, our losses will be negligible, and with the new manager in Atlanta, I foresee profits coming from them in—"

"Mr. Brooks." Mr. Entenza leaned forward. "The fact is, someone has to pay for the loss."

"So, you're scapegoating me? Over the past four years, I've been your top performer." He pointed to the man seated kitty-corner from him. "What about Edwards? Wasn't he responsible for a three million—?"

"Quiet." Entenza raised his voice and sat up straight. "This isn't about Edwards, or Constapoulas, or anyone else. It's about the image you present of ACM Technologies."

Richard laughed. "So this has nothing to do with my performance."

"Our shareholders don't take kindly to having a member of our board with a police record."

"Ahh, I see." Just as he thought. How could he win a battle against the truth? "Let me save you and the shareholders a little trouble." He pushed away from the table, grabbed his briefcase, and stood. Neither a demotion nor an outright firing was acceptable. "I'll have my office cleared in an hour. Other companies have been begging for my expertise. I guess it's time I answer them."

"So be it." Entenza pushed a button on the conference phone. "Patrice, will you send in Cowell?"

"Cowell?" Could this possibly get any worse? "A security escort?"

"Protocol, son. I'm sure you understand."

Richard pinched the bridge of his nose. "Perfectly, sir." He gave Entenza a mock salute and strode from the room, slamming the door behind him.

Happy unbelievable birthday.

Cowell, dressed in a complete security officer's uniform, glanced warily at him and shook his head. "Sorry about this, Richard. Entenza has no clue you're one of the good guys."

"Right. Good guys don't get themselves thrown in jail, now, do they?"

"You paid your dues." Cowell slapped his back.

"I'll be paying for the rest of my life." He muttered under his breath. As well he should. If he were still a drinking man, tonight would have been a perfect time to drown his sorrows with a few Coronas.

With Cowell at his side, Richard hurried through the hallways, keeping his head down. The snickers he heard from passing co-workers told him they already knew of his dismissal. He flew past Verna's desk without acknowledging her. She was the one person he was going to miss.

"I'll wait outside for you." Cowell reached into Richard's office—make that his former office—and closed the door.

Richard fisted his hands. How could he have thrown away everything? One lousy night . . . One moronic choice.

Well, standing here feeling sorry for himself wouldn't solve anything. It was time to move on. Maybe Chicago. Close enough to drive to Minnesota. Far enough to make those drives rare. And with all his connections, he shouldn't have a problem linking up with a Fortune 500 company. Out there, his tarnished reputation wouldn't be slapping him in the face at every turn. Yes, Chicago was a good choice.

After stuffing his laptop in his briefcase, he pulled a copy paper box from his closet and packed the few personal possessions he kept in his office. Some novels, the gift from his girls, pictures of his family, his nephews. What would they all say now? Would his brother laugh that the high and mighty Richard Brooks had been laid low? Again?

No. Not even Marcus would be that small.

He covered the box and took one last look around the office. He wasn't forty yet, and other corporations had frequently sent headhunters his way. This setback wasn't going to stop him. He'd prove to Entenza, and all those finger-pointing shareholders, they'd fired the wrong man.

With a grunt, he picked up his briefcase and the box and carried them out the door.

Verna sat at her desk, sniffling. Tissues overflowed her garbage can. "Richard, I am so sorry. It just breaks my heart to see you go."

"It's been a good run, Verna, and you've been like a mom to me."

She dabbed a tissue at her eyes. "Before you leave, I do have one little smidgen of good news for you. Something I know will bless your heart."

"I could sure use some good news." He propped the box on her desk and managed a smile. "You have another grandchild on the way?"

"That would certainly brighten my day, but I'm afraid all my children are done having babies for now."

"So, what have you got?"

She handed him a pink message slip. "Some much needed mercy."

He read it through once, and his heart dipped. He read it through a second time. The message stayed the same. No. No. No! He balled up the paper and hurled it against his former office door.

Forget New York City.

Forget Chicago.

Much needed mercy? Mercy was the last thing he deserved, and God knew it too.

God couldn't have exacted a more perfect revenge.

TREMBLING, SHEILA PETERSON GRABBED Joe's hand as he pushed away from the restaurant table. "Please, let me explain."

He jerked his hand from hers, disgust darkening his milk chocolate eyes. His silence said more than words as he snatched the velvet box off the table, grabbed his leather jacket, and strode through the dimly lit room toward the exit, weaving around diners with the grace of a natural athlete.

"I had no choice," she whispered, perhaps only to convince herself, and clutched a hand to her chest. Her heart pounded like waves against the shore of a storm-tossed lake.

Joe stopped by the arched exit and turned his head her way.

Her breath stilled. The contempt in his eyes wasn't visible from here, but she knew it was there. He'd made it clear that her offense against him was unforgivable. If he would only listen, understand her perspective, perhaps his ache would ease.

She curved her hands on the edge of the table, about to push back and go to him, but he heaved the box into a planter decorating the door's entrance.

She gasped and covered her mouth.

A second later, he disappeared out the door.

Eyes stinging, she slumped into her chair.

Abandoned. Again.

Joe was just like her parents.

She closed her burning eyes and drew in a trembling breath. Grilled sirloin. Joe's favorite. It sat uneaten. She couldn't blame him.

I will not cry. She opened her eyes and scanned the dining room, a setting groomed for a romantic proposal. Window shades were purposely drawn. An amber glow emanated from candles set at the center of tables draped in burgundy linens. Nearly all the seats held customers, mostly with couples seeking intimacy in a public setting, talking in whispers that created a low buzz throughout the room. Shadows highlighted faces, hiding imperfections.

Joe had no physical imperfections to hide.

Sheila no longer had anything to hide.

How many other couples would end their evening apart? It was too dark to tell. But, it didn't matter. What mattered was that there was no one familiar, no one glancing her way, no one gloating over her humiliation.

He'd embarrassed her.

In public.

Anger tensed her body. How dare he?

Abandoned. Yes. But no longer a victim. Not this time.

She snatched her Kenneth Cole clutch off the table. A link on her bracelet snagged and tugged the tablecloth, knocking over an untouched goblet, and red wine gushed toward her silk sheath. She jumped up, her bracelet pulled free, and she released a grateful sigh. Her new Vera Wang was safe.

Even if her heart wasn't.

Steadying her breath, she laid her mulberry pea coat across

her arm, and with her chin raised, she walked toward the exit intending to glide right past the planter.

But, she couldn't.

Blowing out a breath, she scowled at her professionally manicured nails then squatted and dug into the soil. "Aha," she said softly as her fingers found the box and pulled it out. She wiped residue from its velvet exterior and checked to see if anyone watched before focusing on Joe's unanticipated gift. Her chin quivered, and her eyes moistened as she raised the indigo cover.

She stroked the marquis for only a moment then closed the lid to the box, effectively sealing off her heart.

The ring would never circle her finger. She'd have a courier return the diamond along with a note expressing her apologies, but she couldn't be sorry for what she'd done. It was the only thing that made sense. She didn't regret her actions even if it meant losing Joe.

SHIVERING IN JANUARY'S THIRTY-ONE degree temperatures, Richard zipped up his leather jacket and pulled on gloves. He rested against the U-Haul that stored his surprisingly few meaningful possessions. It had taken him all of one week to pack and sell his Brooklyn Heights condominium, with a nice little profit even. A sure sign he was meant to flee New York.

He stared out beyond the Louis Valentine, Jr. Pier. This would be his final journey here, a rare place of tranquility in this unsleeping city. He pulled the truck's door handle, making sure it was locked, then walked across Coffey Street's cobblestone, down the sidewalk that split snow-coated parkland, and onto a pier quieted by cold. Once upon eight months ago, he'd dreamed of fishing side by side with a son off this pier. Now, that would never happen.

Winter's wind gusted off the water as he leaned into the railing and gazed out over New York Harbor, at the Statue of Liberty rising above it. The country's symbol of freedom.

Freedom, huh! He kicked at a guardrail, and it made a clinking sound. He glanced down. A chain necklace, coated with snow, circled the post.

He squatted and loosened the chain, then stood and ran his thumb over its filthy oval links. This must be a gift from God himself to remind Richard of mercy's shackle. He stared out at the Statue, the chains of tyranny lying broken at her feet, and tugged at the necklace's cold links. They held firm. Unbroken. Perfect.

He shook snow and dirt from the chain, removed his gloves, then pulled a tissue from his pocket and polished the links. It had been exposed to the elements too long for it to have a burnished shine. All the better. He retrieved his keychain and removed the key he should have left alone eight months ago. If he had . . .

No. Not going there.

He unclasped the grimy chain, slipped the key onto it, and then fastened it back together. His palms clammy despite the cold, he grasped the chain in both hands, hefted it over his head, and anchored it around his neck, tucking the key inside his sweatshirt.

In moving back to Minnesota, he would no longer encounter the stabbing reminders that living in New York brought him. But, with this chain forever circling his neck, he'd certainly never forget.

CPSIA information can be obtained
at www.ICGtesting.com
Printed in the USA
LVHW090103230421
685308LV00005B/313

9 781951 664046